DREAM OF LOVE

Marcel returned early; Maggie was eagerly waiting for him. As the guests started to straggle into the ballroom, they went out on the terrace, the only place where they could be alone. They walked slowly, hand in hand, the soft glow of Japanese lanterns casting flickering shadows on these two young people who were rapidly falling in love.

"You must come to Paris, Maggie. I want to show you my world," he whispered into her ear.

"That sounds heavenly," she sighed, "but my work keeps me here."

"We shall see, cherie, we shall see."

Maggie was thrilled by the implication of his words. They had reached the end of the terrace and turned to face each other. Maggie's heart was beating so hard she had difficulty breathing; he was like a magnet drawing her closer by sheer animal sensuality. Marcel bent and placed a light kiss, not on her mouth, but just under her ear; she was afraid she might swoon.

"Hello, you two—come inside before you catch cold," Ellen called.

Marcel placed his hands on Maggie's bare, trembling shoulders.

"Forgive me—you are cold." Maggie shook her head as he continued, "I am so warm with love for you, I didn't realize . . ." He kissed her hand; then, holding it tight in his, led her back to the ballroom where a waltz was playing. "Dance with me so I can hold you close," he ordered. He held out his arms and she melted into them. . . .

Also by Lou Graham:

FRAGMENTS
FANNY G.

THE SEVENTH SISTER

LOU GRAHAM

LEISURE BOOKS   NEW YORK CITY

For Leslie and Gabriella Bova, who love and are loved.

A LEISURE BOOK

Published by

Dorchester Publishing Co., Inc.
6 East 39th Street
New York, NY 10016

Printed in the United States of America

THE SEVENTH SISTER

PART ONE

I

THE FAMILY

Ian Maccrae, middleaged widower and father of seven daughters, moved up the path to his home with long vigorous strides. He opened the door and called his usual greeting, "I'm home, girls."

Annie, the oldest at twenty-four, always answered, "Supper will be ready in a moment." This meant that by the time he washed and had his tot of whiskey, they would all be ready to sit down. Maggie, the youngest, was placing the silver on the long, pine table when he entered. The utensils clattered to the table as she ran to him for their nightly hug.

Ian loved all his daughters, but Maggie had a special place in his heart. Fourteen years ago, her birth had left Mrs. Maccrae an invalid. She lingered for two bedridden years and during that time patiently taught ten-year-old Annie to take her place as surrogate mother, to perform all the household duties and to care for her six younger sisters with love. Annie learned her lessons well, and at the age of twelve she was in charge of home and family. Village gossip, whispered among some of the women of Paisley, was to the effect that Dora Maccrae should not have had another after Robyn, so named for the boy she was hoped to be.

Robbie was taller than her sisters and, unlike them, big-boned with coarse red hair just a shade lighter than her father's; Robbie was the only daughter who resembled Ian. The talk in the town was that Dora had so little strength left after bearing six children that her seventh child, Maggie, was the "runt of the litter." It was unkind and unthinking. She was the miniature of her mother then, and now, fourteen years later, Maggie was a constant reminder to Ian of his beloved wife. Her heart-shaped face was framed by unruly strawberry blonde hair, too fine to stay neatly in braids, or so she claimed, and despite Annie's supervision she never was quite put together in a tidy manner. She was the family's pet and even Mary, a year younger than Annie and a strict disciplinarian, was often secretly amused at her impish disposition. Da had made them read Shakespeare as an important part of their education and Mary had dubbed her little sister Ariel after the mischievous little sprite in "The Tempest," darting here and there and teasing everyone.

When Ian gave her his bear hug it made his great height and broad shoulders look even larger and she was completely lost to sight until he released her. "Little one," he took a deep breath, "I shall truly miss your greeting when you grow up!"

"I'm afraid I will never be as tall as my

sisters no matter what my age, and they will *never* let me grow up," she said petulantly. It was a sore spot with her. She envied Annie's height and auburn hair and the same dark, blue eyes of her father; but more than that she prayed every night that one day she would look like Kate. Kate was so beautiful that most people, including Maggie, were in awe of her. Her titian red hair, wide, violet eyes and slim but shapely figure made her a person set apart She was very popular and used her beauty as a weapon to get what and whom she wanted. Kate was already grist for the gossip mill when the string of broken hearts she left behind her were counted.

By the time Ian returned from washing up, Maggie had dismissed all her envious thoughts and brought Da his whiskey.

Annie came to the table first. She took her place at the foot of it where her mother would have sat if she hadn't been claimed by an early death. The others followed, each dropping a kiss on Ian's fiery red hair. Maggie, late as always, scuttled to her chair at the left of Annie. Her braids had been hastily tied back with a white ribbon bow on which there were finger smudges. Mary, at her father's right, could see them from that distance. She looked to Annie, waiting for her to reprove this un-disciplined child and sighed with annoyance as nothing was forthcoming. Under cover of the table cloth, Maggie had showed her hands to Annie, palms up, to prove they were clean. Maggie liked to draw with charcoal, so everything she touched got smudged and her nails were never really clean. Annie knew why she showed her hands only palm up, but pretended she didn't. Her nod was almost imperceptible. Maggie did not have to leave the table.

The girls bowed their heads and clasped their hands in front of them. Ian spoke. "My daughters, I have had great news . . ." he stopped suddenly as seven pair of eyes looked up at him from their clasped hands. Redfaced, he bowed his head and so did the girls again. Asking forgiveness of the Lord for his oversight, he offered a hasty prayer of thanks for the food they were about to eat.

Except for Annie, the girls thought Da's forgetfulness a matter for giggling. Maggie was shaking with suppressed laughter and as she slid her eyes to Robbie, it became contagious.

Ian looked in consternation from one to the other, which made them laugh harder. He threw up his hands. "What have I done to deserve six silly, giggling daughters?"

Annie clapped her hands lightly and brought them to order. He attempted again to tell his news but Annie said softly, "Da, can your news wait until we have had supper? It is ready and will be cold if we don't eat now." Ian had broken his own rule that they would not discuss anything of importance until after supper. He shrugged and with a slightly impatient gesture, admitted that his news could wait. Annie, her kitchen chores finished with the preparation of the meal, waited for Mary who brought in a huge shepherd's pie filled

12

with chunks of lamb and redolent with the aroma of fresh vegetables and herbs from the kitchen garden. She placed it in front of Ian.

Frances, at seventeen, was the least colorful of the Maccrae daughters; her hair had red lights, but she possessed neither color nor facial expression to set them off. She was content to be Mary's shadow. If Mary had been in the kitchen, she would not have let Kate usurp the pleasure of serving Da his favorite dish, but Frances did not have the energy to make a fuss; therefore she was assigned the task of bringing in the warmed plates while Kate emerged from the kitchen with a large-lidded bowl. She carried it at arms' length like an offering to a king. As she reached her father she made a flourishing gesture as she uncovered the dish. "Look, Da, Annie made a treat for you."

"Colcannon! This is just the night for a special treat." His eyes followed the dish of potatoes mashed with butter, cream, sauteed cabbage and a sprinkle of chopped young onions, as Kate placed it in front of Annie. He put a good-sized portion of the pie on his plate and started it on its journey to Annie who filled it with an overgenerous helping, then sent it back to him up the other side of the table. As soon as the last plate reached Kate on her father's right, he spooned up a mouthful of colcannon, ate it slowly as he savored it, then raised his eyes heavenward. "What would I ever do without you, Annie?" He added to himself, "What will I do without any of my

13

girls?" It was a question heavy on his mind at the moment.

Supper was usually a time for chatter and relaxation. Mary, Kate, Frances, Laurie and Robbie all worked as weavers at their father's mill and brought to this hour amusing stories and bits of gossip. Da, removed from their part of his business, joined in their lighthearted laughter. Tonight, however, he consumed his food quickly and quietly and did not indulge in banter. His preoccupation had its effect and soon they were all eating silently. Frances and Laurie cleared the table while Robbie went into the kitchen to bring the dessert, a steaming fruit dumpling, to the table.

"You're very quiet, Da," said Annie. "Your news must be serious and important."

"Not serious, but important, yes. I'm bursting to tell you." It was a wistful sound to come from this giant of a man. "Now, Annie?"

"Of course." She was about to call Frances and Laurie but they had heard and were in their chairs just a second before Robbie.

Ian sat tall in his chair as his gaze swept over his lovely daughters. In their dark cotton dresses with the white aprons, which Maggie had begged Frances to make with "angel ruffles" and sketched for her when she professed not to know what she meant, they looked so young and vulnerable and—yes, like angels. There was a lump in his throat and as he did so often, he wished that his beloved Dora had lived to see their red-haired daughters, each of a different hue, each of

14

them so innocent—his head cocked a little and his eyebrow was raised in speculation as he came to Kate; he wasn't quite sure she belonged in that category.

The girls were fidgeting under his long scrutiny. Annie reached over and straightened Maggie's shoulder ruffle as Mary spoke in a low, stern voice and told her to stop wriggling; it was enough to settle them all. Ian had their rapt attention.

It was almost as if he had rehearsed it. He started as he had before. "My daughters, I have had great news today." He paused dramatically.

"What is your news, Da?" Annie asked.

He answered slowly and with emphasis, "We . . . are going to have . . . a visitor; *a very distinguished* visitor."

"Da, don't tease. Who?" Maggie dared to show her impatience with his slow delivery.

He smiled at her to soften his words. "I'm sorry to tell you, little one, the news will be of the least importance to you."

She pouted and sat back in her chair, then, grinning, she pointed to Mary. "Another suitor for Mary!"

Mary was embarrassed and angry. A bright pink flush spread from her neck to her hairline. "Annie, you would be doing us all a favor if you would teach that . . ."

She didn't continue as Da put up his hand for quiet. "Girls," he raised his voice slightly, "if you want to hear the rest of the news you will have to be quiet. No more interruptions."

They nodded and he continued. "A gentleman, from North America across the sea, is coming to visit us." Robbie opened her mouth but at a frown from her father closed it. "The gentleman owns the largest silk mill in America and," he went on quickly to avoid further interruptions, "he is going to honor *us* with his presence."

Annie was mature beyond her years but even her curiosity had come to the fore. "Do you know him, Da?"

Ian shook his head. "I have never met him but we have corresponded."

"Then why is he coming to visit?"

"That, my dear Annie, is the reason it is such an honor. Mr. MacConnack has heard of the artistic paisley weaving done by the Maccrae family. He is coming to invite some members of our family to return to America with him to teach the art to his mill workers." He paused, waiting for a response to his tremendous news. Not quite sure what it portended, he was met with dead silence—not a sound for seconds. Then they all exploded into speech at once. He tried to sort out the snippets of words flying around the table. "How wonderful!" "Oh, no!" (Was it Annie who'd said that?) Some of the girls gasped with shared excitement, he was sure, at the great honor being bestowed upon them.

Robbie could no longer contain herself. "*All* of us?"

"No, Robbie, just two. And as we have always done, the offer goes to the two oldest."

Annie knew that didn't include her. "Mary and Katherine." It wasn't a question. Kate took a deep breath and held her clasped hands to her heart in joy.

"What do you say to that, Mary?" Ian asked. Avoiding her father's eyes, she looked down at her hands nervously plucking at her napkin. "Mary?" He could see she was troubled. "What is it?"

She answered hesitantly, "It is very sudden, Da, to go so far away with strangers in a strange country." She looked up and tears shimmered in her pale blue eyes. "And . . . and . . ." she was biting her lips to stem the tears, "and . . ."

Maggie impishly finished the sentence for her, " . . . And then she couldn't marry Scott Durant!"

"Durant? My assistant?" Mary lowered her eyes. "What is this?" He turned to Annie. "Did you know about Mary and Scott?"

She sighed. "Yes, Da. They have been walking out, but I *didn't* know," her manner was severe as she spoke to Mary, "you didn't tell me you were serious. He has spoken neither to your father nor me."

Mary was crying openly. "We've only just spoken to each other. Da, please don't make me go," she implored.

Her unexpected reaction had deflated his enthusiasm. "I will make no one go." He turned to Katherine, and a note of doubt could be heard in his voice. " . . . And you? Would you like to go?"

"More than anything I can think of!" she said with great enthusiasm. "Of course I'll go. Mary, how can you pass up such a wonderful opportunity for Scott Durant?" she was lightly contemptuous.

Mary cried harder. Mary was not pretty when she cried, though she had the fine features of her sisters. Her face was flushed, her almost colorless eyes were red rimmed and her brick-red hair was an ugly contrast. No one had ever seen her cry before.

Annie intervened. "We will have no bickering, Kate, before you answer too fast, think it through. It is a long and possibly hazardous journey and you will be going to a land of unfamiliar ways."

Kate answered quickly, "I don't have to think any further. If Da's American gentleman finds me acceptable, I will most certainly go!" Her voice was modest but she didn't for a minute think that any man could find her less than desirable. "Anyway, Da has already given his permission." Her remark was addressed to Annie with the full implication that she didn't need her approval.

"That's correct. Before I accepted Mr. Mac-Connack's offer, I thought about it for a long time. I had him investigated as far as I could. He has a fine reputation as a man of honor and a thorough gentleman. You know," again his eyes embraced them, "we have much love in this family and with two of you absent it will leave a terrible void. Kate, Annie is right—the voyage is long, six to eight weeks depending on the weather. But if I thought it hazardous, of course I would not have considered it."

Annie argued no further. "You wouldn't let her go alone?" she asked tentatively.

Mr. Maccrae shook his head. "That's out of the question. Would you like to go, Frances?"

As happens in large families, the girls had paired off each with a compatible sibling. They were close friends as well as sisters. Tears had trickled down Frances's cheeks as she felt Mary's anguish and she swallowed hard before she answered. "I am mindful of the honor the American gentleman has conferred on us, but Da," she made another effort to swallow her tears, "I don't want to leave you and my family and my home. If Mary had said 'yes' I would have gone to be with her and to please you."

Ian understood but was visibly disappointed. "Well, I guess that settles it. When our guest arrives I'll tell him to speak to another family. Laurie, at sixteen you are too young to leave us."

Relieved, Laurie thanked her father, saying, "I have no wish to go to America." Frances and Laurie were the good, obedient children of the family, though Laurie was slightly more independent than Frances, who looked to Mary for direction in everything she did. They never had to be reminded about their chores and rarely offered an opinion. Laurie was everybody's friend.

Katherine turned on them, her voice loud with temper. "What kind of cowardly girls do I have for sisters? Don't you realize you are depriving yourselves, *and me*, of the only chance we'll ever have to see the world? You're selfish, that's what!"

Sharing her temptestuous outburst, Robbie jumped to her feet. "*I'm* the one who should go —after all, I won the Gold Ribbon at the Edinburgh Fair." A scowl settled on Ian's face but she was saved a sermon about her tender years by Kate, who took quick advantage of the moment.

"True, Robbie is only fifteen, but she did win first prize at the Fair. We would do well together. If you have faith in me, trust me to see that she will be well taken care of."

Stung by her sister's accusation of timidity, Mary was indignant. "Do you think Robbie would let you tell her what to do? She is self-willed and heeds no one."

Under the raised voices at the other end of the table no one heard Maggie's protests. "Da . . . Robbie, I helped you win the prize! It was *my* design you followed. Please, listen . . ."

Robbie's crisp red curls came loose and her green eyes glittered; she looked like a cat ready to pounce. "I don't pay any heed to *you*, Mary, because you have no right to tell me what to do. You stay and marry your namby-pamby Scott and have lots of babies and don't concern yourself with me."

"Stop!" Annie clapped her hands. "Enough of this." She had been sitting quietly up to this time, unsettled in her mind. It was hard for her to believe that her father would have accepted such an invitation without consulting her, and she disapproved. But while she had authority, his word was the final one. "I think," she suggested, "that Robbie and Kate are both too young to travel alone to a primitive country across the sea."

Ian Maccrae had retired into his own thoughts and let his eldest take care of the small bursts of temper that surrounded him. Now he directed his words to her. "They will be well chaperoned. Mr. MacConnack's sister has accompanied him and," he paused to give weight to his words, "not only is it an honor for us to have been chosen, but also a great opportunity to introduce the art of paisley weaving to a far flung part of the world." He paused again. "Now, Robbie," he was thinking aloud and he spoke slowly, "if you can control your temper and promise to obey your sister and accept her judgment in all things, I'll consider sending you along with her."

Robbie, who always got her own way or did as she pleased anyway, had won again. She ran to her father, threw her arms around him and planted a hearty kiss on his cheek. "Thank you, thank you, Da!" Then she hugged Katherine. "Thank you Kate, you won't be sorry."

"Sit down, Robbie. That kind of impulsive behavior is precisely why you should *not* be allowed to leave home." Annie was torn between surrogate motherhood, which had been forced on her at an early age, and her stifled longing to escape, a longing which she had managed until now to submerge. This new turn of events had brought it to the surface. Her demeanor reflected the responsibilities she carried for the welfare of home and family, with no thought of self. Her auburn hair was pulled back in a severe knot and always covered with an immaculate white cap. Her dress, except for prayer meeting on Sunday, was of black homespun, covered with a white apron. There had been suitors but her father had discouraged them quickly, and she had never questioned him. As the eldest of the motherless family, who else would care for them? Resigned to spinsterhood at the age of twenty-four, she was ashamed of the little tongues of envy that were licking at her.

"Are you still against it?" her father asked.

Annie struggled with her thoughts for a moment. "*If* the girls are properly chaperoned and *if* we can be assured they will live with a family I . . ." she faltered, "I guess it will be all right."

Katherine tried to keep Robbie in her place with a long look; to make sure, she pinched Frances and whispered to her to pass it along. Robbie understood the message. She clasped her hands on her lap and said a silent "thank you" to God. Kate, unaccustomed tears in her eyes, placed her hand over Annie's and said a heartfelt, "Thank you for your trust. I promise it will not be misplaced." She and Robbie approached their father and thanked him, too. Kate took one of the large empty platters from the table, handed it to Robbie and they walked majestically into the kitchen, where they hugged and kissed and cried together.

Overcome with the confusion of emotions, Annie rose and motioned to the others to help clear the table. She put her hand on her father's shoulders as she passed and he patted it. "You didn't tell us when your Mr. Mac-Connack is going to arrive, Da."

"So I didn't! Saturday at two o'clock." She let out a small shriek and hustled the girls along with the last of the dishes.

No one noticed that Maggie was crying.

II

THE VISITORS

Shortly before two o'clock Saturday afternoon, the girls had gathered for Annie's approval and then for Da's. There was no mistaking the look of pride in his eyes as he first inspected Annie (although he really didn't consider her one of the girls), then looked down the line of his daughters all clad in the tartan plaid of the Maccraes, a striking turquoise on a field of black. Once again he had a fleeting moment of sadness as his eyes lit on Maggie; so petite, so much like her mother except for her eyes, which were not clear blue but a gray-blue which changed with the different colors she wore.

Never a demonstrative man, Ian was not much given to compliments but, carried away by the moment he recited a stanza from a poem of one of Scotland's favorite poets, Robert Burns:

> "Auld nature swears, the lovely dears
> Her noblest work she classes, O
> Her prentice han she tried on man
> And *then* she made the lasses, O!"

The girls clapped their hands and blushed at the unaccustomed tribute. Annie said, "Turn around, Da; let us see how *you* look."

Ian Maccrae had been acclaimed the caber-throwing champion of Glasgow for the past five years. The 18-foot, 120 pound pole took great strength to throw and the clan plaid kilt showed his well-muscled body to great advantage. His eyes were a deeper blue and his hair a brighter red than any of his daughters; it marched down his face in side whiskers and joined under his chin in a short beard. He strutted and preened under the adoring scrutiny of his girls. Kate gave him a hug. "You're a handsome laddy, Ian Maccrae!" she teased.

There was no time for an answer. Maggie had darted outside and now came running back. "The carriage is coming—they're here, they're here!" She was shrill in her excitement and stationed herself alongside Annie who gave her a love-tap spank and sent her to the end of the recieving line. Maggie's high excitement fell flat, and her father felt sorry for her. "Stand forward, little one, no one can see you there." Shaking her head stubbornly, she took a step back.

Ian strode out to meet his guests. "Welcome, Mr. MacConnack," he boomed. Donald MacConnack, hand outstretched, walked rapidly toward him. After a hard American handshake he turned back, waiting for his sister who followed more slowly. "This is my dear sister Amy, who has proved herself an excellent sailor." She smiled and curtsied but her eyes were on the long line of redhaired girls, moving from one to the other—from cute to pretty to beautiful, she quickly assessed. At the same time they were awestruck by this lovely creature dressed in clothes only Kate, and secretly Maggie, realized were the height of fashion. As they discovered later, Amy at fifteen was three months older than Robbie and fifteen years younger than her brother. Their mother had died when Amy was born and their father shortly after. Like Annie, Donald was a surrogate parent and Amy looked to him for all her needs. Also like Annie, he took very good care of his little sister.

Still annoyed at being sent to the end of the line, Maggie had planned to disappear for a while, but the sight of Amy in a fawn velvet dress and tight-fitting jacket with a nipped in waist, a round mink collar and a little muff to match, was more than she could walk away from. Amy wore a soft fur hat and the face under it was that of an angel with long, dark finger-curls, laughing brown eyes, a complexion not as fair as the Maccraes but fair nevertheless, and a cherry red mouth which showed very white teeth when she smiled.

During these few moments of silent inspection, Annie stepped forward as did Donald MacConnack. He was slim and as tall as her father. She had to tilt her head back slightly to meet his eyes, after which she found it difficult to breathe normally and maintain her poise; he was the most darkly fascinating person she had never encountered. Her good training came to the fore and she extended her hand. "Welcome to you and your sister, sir." Faint color crept up her cheeks as he kissed the back of the extended hand. She stiffened slightly and he released it. She then turned and introduced her sisters. "Mary, Katherine, Frances, Laurie, Robbie and Maggie . . . Maggie, where are you?" Reluctantly, Maggie peeked out from behind Robbie.

Amy, whose manner was as easy and open as her brother's, broke the silence with a giggle. "How do you remember all the names? Let me see if I can!" She started with Maggie and with a little prompting managed to get them all right. It was an auspicious beginning and in the days that followed it became a game. One of the girls would step in front of her and say, "What's my name?" A mistake sent them into gales of laughter.

Maggie offered to relieve Amy of her muff and jacket, on top of which she piled her hat. She hugged the soft fur and surreptitiously stole into Kate's room, the only one with a mirror, where she tried on the hat and held the muff just under her chin. "Oh, yes," she told her reflection, "this is what I want! I *will* get to America some way and have a fur muff and grand clothes, too!"

Maggie was exuberant now as she ran back to join the others who were chattering and laughing and on their way out of the house,

Amy wearing a shawl Mary had given her. Scotland in late summer is cool—chilly, Amy said—and the Shetland shawl was warm. Maggie slowed her steps and stopped in the doorway. She called to them but no one heard her. Completely forlorn, Maggie closed the door and went to her private hiding place in the attic to sulk.

Annie excused herself and enlisted Katherine and Robbie to help her with the tea table while Da led Donald into the parlor. "A comfortable room, Mr. Maccrae," he said as he walked over to the stone fireplace where a fire already blazed in the grate. He warmed his hands, then accepted the glass of whiskey Ian held out to him. The men had much to discuss and did so easily, forging a bond of friendship which, both knew, would never change except to grow stronger.

At last Annie called them to tea, and as the girls trooped back into the house, Amy said she was famished and proved it by eating a half dozen scones dripping with home-churned butter and lots of fruit jam. There was no rebuke forthcoming from her brother; he was pleased to see her enjoy the family as he was doing. They finished the light repast and once again the younger girls, all but Maggie, swept Amy outdoors. Frances and Mary cleared the table and went into the kitchen.

Ian asked Katherine and Robbie to join them in the parlor. "Mr. MacConnack would like to speak with you," he told them. Annie and her two sisters settled themselves expectantly.

"First," Donald said and he looked directly at Annie, "I would like to explain that we are an informal household. Unless you object, I would like to address you by your first names. Do you mind?"

"If that is the custom," Annie replied stiffly, "I am sure the girls can comply." To herself she thought, "The first of the primitive customs," but her sisters rather liked it.

"Your father has given his permission to have you, Katherine, and your sister Robyn come with us to America," said Donald. He directed his next remark to Robbie. "I am mindful of your age, but Amy is only a few months older than you and she withstood the voyage very well. You look quite capable." She murmured her thanks for his confidence. "I have also learned that you won the gold ribbon at the Edinburgh Fair last September. Had you planned to exhibit your work again?"

"Yes sir, but Mary will present the piece I have done," said Robbie quickly.

He smiled and nodded. "That is good. I would not like to have you deprived of further honors."

Robbie's forthright approach to all things stood her in good stead. "Would you like to see a sample of my work?" she asked.

"Yes, indeed." He turned to Katherine. "Do you have a sample, too?"

"I'll fetch them, Kate," said Robbie eagerly. The girls had been prepared to display their work and she was back in a minute. Mr. Mac-

Connack, an expert at textiles, was impressed with the design and exquisite colors, all hand-dyed.

"Paisley is even more beautiful than I had imagined," he said. "Mr. Maccrae, you must be very proud of your artistic family."

Ian Maccrae smiled broadly. "I am, indeed."

"Now, young ladies," Mr. MacConnack continued, "have you thought deeply about leaving your homeland and coming to America?"

Kate answered immediately, "We love our home and family, Mr. MacConnack, but Robbie and I would like to see your part of the world. We are proud that we have been chosen, and will do our very best not to disappoint you."

He was about to respond when Annie interrupted him, her anxiety overcoming her natural courtesy. "Would you be good enough to tell us exactly how the girls will travel and where they will live when you reach America?"

"Let me put your mind at rest, Mrs. Maccrae . . ." Donald began.

He got no further. Both Annie and her father exclaimed, "No, oh, no . . ."

He looked in dismay from one to the other.

Ian took over. "Forgive me, Mr. MacConnack, for not making Annie's position clear. She is my eldest daughter. My dear wife died when Annie was but a little lass and she has taken charge of her sisters and the household since then. I have tutored the girls and they have a fair education as well as an artistic bent, but

31

Annie has seen to the welfare of us all."

Donald MacConnack turned to Annie. "It was an awkward blunder and I humbly beg your pardon."

"Not at all. There was no way for you to know." But Annie's heart was breaking that he thought her old enough to have borne her six sisters. It didn't help that he was studying her closely. Ian felt suddenly as if he had become invisible.

"Just looking at you should have told me," said Donald softly. Quite out of character with the deference he had paid her as his host's wife, he blurted, "Why do you hide your youth?"

Though dressed in her best, Annie had covered her hair with a matronly ruffled bonnet. She could feel herself blushing and as she put her hand to her face, a tendril of auburn hair escaped the bonnet. Donald may not have known but if he did, he completely ignored the fastidious rules of a Scottish household where beauty of feature was never spoken of. "You are very beautiful, you know."

Ian felt the situation was getting out of control and he pursed his lips and made a clicking sound of tongue against teeth. "Mr. MacConnack, we'd better get back to the business at hand," he suggested.

"Again, I beg your pardon. I was carried away with relief and surprise." It was an enigmatic statement which neither Annie nor her father asked him to explain.

Annie had taken a few moments to dispel the

confusion his compliment had raised. She relaxed her tightly clasped hands, smoothed her dress, then said as if there had been no other conversation, "You have not answered my question, Mr. MacConnack."

"Oh, yes, your question," he paused. "About the chaperone—well, on the voyage the girls will have their own cabin next to my sister's and her maid, who will supervise them all. When we arrive in America, they will live at my home. I have a large estate and they will have a wing with their own sitting room to share and each her own bedroom. They will be treated as my sister is. I'm sure we can make them comfortable and happy. They will be driven to my mill every day where I will have a separate space for them to teach a selected handful of my workers." He paused again. "Have I reassured you?"

"Very much so, thank you." She wanted to say more but something strange happened every time he looked at her. She was vastly annoyed with herself; her heart was fluttering and her tongue seemed tied. To turn his attention away from her, she said, "Katherine, I'm sure you and Robbie have some questions for Mr. MacConnack. If you'll excuse me, I'll call the rest of the girls." She had to escape his intent gaze.

Katherine suspected what was happening. During the by-play between them she had wondered what on earth he could see in Annie, of all people? Kate knew she was far prettier than her sister, and was annoyed that Mr. Mac-

Connack had said nothing about her. At any rate, she would soon have a better opportunity to know this handsome American. She would see to it that he forgot Annie. These thoughts going through her head brought her to a question. "How long will we be in America?"

"I'm glad you asked that, Kate. That's the one thing we haven't discussed. How long do you think they will have to be away?" Mr. Maccrae asked.

"I don't think we can set a time. It will depend on how rapidly my people learn. By the way, will we be able to take some of your looms with us?" Donald asked.

Ian Maccrae's good living was earned by the manufacture of special looms which were used to produce the complex paisley design woven at his mill. "We have six of our very latest, ready to put aboard ship with you. Mr. Durant, my assistant, and I have made improvements and the girls are familiar with them. I'm sure they'll be satisfactory."

"Good. If everything goes well, let us say your daughters will spend approximately six months with us. Is that agreeable?"

Ian sighed heavily. "So be it!" He was thinking, a month to travel to America and a month back and six months there—almost a year. He hoped he hadn't made a mistake in giving his consent. "When will you be leaving?"

"Our ship leaves next Saturday. We have a week here." Donald turned to Robbie and Kate. "Will you girls be ready?"

"It will give us just enough time to get our

clothes sorted and packed," Kate assured him.

"With the help of your maid, that shouldn't take too long. By the way, if you wish to bring her along there will be room for her as well," said Donald.

Kate and Robbie exchanged glances of consternation. "We don't have a maid, Mr. Mac-Connack," Robbie said. She didn't suffer the embarrassment of Kate who was ashamed to admit it. "We do these things ourselves. We're just not sure what to take."

"Don't worry about that. Tomorrow Amy and her maid will come over and between the four of you, everything will work smoothly. When we reach my home we'll get someone to help you."

Maggie had not gone outside with the other girls, but had hovered in the open doorway all this time, out of sight but within earshot. She heard one phrase and repeated it to herself to keep from shouting with joy. "That's it! I *can* go to America; *I'll* be the maid!" She twirled around singing the words to herself, but Annie spotted her.

"What are you doing, Maggie? Why aren't you with the others? They're ready to leave now. Come and say goodbye." She started away quickly but Maggie held onto her sleeve.

"Wait, Annie! Kate and Robbie can bring a maid. *I'll* be the maid and then I can go with them! Isn't that the most wonderful thing you've ever heard?" Maggie's face glowed with the ecstasy of the mere thought.

Annie put her hands on her hips. "What

35

makes you think they would want you with them? It's the silliest thing you have ever said! Now stop your nonsense and come along." She pulled out of her sister's grasp and headed for the door.

Maggie, furious and rejected once more, decided there was no reason for her to be friendly with the whatever-their-name-was. She would never see them again. She returned to her private thinking spot, which was really her sulking spot, where she went to brood over important thoughts, evil thoughts, and soothe her wounded feelings. But today the magic didn't work and she finally cried herself to sleep.

The family was at supper when she awoke. Maggie knew she had to make an appearance. She washed her face, tidied her hair and sullenly joined them.

"Well," Da said cheerfully, "here's our long-lost child. Where have you been?"

Angry enough to be rude, she answered, "I'm sure I wasn't missed!" Annie and her father exchanged knowing glances.

"What's wrong with your nose, little one?" her father asked teasingly, though at any other time she would have been soundly scolded for her surly manner.

"Don't call me 'little one!' I'm almost as old as Robbie and that Amy person!" She rubbed her nose. "What *is* wrong with my nose?"

"I think it's crooked, a little out of joint," Da teased, which didn't help at all. Maggie ate very little, then asked to be excused. She went to bed but not to sleep; her mind kept running in circles. All she could think about was a sailing ship taking her to America. Suddenly she sat up straight and smiled a wide smile. Da always said, "Where there's a will, there's a way." And Maggie had a very strong will.

The next morning she was her usual sunny self and everyone was thankful that another crisis had passed.

III

BON VOYAGE

The ensuing week was hectic but, under the supervision of Annie and the helping hand of Amy's maid, Birdy, the activity was kept orderly. Maggie was always underfoot trying to be of assistance, which no one appreciated. She watched Birdy closely and made mental notes of the proper conduct of a maid.

Bringing Amy and her maid each day to help with the sorting and packing of clothes gave Donald MacConnack a valid reason to spend a great deal of time at the Maccraes'. Ian Maccrae, Mary, Frances and Laurie were all working at the mill and Kate and Robbie occupied most of their time packing the two trunks. All this activity made it easy for him to find excuses to see Annie. He was curious about her and at the same time, fascinated. He stole every possible moment to ostensibly consult with her about her sisters' future. Annie found no reason to avoid him and as the week wore on, their "consultations" took on the aura of trysts. A touch on the hand became a warm clasp; a meeting of the eyes left hers dreamy and his, hopeful. Toward the end of the week Annie's unspoken depth of feeling left her bewildered. She wasn't sure what was happening; she had never felt such intense emotions before and became terribly self-conscious whenever Donald was near.

As for Donald, he knew he had fallen in love.

The day of departure arrived at last. The carriage was at the door and Annie was supervising the hand luggage to be carried with the girls. The trunks had been sent on ahead.

Donald approached her. "Annie, let the girls take care of their own things," he said firmly. "I want to talk to you."

They walked a little distance away, out of sight of the others. "Annie, I am considered by those who know me, to be a 'man of the world' . . . a bon vivant." He laughed lightly, then turned suddenly serious. "To a certain extent, I guess I am, but," he hesitated a moment, looking deep into her eyes, "I have never, ever, fallen so completely in love with anyone as I have with you these past few days. I don't mean to be bold, but there is so little time; we have only these moments. I love you, Annie Maccrae!" She gasped. "I am desolate that your life is being sacrificed to the needs of your family. I have been wretched trying to devise an excuse for you to come to America with us, to no avail." He paused and looked for a response in her eyes. "Am I wrong in thinking you return my feelings?"

"No," she said slowly, "you are not wrong. I have never been in love so I'm not quite sure what it is I feel, but I am—strongly drawn to you. I should feel shame in answering you in kind, but I do not know. I . . . " in spite of herself she faltered, "I . . . think I love you, too."

40

He clasped her hands in his and kissed them, then held them to his heart. Her upturned face glowing with love was more than he could resist. He swept her into his arms, pressed her hard against him and kissed her passionately. For a brief, ardent moment they were lost to their surroundings.

Mr. Maccrae's voice calling Annie fortunately preceded his footsteps and by the time he came upon them, they were engaged in conventional conversation. As they followed him out to the carriage, Donald whispered to her, "I will be back, Annie Maccrae. Wait for me!"

"I will, Donald, I will," she, too, whispered.

Donald climbed onto the carriage next to the driver as the sisters kissed each other goodbye once again. Kate however noticed Annie's white cap was askew, and suspected something of what had gone on between her eldest sister and the handsome mill owner; it strenghened her determination to make him notice her as soon as possible.

After the last farewell had been said, Annie and her father walked back to the house with Maggie tugging at his arm. "Da, please?" she begged.

He sighed deeply, then called the others, who remained. "Maggie is pestering me to go to to the ship to say goodbye again. I'll take the carriage and we can all go." There was much eager chattering as the girls got ready. Maggie brought a little knapsack of goodies which she said she had saved for Kate and Robbie and forgotten to give them.

"It will be too late, Maggie—they'll be on the ship by the time we get there." Laurie, usually the silent one, let her know she was being foolish.

"I'll find them, don't worry," said Maggie smugly.

"If you don't mind, Da," Annie said, "I'll stay here and just see that everything is in order. Mary can take charge."

"It's been a difficult time for you, daughter. The girls will help when they return. You should rest, you look pale and tired," said her father sympathetically.

Annie welcomed this opportunity to be alone, to sort out all the wonderful things that had happened in the last week. She could see Donald's handsome face as she dreamed—but suddenly the reality of the situation struck her. It wasn't wonderful, it was terrible! He was gone! "Dear Lord," she prayed, "give me the strength to go on without him." The more she thought, the more hopeless she became. She berated herself for being thoughtless, forgetting her obligation to her father and the girls and thinking only of herself. Her little glimpse of heaven had blinded her to the people depending on her. She had found love, only to have to push it away and live the rest of her life unhappy because of it. Donald had asked her to wait for him and of course, even though she had promised, she could not. She could never leave Da and her sisters. She would have to write to him and break her promise. Annie had worked herself into a terrible state. It seemed that demons hammered at her skull. She crept off to bed too drained to cry, and finally slept, but with tortured dreams.

* * *

There were two ships in the harbor and another was sailing away as Ian Maccrae and his family arrived at the pier. Maggie was the first one out of the carriage. Mary called after her, "I think we're too late. Come back, Maggie!"

Maggie stopped just long enough to call back, "That isn't the ship—it had a flower name . . . I'm going to see if they're on that one." She pointed vaguely to one of the two ships still in the harbor and kept running. Meanwhile, Ian made some inquiries and discovered that the *Tulippe* had already sailed. He was disappointed and knew the girls would be equally so at having missed the chance to wave a last goodbye to their sisters. "Sorry, daughters, we might as well go home. Are you ready?"

They resettled themselves in the carriage, all a little sad and irritable because they had delayed too long at home. "Well, this time we can't blame Maggie!" sighed Mary. The words were no sooner out of her mouth when they all looked at each other. "Maggie! She's not here!" Mary was now angry and upset.

To soothe her, Frances volunteered to look for her youngest sister. She hurried over to the two ships. People were embarking on the first and only a few sailors were lounging around near the gangplank of the second. Gathering all of her courage, she approached one of them and asked if they had seen a young girl, but none of them had. She ran back to the carriage and enlisted everyone's help. They spread out in all directions. They called, they asked everyone, and were even permitted to search the ships, but no Maggie! They looked to their

43

father for an answer. He was completely non-plussed, but to lessen the despair of his daughters he suggested that Maggie might have met someone of their acquaintance and gone home with them. He didn't say it convincingly and no one was convinced but the only thing left to do was to return home. To cover up their fears of what might have happened to her—an accident, a kidnapping—they all agreed that Maggie should be punished severely for upsetting them so.

The stillness of the house was broken by the girls who came running in, calling Maggie. Annie woke with a start to find the house in turmoil. The girls burst into her room, all talking at once.

"Please, girls, my head aches. Can't we talk about whatever it is later?" she sighed. She went over to the basin and bathed her face in cold water. The nap had lightened her headache but now it was in danger of returning. Then she noticed their stricken faces. "What is it? What has happened?"

Her face streaked with tears, Mary sobbed, "It's Maggie! She's missing! I should have watched her more carefully."

"What do you mean, she's missing?" Annie's voice hit a slightly hysterical note. Frances took it upon herself to explain.

Annie sat very still as she listened, her fingers to her temples which were beginning to throb. "Let me think . . . I know where she is! She has a special hiding place. I'm not sure where it is, but it's somewhere in the house. I'm sure that's where she's gone," she said at last.

Laurie spoke up. "I know, I'll show you." She led Annie, with the others following, to Maggie's so-called hiding place in the attic, although no-one had figured out how she could have got there. Again, no Maggie. Annie reached down into a corner by the dormer window and picked up several drawings. They were designs she had drawn—original paisley designs, a ship. The next had two people going up a gangplank and a very small person at the bottom waving and standing in a puddle of tears.

Mary exploded, "She's probably on the ship we saw sailing away, the little beast!"

Frances put her hand on her sister's shoulder. "You are too hard on her, Mary. You're forgetting the ship was underway when we arrived. She's not on *that* ship."

"When do the other ships sail?" Annie asked frantically.

"I inquired," said Frances. "Tomorrow the *Red Rose* sails at dawn, the other the next day."

Da said, grimly, "I'll go back and try to board the ship again. If not, I'll wait there until morning."

"No, Da. Nothing can be accomplished to-night. I will wake you at four tomorrow morning, and if she has not returned by then, we will both go and search the ship," said Annie.

Ian Maccrae reluctantly agreed. No one was hungry, but they were all exhausted and managed to sleep; all except Annie and Da. She was up at three and her father just a little after. At her insistence he ate the porridge she set before him. They left without disturbing the others.

The day was half gone when they returned. No one at the docks had seen Maggie and they had searched, with help, in every corner of each ship. They didn't leave until the *Red Rose* had set sail. By that time they were convinced that Maggie had managed to board some other ship and was even now on her way to America.

Annie thought of writing to Katherine then decided against it. If Maggie caught up with them they would be the first to mention it. There was no point in worrying them. All thoughts of love for Donald MacConnack had been forgotten with the added burden of Maggie's sudden disappearance.

IV

THE STOWAWAY

When Maggie darted away, she had every
intention of secretly joining Kate and Robbie.
Her sack of goodies was actually a small
bundle of clothing, a few leftover scones and
bits and pieces of food, enough to keep her
until the ship was at sea, at which time she
planned to disclose herself, thus ensuring that
it would be too late to be sent home. It was the
kind of foolproof scheme only a determined
fourteen-year-old would think of. Her only
fear was that she would be found before the
ship sailed. She found a hiding place on the
dock behind crates and trunks that were still
to be loaded.

Maggie put her fingers in her ears to shut
out the sound of her sisters and father calling
her. It seemed hours before they gave up and
left. Unmindful of the distress she was causing, her sense of relief at the silence was soon
replaced by worry as footsteps came close and
crates were carried off to be loaded on the
ship. She had hidden herself in the farthest
corner behind a large coil of rope. Now she
heard several voices coming nearer and looked
around wildly for another place to hide, but it
was too late. They were standing directly in

front of the rope when one man said to the others, "I think we've done it for tonight, men. We can load the little that's left in the morning." Her heart slowed down to its normal beat as the footsteps receded.

Maggie felt asleep for a few hours and was awakened by the noise of men calling to each other. It was still dark. Again her heart picked up a fast beat as she decided to take a chance and make a dash for the gangplank. She got to the foot of it when she felt a hand on her shoulder, and a deep voice said, "Well, lass, where do you think you are going?"

Maggie let out a startled yelp. It took her a few moments of heavy breathing before she could gather her wits and get enough breath to answer. "Oh, sir," she addressed the sailor who had stopped her, thinking fast, "I am nursemaid to a lady who is sailing on this ship. I was to meet them here but the carriage I was in had a broken wheel. We arrived late and I couldn't find them." It was easy to call up tears as frustration and exhaustion crowded in on her; she looked so bedraggled that she was very convincing.

"Are you sure this is the right ship?"

"Oh, yes sir," (she had seen the name painted on the side). "It was the *Red Rose*. They were to board the ship last night and sail early this morning."

"Well," he said reluctantly, "you can't stay here. Go on board and when you find your mistress, see that you stay close."

Maggie curtsied and said thank you, then scrambled up the gangplank and lost herself in the many corridors until she found the one where the passenger cabins were located. She listened at each door until she heard the sound of restless children in Cabin 10. There was no one in sight, so she scrunched down to one side behind a large trunk and slept very lightly, awaking each time some sound came near. She had heard footsteps very close at one time but they didn't pass her; they turned around and walked away. They belonged to Annie and her father.

The second time she was caught, by the same sailor who had stopped her at the gangplank. The crying children could be heard through the door and Maggie stood as if waiting to be admitted. "Well, I see you found your mistress. From the sound of those children, she must be very glad you did." Afraid of being heard inside, Maggie just nodded as he passed.

A woman's voice was heard over the din in the cabin and Maggie quickly moved away as the door opened. "This voyage is going to be a disaster for me!" the woman was moaning. "Nurse Gilmore had such wonderful references, but she's no better than any other servant. They always get sick when you need them most."

"Don't fret, dear," said a man's voice. "We can probably find someone on the ship to take care of the children."

"I hope so. Not only am I deprived of her services, but here we have paid for Cabin 6 with no one to occupy it."

Maggie walked to the opposite end of the corridor and waited until the couple disappeared. Making sure she wasn't seen, she ran back and tried the door of Cabin 6, which was providentially unlocked. She found a basin of water, dipped one end of her shawl into it and washed her face and hands. She also found on a small table a basket of food, ostensibly, she assumed, for the nursemaid and the children. She broke off a piece of bread and found cheese which she ate, wrapped up the rest in a napkin she found there, and quickly returned to the far end of the corridor. It might have been her awareness of the position she was in or just good luck but she managed the first day very well.

The second day at sea Maggie contrived to walk along the corridor just as the family emerged from Cabin 10. The husband and wife were at odds with each other; he was tired of her complaining and she felt very much put upon. One of the children dawdled behind the others. Maggie caught up with the child. "Is he your little boy?" she asked in all innocence.

"Dear Lord, yes!" sighed the woman. "I just cannot keep up with the task of caring for three children all by myself."

"May I offer my help? I'm well used to little ones," said Maggie with a winning smile. Not quite true, but she *had* taught a Sunday school class.

"You are a *nursemaid?*" the lady asked almost prayerfully.

Maggie avoided the lie. "I am traveling to the States and hope to find a position there."

"Would you consider being nursemaid to my children for the voyage?" the woman asked eagerly. She explained about Nurse Gilmore's illness, and added, "We hope she will be able to sail on the next ship."

"I'm sorry about your nursemaid. I would be grateful for the work. I love children. The only problem is that I have a very small cabin and I couldn't bring the children there," said Maggie.

"My dear young lady, what is your name?" Before Maggie could reply, she rattled on, "We have an empty cabin with room enough to house you and the children—that is, if you . . . ?"

This was a new role for Mrs. Henderson. She had never catered to a servant before; it was obvious that she was desperate.

"My name is Margaret Anderson," Maggie informed the woman. She was thinking fast. A lot of what she was about to say had been prepared in advance in case someone questioned her. "I have references, but they are in my trunk—and I would love to take care of your children."

"Don't worry about references, Margaret. I can see you have been very well trained. I am Mrs. Henderson and my husband is Dr. Henderson. We are about to have breakfast. Can you begin now?"

The word "breakfast" was music to Maggie's ears. "If it is agreeable to you, Mrs. Henderson, perhaps you can ask for a small table to be set up in the cabin and I will feed the children there." This of course gave her the freedom to eat as much as she wanted, without being observed by her new employer.

"I am sure that can be arranged. It is very bright of you to suggest it. Come, children!" Her voice had become almost affectionate as she herded them into the cabin. On their way to breakfast shortly thereafter, she told her husband. "That girl is a jewel! Perhaps we should ask her to stay with us permanently.

"Perhaps, but let us not be hasty," said Dr. Henderson. "Nurse Gilmore will be along on the next ship, after all."

In the little free time afforded her, Maggie looked for her sisters and the Americans. They had to be in one of the first class cabins, as she was, but they were nowhere to be found. Taking her courage in both hands, she timidly knocked on the door of the wheelhouse. The Captain received her graciously, listened to her story (which by this time was somewhat garbled because of her employment with Dr. and Mrs. Henderson.) He promised to look over the passenger list and let her know, although he was sure they were not on board. He confirmed it the following day. It posed a terrible dilemma for Maggie. In her wildest scheming she had not envisioned herself in America without Kate and Robbie. She feared she would not be able to enter the country without the proper identification.

For the first week, everything went smoothly. Maggie and the children got along very well, the food was plentiful and with just a few exceptions, she was able to sleep all night. Dr. Henderson was fast becoming a father figure to her. He stopped at her cabin each afternoon to see that she and the children fared well and was most solicitous. As for Mrs. Henderson, she left the complete responsibility for the children on Maggie's slim shoulders.

By the second week, Dr. Henderson's fatherly pats were becoming more like caresses. Maggie was becoming wary but didn't know what to do about it. On the tenth day of the voyage he stopped by as was his wont. "Mrs. Henderson is taking a nap, Margaret, and I thought it was time for us to have a serious talk," he said firmly.

"About what, Dr. Henderson?" His voice was low and she felt herself stiffen.

"We don't know anything about your background or your state of health. We would like you to stay on as the children's nursemaid, but before you make your home with us, you should have a physical examination. The children seem to be sound asleep; I think this would be a good time." He put his arm around her shoulders and began to unbutton the bodice of her dress.

Eyes wide with fear, Maggie protested, "I am *very* healthy, Dr. Henderson. As you have seen, I'm not even bothered by the motion of the ship."

"Don't be afraid, Margaret dear, I wouldn't hurt you," soothed the doctor. He tightened his grasp and tried for the second button. Maggie wriggled out of his grasp and he lunged for her. She tried not to panic and dodging his hands, sat down hard on the bunk of the eldest child. He woke with a loud cry of fright.

"I'm sorry, Eric, I tripped. Did I hurt you?" she asked solicitously. He blinked his eyes sleepily and she sat him up. "Your papa is here to visit with you."

The doctor's eyes blazed with anger. "I can't stay now, son. Go back to sleep." But Maggie took the child on her lap. "If you're going to stay with us, Margaret," he continued, "you will have to submit . . . to an examination. We'll talk again." In a temper, Dr. Henderson left, slamming the door as he went and leaving behind a very bewildered young lady. She knew nothing of the ways of men with women. There had been whispered scandals in Paisley, but never anything explained. At home she had been babied and protected. All things sordid had been kept from her as was usual with young girls.

Maggie lay down in her bunk, trying to sort out what had happened. Dr. Henderson's touch on her neck as he unbuttond her dress had stirred strange emotions; fear, anger—and, what bothered her most, a desire to let him continue. Her imagination couldn't carry her far enough to guess what might have happened if he had. She was breathing heavily, giving herself up to the tiny spark that had run the length of her body.

She didn't have time to think further along those lines, however, for the ship rolled sharply and the youngest child started to cry. She soothed the child, then put a chair against the door. She had to protect herself against Dr. Henderson—and perhaps against herself. She couldn't tell Mrs. Henderson. That would make it impossible to retain her position with them; and yet, she knew she couldn't live in the same house. Her main concern was to get to the end of the voyage without further problems. She finally evolved a plan, not perfect, but worth trying.

The next day, when the children were napping and after she had watched Dr. Henderson leave to visit the Captain's pregnant wife, she knocked on the door of Cabin 10. Mrs. Henderson welcomed her.

"You look tired, my dear. Are the children proving too much for you?"

"No, Mrs. Henderson, but I would like to have some little time for myself. Would it be possible for you to visit with them in the afternoon? They miss you very much and ask for you so often. That would give me time to walk on deck and get some air and exercise which I sorely need."

Mrs. Henderson's eyebrows shot up. Servants didn't usually speak to the mistress this way. She was a beautiful woman, proud and haughty, but at heart, good natured. "Margaret, I have been selfish. I know children can be demanding and at the same time, often boring. But now that I think about it a little, I guess I miss them, too. Suppose I visit every afternoon and give you a half-hour to be on your own? Would that be satisfactory?"

"You've very generous and I thank you," said Maggie gratefully. "The children will be so happy to have you with them. They will be waking now—I must go back."

Dr. Henderson didn't find out about the new arrangement until he tapped on the door of Maggie's cabin later that day and found his wife with the children. There were no recriminations from her, so he guessed Maggie hadn't told his wife about the episode the day before. He recognized that he had been outsmarted—but only temporarily, he assured himself.

V

FRIENDSHIP

Mrs. Henderson was surprised and pleased to see her husband when he dropped in two days in succession. He had trapped himself and each time he stayed to help her, as she said, "entertain the children." She suggested that he continue to come each afternoon. "It's fun for the children and gives poor, overworked Margaret a few minutes to herself," she said. Her remark told him all he needed to know. Margaret was a smart little minx and he was determined that she wouldn't get away with it. He could wait until he was in control of the situation at home; there he was master and all the servants knew it . . . particularly the female servants.

Maggie was breathing more freely. She had two more weeks before the ship reached its destination and Mrs. Henderson said she would give her the wages she had earned during the voyage before they docked in New York. With money in her pocket, her vague plans to lose herself in the crowd of passengers disembarking became more of a reality. She spent a lot of time figuring the best way to accomplish her separation from the

Hendersons. She decided she would start off the ship, pretend she had forgotten something, and hide somewhere until they left—which was exactly the same way she had come aboard. Dr. Henderson no longer paid visits when she was alone with the children, and her daily walks on the deck revived the vitality she had lost by staying in the closed quarters of the cabin. Her fears were allayed and she ignored the threat still posed by the doctor.

On one of her walks, she met the Captain who was standing at the rail, head bowed.

"Good afternoon, Captain Colton," she said politely. He didn't raise his head. "Is there anything wrong? Are you ill?"

"What are you doing here, Miss? No one is allowed to come this far. You have intruded on my privacy!" His face was drawn and his voice was harsh.

Embarrassed, Maggie replied, "I did not know. I am sorry, I will leave immediately."

"No, no, forgive my rudeness. I am not ill, but I am troubled."

"Can I help?" Maggie asked.

"Bless you," the Captain sighed. "It's my wife. She's with child and not well. The doctor says the birth will be difficult. She is lonely and dispirited. You see, we did not expect the child for another month. It was to be born in America but now . . ." He turned and for the first time looked at Maggie. "My dear young lady, forgive me! I am so full of my own problems that I have forgotten the dignity of my profession." He begged her pardon again as he turned to leave.

"Please, Captain Colton, I am the nursemaid for Dr. Henderson's children. I am permitted a half hour for a constitutional every afternoon. Perhaps your . . . Mrs. Colton would enjoy some company. I could spend some time with her each afternoon.''

"That is very thoughtful, my dear," said the Captain, "but you're just a child."

"Don't let my small stature deceive you. I will soon be seventeen years old," said Maggie briskly. She didn't have to cross her fingers to tell that lie. She didn't say *how* soon she would be seventeen.

"Thank you, Miss . . . ?" He raised his eyebrows in question.

"Miss Margaret," she supplied.

"You say you have some free time now?"

She nodded.

"Come with me." He led the way to a large and well furnished cabin where Mrs. Colton lay on a couch in the living quarters, looking as miserable as she felt. The Captain introduced Maggie and asked, "Would you like some company for a few minutes? This is the nursemaid of Dr. Henderson's children. She would like to sit with you for a bit."

Mrs. Colton extended a feeble hand and smiled, her husband noted, for the first time in days. "Do sit down, my dear. I welcome some feminine company." She said to her husband as he was leaving, "You are so thoughtful, John. I have been so longing for a woman to speak with!" He turned back, kissed her cheek and left.

"I am sorry I did not know of your . . . condition before, Mrs. Colton. I am given thirty minutes each afternoon and I could have dropped by to see you. As it is, today I have only a few minutes left. Would you like me to comb your hair? It is quite beautiful, like gold, but it must annoy you hanging down your back," said Maggie, smiling.

In just a few moments, Mrs. Colton began to look more like her attractive self. Maggie washed her face with cool water, combed her hair and suggested that she pinch her cheeks just a little to bring some color to her face, which made her laugh out loud. She found a pink shawl to drape over her shoulders and by the time the Captain returned, she looked more like the girl he had married than she had on the entire voyage. Maggie had even prepared tea and had a cup ready for him. Gratefully he stumbled over his thanks. "Miss Margaret, if there is anything I can do to make you more comfortable, you have only to ask!"

Acknowledging his gratitude with a nod, she said to Mrs. Colton, "I'll be here tomorrow and spend a little more time with you, if you wish."

"I'll be waiting for you," she called after her. After Maggie had left, she turned to her husband. "I do hope she comes tomorrow." She sounded wistful.

"I'm sure she will. She's a sweet and thoughtful person." John Colton knelt beside his wife, put his hands on her shoulders and said, "Here, let me look at you." A wave of emotion swept over him at her improved appearance and he buried his face in her lap. This brave, strong man, with a shipful of people in his care, was weeping.

"Don't, John, I'm fine, really I am. You must not worry so," she said softly.

"I feel so guilty, my love, to have done this to you," Colton sighed. "Only a year ago when we were married you were vibrant with health, and when I think that this is my fault . . ."

"Say no more. I want a child as much as you do. And I'll go through it again," she said as she put both hands on his face and lifted it so their lips could meet. She added lightly, "You'd better get used to it!" She gave him a little poke in the ribs, making him laugh. "Who's having this baby, anyway?" She kissed him again. "*Mon Capitaine,* I think the ship is in need of your guiding hand. It seems to be rolling more than usual." He helped her back to the couch, not admitting she was right about the ship rocking. For the first time in many days he had a smile on his face as he saluted her and left.

A pattern had been established and every day Maggie walked for ten minutes, met the Captain and accompanied him to his cabin. Mrs. Colton had become interested again in her appearance and was coiffed, washed and dressed when Maggie arrived, giving them time for a chat. They had known each other less than a week and yet had become fast friends, each filling a need in the other. Maggie hadn't realized how much she missed her sisters and Ellen Colton needed a woman friend.

Dr. Henderson was pleased with the improvement in his patient's condition. He had been visiting her every day, and each day she seemed stronger. Today when he arrived she was waiting for Maggie in a comfortable chair on the deck outside her cabin; she found the slight breeze and the sunshine invigorating.

"Well, Mrs. Colton, I must say I have not seen you look as well since we started this voyage. What magic are you employing?" the doctor asked.

"Here comes my magic!" She pointed to Maggie who was coming towards them.

His smile was immediatedly replaced by a scowl. "What are you doing here, Margaret? Aren't you supposed to be with the children?" He forgot his patient, grabbed Maggie by the arm and pushed her ahead of him. "It's time we learned something about you, Missy! You're not supposed to be associating with the passengers, particularly the Captain's wife. How did you get here?"

Maggie pulled herself free, her eyes narrowing in anger. "Don't you ever put a hand on me again or I will have to speak with Mrs. Henderson about your behaviour!" she hissed. She could not let him know how he intimidated her.

"You're threatening me?"

She ignored his question. "Furthermore, you are intruding on the time I have to myself. I am here because the Captain and Mrs. Colton have invited me. She is waiting for me—as Mrs. Henderson and your children are waiting for *you.*"

His chin jerked up and dark blood suffused his face. He glanced quickly in Mrs. Colton's direction and could see she was watching them with a puzzled expression. "You'll play for your insubordinate attitude, Margaret! You'll find living in my home will make your situation very different." He nodded to Mrs. Colton, turned on his heel and walked rapidly away.

"I'm sorry for the interruption," said Maggie as calmly as possible. She sat in her usual chair opposite Mrs. Colton and folded her hands in her lap to hide the trembling.

"Margaret—may I call you that?—What did Dr. Henderson say to you? He frightened you, didn't he?"

"Oh, Mrs. Colton . . ." Maggie began.

She interrupted, "We are friends; please call me Ellen."

"My friends call me Maggie, Ellen. I hope you will, too," said Maggie promptly.

Ellen Colton leaned over and pressed her hand to give comfort. "Tell me about the doctor, Maggie."

Maggie wanted desperately to tell her everything, including about stowing away, but as the Captain's wife, her first duty would be to inform her husband. So she said nothing about her unorthodox manner of boarding the ship and told her as much of the truth as she dared. "I met Mrs. Henderson quite by accident and she was having a struggle trying to care for the children. It seems that her nursemaid was ill and couldn't join them on the voyage home. She offered me the position, just for the trip, and I gladly accepted. She gave me the accommodations she had already paid for and the children and I share a cabin. She has since offered me the job permanently. I suppose I have to take it, as it is the only way I can live in America."

"Have you no family?" Ellen asked,

concerned.

"Yes, I have two sisters who are in America. I hope to find them."

Puzzled, Ellen asked, "Do you know where they are living?"

Maggie sighed deeply. "I have lost the address. They are, I'm sure, somewhere in New York City."

"My dear Maggie, that's like looking for a needle in a haystack! Let me think about this for a bit . . . Why did it seem to me that Dr. Henderson was threatening you?"

Tears brimmed in Maggie's eyes and she bit her lip to stop them from spilling over. "He . . . he wants me to . . ."

Ellen understood immediately what was bothering Maggie. "You mean he's forcing his attentions on you?" Maggie nodded. "The beast!" Her anger was showing and Maggie worried about getting her upset. "I'll speak to my husband!"

"No, please don't do that! If it is necessary, and I just told him so, I will speak to Mrs. Henderson." She grinned momentarily. "He doesn't want that!"

"What did he say?"

"That's what worries me. He said when I am under his roof I will understand that servants are in his charge and do *his* bidding. Ellen, I know little of men and their ways, but he frightens me." She looked at the little watch pinned to her dress. "I must go. Forgive me for worrying you. Are you feeling well? Have I upset you?"

Ellen shook her head. "No," she said slowly, "but we'll talk again. Meanwhile, if he bothers you, let me know." Maggie kissed her on the cheek and left.

It was good to have a friend.

VI

THE STORM

As Maggie made her way to the Coltons'
cabin she had to hold on to the railing to
balance herself against the pitching of the
ship. This was the second day the skies had
been gray. Today they had turned very dark,
like a pall of black smoke from which the ship
couldn't escape.

Ellen Colton was feeling the effects of the
rolling and suffering a severe case of *mal de
mer*, which doubled her problem of nausea
due to pregnancy. She welcomed the sight of
Maggie, who immediately helped her into bed.
Maggie made light of the fact that she had to
struggle to keep herself upright and made a
joke of tying down some of the loose objects in
the cabin. The oil lamp was first—it was swaying dangerously. Ellen agreed it would be
better to be in the dark than to have the oil
spill over. Maggie supported her with pillows,
then washed her face with cool water and gave
her a shallow basin in case of emergency. The
ship's motion was getting more severe. When
it was time for Maggie to leave she tied a sheet
around Ellen, anchoring it on both sides of the
bed.

"I wish you didn't have to go, Maggie." Ellen

was pale and drawn and started to retch.

"I'll be back. I'm going to get the doctor and I'll just tell Mrs. Henderson to stay with the children."

Ellen closed her eyes, hoping sleep would still the awful nausea which had seized her.

There was only ten feet between Maggie and her cabin when a tremendous wave broke over the side of the ship, drenching her and plastering her against the outside wall. One of the sailors came along, tied to a rope. He scolded her soundly and when she managed to make him hear her above the howling wind, she told him about Mrs. Colton. "She has to have the doctor. He's in that cabin." She pointed. He wrapped the end of his rope around her and at last they made it to the door. Dr. Henderson was tending a cut on his little boy's head; the child had been thrown out of his bunk. Mrs. Henderson was hanging on to the side of it, terrified.

When the message had been delivered, the doctor turned to Mrs. Henderson. "You'd better come with me. I'll need help."

"*Me?*" she shrieked. "I'm not a nurse! Get someone else to help you."

He knew how she would react to that request but it gave him the excuse he needed to take Maggie with him.

"You can't take Margaret; you think more of your patients than you do your own family. I can't take care of the children and myself, too, in this storm. Maggie stays here!" Mrs. Henderson wailed.

Meanwhile, Maggie was busying herself getting out sheets and tying the children securely in their bunks. "Sit down, Mrs.

Henderson," she commanded as she tried to pull a chair close to the children's bunks. The sailor pulled it over for her. Although protesting, Mrs. Henderson was tied securely to the chair and the chair tied to the bunk post with a knot fastened in such a manner that she could open it if necessary. Maggie told the doctor to go on ahead to tend to Mrs. Colton and she would follow. Finally, everyone was in a more or less secure position. With a great effort, the sailor opened the door. Although a short length of rope held them together, Tommy, the sailor, put his arm around Maggie and held her tightly as they fought their way against the raging storm, being swept back two steps for every one they took forward. They had almost reached their destination when they could see dimly through the sheets of rain, a figure sprawled on the deck outside the Coltons' cabin. It was Dr. Henderson—he had fallen and was trying to keep from being washed overboard. Between them they managed to raise him to his feet; he was uninjured but shaken. The two men then used their combined strength to open the door of the cabin, to find Ellen hanging half out of her bunk, kept there only by the sheet which Maggie had tied around her. She was in great pain and crying.

If Maggie knew nothing of men and their ways, she also knew nothing of birthing. Dr. Henderson, for all his peculiarities, was a fine physician and his orders were precise. Maggie followed them without thinking about what she was experiencing.

The ship pitched violently, first topping the crest of a gigantic wave, then slamming down into the trough of it. It was more than any normal pregnancy could withstand and certainly Ellen was so fragile that it portended the too-early birth of her child.

As Ellen was fighting for her life, so Captain Colton was fighting for the life of his ship. He had been through violent storms before and it took all his concentration plus the strength of two men to keep the wheel in his hands. He had no time to think of Ellen. With the first lull, however, his thoughts were only of his wife. The seething waters diminished. The angry air bursting cannon-like through the sails had calmed somewhat and now the wind vibrated among the shrouds like a song. John handed over the wheel to his First Mate and literally ran through the stinging rain, praying that Ellen had withstood the severe tossing of the ship. There was a break in the black clouds as he opened the door of his cabin and a beam of dying sunlight broke through. He heard a sharp slap and then the first cry of his son. For a moment he stood in the doorway, confused by the number of people in the cabin. Dr. Henderson was working desperately to keep his patient alive; Maggie was giving Tommy orders to bring her blankets to swaddle the tiny creature in, and to try to heat some water to bathe the infant. No one noticed John until he dashed forward, tearing off his oilskins and about to throw his arms around Ellen.

Dr. Henderson shoved him out of the way and continued his ministrations. John stood there, mute, aching to embrace her. He hadn't noticed Maggie, who had disappeared with the infant to the other room. The sailor pushed past him and left the cabin; he returned with a barrel cut in half lengthwise, blankets and several warming pans, used only in the coldest winters to warm the bunks. With very little knowledge but deep instinct as to the needs of this tiny creature, Maggie made a warm nest for him . . . blankets folded over several times, the warming pans filled with hot coals Tommy had filched from the galley, more blankets and then the child, bathed and with eye and nose passages cleared by Dr. Henderson, was ready for his father's inspection.

"He's so tiny, so red and wrinkled," was the only thing John could think of to say.

"He wasn't quite ready to make his debut. He's a fine fellow and strong—a fighter like you, sir," the doctor said sincerely. "He'll be just fine."

"Thanks to you . . . and Margaret. How do I thank you?" said the Captain. "Margaret, I didn't know you knew about these things."

"I don't . . . didn't. I just followed the doctor's orders and well, I guess there are some things you do by instinct. He's a beautiful baby! Congratulations."

He said a vague "thank you," turned on his heel and went back to Ellen. Dr. Henderson was just finishing with his patient.

"May I sit with her?" John asked.

The doctor pointed to the chair he had been occupying. "She should have someone with her. She's been through an ordeal."

John sat down and took his wife's hand in his. "Ellen, sweatheart, can you hear me?"

She opened her eyes. "Oh, John, I'm so glad you're here! The baby . . . ?"

"I just saw him. He's . . . he's" he gulped "wonderful! Are you all right?" She was white as paper and it was obvious she had no strength left. John sat alongside her, held her hand and kissed it repeatedly. "May I stay?" he asked the doctor.

"Yes, of course," he answered. "Continue to bathe her head and face; she's slightly feverish." A knock at the door interrupted any further instructions he might have issued.

Tommy opened it and held a low conversation with the deckhand at the door, then beckoned to the Captain. Dr. Henderson had just told Maggie to go back to her cabin. "Wait, Margaret. Doctor, I am needed, I cannot stay. May we keep Margaret here a little longer?"

The doctor sighed deeply and then decided the greater necessity for her services lay with Mrs. Colton. He knew his wife would be furious, which was the reason for his sigh. He nodded his consent. "I have to see if there are others needing my help."

"I'd like you to come with me first if you will, Dr. Henderson," said the Captain. "We have some casualties among the crew, it appears." There was urgency in his voice. As they walked, Captain Colton explained that one man had been washed overboard and another was in serious trouble. He pointed to the mast where a sailor, who had lashed himself to the rigging when the storm hit, was hanging, unconscious or dead. Although the clouds had broken, the light was dim and the men watched apprehensively as sailors swarmed up the mast to free him. The fury of the sea had quieted but the ship was still rocking and the men had a difficult time bringing him down.

The doctor didn't have to examine him very thoroughly to determine that he was dead. At the Captain's orders a canvas was brought immediately and the dead sailor sewed into it. A ragtag-looking crew assembled, a brief service was read, and the sea received the body. They were all too exhausted to show emotion. The crew were dismissed and Dr. Henderson gave each a cursory examination, putting a patch here, a bandage there. Fortunately there were no broken bones and the crew went back to work.

The Captain left the First Mate at the wheel and returned to his wife. Tommy had managed to bring some soup from the galley and Maggie was about to spoon-feed Ellen when he came in. "I'll do that, Margaret. Perhaps you should get some rest. Why do't you lie down before going back to your cabin?"

"Thank you, it will be best for me to return right away. Mrs. Henderson will be upset at my absence and I'm not in a position to make her angry with me."

John was wringing out a cloth to put on Ellen's head when he turned and said, "I have felt that you are afraid of Dr. and Mrs. Henderson. Why?"

"It's a long story, Captain Colton, and we're all too tired to hear it now. Suffice it to say that I am dependent on them to be allowed to land in America," said Maggie quietly.

Ellen summoned the strength to speak. "We'll talk about it later, John. We have much to discuss. Thank you, dear Maggie! Try to get some rest and come back when you can."

Maggie kissed her cheek and waited until she had seen Ellen accept her first spoonful of broth, then left, steeling herself for the scolding she knew she would get from her employer.

She wasn't disappointed. A wild-eyed Mrs. Henderson heaped abuse on her until the doctor walked in and told her to "shut up." The expression was so shocking, that she did. He then escorted Mrs. Henderson to their cabin, gave her a drop of laudanum and told her to rest, after which he returned to Maggie. She had quieted the children and was about to change her clothes when he walked in. She quickly buttoned her blouse as he took one long stride forward, put his arm around her waist and pulled her towards him, trying to cover her mouth with his, but she fought hard and finally managed to stamp on his foot. He let go with a cry and sat down, rubbing his foot.

"Dammit, Margaret. I don't believe you've ever been in service! A pretty girl like you ought to know how to treat the master!" Maggie was breathing hard and her eyes flashed sparks of hatred. "Anyway, that was only a reward for being such a fine nurse. I have decided to have you work with me. You'd be wasting your talents as a nursemaid; we can always get someone to take care of the children. Your wages will be higher, your hours better and you'll be in my office with me. When you get to know me better, you'll realize I'm a fine fellow."

Maggie had remained quiet, standing at some distance from him. She was dismayed at his offer and didn't know how to answer him.

"I like a spitfire, Margaret, but only at certain times." He winked as he replaced the boot he had removed to rub his toes. "Think about my offer. It will be to your advantage to accept it."

Maggie didn't breathe until the door closed behind him. The palms of her hands were sore from digging her nails into them. She locked the door against further intrusion and gave vent to the tears she had so fiercely held back. She thought of complaining to the Captain but, again, she would have to disclose her stowaway status and she was afraid of the resulting punishment.

Despite the torment of her mind, exhaustion took over and she sank into a deep sleep.

VII

THE INVITATION

When Mrs. Henderson came to the cabin the next day to relieve Maggie for her walk, she was puffy-faced and red-eyed from weeping. "Are you feeling ill?" Maggie inquired.

"I am upset, Margaret. Dr. Henderson has no idea of the work entailed in taking care of the children. He's told me he wants you to work with him and his patients. I want you to stay with me. He is selfish and inconsiderate and I don't know how I put up with him!"

"Don't worry, Mrs. Henderson, I'm sure everything will work out well," Maggie soothed, while wondering how she could escape both of them. Her sense of security was somewhat restored when Mrs. Henderson brought out her purse and counted out twenty dollars. Maggie did not know about American money and how much each bill was worth, but she sensed it was a good sum—and a bribe. She did not refuse it.

"You have helped me tremendously, Margaret, during this voyage. We'll be in the harbor in two days and I want you to have this now." Mrs. Henderson peeled off five more one-dollar bills. "That is a token of my appreciation and an indication that I want you to continue as the children's nursemaid." She waited for a reply.

"Thank you, Mrs. Henderson, you are most generous," said Maggie. "I must go now, but after I've had some time to think about all this, perhaps we can talk again?"

"By all means, child. Think well on it."

Maggie rolled up the money and put it in her purse. She had to find out how much it would buy, such as lodging and food, and for how long. A vague plan had been forming; the only thing holding it up was money.

As usual, she saw the Captain as she neared his cabin. "How are Mrs. Colton and the baby?" was her first question.

"Margaret, it's good to see you." He had been deep in thought. "My wife is feeling better than she did yesterday, but I wouldn't say she's well. Young John, however, appears to be in fine fettle."

"I'll go to her immediately—but I have a question to ask of you. May I speak to you later?"

"By all means. I'll stop by before you leave. I have asked Dr. Henderson's permission for you to stay longer today. We'll have time to talk."

Maggie thanked him and ran off to Ellen, whom she found much improved. She brought little John to his mother, and for all that he was tiny, he was also lusty and screaming with hunger. Following the doctor's instructions, Ellen nursed him as she admired his minuscule fingers and watched his innocent eyes close as his demands were met. At last Maggie took the contentedly sleeping bundle from her.

"Oh, Maggie," Ellen sighed, "this is the most joyous moment of my life! I hope you experience it one day."

Maggie smiled and laid the baby back in his barrel crib after changing him into a dry nappy. He was a beautiful baby, but she wasn't sure she wanted to go through all that Ellen had in order to have one like him. She shrugged; she had plenty of time to think about that. She looked for and found a pretty, pink sleeping jacket and nightgown to match from Ellen's little-used trousseau. After she had given her a sponge bath and combed her hair, the pink jacket brought a touch of color to Ellen's otherwise pale face.

The Captain was very pleased when he joined them. Maggie brought him tea and some cookies that had been baked especially in honor of the new babe. Twenty minutes had passed. Maggie looked at her watch. "I should get back."

"You said you wanted to speak to me about something. What is it, Margaret?" John Colton asked kindly.

"I don't want to burden Ellen now. She should take a nap." Maggie didn't want to open a serious conversation in Ellen's presence.

"Go ahead, Maggie, I'm all right," Ellen encouraged.

She took a deep breath and, hesitantly at first, explained her dilemma. "I'm afraid of Dr. Henderson and if I work in his office I don't know what will happen. If I continue as nursemaid I'll be living in the same house with him. I'll never feel secure." She opened her purse. "Mrs. Henderson paid me for the voyage and gave me extra, as she said, to influence me to stay with her. See? I don't know how much it is or if it will permit me to find a place to live until I can find some kind of employment." She spread the money on Ellen's bunk.

"Good Lord, she really must be anxious!" John said. "Some men support their families for a month on twenty-five dollars."

Ellen was sitting up straighter and her eyes were bright as she urged her husband, "Tell her, John."

"My darling wife, I wouldn't deprive you of that pleasure. Margaret, Ellen and I have had a long talk and we have a suggestion to make. Go ahead, dear."

Mystified, Maggie looked from one to the other.

"I will not be traveling with John now that Baby John is here," Ellen began, "and it will be lonesome for me. I would dearly love to have you come home with us as my companion. Not as a servant," she added hastily, "but as a friend. I have a house-keeper and will have a nursemaid but I need someone to help me supervise the house-hold and keep me company. Would you con-sider it?"

Maggie covered her face with her hands and broke into tears. She tried to control her sobs as she thanked Ellen. "I . . . don't . . . know how to say thank you! Oh, you have saved my life! Of course I'll come." She turned to the

Captain. "I can promise you, Captain Colton . . ."

He interrupted her by putting up his hand. "From now on you must call me John."

Smiling, she repeated, "I promise you, *John*, you will never have to worry about the welfare of your wife or child. I shall dedicate myself to them both." Maggie, not quite fifteen years old, had attained in a little over a month at sea the maturity her eldest sister had achieved at an even earlier age. Gathering up the money still spread on the bed she said, "I will return this to Mrs. Henderson."

Shaking his head in disagreement John said, "No, you have earned that money by working very hard in unhappy circumstances. Keep it and if you wish, I'll speak to Dr. Henderson about our plans."

Before replying to John's offer she asked, "When do we get to our destination?"

"We dock in New York harbor in two days, Friday, about four in the afternoon."

"The day after tomorrow?"

He nodded. She continued, "I would rather not say anything to the Hendersons until Thursday night. There will be packing to do and I'll help them get ready to leave the ship. I'm sure they can manage without me until they reach their home." She was silent for a moment. "I think, John, it *would* be best if you tell the doctor. I'll speak to Mrs. Henderson myself. Is that fair?"

They all agreed it was the best way to handle the situation.

That night after the Henderson children had been put to sleep, Maggie wrote a letter to her family. She did not disclose where she would be since she wasn't sure herself, but told them she was on her way to America, well and happy and that she would write again. She also expressed regret at the worry she knew she had caused. "I have not found Kate or Robbie but feel sure that in the not too distant future I will. I love you and miss you, but I'm sure I'll love America, too. I hope you understand my great desire to be here." She signed it with love and kisses and a little blur that might have been a teardrop. To spare her father the shock of receiving her first letter, she addressed it to Annie.

The next day she waited until she saw her sailor friend, Tommy. "You've been so kind to me, Tommy, I feel I can ask you to do me a very important favor," she said.

"Anything, Miss, anything at all."

Maggie gave him the letter and asked him to post it when the ship returned to Glasgow, which he said would be just before Christmas. "I'll hand deliver it, if you wish," he offered.

"No," she said quickly, "you may be questioned. It is better this way."

Ah, little lass, I thought you were a runaway, he said to himself. It confirmed his well-formed opinion of her tender years. "I will post it, as you wish."

"You won't forget?"

"Have no fear, I'll not forget!"

At four o'clock the following afternoon, two stocky, muscular crewmen placed Ellen on a chair and carried her off the ship. Maggie followed with Little John in her arms. Tommy, who had children somewhere in the world but had never seen them, felt privileged to bring up the end of this little entourage. John had to stay with his ship.

Maggie had arrived in America.

PART TWO

VIII

TARRYTOWN

For Maggie's two older sisters, traveling on the *Tulippe* with the MacConnacks brought no hardship. Only one day ahead of the *Red Rose*, even the sea performed for the prestigious passengers. Their cabins, four in all, were second in elegance only to that of the Master of the ship. Amy, Robbie and Kate revelled in the sunshine, played games on the deck and neither saw nor thought of steerage and the people therein. Formal dinners, sometimes with the Captain and his wife, served to break the monotony. The voyage, which usually took forty days, was shortened by fair winds with no indication of the storm they had so providentially escaped.

On arrival in New York City, the Maccrae girls were admitted as part of the MacConnack party. Their names were not recorded in the hand ledgers of entry. They were met by the MacConnack carriage harnessed to four handsome horses and attended by footman and driver, both in livery. It was a large carriage with more than enough room for the four of them and Amy's maid. Kate didn't have to maneuver to sit next to Mr. MacConnack. Her seniority placed her in the back with him while the younger girls sat facing them. Kate took advantage of every bump in the road that sent her in his direction, savoring the physical contact.

Donald MacConnack had turned to speak to her just as she closed her eyes in deep appreciation of the intimacy of the moment. "Do you feel ill, Katherine?" he asked.

She had never felt better in her life but took advantage of his solicitude. "A trifle faint, Mr. MacConnack. The excitement of being in America with you . . ." she saw his eyebrows raise slightly and hastily added, " . . . and Amy is overwhelming!"

Robbie wondered what kind of a game she was playing. She knew there was nothing wrong with her sister, who had the face of a flower and the constitution of an ox. Amy claimed Robbie's attention as they traveled swiftly along and Donald obligingly adjusted his position so Kate could put her head on his shoulder. "Lean on me," he said, which she did, gratefully. She winked at Robbie who wanted to slap her.

They had been traveling almost an hour when Robbie leaned forward. "Kate? Kate!" She patted her sister's knee. Not getting any response, she pinched her under the guise of shaking her slightly. "Kate, *dear*, you had best wake up now."

Slowly Katherine opened her eyes, appeared bewildered, and then apologized for having fallen asleep. "I didn't know how tired I was. I hope you'll forgive me." She spoke to Donald MacConnack, batting her long lashes.

Robbie bit her lips to keep from venting her annoyance at Kate's manipulations.

Donald asked, "Are you feeling better, Kate?"

"Thank you, yes," she said with a gentle smile.

"I'm glad. You are missing a lot of the countryside I wanted you to see."

Kate murmured, "Oh, dear, I *am* sorry."

"Do you ride?" he asked.

"Oh, yes . . ."

Before she could finish the sentence Robbie interjected, "We all do."

"Good. We're not too far from home. We'll ride this way one day so you can see what you've missed."

"That's very kind of you, Mr. MacConnack. I'd like that," said Kate.

"I want to remind you both that we are to use first names. Please remember, mine is Donald."

Robbie opened her mouth but Kate answered first. "We'll remember, *Donald*." She put her hand on his arm to emphasize her words while Robbie silently seethed.

The carriage entered a long drive to the stately mansion set in the middle of a bower of autumn flowers as far as they could see. The grass had lost its summer green but the blue spruce and pine trees gave promise of Christmas a little more than a month away. The drive was lined with red cannas, so tall they looked like dwarf trees; pale yellow chrysanthemums bordered the veranda.

Robbie's eyes widened as she turned to Amy. "This is where you live?" She was thinking of her own quarried-stone house built by her grandfather and added onto by her father as the children arrived, and comparing it to this mansion which was so big you couldn't even guess at the number of rooms.

Standing on the veranda of this sprawling, very white house, the servants were lined up with the housekeeper, Mrs. Wheeler, at the head of the line to greet the new arrivals. She embraced Amy and was introduced to Kate and Robbie, as was Jeffrey, the head butler. The girls were speechless and could do no more than nod in acknowledgment. Mrs. Wheeler led them past the curtseying maids and bowing male servants, who scattered at a signal from Jeffrey to take care of the luggage.

They were then led into the Grand Hall; the floor they crossed was of highly polished wood laid in patterns on top of which lay an exquisite Persian rug. Hanging over all in the center of the hall was a tremendous crystal chandelier. Robbie kept her eyes on Mrs. Wheeler's back as they followed her but Kate managed a quick glance to either side and was struck with the spaciousness of the rooms she could see through the high-arched entrances. They ascended a long, winding mahogany staircase, carpeted to match the Persian rug which, in turn, was matched in color by the stained-glass wall sconces which lit the way to the top of the stairs and then continued to light the corridor which led to the many bedrooms and sitting rooms.

Amy left them at the entrance to their rooms. Robbie, her irritation at Kate dissolved and feeling like a little girl in fairyland, reached for Kate's hand as they entered, wide-eyed and unbelieving.

In awe they walked around the three rooms alloted to them—a bedroom and bath for each and a sitting room to be shared. The elegance of their surroundings was enhanced by the tall curtained windows and the colorful wallpaper, which they had never seen before. Kate's was white with pink roses and Robbie's was patterned with yellow daffodils. The brass beds were covered with spreads to match the color of the flowers in each room. A fire had been laid in the sitting room's white mantelled fireplace, and bouquets of flowers from the greenhouse were placed around all the rooms. The finishing luxury was the thick wool rug. There was no comparison here to the rugged weather they had become accustomed to in Scotland but the late October frost had set in and it was good to feel the warmth of their rooms.

They heard a light knock on the door and Amy entered, asking if they were quite comfortable. The sisters found it hard to express their wonder at their new and luxurious surroundings. Amy wanted to know if they would like to have dinner in their rooms. They had always had "supper" before, but were quick to catch on to the new word. Kate answered for both of them. "Yes, Amy, we are tired and would like that very much. Shall I fetch it?"

"Let me explain something," Amy answered softly. "Our way of living is very different than you have most likely been accustomed to. Here, you will have no household duties. When you want something, just pull this cord; it rings a bell in the servants' quarters and someone will respond to do your bidding." Kate and Robbie exchanged wide-eyed glances. Amy continued, "Birdy will fix a bath for you tonight, and tomorrow we will have a maid for you both to share . . ."

Robbie started to protest that it wouldn't be necessary. "Really, Amy, Kate and I are quite used to doing for ourselves . . ."

But Amy stopped her. "Robbie dear, I know that very well. However, this is the way we live and it would make us very happy if you do not object."

"We're grateful," Robbie said, "but we don't want to put your household to further inconvenience. After all, we're here to teach and work. We're not exactly guests and we do not expect to live like you, the lady of the manor."

"Shame on you, Robbie! You'll never know how happy you have both made me by being my friends. Now," Amy changed the subject abruptly, "Birdy is putting her fifteen-year-old sister, Bessie, into service. She will arrive tomorrow. You will learn, along with her, the ways of our society. It will be an easy lesson, take my word for it!" Doubts remained with the Maccrae sisters but they nodded in agreement. "I am tired, too," Amy added. "I'll have dinner in my room, and retire early." Before she left, she pulled the bell cord which was a prearranged signal to bring the dinner upstairs.

Meanwhile, Birdy had filled white enamelled tin tubs with warm sudsy water. Nightclothes (not theirs) were laid out for them and a table was set in the sitting room. Both girls emerged from the bath rosy, relaxed and wearing silky, lace-edged fine flannel nightgowns with robes to match just as Birdy finished laying the table and placing covered dishes on it. She showed them the sideboard which held a pot of tea and little pastel confections—bon-bons, she called them. The girls seated themselves and when the maid left, she told them to ring if they wanted anything else. They avoided each other's eyes until they heard the door close and then, awestruck, tired and nervous over all these exciting events, burst into laughter which they tried to stifle. "Oh, Robbie, if Da and the girls could see us now!" crowed Kate.

"And if Mary and Frances knew what they missed!" Robbie would never understand that her sisters' desires ran in different directions and that they would not have enjoyed being pampered and catered to. But Kate and Robbie were the perfect pair for this extravagance. Suddenly Robbie said, "Maggie would have loved it! If only we could send her some of these bon-bons ...." They were lost in thoughts of home for only a moment, then ate all the food that had been set before them, including the last bon-bon which Robbie popped in her mouth.

Kate wasn't quite sure what they should do about the soiled dishes. "I suppose this is the time to pull the bell cord," she said doubtfully.

"Of course. Go ahead," Robbie urged.

"Why me? Just because I'm the oldest doesn't mean I have to do everything first. *You* do it!" said Kate, suddenly apprehensive.

Robbie, more daring, grabbed it, held it in her hand like a hot poker, and closing her eyes, gave it a determined yank. A maid responded a few minutes later and when she left, they congratulated themselves that they had learned their first lesson about living in polite society.

As they had every day of the voyage to

America, the girls had written a letter home that night. Kate added a note telling of their safe arrival. She would find out where to post them in the morning.

While they were eating, their beds had been turned down and warmed and they were too tired to resist the inviting softness. "Don't forget to say your prayers and pray for the family, too," Kate reminded Robbie.

"You, too, Kate."

"I can promise you I will. I have a very *big* thank-you to say. Maybe one day we can bring them all here. I'll put that in my prayer, too."

The mention of the family brought nostalgic tears to Robbie's eyes. "We had better wait a little before making any great promises. Don't forget, we're here for just a little while to work."

"I won't forget, little sister," Kate murmured sleepily. Robbie didn't hear the rest of the sentence; "If this is the way it is in America, I doubt that I will ever leave!"

IX

THE STUDIO

Amy's prediction came true. Although Katherine slid into the life of luxury and servants more easily than Robbie, it wasn't too long before pulling the bell cord and summoning assistance for any reason, trivial or otherwise, became second nature to both girls.

Amy, and occasionally Donald, saw to it that they became acquainted with the countryside. The girls had their choice of horses. They were both excellent horsewomen, though Robbie considered her skill superior to Kate's, in spite of which Kate chose a highly spirited dapple gray, over the objection of the stable master. Before she had a chance to mount, he reported her insistence on riding Gray Beard to Donald who told her at dinner that night that Gray Beard was not for her. The next morning he accompanied her to the stables and chose an appropriate horse. "You'll enjoy riding Dawn and you won't have to battle her all the way as you would Gray Beard. Why don't you try her tomorrow?" he suggested.

"I'd like that."

"I'll ride with you. I think I should know how you handle a horse before you go off on your own. And I can show you some of the country you missed on the way from the ship."

"I thought you had forgotten," she said shyly.

"Not at all." He looked at his pocket watch. "But I must leave you now. I don't want to get to the office too late."

"You're very kind to me, Donald. Thank you." Kate raised herself on tiptoe, kissed him lightly on the cheek, then turned and quickly ran from the stable. He stood there, raised hat in hand, and looked after her speculatively.

As Kate ran to the house, she rejoiced in the sense of power that had surged through her as she had maneuvered Donald into the invitation to ride with him. The unplanned kiss was an inspiration. She looked for Amy when she returned and when she couldn't locate her, left word with Mrs. Wheeler to have her come to her room as soon as she was available. Robbie was nowhere to be found either.

A half hour had passed before Kate heard the girls laughing softly as they came up the stairs. She addressed Robbie, although her impatience was aimed at both. "Where have you been? You two are always disappearing and I think, Robbie, you should let me know . . . what have you got there?"

Robbie held up her cupped hands. A tiny peach-colored head with tremendous blue eyes peeked out over her fingers. "A tiny kitten. She's mine," she said as Kate reached for it. "Amy said I can keep her."

Kate melted. "Oh, let me hold her! You sweet little darling baby cat—can't we share her, Robbie?"

Amy was pleasantly surprised at Kate's

response to the little bit of fluff she held close to her cheek. "You may have one of your own, if you like. I'll take you back to the farm later."

Robbie waxed enthusiastic. "It's beautiful, Kate. They have great, round orange pumpkins sitting on the ground in the fields and stacks of—is it corn shucks, Amy?"

Before Amy had an opportunity to answer, Kate returned to her earlier irritation. "Yes, yes, I would like to do that very much, perhaps this afternoon if you have the time. But now I have a problem, which I hope you can help me solve, Amy." Amy waited for her to continue. "I would like to ride tomorrow and I did not bring any riding clothes with me. Is there any place where I can shop for them?"

"Oh, that. You won't have to shop. We keep a wardrobe of clothes for our guests. I'm sure you will find something to fit. Come, I'll show you."

Kate reluctantly gave up the kitten to Robbie, who had already named her Peaches, and followed along. They went to the third floor and Amy led them into a room that had the appearance of a specialty shop. Rows of daytime dresses, evening dresses, nightgowns, robes and an extravagent collection of riding clothes and boots were displayed when the muslin cover was removed from the racks. "We entertain quite a bit and often we will decide on some entertainment or sport for which the guests are not prepared . . . *voila!*" She waved her hand to the wonderful selection of clothing.

The sisters were overwhelmed by such abundance of luxury and Kate readily accepted the invitation as she slid garment after garment along the rack. Her eye had fastened on an exquisite black riding skirt and jacket to be worn with a high-necked ruffled blouse, but she decided this was not right for the first excursion with Donald. A dark blue serge outfit, the jacket with velvet lapels, and a matching derby were chosen. She even found soft, dark leather boots in her size. She sighed with relief as she realized she was ready. She would look smart and, as always, beautiful.

Robbie looked at her with envious eyes. "Kate, you make me so jealous!" She held up a jacket. "Look—these shoulders are so narrow I can't even get both arms in . . . and if you think I can find a pair of boots to fit my clodhopper feet, you are sadly mistaken."

Amy flew to her rescue. "Don't fret, dear, it's true Kate is easier to fit, but we'll go into the city tomorrow and have you measured for a riding habit and boots of your own."

Now it was Kate's turn to be envious. She would have loved to be fitted for her own clothes, but not at the cost of giving up spending time alone with Donald. Tomorrow was an important day.

After lunch, at Kate's request, they went to the farm. Although Amy would have denied it, she was somewhat intimidated by Kate's beauty, self-confidence and arrogance, and had difficulty adjusting to the startling change in personality that took place when they reached the farm. There were dogs and cats and cows and pigs, and fields to run in. Kate borrowed a pair of workshoes, whistled to the dogs to follow and trudged through the muddy fields. Then, shedding the shoes, she ran barefoot, throwing sticks for the dogs to fetch. She was permitted to feed the pigs and was taught to milk a cow. She pulled her skirt up to her knees, rolled her sleeves up, pushed the tendrils of hair out of her face with the back of her hand and, sitting on the low stool, knees spread and leaning foward, soon picked up the rhythm for successful milking. She liked the feel of the soft, pink udders and closed her eyes as she enjoyed the sensuality that swept over her unbidden.

Robbie's cry, "You've done it, Kate, good for you!" snapped her out of her euphoria that was enveloping her. She kicked the stool aside and gave the cow a brisk pat. "Thank you— you're a good girl," she said, and held up the half-full pail, laughing a rowdy, peasant laugh. "See how much is here!" She took a dipper which had been hanging on the side of the pail, dipped some of the milk from the bucket and handed it to Robbie, who tasted it and didn't make a face until Amy declined and Kate put the dipper to her lips. She had difficulty swallowing it and wrinkled her nose as she looked at Robbie, who permitted herself a guttural, "Ugh! That's terrible!"

"I must admit," Kate said sadly, "I thought it would be delicious."

Amy was laughing heartily. "It's much better when it's chilled. You've been drinking it every day. It's almost time to go back. Are you ready, Kate?"

She nodded. "Except for one thing . . . my kitten!"

There were four kittens left from the same litter Peaches had come from, a tan, a darker tan with a white stripe, and one like Peaches, all females. There was another tucked under the mother cat, nursing greedily, black as coal with a white blaze, white socks and bright green eyes. "*That's* the one I want! What a beautiful little devil," Kate cried.

The farm manager standing with them said, "Take him."

"*Him?* A tomcat?" He nodded. "I might have known it," she murmured. "I can't take him, he's . . . busy."

"If you wait for him to finish you'll never get him. He's a greedy little fellow." He bent down and plucked the kitten away from the mother cat which let him go without a fuss. The kitten then jumped onto Kate's shoulder, dug his claws into her, opened his mouth and let out the loudest cry he could muster—which wasn't very loud. With a little tugging she managed to get him into her hands where he wriggled and scratched and put up quite a fight. But Kate's soothing finger stroking his head finally calmed him down and he snuggled close to her. She ignored the little pin-dots of blood that showed through the shoulder of her shirtwaist. She had a broad smile for the farm manager and was effusive in her thanks to Amy for bringing her to the farm.

"What are you going to name him?" Robbie asked.

"He's named himself—Little Devil."

"That seems appropriate," she answered dryly.

The week ended on a note of gaiety. Donald had arranged a dinner party at the Hunt Club. He introduced Kate and Robbie to some of his neighbors on the far-flung estates which comprised the social life of Tarrytown. Robbie was torn between envy and admiration as she watched Kate flirt and tease and dance every dance. None of the under-sixteen group were eager to dance. Young J. Horton Smythe led them into the billiard room where he taught Robbie the game. Before the party was over, Robbie, who excelled at so many sports, was an expert and J. Horton Smythe her first admirer.

Tired and happy when they arrived home, they shed their wraps, and the Maccrae girls thanked Donald for the enjoyable evening. He acknowledged their gratitude, then added, "get a good rest tonight and sleep late if you wish tomorrow because on Monday you will be accompanying me to the mill."

At seven o'clock Monday morning, Donald and the girls were on their way. The first sight of the mill was impressive. It was a two-story, clapboard building painted white and set on a good-sized lot. Half the second floor had been designated for paisley weaving and Ian Maccrae's looms had been set up. Donald shepherded them inside and introduced them to a tall, blonde young man. "May I present my chief engineer, Gunther Crismann? Gunther, meet our esteemed paisley weavers, the Misses Katherine and Robyn Maccrae."

Gunther's dark blue eyes absorbed the sight of Katherine with obvious appreciation as he gave a crisp bow of his head. "I have been waiting to meet the artists who weave such beautiful designs." He included Robbie, who flushed and lowered her eyes; Katherine returned his very direct and interested gaze and murmured, "Thank you."

There was an oval table with chairs around it in one corner of the office. After Donald left, Gunther brought out his plans for building more looms as he had copied them. Robbie studied them carefully and pointed out a few changes to be made in the drawing.

"You are very astute, Miss Maccrae," he said. They both looked up. "I can't go on calling you both Miss Maccrae—you'll never know who I'm speaking to."

"I don't know too much about your informal American ways, Mr. Crismann, but Donald has suggested we call each other by our first names," said Kate.

He nodded. "We are informal, true, and the MacConnacks to a slightly greater degree than most. We work in the factory pretty much as a family and use first names except for circumstances of extreme formality. May I call you Katherine?" With her head still bowed, Robbie raised her eyes slightly, watching her sister.

"My family calls me Kate," she smiled back. "If we are going to be a family, perhaps you should, too."

Robbie was shocked. Kate was flirting with this young man! She forgot that, at eighteen, Katherine did not socialize at home in the presence of her fifteen year old sister; nor did she know Kate had a reputation as a flirt. Robbie envied her easy manner but wished her sister wouldn't appear so forward.

Gunther sat between them and Robbie felt easier as she helped to explain some of the needs they would have in order to teach properly. Forgetting her self-consciousness, she turned to him. "Is there any way we could have more light? At home when the weather permits, we set up looms outside the mill."

He nodded thoughtfully. "How would it be," he was thinking out loud, "if I put some glass in a portion of the roof, up there . . ." he pointed to the back wall of the room.

"Could you do that?" Robbie asked.

"Definitely."

Kate clapped her hands in delight. "It will be like the artist's studio I saw in a magazine the other day! Oh, Gunther, could you?"

"For you, Kate, a glass house if you wish." His eyes said what he would not allow himself to voice. Even so, Robbie gasped at his implied familiarity. Kate's smile of gratification turned to one of amusement as she raised an eyebrow at Robbie.

Gunther quickly regretted his outspokenness. "Oh, Robbie, I meant no disrespect. One can't help but admire two such talented ladies." Again Robbie dropped her eyes in utter confusion; she didn't know why, but she felt his many compliments were too familiar.

The morning passed with the three of them deep in the plans for a more efficient "studio," as they automatically named it, and at noon Donald stopped in to invite them to lunch in his spacious office. After lunch, he went over the plans and approved them. Gunther estimated the renovations would take about two weeks to accomplish. Meanwhile, two of the looms were transported to a large room off the executive office and instead of starting with six students, they would start with two and expand when the studio was ready.

At four o'clock Donald suggested it was time for them to leave. "Mind you, this is only because it's your first day here. We work until six o'clock six days a week," he said lightly but honestly.

"Well, Donald, I must say, if every day passes as quickly and as pleasantly as this one, we have nothing to worry about," Kate sparkled.

"I'm glad you feel that way. How about you, Robbie?"

"Oh, yes sir, I do, too." Gunther escorted them to the carriage which was waiting, and Robbie's jaw jutted angrily as she noted how long Gunther held Kate's hand when he bade her goodbye. She was silent and glum as they travelled the few miles to home.

"Don't you feel well, Robbie?" her sister asked with concern.

"I'm all right," Robbie muttered.

"Is something bothering you?"

For an answer she clenched her teeth until her mouth was a thin line.

"Don't you like Gunther?" Kate persisted.

Robbie couldn't stop the retort that came involuntarily to her lips. "Not as much as you do!"

A brief, high note of irritation underlined Kate's next question. "What do you mean by that? Robbie, you're acting like a child. Stop sulking and answer me!"

"I don't want to talk about it." And there was no further word spoken.

Music emanated from the conservatory; Amy was having her daily piano lesson. Kate peeked in and, not disturbing her at her practice, gave a slight wave to the professor, whom she did not know. Robbie was too angry to stop and went quickly to her room. She took off the white blouse and plaid jumper she had been wearing all day, bathed her face and threw herself down on the bed. She was trying desperately to control her anger; nevertheless, tears rolled down her face. Kate's behavior was embarrassing! If only Annie were here. *She* would see that Katherine behaved properly. She pretended to be asleep when her sister came in, pulled the bell cord for Bessie and told her to draw a bath. When the maid arrived, Kate told her, "Bessie, after today we'll be home about 6:30. Will you have a bath ready for me? Robbie too."

It was an unusual request. Birdy had instructed Bessie to have their baths ready at night before the girls retired. "As you wish, Miss Katherine. Will you want another one before you go to bed?"

She shook her head. "No, but be sure there's warm water in the basin." The maid nodded and went out.

Hearing all these orders, Robbie sat up and came into the sitting room. "Kate, you're changing the schedule of the household. Why don't you find out if it's all right before you issue different orders? . . . And besides, you didn't say 'please'."

Kate sighed elaborately. "I know we've only been here a week, but you should have learned by now, Robbie, that you don't say 'please' to a servant."

"I don't know what's happening to you, but if Da could hear you, you wouldn't say things like that," Robbie grumbled.

"I'm beginning to think I made a mistake asking you to come," Kate snapped. "You refuse to listen. You'll *never* know how to handle wealth."

"What makes you think any of us will have enough of that to worry about? You seem to forget that you're here to work," Robbie snapped back.

Kate put her chin up with her nose in the air, looking at her sister under lowered lids. "Don't be naive."

"I don't know what you mean."

"One day I will be mistress of this . . ." she hastily amended, "of a house and servants."

"How do you expect to do that?" asked Robbie.

"Just watch me!"

There was a timid knock at the door. It was Bessie, come to help the girls dress for dinner.

"Thank you, Bessie, *I'll* take care of myself!" Robbie went to her room. She didn't want to hear Kate giving more orders in her newly assumed supercilious voice.

Amy and Robbie went downstairs to dinner together. Kate wasn't ready. At Robbie's request, Amy sat down at the piano and played one of the pieces she knew very well; soon Donald joined them. He had a glass of sherry and permitted the girls to have lemonade with just a drop of claret. He succeeded in making them both feel quite sophisticated. Katherine wasn't missed, at least not by Robbie.

The butler had announced dinner as Kate descended the staircase. Her long toilette earned her a sincere compliment from her host. "You look beautiful, Kate. You are, indeed, a woman of many talents, toiling during the day and this evening looking as if those delicate fingers never touched anything heavier than a tea cup." He offered his arm and escorted her to the dining room. She accepted the compliment with a half-smile and a gracious inclination of her head. He seated Kate at his right and Robbie to his left. Amy was at the foot of the table.

There was much to talk about this first night of their new career; before dinner had finished, Katherine had usurped all Donald's attention with a serious discussion of the new studio, while Amy and Robbie chattered of lighter things.

The studio was finished at last and christened with a party. The guests of honor were Robbie and Katherine and the two students they had been training, Tom Henderson and Rory Sullivan, who was the foreman of the mill. Tom was his assistant and Donald's thinking was that they should know the craft in order to handle any problems that might arise when the Maccrae girls were no longer present; thus, they were the first trainees.

All the millworkers were invited to inspect the new weaving room and walked through, awed that this pristine room with its walls painted white and the north wall windows reaching almost to the floor could be a workroom. Most of the weavers paused longer in front of the large frames, which were different than the ones they were using. On the looms were samples of the paisley designs woven by the two men. Gaslight had been piped in and instead of the fixtures near the ceiling, there was one glass globe over each machine, hung by a fine white enamelled pipe, conveying the gas to the jet.

The scalloped, bell-shaped globe had been Kate's suggestion, as were the high-backed stool-like chairs; Rory Sullivan made sure his fellow-workers were privy to her talents. Not wanting to deny her suggestion, Gunther, with Robbie's aid, had added rollers to the chairs that could be locked in position. Most weavers stood while working and although he thought them superfluous, Robbie persuaded him the chairs were good for the morale of the employees.

As the workers filed back to their own (dingy by comparison) part of the mill, they were pleasantly surprised to find a long buffet table spread with sandwiches, tea and coffee and a large, square cake set in the middle. No one but Amy would have thought of having them participate in the celebration; it alleviated the resentment that some were harboring because only a special few would enjoy the light, airy studio with innovative, modern equipment. Donald said a few words, telling them that in the near future the entire mill would be renovated in the same manner, with better light and more comfortable work surroundings. Gunther took a bow and was applauded for his inventive engineering. He made it a point to tell of Robbie's knowledgeable assistance. Tom and Rory stayed with their friends until Kate missed them.

"Where is that handsome Irishman?" she asked Amy.

Gunther's eyes followed her as she left the Studio. When she returned, she had Rory by the hand and, noting Gunther's hard stare, she slid her arm through Tom Henderson's, to avoid any comment on her behaviour.

Champagne was served and Gunther raised his glass in salute to Robbie, then made a a toast to Kate. Donald made a toast to Robbie's grasp of engineering. Amy claimed Gunther whenever he moved from Kate's side. He was quite deferential and danced with her twice to the music of one of the first gramophones in Tarrytown. Robbie was too shy to participate in their style of dancing, of which she knew nothing. Katherine, on the other hand, was as light as a feather and had no problem following her partner's lead, whoever that partner happened to be.

Both girls were exhilarated over the celebration but Amy seemed withdrawn. "Amy, will you come into my room for a minute before you go to bed?" Robbie asked. "I'd like to talk to you."

"I'd like to talk with you, too, Robbie, but I'd rather you come to my room. Is that all right?"

Robbie said it was and when she had undressed and put on her nightclothes, she joined Amy.

Birdy had left a pot of hot chocolate and cookies for the girls.

"Amy, I know you must feel a little left out of things because of Kate and me. I want to make you feel better about us," Robbie began.

"It isn't you, Robbie, truly it isn't."

"Then what? Who?" asked Robbie, bewildered.

Amy kept her eyes down and almost whispered, "I . . . I can't tell you."

"If it isn't me or the fuss that's being made

about our teaching, then what?" Robbie took a deep breath as the thought hit her. "Is it Kate?"

Amy bit her lip as she slowly nodded.

"Of course," Robbie sighed. "I thought I was the only one who noticed that all the elegance we're living in is affecting her. But don't forget, Amy, we're here for only a little time and I hope she'll get over it. She'll have to. We live very differently at home. Please don't let her worry you."

"It isn't that, Robbie. It's . . . it's . . . I don't know how to say it without sounding foolish." Robbie urged her to continue. "Well," she drew it out, "I am going to be sixteen on the first of January. Until that time I am considered a child, but sixteen is the magic number. I will be permitted to have gentleman callers and attend some of the functions I'm not allowed to go to now."

"I know what you're saying, but I don't understand . . ."

"This is the silly part, I'm afraid. I have known Gunther since he came to work for my brother three years ago and I . . . I have always . . ." she hesitated over the next work "*liked* him. I have hoped that he . . ." her voice was so low that Robbie had to lean foward to hear her "would be my first caller."

Robbie slumped in her chair. "I see. And you think he likes Kate?"

"How can he help it?" she asked wistfully. "She is so beautiful."

" . . . And vivacious . . . and flirtatious . . . and popular . . . and . . ." Robbie took a a deep breath. "I have never said anything bad to anyone about my sisters. Oh, of course, when

110

you consider we are seven sisters—although I don't think I should count Annie—you must know that we bicker and sometimes argue with each other. Kate is the third oldest and, *I* think, the most beautiful. Now," she paused to get the order of things clear, "Kate and I have never been very close because I am next to the youngest and still considered a child. The age difference divides us socially. I have never attended any outside parties, not even church socials with her. I hate to say this, but I think Kate is a flirt. She flirts with Gunther, but she also flirted with the two men students and even your brother. I don't think she will take any advice from me but I'll try to make her behave. Meanwhile, remember what fun she can be—the way she was at the farm and with the kittens—and perhaps, if you're willing to try, you can make her your friend. We'll be here only another few months and then you'll have Gunther all to yourself."

Amy was so relieved to have been able to talk about her problem that she quite unexpectedly let out a nervous titter which grew into a giggle, and before too long both girls were laughing hard as they fell into each other's arms, though there was a hint of tears as well.

X

AMY

By the second week of November all the
students had mastered weaving the intricate
paisley design. Although they were ready for
the next step, the holidays intervened and it
was time for festivity. The Maccrae girls had
their first taste, literally, of a Thanksgiving
feast. They attended church in the morning
then came home to the most beautiful table
they had ever seen. The turkey was a sight to
behold and Katherine took great pride in
Donald as he expertly carved the mammoth
bird. As was the custom, they gorged themselves on the stuffing and cranberries and
something called "southern sweets," a yellow
potato baked with syrup, an apple drink called
cider, quite different from the cider they knew
at home, the like of which they not only had
never tasted, but had never heard of; nuts and
fruits finished the meal.

Gunther had been invited and he and Donald
took a long walk in the crisp air after dinner.
Amy and Robbie wanted nothing more than a
nap, but Katherine wrapped herself in a warm
cloak; she wanted, she said, some fresh air and
a little exercise. When the men returned she

managed to arrive at the door at the same time.

"My dear Kate, come in before you catch cold! This weather is hard enough on us—you will be chilled through."

"You forget, Donald, I come from a country where the climate is cold and damp most of the time, but I will be glad to go inside now." She rubbed her hands together to warm them.

"Come into the drawing room, Kate, we'll have a glass of hot cider." It was the invitation she had been looking for. Much to her dismay, it was Gunther who helped to rub the circulation back into her frozen hands. It was a cozy time for the three of them even though they talked "shop." Kate could feel Donald's eyes on her and knew she made an impression. What she didn't know was that he was speculating on her easy familiarity with Gunther; it relieved him, as he was well aware of her efforts to attract him and any other male who happened to be within her line of vision. He wanted desperately to talk about Annie but had so far been held to silence.

"I noticed letters from Scotland in this week's mail. What do you hear from home?" he asked at last.

Kate regaled them with the happenings at home, making them sound witty and interesting, but did not mention Annie. Gunther listened with his eyes.

Donald had also received a letter from Annie which carried sad tidings. Maggie had run away. A letter had been received from her, posted at Glasgow, saying she was in America, had not been able to find her sisters but was living with a fine family and very happy.

114

"If there is any way, Donald, that you can search for her, will you do so? I am not telling Kate or Robbie. I have had letters from them and know they would have written if they had seen our little sister. Mary had planned to be married at Christmas but became so ill when Maggie disappeared, feeling it was her fault, that the marriage has been postponed. My father's health has not been good. He is not ailing but has lost the vibrancy that was so much a part of him. Both Da and Mary picked up after we learned that Maggie is alive, not kidnapped, or not had any other dire thing happen to her. She will never know what a blight she has put on our family. If I thought I could find her and were free to do so, I would come to America and look for her myself. For many reasons I cannot. I am trying to restore the family spirit. Although my heart is sore, I still have to take care of them.

"Added to that, dear one, is the fact that our plans have to be forgotten. I cannot leave these heavy burdens and join you. Please understand. My feeling for you has not changed but my responsibilities have increased. Think of me sometimes. Ever yours, Annie."

Donald had been hard put to get through this day and pretend to enjoy it. He understood the role that Annie had to play; he had the same responsibility to his home and family, even though he had only *one* younger sister to protect. His mind had only been partially with the festivities. The other part was planning a search for Maggie and undertaking a trip to Paisley to convince his beloved that there were other ways to handle the problem. He was determined not to let her go, either in mind or body. Lost in thought for some time, the laughter of Amy and Robbie brought him back to the company at hand. He joined them and played a word game for a while, but his heart was not in it.

In spite of the huge midday meal they had eaten, they were all ready for the sumptuous buffet that had been prepared later that evening. "We," Robbie announced, after she had stuffed herself, "have dealt our father's upbringing a terrible blow. Gluttony is one of the major sins in all Scottish households. We eat well but sparsely, *but* . . . I feel wonderful!" She groaned and pretended to collapse in one of the comfortable chairs. Amy did the same and pulled Gunther by the hand so he fell next to her. He tried to grab Kate's hand but she, with a quick little turn, ended up next to Donald. She tripped and he had to catch her or she would have fallen. Only Gunther was worried; the others knew it was a not-so-clever maneuver to focus Donald's wandering attention.

Shortly thereafter, Donald said goodnight. "I have some papers to look over before I retire; the rest of you, don't stay up too late." He left.

Kate would have lingered but Robbie took her by the hand. "Come on, sister, it's been a long day." Kate looked resentfully at Robbie and regretfully at Gunther, then decided not to put up an argument. Robbie managed a slight wink at Amy as she and her sister left the room.

Amy took advantage of the time alone with

Gunther to ask him to come to her birthday party. In her own innocent way, she was applying Kate's tactics . . . entrapment.

"I'm flattered to get a personal invitation, Amy. I will be delighted to come," Gunther told her.

When she said her prayers that night, Amy added a request—to show her the way to do something special for Robbie.

The next morning, buoyed with self-confidence, Amy stood at the foot of the staircase waiting for Kate. She was determined to do as Robbie had suggested and make a friend of Kate. When Kate finally descended, she was dressed all wrong for the season—which didn't detract one whit from the picture of loveliness she had so artfully contrived. Amy gazed in fascination at the white, silk clad feet that moved with grace down the stairs. Draped over the shoulder of the white batiste dress (although she didn't know it, a garden-party dress) was her kitten.

"Good morning, Kate, you look lovely," said Amy sincerely.

"Thank you." For a reason she couldn't fathom, Amy made her uncomfortable, insecure. "I hope you don't mind that I raided your guest closet. We really do not have appropriate clothes with us. Isn't there a possibility of buying a few dresses so that I wouldn't have to use yours?"

"We'll go into the city as soon as you have free time, Kate. Meanwhile, use the guest closet as often as you wish."

Amy was being the gracious hostess but

Kate felt she was being patronized. "I have money, you know," she said defensively. "I can pay for new clothes."

To cover her confusion at the uncalled-for remark, Amy bent forward and put out her hand to pet Little Devil. The kitten unsheated his claws as he struck, ripping open one of her fingers. '

"Oh, Amy, I'm so sorry! I thought you knew that he wouldn't let anyone but me pet him." Amy was holding her finger, watching the blood flow profusely. "You'd better get that attended to." She spoke to Amy's fast disappearing back as she raced to find Birdy, tears streaming down her face as much for her thwarted offer of friendship as for her bloody finger. On the way to the breakfast room, Kate petted her little friend. "You're a good boy and you have my permission to scratch anyone who is not kind to me," she said smugly.

Donald and Robbie were at the table. "What was all that noise about, Kate?"

"Amy hurt her finger. She'll be all right." She thought she had dismissed the subject, but Donald persisted.

"How did she do that?" Robbie eyed her sister suspiciously. Donald's concern was evident and she was almost afraid to hear Kate's answer.

"Well, Donald, I thought I had told everyone that my baby cat doesn't like to be petted; I am so sorry that Amy didn't know . . ." She sounded contrite.

"You mean that . . . cat scratched her?" Donald asked. She nodded.

"I'll see if she's all right." Robbie started to rise.

"No, Birdy will take care of her—but it brings me to something I've been wanting to say to you, Kate. Please don't bring that animal downstairs again, at least, not in our living rooms. You can play with it in your own room but feed it in the kitchen then let it outside. I particularly dislike having it at the table and will ask you to remove it now."

Kate's temper had been rising. Although she strove to hide it from Donald, she wasn't successful. "He's only a baby, Donald! I'll feed him in the kitchen if you insist, but he's too young to be put outside and besides, he's a *him*, not an it!" She pushed her chair back so hard Little Devil's back rose and he spat at no one in particular. Kate put her hand up to calm him as she stalked out of the room.

Robbie, shamed by her sister's behaviour, apologized to Donald. "I don't know what has come over Kate. She has a temper but she would never dare display it this way at home. Neither Annie nor Da would permit it. I'll try to talk to her."

"No, Robbie, don't bother yourself over this tantrum. I think Kate is angry at herself . . . she'll get over it."

After Donald had finished his breakfast and excused himself, he was about to go in search of Amy when she entered the room, finger bandaged thickly. "Is that a serious injury, Amy?" he asked gently.

"No, this bandage is Birdy's idea. You know how she fusses."

Donald put his hand under her chin and raised her face. "Are you sure?"

She smiled. "I'm sure. Don't worry about me, brother. It's just a scratch." She changed

119

the subject. "I thought the mill was closed today. Do you have to go to work?"

"I'll stay home if you want me to, but Gunther and I have a lot of details we need to go over. With the studio and all the work going on in there, we haven't had much time to get together." He paused. "Shall I stay?"

"No, no, dear, you go ahead. Robbie and I have things planned for today." He kissed her cheek and told Robbie not to worry. No one mentioned Kate.

For the next three weeks everyone settled down, learning the finishing touches of the course the Maccrae girls were teaching. When the students returned to their regular work, Robbie and Kate were given a vacation to shop for Christmas gifts.

Another thrill was in store for the girls when several families hitched their horses to sleighs and they all set out to seek, each one, the perfect Christmas tree. The week before Christmas was a joyous time. The girls helped to string popcorn and cranberries; the crowning event was the trimming of the Christmas tree. On Christmas eve, all the local families came together to sing Christmas carols, wandering from one estate to another, and finally returning too full of eggnog and the goodies served at each house to do anything more than sleep until the great day dawned.

Christmas day was a different and exciting event for Robbie and Katherine. Both girls had been industriously knitting every spare moment they could find and after they had attended church services, it was time to exchange gifts. The Shetland wool the girls had brought from Scotland stood them in good stead. Donald and Amy received creamy wool sweaters with scarves to match from Kate. Robbie knitted a matching bonnet for Amy. The off-white color against her dark hair and eyes made her look like a Christmas doll.

Amy gave each of the girls a crystal bottle filled with perfume imported from Paris. Donald waited until all gifts were distributed before he gave his. Each received a small velvet jewel case. Amy's held a string of pearls which had been her mother's. Robbie and Katherine each were presented with a small cameo on a gold chain. "A story goes with these gifts," he said. "You have long looked forward to having mother's pearls, Amy." She thanked him gratefully; they meant much to her although she did not remember her mother.

"The cameos," he continued, "were made in Florence, Italy, my mother's birthplace. They are precious to me and I hope you will accept them as a token of my affection for you both."

Robbie admired her gift and thanked him graciously—"for your affection and trust, Donald, and for making us a part of your family."

Kate kissed him. "I shall treasure your gift always! I have wondered about your dark hair and eyes, Amy's too, and now I understand." She turned to Amy and said softly, "Your mother must have been a beautiful woman."

"You haven't seen her portrait?" Donald asked.

Both girls shook their heads. "Take the girls into the gallery, Amy, and show them our fore-bears. My father was a Scot, and thus our

121

name. We have a long line of ancestors, English, Scottish and Italian."

Katherine took her chain out of its box and held it for him to fasten. The touch of his hand on her neck sent sparks flying through her; the touch of her skin made Donald think longingly of Annie; but Kate misread his reaction.

Following Amy up the staircase, they turned right when they reached the top, which led to the wing occupied by Donald. Ahead was a long, windowless corridor lighted by gas lamps with white porcelain globes, one over each of the ornately gold-framed portraits which hung below. The first four depicted the MacConnacks' great-grandparents, maternal and paternal, the women exquisitely delicate, the men dashing and virile.

Robbie had passed on to the portrait of Amy's mother and father. While the father seemed a bigger man, he reminded her of Da. Amy's mother, all black curls and sparkling dark eyes and red of cheek, was more beautiful than any of her ancestors. Robbie gasped as she gazed at the portrait. "Amy, that's you!"

"No," she answered with reverence, "that's my mother. I know I resemble her."

"You're her very image, you must know that. Kate," she called, "come look at this portrait."

Kate was still examining the first picture, or so it seemed. Actually, she had angled herself to get a better view of Donald's sitting room. A maid was inside cleaning and, unused to visitors to the wing, had left the door open. Robbie's insistent voice finally broke through her concentration. "I haven't seen the others yet. I'll be there in a moment."

"No, come here *first*. You must see this uncanny likeness!" Kate shrugged and joined them. "Have you ever seen two people look so much alike?"

Kate put her hand to her heart. "Oh, never. Donald looks exactly like her!"

"*Donald!* Kate, look, look at the portrait," Robbie said impatiently. "Now look at Amy."

Kate dutifully did as asked. "Turn around, Amy." She did so reluctantly. It was difficult to stand there and have Kate examine her so coolly, then hear her say, "Well, yes, I suppose there is a resemblance." Kate turned away and walked back to the first painting, only to discover that the maid had closed the door to Donald's rooms. She was bored with the ancestral hall and gave only a cursory glance at the other portraits as she passed the younger girls and waited for them impatiently at the top of the stairs, then preceded them down.

Robbie could see that Amy was discomforted. She grabbed her hand and squeezed it. "Don't pay any attention to her. She'll only spoil this wonderful day."

"You're right. It's Christmas and we shall enjoy it! In fact, I think Jeffrey just announced dinner." She held out her arm which Robbie accepted and the two of them followed Donald and Kate into the dining room.

The Maccrae girls thought they would never see a table more bountifully laid than the one at Thanksgiving. However, the Christmas feast was even more elaborate. "It looks too beautiful to eat," Robbie said, admiring the Christmas china and the horn-of-plenty centerpiece filled with gold, red and green wrapped chocolates. Just then Gunther rushed in, brushing the snowflakes from his hat. "My apologies," he called out as he struggled out of his heavy coat. "I was almost snowed in. Merry Christmas, everyone!" They returned his greeting as he took his now accustomed seat between Kate and Amy and raised his glass in a toast to "my host and all the lovely ladies who grace this table."

Jeffrey and the serving maid came round with platters of sliced pink ham that had cloves stuck in the small, tiny diamond cuts that had been scored in the top of it, and turkey with the same wonderful bread stuffing the girls had enjoyed before. There were two kinds of potatoes, one that had been boiled and mashed until it was fluffy with cream and butter, and the other, the sweet potatoes they had had before but this time mashed with butter and marshmallow made from egg whites and sugar and some drizzled on the top, and all kinds of vegetables and cranberry conserve and . . . Robbie was rehearsing all the wonderful dishes that she would write home about. Just maybe, they would be able to find some of the ingredients and try to duplicate it. If not, she would do it when she got back to Paisley.

For a brief moment Robbie was overwhelmed with a longing for Christmas at her own fireside, with Da and Annie and all her sisters. Less lavish and more spiritual, Christmas at home was perhaps a more joyous celebration. Her eyes were open but her thoughts miles away when she was conscious of Gunther saying, "Robbie?" He was almost crooning. "Where are you? Come back to us,

Robyn Maccrae." She blushed furiously when she realized how far her nostalgia had taken her.

"I do beg your pardon. I was thinking, Kate, of Christmas at home." Kate nodded but wished Robbie hadn't mentioned it. Their Christmas was so puny compared to this. However, Amy insisted that Robbie tell them all about it and the rest of the dinner was spent listening to Robbie sing her song of praise for home. Afterwards they bundled up, went out in the snow, had a snowball fight and built a giant snowman holding a little fir tree in his arms, to which they sang their last Christmas carol.

The sense of fun that had enveloped the Christmas festivities diminished as the Maccrae girls went at last to their rooms. Kate closed the door behind them and said irritably, "I know, Robbie, you are younger than I am and probably miss our family more, but in future, I do wish you would be more discreet about mentioning our homelife in comparison to how we live here."

"I'm glad you brought up the subject, Kate, it makes it easier for me to say what's on my mind. May I?" Robbie pointed to the silver pot of chocolate Bessie had left for them. Kate waved her hand in consent as she sat opposite her at the little table and waited.

Robbie plunged ahead. "I'm glad you mentioned the difference in our ages, Kate. It's something I was about to apologize for." She took a deep breath. "When Da gave his consent for me to come to America with you, he said I should abide by your judgment at all times."

Kate nodded in agreement. "I know," she was quick to add, "because of my age, I see things differently than you do. It seems to me, however, that you have turned things upside down and I always have to explain, and yes, apologize for your behaviour."

"You little snip!" Kate gasped. "How dare you? What do you mean, explain and apologize for my behaviour?"

"Ah, Kate, please try to understand," Robbie pleaded. "We are guests of a generous and loving family. I know you enjoy it . . ."

"Then what are you talking about?" Kate snapped.

Robbie hesitated. "This is difficult for me to say but . . ." she blurted out, "why are you so mean to Amy? *Why?*"

Stung by the accusation, Kate retorted. "That child! Spoiled and pampered, she would drive anyone mad with her snobbish airs."

"That isn't true! She is loving and sweet and has tried to be your friend. You have rebuffed her every time. Won't you try to change your attitude?"

Kate was silent, thinking about what her younger sister had said. Drawing a deep sigh, she shrugged, then answered honestly, "I hate to admit it, but I *have* been mean, mostly deliberately but sometimes not. I *am* older and I *do* know better, but I guess I'm envious of her breeding, her wealth and her position in the household."

"That's not your true self, Kate. I want Amy to know you as you really are."

Kate sat, elbows on the table, making a steeple of her fingers against her pursed lips. Robbie couldn't tell what the remote look in her eyes conveyed. She couldn't be sure Kate was even listening. Not getting any response, she pressed the point. "Amy has lived a sheltered life and no one has ever been unkind to her." Kate was about to shrug off her sister's criticism but her next words caught her full attention. "You must know Donald has dedicated himself to her and he would protect her against anyone who made her unhappy."

Kate slapped her hands down on the table. "Has she complained to Donald?" she asked sharply.

"No, and I don't think she will unless you push her too far with your unkind remarks."

Kate rose. "Well, little sister, you've given me something to think about." She walked toward her bedroom. "Go to bed now, we'll talk more in the morning."

Robbie had to be satisfied with that. It was less than she wanted but more than she had expected. Some of her anxiety had been lifted and after some tossing and turning, she fell asleep.

Kate, on the other hand, spent a long time deep in thought. Robbie was right. If Donald found out that she had made Amy unhappy, she would probably be shipped home. She resolved then and there to give up the fun of making soft, weak, little Amy the butt of her sarcasm. Amy reminded her of Robbie's cat Peaches; gentle, content to play by the hour with a piece of string. "I need a more worthy opponent, anyway," she said aloud, "and I can't afford to offend Donald."

Slowly she started to undress. She didn't put on her nightgown immediately, but walked over to the full-length mirror in glorious nakedness. "Oh, Donald," she said softly to herself, "see what you could have, just for the offer of your name and wealth!" Slimmer than most of the fashionable ladies and a mite taller, her body was delicate, milky white with full, firm breasts—again not as ample as fashion demanded but perfect. Her expression became soft and dreamy as she traced the rosy-brown aureoles surrounding the pink nipples, which now stood taut at her own touch. "Donald, one day you'll see." Suddenly conscious of her own sensuality, she shook her head to break the trance she was slipping into. "Kate, my girl, time to change your attitude. From now on, not sweet, exactly, but *nice* to Amy."

She reached down and scooped Little Devil out of his basket. He struck out, angry at having his sleep disturbed, but she kissed him on the top of his head and he started to purr. "*You're* a worthy opponent, little fellow," she said as she settled him in bed with her. "I'm glad you're here. Tonight I need company."

They both slept well.

The next morning Kate contrived to leave her room as she heard Amy's door close. She called out, "Good morning, Amy, wait for me." Steeling herself for one of Kate's usual verbal assaults, Amy waited with a stiff smile on her face.

"Good morning, Kate," she said as they started down the staircase together.

"You look so pretty this morning. After all the food we had yesterday I'm ashamed to say I'm famished." Amy nodded her understanding but could think of nothing to say. "What are your plans for today?" Kate continued. "Perhaps you and Robbie will spend the afternoon with me."

Kate's smile was beguiling and her warm sincerity could be felt. Amy responded in kind. "Oh, Katherine, we already do have plans to do something together this afternoon. We are expected by Mrs. Oakley at two."

"Mrs. Who?" Kate had drawn a blank.

"My dressmaker."

"Of course—how could I forget, the final fitting on our ballgowns. Donald is such a kind man, and so considerate. Just think, Robbie and I will have our very first ballgowns for New Year's Eve!"

" . . . And my birthday party. I was born on January first, and this year the holiday party will end on the stroke of twelve. Five minutes after, my birthday party will begin."

Kate clapped her hands in delight and impulsively hugged her. "Oh, how lovely, dear Amy! Why, the party will probably go on to the wee hours of the morning."

Robbie joined them and the three girls chattered about the forthcoming party—what they would wear, who would attend, and all those exciting things young girls talk about. Robbie, after a bit, was convinced that Kate had indeed changed her attitude toward Amy, who had let down her defenses and was responding to Kate's charm.

For the next few days their conversation was only of the two parties, and good will prevailed.

During this time, Donald had absented himself on the feigned excuse of business meetings in New York City. He visited all the shipping companies, trying to find some trace of Maggie's name on a passenger list. Although he was given every cooperation, her name appeared on none of them.

He wrote Annie to tell her, reluctantly, that his search had been disappointing. "It is most probable, darling, that she was included as part of the family she had mentioned in her letter and until we know who they are, we will have some difficulty finding her. Don't worry, dearest, she's an independent young lady, obviously not the child you think her. You know she is alive and well and if she is here I will find her. I beg you not to close your mind to our future together. I love you. Yours always, Donald."

He continued his search until the morning of New Year's Eve, when he had to turn his mind to the ball. It was Amy's night and he would do nothing to spoil it. . . .

Amy descended the staircase, ready to receive their guests. "Is this my little sister?" gasped Donald. It was, definitely a compliment. Her long dark hair had been combed back into silky curls and tied with a flat red velvet bow. She had poked through the antique jewelry which had been her mother's and found drop earrings to wear with the pearls Donald had given her for Christmas. Her dress was of *peau de soie*, white with holly berries embroidered here and there. Her eyes sparkled and her cheeks and lips were red from excitement. She was indeed a picture of young, innocent loveliness. In her, Donald had a glimpse of their own mother as he remem-

130

bered her. He kissed her on the forehead and, holding her hand, drew her proudly to the entrance of the drawing room.

Guests were arriving by the time Robbie came downstairs. She, too, looked grown-up, also in white *peau de soie,* wearing a pair of jade earrings Amy had found for her. They matched her eyes and with her red hair brushed to one side in a long curl, she too, was quite a charming sight to behold. Donald was quick to tell her so. This time she knew she looked pretty and did not lower her eyes.

Kate came down after most of the guests had assembled and every eligible man in the room quickly surrounded her until she had to rescue her dance program in order to leave several empty spaces for Donald to sign his name.

Gunther came late. "Ah, my beauty," he greeted Amy and kissed her hand. "I came late in the hope you would have finished receiving. I would like the first dance with the birthday girl." She looked at Donald with a mute plea. She knew it should be his dance.

Donald didn't mistake her meaning and rose to the occasion. "I think it fitting that you should open the dancing with our very good friend. It's time for us to join the others anyway." He motioned the band to strike up and Gunther led Amy through the intricacies of a waltz. They looked very handsome together and gave Donald something to think about as he gazed after them.

He waited until others joined the dancing, then went toward the group where Katherine had just given a young man her hand to be escorted to the dance floor. When she saw

Donald coming toward her, she almost panicked and was about to turn away from her partner when Donald brushed by. "You look beautiful tonight, Kate. Save a dance for me," he said as he passed. She did, indeed, look beautiful. She had chosen an off-the-shoulder dress, cut very low over the bosom, in dark green velvet. Her always white skin looked like alabaster. She had combed her titian red hair back quite simply and fashioned it into a soft chignon at the nape of her neck. Her only adornment was the cameo pendant which nestled in the cleavage of her breasts. But much to Kate's chagrin, Donald stopped before Robbie. "May I have the honor of this dance?" he asked, bowing low. Her eyes widened and she bit her bottom lip nervously. "Don't look so scared, Robbie," laughed Donald.

"I—I don't know how to dance the way you do," she stammered. "I'd step all over your feet!"

"Then it's a good thing your first dance will be with me. I am a good dancer and an excellent teacher." He put his arm around her waist. "Now, come with me, and let my arm guide you. Don't let anyone see you counting, but it's one-two-three, one-two-three . . ." Before the dance was half over Robbie was relaxed and gliding over the floor. When the music stopped, Donald was about to bring her a glass of punch when young John Horton Smythe came over. He and Robbie had played as a team in several of the games at the Hunt Club and won each time. They liked each other and were comfortable together because there was no thought of romance between them.

When John asked her to dance, she looked questioningly at Donald. His smile reassured her. Before the night was over, Robbie had danced with several young men, but most of her card was filled in by J.H., as she called him. She promised to teach him the Highland fling at a later date.

Gunther managed only one dance with Katherine, much to his disappointment. He breathed flowery compliments while they were dancing, which she accepted with a smile hoping to cover the anxious frown that was fighting to emerge. The night was almost over and Donald had not approached her for a single dance. True, she rationalized, as host he had to perform his duty by dancing with all the ladies, particularly those whose mothers fawned over him; he was every mother's ideal son-in-law. He performed his duty with a smile and a jest but never paid particular attention to any one young woman. Katherine, so beautiful, became the enemy in their eyes, and the women were hard put to hide their hostility, many of them asking, in a roundabout way, how long she intended to stay. Their fears reassured her of her beauty and charm.

At three minutes to twelve, the guests were called to order, champagne was passed by the maids and the new year was brought in with the singing of Auld Lang Syne. As the last notes were heard, the band struck up "Happy Birthday." Donald escorted Amy to the center of the floor as the assembled guests sang their tribute. She was ringed with people wishing her well for now and the future. Gunther's congratulations overwhelmed her.

"Now that you are no longer a child, my

dear Miss MacConnack," he said earnestly,
"you will be accorded the homage your beauty
demands." He bent to kiss her forehead as
she raised her face. It was a pleasant surprise to them both when his kiss landed on
her mouth. Amy turned peony pink and he
covered his own confusion by asking her to
dance.

It was one o'clock when the last dance was
announced, and Donald made his way to
Katherine's side.

"I hope you have reserved this dance for me,
Kate," he said gravely.

"I have, Donald. I couldn't believe we
wouldn't have at least one dance before the
evening ended." She held up her arms and he
waltzed her out to the floor. The focus of all
eyes shifted from Amy and Gunther to Kate
and Donald. They were indeed a handsome
couple. As they whirled in graceful unison,
hope died in the hearts of the ambitious
mothers of available daughters.

For all his conservatism, Donald loved to
dance. As he had told Robbie, he was an excellent dancer. Katherine was as light in his arms
as a feather, letting him guide her to the
strains of a Strauss waltz. They observed the
conventional four inches between them;
Kate's hand rested lightly on his shoulder and
her eyes were on a level with his mouth. As the
dance progressed, the orchestra stepped up
the tempo ever so slightly. The floor cleared
and the guests became their admiring, envious
audience. Caught up in the music and the
swaying rhythm, Kate threw her head back
with eyes closed. Donald grasped her waist

more firmly and drew her close; her soft, pliant body which responded to his lightest touch enveloped him in a sensual warmth. When the dance ended, she opened her eyes to find his face very close to hers. There was no mistaking the glow in his eyes; applause from his guests brought him back to reality. "You are an enchantress, Kate," he said softly. "For a moment I forgot the rest of the world."

Kate smiled seductively as she grasped his hand and curtsied modestly. He returned her smile and bowed to her; his hand tingled as her warm, soft fingers curled around his. Kate was satisfied; she knew now she could seduce Donald. She sensed passion under the cool exterior he presented; it would be thrilling to arouse that other, hidden self.

Amy's good-night to Donald was solemn. "Thank you for all you have done for me, dear brother. Now I shall take my rightful place as mistress of the house and relieve you of most of the household supervision." He kissed her hand in acknowledgment of her new adult status, realizing with a pang that Amy was no longer a child.

On Monday morning, January 3, 1881, Robbie and Katherine had accomplished their mission. Now that their students had learned the intricacies of weaving the paisley pattern, it was time for the girls to learn how to use the machines Gunther had designed to produce the pattern mechanically. They sat alongside their former pupils and with them were taught by Gunther. He was pleased with their quick minds and aptitude for machinery. Donald was satisfied that everything was going smoothly at the factory, and Amy had taken hold at home and was helping to run the household with efficiency.

They had all gathered in the drawing room after dinner one night. Gunther, at Donald's invitation, had joined them. The only reason it was by special invitation was that, although Gunther was with them for dinner four nights out of seven, tonight Donald wanted to have an informal meeting with him and the girls. Amy had discreetly withdrawn to the music room where she played softly so as not to intrude on their conversation.

"Gunther . . ." Donald paused and sipped at the demi-tasse Amy had sent in, "how much longer do you think it will be before Robbie and Kate know enough about the machines to be capable of teaching the weavers at home?"

"At home?" Kate asked quickly. "What home?" Her voice was sharp.

"*Your* home, Kate, with your family in Paisley. You remember, I promised your father it wouldn't be more than six months and that time will soon have expired."

For the second time since leaving Scotland, Kate was angry. Robbie grasped her hand to calm her.

Donald waited for Gunther's reply. "I would say," he said slowly, "that before they return to Scotland, the girls should be completely knowledgeable about taking the machines apart and putting them back together again." He laughed and paused, his eyes on Katherine. "About another two months should do it." He could see the delight on her face and knew she didn't want to go home.

Kate put her hand to her eyes. "May I be excused?" she asked, overcome with relief. "I have a headache and it's getting worse."

"I'm sorry, Katherine. Stay just a few more minutes—I want to tell you my plans," said Donald. Afraid of what she might hear, she sat stiffly on the edge of her chair. "I have an appointment in Paris to see one of the top designers there. Now that our ships are running on steam, the trip will take three weeks or a little less. I'll go to Paisley from there. I want to see your father and Scott about the machines, so I am planning to leave the day after tomorrow and I can be your courier. I thought you and Robbie would like to have letters prepared. I can take them along."

"Wonderful, Donald." cried Robbie eagerly. "I have so much to tell, it will take me all day tomorrow to write it!" Jokingly she added, "You may not be able to carry it."

"If we both write, Robbie, you'll have to leave something for *me* to tell the family," Kate teased.

The mood was light and as she got up to leave Robbie did, too. The men also rose and Donald put his arm around Robbie's shoulders as they walked to the door. "Did I detect a note of homesickness?"

She measured an inch with her fingers and smiled wistfully. "Maybe just this much. Goodnight, Donald. Are you coming Kate?"

Gunther walked with Kate and as they neared the door, lifted her hand to his lips.

"Sweet dreams, Kate." She smiled and said a whispered thanks. Gunther understood.

Donald breathed a sigh of relief as he poured

himself a glass of sherry and sank into his large comfortable chair in front of the fireplace. In retrospect, it had been a good Christmas and Amy's party truly memorable. Still, he was glad it was all behind him. Now he had to turn his mind to finding the youngest Maccrae girl, Maggie. He thought long and hard and came to the conclusion that it would be a mistake to leave for Scotland before making another try. His thoughts turned to Annie. He put his head back and closed his eyes. Soon he slept and dreamed of her snuggling in his arms, brushing his face with butterfly kisses and arousing him in a way he had never known . . .

He awakened with a start and was conscious of the scent of perfume surrounding him. Not quite awake, it took him a few moments to realize that Robbie and Kate had been wearing the fragrance Amy had given them. He thought about Kate. Poor Kate—he knew about headaches and wondered if hers had gone. As he started up the stairs he decided to offer her some of the medication he used when he was similarly afflicted. Trying to convince himself that he felt sorry for anyone who was thus distressed, he denied the thumping of his heart as he neared her door. Ever since he had held her in his arms when they danced, he had avoided her as much as possible but her magnetism had drawn him to her.

He tapped lightly at her door and, conscience-stricken, was about to turn away when she opened the door. In a flimsy pink night dress and robe she was so exquisite she took his breath away.

"You are . . ." he caught himself, "still

138

suffering with a headache?" he finished rather lamely. Asserting his own dignity, he added in a controlled voice, "I have brought you some medicine that will relieve it. Take it with water then go directly to bed."

Kate thanked him for his very kind consideration, then smiled faintly and leaned against him as she kissed his cheek. The feel of her barely covered breasts was almost more than he could stand. He muttered, "I hope you feel better in the morning," and turning quickly, crossed the corridor to his own quarters where he tore off his clothes and doused himself with cold water. Bracing himself with both hands on the basin he looked in the mirror above it and berated himself. How had he fallen under Katherine's spell? He remembered he had called her an enchantress; she wasn't just an enchantress, she was a witch! If she had not been Annie's sister . . . it would have been a fascinating way to while away the time until he could bring Annie to America.

He fell into bed, pulled the covers over his head and muffled his face in the pillow so no one could hear his anguished cry for "Annie, sweet Annie!" He had taken some of the headache medicine himself and before too long he fell into a sleep of exhaustion.

The next morning he awakened feeling a little groggy but his head cleared with the first cup of breakfast coffee. He ate hurriedly, not wanting to see Kate before leaving. He was no longer afraid of what she might do—he was now afraid of himself. He felt guilty and ashamed. He left instructions for Jeffrey to see that the Maccrae sisters were taken and picked up at the silk mill and also left a note

139

for Amy telling her he was going to stay in the city for a few days before leaving for Scotland. He had decided to cancel his trip to Paris.

His bags had been taken to the carriage and he was about to walk out the door when he heard Kate's voice behind him. She slid her arm through his, but he pulled away roughly. Only Jeffrey was near and he was busy stowing the luggage. Instead of being angry, Kate was, in fact, rather pleased that her touch bothered him. "I'll see you later, Donald," she said softly. He tipped his hat politely and didn't look back.

Kate was privately furious when she found out exactly how much later it would be.

XI

THREE WEDDINGS

Donald had arranged his schedule to arrive at the Maccrae home when the three girls and their father were at work. He had written to Annie that he was coming, but because of the slow mails she did not know exactly when. She opened the door to his knock and almost fainted at the sight of him. He stepped in quickly and held her to him. "My dear, my dear!" he whispered as he smothered her with kisses.

She clasped her arms around his neck and for a few moments gave herself up to him as he poured out his love. "Donald, my dear one, I am so glad you have come!" At last she pushed him gently away and led him into the parlor. "We have so much to talk about."

"That's exactly why I am here, Annie darling —to put away all foolish notions of your not coming to America with me." She shook her head sadly. "Don't say no, it doesn't have to be this minute."

She took his hands in hers. "Donald, we were a miserable household after Maggie disappeared. It has taken us all this time to resume our lives. Knowing that she is safe has made a great difference, but I cannot leave the family. Mary and Frances are planning a double wedding the first of May, and Laurie's young man is going to speak to Da. Robbie has written that when she returns, she probably won't be living here in the house." Her voice faded, "I can't imagine what she means."

"I can tell you about that," Donald said. "We used to joke with our chief engineer, Gunther Crismann, that when he finished teaching your sisters how to run the machines which have been adapted from your father's paisley hand looms, they would be capable of taking them apart and putting them together again." Sitting in the circle of Donald's arm, Annie felt secure. She settled back as he continued. "As it turns out, Robbie has a brilliant mind and is literally learning to do just that. In fact, she has suggested a few improvements. I have told her that I would sponsor her at Edinburgh University so she can become a bona fide engineer."

Annie looked shocked. "A *female* engineer? She would have trouble getting into the University because she's a female, let alone to study engineering!"

"With my recommendation and Gunther's, and with the time she's already worked as a semi-professional engineer, she could get in. She knows it won't be easy but Robbie's very excited about the prospect."

"Well, that *is* news," said Annie faintly. "And Kate? What about her?"

"She's bright, too, but Katherine is looking for something else . . . a husband."

"She'll have no problem there. She's left a string of broken hearts among the local boys.

They're all waiting for her return," Annie said with a slight smile.

He was about to tell Annie that he was sure none of them would meet her sister's new set of values, but thought better of it. "I'm sure. Now, let us talk about us." He pulled the pins out of the tight knot of hair and as it fell she shook her head, causing the shimmering mass to fall over her shoulders. "Your beautiful hair! Promise me when we're married you will never pull it into a tight knot again." Putting both hands under it and lifting it like a curtain he kissed her neck, the tip of her ear and then, unbuttoning her dress, he kissed her breast. His warm moist mouth stirred her as nothing ever had before. Rather than resist him, she pressed him closer. A little moan escaped her parted lips. She was ready to give herself to him completely. Donald sat up straight. "Oh, my dearest, forgive me!" he groaned. "I want you so much, I love you and want you close to me."

"Donald, there is nothing to forgive. I want you too. I might have stopped you if we had any future together—but this is as close as I will ever come to your lovemaking. I wanted something to remember," she whispered, half ashamed.

"You're talking nonsense, Annie. You don't know me very well—I always get what I want and I . . . want . . . *you*. But not like this. We'll work it out and you *will* come to me as the mistress of my home."

"Listen to me," Annie pleaded. "With Mary, Frances, Laurie—and I'm sure Katherine soon after she comes home—all getting married and, as naturally follows, having their own families, that will leave Da very much alone. I will not allow that to happen. I love you more than life itself, Donald, but I will not abandon my father. Can't you understand that?"

For answer, he kissed her long and hard on the mouth, retrieved her hairpins, handed them to her, and excused himself. He went into the kitchen. Annie dejectedly followed him, poured very cold water into a basin, gave him a towel and retired to her own room to repair her hairdo and to cry in private.

Some time later Annie was composedly pouring tea as her father walked in. He and Donald respected and enjoyed each other and his greeting was warm. "How good to see you, Donald!" He turned to Annie, "I'm surprised at you, daughter. What kind of hospitality is it when you give a man tea instead of a drop of whiskey?"

"Now, Da, don't go on. I thought it best to wait until you came home before pouring whiskey—and don't think for a moment, Donald MacConnack, this man wants only a drop," Annie teased. The affectionate humor was not lost on Donald. Soon, Mary, Frances and Laurie arrived and the evening was spent listening to Donald tell about Robbie and Katherine's success in America, and in turn, telling him all the news they wanted him to bring to their sisters.

Donald spent the next morning at the mill and invited Ian to lunch at the Glasgow Inn where he was staying. Ian had not been able to get over his sadness over the disappearance of Maggie; even though they received word from her each month, his sense of loss was tremendous. "I could not add to Annie's sorrow, neither could I speak with Scott, Mary's fiance. He blames Maggie for the postponement of his marriage and shares Mary's anger."

"I'm sorry I was not here to share your grief; it is difficult not to have another man to speak with," said Donald. "I hope one day life will be smoother for you." The confidential conversation continued. Both men had a lot to discuss which they could do only with each other. At the end of that time, they shook hands in a sincere gesture of friendship and brotherhood. "I am leaving for America the day after tomorrow, Ian, and I would like your permission to have dinner with Annie here at the hotel tomorrow night," Donald told him.

"That would be a rare treat for her and one she richly deserves. It's fine with me." Donald scribbled a note which Ian was to deliver, asking her to be ready at seven when he would pick her up.

Annie tried to suppress her inner excitement but her high color as she readied herself for the evening belied her outward calm. All the girls took a hand in helping her dress and when she finally presented herself for her father's inspection, she was more than pleased. "Well, who is this pretty lass we have here?" was his comment. He wondered why he had never noticed before that she was a beautiful woman. For the first time in many months, his heart and his mind were at ease.

Annie held onto Donald's arm tightly as they entered the Inn restaurant. She looked around nervously after he had seated her.

"Is anything wrong, dear? You seem to be nervous," Donald said.

"Donald, I *am* nervous. I suppose I should be ashamed to admit it, but this is the first time I have been out alone with a man," Annie confessed blushing.

"I don't believe it! My dear, sweet Annie, there's so much to see and do, and I'm just the person to make sure you don't miss anything!"

"It's going to be a wonderful evening, Donald. I want to enjoy every minute." She relaxed after the first glass of champagne and relished the superb dinner Donald ordered. They held hands all the way home and managed a long, loving kiss before he said goodnight.

Ian had waited up for her. She kissed him on the forehead and thanked him for allowing her the most wonderful night of her life.

"It's time, dear daughter. I've never realized how close we have kept you to hearth and home. You deserve more," he said.

Donald came early the next morning to say goodbye. "Remember, my love, you are not to fall in love with anyone else," he warned Annie. "I will be back for your sisters' wedding with Robbie and Kate in not quite two months' time. Will you promise?"

"There will never be anyone else for me, dearest, but I won't hold you to that same promise. You have a name to carry on and must do so."

"I plan to. Think about me while I'm gone." He pulled her into the circle of his arms and held her close.

"You're never out of my thoughts," Annie

assured him. It was true—he was always on her mind.

The first few days after Donald's departure, she lived in the euphoria his visit had created. But as time went on she became frustrated knowing that her memories were all she would ever have. Still, her thwarted desires were forgotten in the weeks that followed as she became caught up in the preparation for her sisters' double wedding.

At the beginning of April, with the ceremony only one month hence, Laurie's young man, Malcolm MacGregor, approached Ian. "Mr. Maccrae, Laurie will be seventeen on the fifth of June," he began.

"I know that better than you do, young man," Ian barked.

Slightly disconcerted, Malcolm continued, stumbling just a little, "Would . . . would you consider having a *triple* wedding?"

Ian slapped his forehead with his hand. "Oh, my dear Lord!" was all he could manage. He took a deep breath and was about to continue when Malcolm hastily interrupted him.

"Well, we thought you wouldn't have to go through all the preparation again, and—and besides . . . we would rather not wait."

Ian had gathered his scattered wits. "The church and the minister have been reserved, the invitations have gone out. It's too late to make any change now."

It took all Malcolm's courage to continue. "Mr. Maccrae, sir, we have spoken to the girls, and the minister, and both Mary and Frances, and Scott and Charles said they would join us in sending out personal notes to everyone on the guest list. All we need, sir, is your approval."

Almost in a state of shock, Ian stalled for time. "Let me think about this, Malcolm. It does have some merit but I thought Laurie would wait at least a year before getting married." He stared intently at the young man before him.

"Perhaps you should explain a few things before you leave. How old are you?"

"I'm twenty, sir."

"Do you think you could support a wife and no doubt a family very soon?"

Finding some encouragement in Ian's words, Malcolm warmed up to the subject. "Yes sir, that I can! My father, you know, owns the largest bank in Edinburgh. When I am married, he has said he will make me assistant manager, with a promotion to manager with the first child."

"Of course—MacGregor the Banker. I never made the connection before," said Ian thoughtfully. "That certainly insures a good future for you and Laurie." He paused, trying to get his thoughts in order. "I shall have to speak to Annie, and of course, to Laurie. Then I will speak with Mary and Frances. Why don't you come for supper tonight? But I won't promise anything, Malcolm, except to give this matter my most serious attention."

"Thank you, sir, that's all we ask!" Malcolm, beaming, bowed himself out as if he had been visiting royalty. Once outside he jumped in the air and let out a loud whoop. Laurie, who had been waiting, ran to him. He took her by the shoulders and danced her around.

"Da said yes?" She couldn't believe it had been that easy.

"Not quite, but I'm sure he will. He wants to speak with you and the others and asked me to supper tonight to give me the verdict. My sweet Laurie, it's going to be fine!"

Annie had been privy to Laurie's wishes. It saddened her to think that her marriage would leave only Katherine at home. "It will be an empty nest, Da, when the girls leave," she sighed.

"But one of the good things will be that Robbie won't be alone in Edinburgh."

"You approve, then?" Da asked.

"Yes, I do. It is only a matter of a few months and, Da, I'm not sure I could go through this all again so soon."

"So be it!" Ian felt a measure of relief. His decision had been conveniently made for him.

That night at supper, joy reigned supreme. Malcolm presented Laurie with an exquisite diamond ring and the celebration continued as six happy people knew their dreams were coming true. Da and Annie rejoiced with them, although there was an undercurrent of sorrow in her forced happiness. She knew that once Kate returned, she wouldn't be with them for very much longer and it left her without a brood to care for. She tried to console herself with the thought that Da would still need her.

Immediately after dinner the three couples sat down to write notes about the change in plans to all the wedding guests. The wedding date had also been changed to the seventh of

June. Annie wrote to Kate and Robbie and a private, personal note to Donald. She had never felt so alone.

XII

PAPER CHASE

Donald, rather surprisingly, suggested to Katherine and Robbie that they postpone the trip they would have made for the weddings of Mary and Frances. Katherine was delighted at the respite but Robbie, thoroughly homesick by now, was disappointed. She had to admit, though, that the extra time would give her the opportunity to finish the machine she had started to construct, and the slight delay would be to her benefit. Donald happily hugged a secret he shared only with Ian Maccrae and did not mind putting off the return to Paisley. He made several trips to New York, ostensibly on business, and was more jovial, Katherine thought, than she had ever seen him, but also more elusive.

The time passed swiftly, too fast for Katherine. And then it was time to go home to Scotland. A party was arranged for the day before their departure. After much planning, it was decided the spring weather was perfect for a hunt, although they were all against chasing a fox, or any animal. Gunther suggested a paper chase.

"How do you do that?" Amy asked.

"It's a game that's played in Europe, mostly

in England. You have to follow a trail of paper. It can be done on horseback. You have two teams—the leader has a bag of cut up paper and strews it as he rides ahead. The rider who successfully follows the erratic path and gets to the end first, wins for the team."

The girls were delighted with the game, and the rest of the day was occupied by tearing up paper. Amy and Mrs. Wheeler made arrangements for the Hunt Breakfast which was to be held on the grounds of the Club.

The day dawned bright and the air was cool and fresh. Robbie had wished more than once she could ride astride, but bowed again to convention and donned her riding habit. The long skirt bothered her but she was still the best horsewoman of the girls. Katherine adored her formal habit and wore it at every opportunity. She, too, was an excellent horsewoman, second only to Robbie. The three girls made a striking picture as they joined the large group of riders.

Robbie, the appointed leader, started out alone. Ten minutes later the signal was given for the rest to follow. Amy at the head of one team and Kate at the head of the other started off at a fast gallop. Katherine, determined as always to be the winner, mercilessly used her spurs and applied the whip. Her mare shot ahead, disappearing behind a clump of trees.

It was Gunther who found her some time later, barely conscious and in great pain, one leg folded at an unnatural angle under her. Young John Horton Smythe carried the word to Robbie who raced back to the scene of the accident. "I can't believe the horse threw her," she cried, but she had to believe it because Kate's leg was obviously broken. Dr. Wilson, a neighbor who was a member of the group, administered first aid. Gunther was beside himself with anxiety and every time Kate moaned, his anguish increased. Donald organized a party to find tree branches for a temporarily splint, and a litter of sorts was made so Katherine could be carried back to the Club, then came the painful carriage ride home. Kate made such a fuss about the pain that the doctor prescribed laudanum, which eased her discomfort but kept her drifting in and out of consciousness. Robbie sat at her bedside waiting for a lucid moment.

"Kate, can you hear me?"

Kate's eyelids fluttered, then opened slowly. "Robbie? Oh, Robbie, I feel terrible!"

"Try to stay awake, Kate—we have to talk. Do you remember that we're supposed to be leaving tomorrow to go home?" she asked urgently.

"How can you even *suggest* such a thing? I can't move!" Kate's voice, though weak, was indignant.

"We *have* to leave tomorrow or we won't be home in time for the wedding—*three* weddings, Kate. We *have* to be there!" Robbie insisted.

Katherine moved quickly and the pain brought tears to her eyes, which she used to good advantage. "I know, Robyn, I know, but I can't possibly make the trip. I'm in agony!"

But Robbie wouldn't give up. "Gunther says he can construct a chair for you that will keep you fairly comfortable. You can be carried to the ship and your leg will be much better by the time we get to Scotland. It is only a slight fracture and should heal quickly."

"*No,*" Kate wailed and covered her eyes with her forearm. "I wouldn't risk it. Suppose there is a storm while we're at sea? Robbie dear, you'll have to take my love and my excuses to the girls. I want more than anything to be with them, but it just isn't possible."

Intuitively Robbie knew Kate had deliberately *fallen*, not been *thrown*, from the horse. Knowing full well what her answer would be she sighed as she said, "Well, Kate, I can't stay with you. I wouldn't miss the wedding of our three sisters for anything in the world . . . besides, I'm homesick and I can't wait to see the family."

Kate pulled herself higher on her pillows; her voice was stronger and her eyes brighter. "Of course I don't expect you to stay. Amy is here and the whole staff will be here as well to take care of me. I'll come as soon as I am stronger."

"Get some rest, Katherine," said Robbie, defeated. "I'll stop in tomorrow morning. Call me if you need anything during the night."

Kate nodded, and closed her eyes. A fractured leg was a high price to pay for remaining in America, but it was well worth it. By the time Donald returned she would be walking again. Meanwhile, there was Gunther . . . and for variety, Rory Sullivan. He had been her prize student and was an exciting man. She smiled as she drifted off to sleep.

Very early the next morning Robbie, dressed and ready to leave for the ship, stood at Kate's bedside. Kate was asleep and, considering the condition of her leg, she looked quite content. Robbie didn't want to disturb her, so she bent down and placed a soft kiss on her forehead.

"I'm awake, Robbie. Are you leaving now?" Kate asked, opening her eyes.

"In a few minutes. How do you feel?"

"I don't know . . . I didn't sleep well." (Actually, she slept like a baby.) "Have a good voyage and give hugs and kisses all around, and my wishes for everyone's happiness." She felt she had to extend that further. "Tell them I'm *desolate* that I have to miss their weddings."

"I will, dear. Now I have a few things to tell you," said Robbie. "One is that Bessie, as you know, will be accompanying me as chaperone. Birdy is going to sleep in my room until you can help yourself." Kate nodded. "The other thing I want to ask about is, what will you do about clothes? Our trunks went off a week ago."

Wide awake now, Kate answered airily. "Oh, I only sent my old things home. I didn't want to keep the good ones in the trunk so long. Birdy said she would send them after we left. So you see, I have plenty of clothes. Thank goodness I don't have to worry about that!"

Robbie saw more than her sister had intended. She had just confirmed what Robbie had suspected—that Kate's "accident" had been deliberate and she had never had any intention of going home.

"I see." Robbie stood up and straightened her dress. Kate reached up to kiss her again. She tried to squeeze out a tear but couldn't manage it, so brushed away an imaginary one.

She looked pathetic until Robbie closed the bedroom door—then she had to bury her face in the pillow so her triumphant laughter wouldn't be heard.

Amy had a sad leave-taking with Robbie, who extracted promises that she would come to visit. "I'll come with Kate when she goes home," she said.

"I wouldn't wait for that, dear friend," said Robbie dryly.

Amy returned her slightly sardonic smile. "You're right. I don't think she'll ever leave, either. Then I'll come on one of Donald's trips to Europe. Oh, I shall miss you!"

After an uneventful voyage, on which Robbie spent most of her time trying to read, with the help of a German language dictionary, the engineering textbooks Gunther had given her as a parting gift, they were almost there. Her heart beat hard as the carriage neared the house. Family and friends had gathered on the lawn to greet Robbie. She was out of the carriage almost before it had stopped, and was enveloped in Annie's arms. By the time she turned to her father she was sobbing uncontrollably with joy. "Oh Da, I am so glad to be home!"

Annie then walked toward the carriage, her eyes on Donald while waiting for Katherine to alight. They held a question as he came to her and kissed her hand. She tightened her grasp on his in response. "Donald, where's Kate?" she asked fearfully.

"Don't be alarmed, Annie. She's not with us."

His words only served to make her more

apprehensive than she might otherwise have been. "What do you mean . . . is she ill? Has something happened to her?"

"Hush, darling," he whispered. "Why don't we go inside and I'll tell you all why she isn't here. Please don't get so excited." The friends and neighbors dispersed as he took her by the arm and they followed Ian and Robbie, Mary, Frances, and Laurie with their fiances into the house. Donald could hear Ian's questions to Robbie. The three girls were talking among themselves and a low hum of anxiety hovered over the gathering.

"Please, everybody." He raised his hands for quiet as they seated themselves. "Kate will be along soon, probably before the month is out. Unfortunately, she was thrown from a horse and has a simple fracture of the right leg."

He got no further. The entire Maccrae family expressed their disbelief. "Kate thrown from a horse?" "There isn't a horse born that she couldn't ride!" "Next to Robbie, Katherine's the best horsewoman in the County. She could never be thrown." "What is *really* wrong?" This last from Annie.

Robbie rose to assist Donald, who was somewhat overcome by the comments and quetions being thrown at him. "Wait, folks. It *is* true." She went on to explain about the paper chase at the Hunt Club and how they found Kate on the ground. "She more than likely was *not* thrown, but more likely her horse stumbled and she fell off hard with her leg bent under her. It's not serious, it just means she has to stay off her feet until the fracture heals. The doctor said it was a matter of a few weeks. I have messages from her, though, for all the brides-to-be and," she giggled, "their husbands-to-be."

Annie looked to Donald for assurance. "That's the truth, Annie," he told her. "Anyone else in your family would have come anyway, but Kate pampers herself." They walked toward the kitchen, arm in arm.

Annie nodded, resigned. "Yes, I know. I suppose it is hard for her to give up all that luxury."

But Donald was tired of talking about Kate. "Can we be alone for a few moments? I'd like to talk to you. I'll be here until the morning after the wedding—that is a week from today?" She nodded. "Good. We'll have to find time before I leave. Perhaps tomorrow?" he asked again hopefully.

She took him by the hand, led him to the doorway of the parlor, and lifted her hands palm up in a gesture of helplessness. "Look around." With hers, his gaze swept the large family group assembled there.

"I understand, but before I leave we *will* manage it."

Shortly thereafter, Ian left the others and walked Donald outside on the grounds for a bit. Donald reassured him again about Katherine, and Ian said, "It's strange, Donald. I feel it's my fault that my family has started to go their separate ways. First Maggie and now Katherine . . . If I had said no to your invitation, this couldn't have happened."

"Try to think of it this way. Katherine and Maggie are both strong and daring, with a great sense of adventure. They would have left, sooner or later, anyway. Robbie is also adventurous and has an astonishing mind. The trip to America gave her a direction she would not have had otherwise. She will do you great credit one day. To return to Maggie . . . aside from the fact that she is so young, she has proved that she can survive on her own, and well, if what I hear is true." Ian nodded in agreement. "Have you heard from her lately?"

"We get a letter once a month. She says she is well and happy, misses us, but it not ready to return although she says she will someday. What we can't understand is why the letters always come from Glasgow."

"Have you searched there for her?" asked Donald.

"Oh, yes! I have even employed people to try to find her. She's not there." Ian sighed heavily. "And now, three more girls will be gone."

"Ah, but just think, you now have three sons."

Ian slapped his thigh. "By God, I never even thought of that! And finer men I couldn't have bred myself." He was more at peace than he had been in months. "Will I see you at the mill tomorrow?" he asked Donald.

"Yes, I want to talk to you about the new machinery. I think you will find our machines extremely helpful and Robbie will be here to instruct your weavers."

"I'm not sure they will like the idea of working with machines, Donald, but I'll certainly give them a chance to find out."

"Good. I also have several things I'd like to speak to you about—personal things. We can't talk in private at the mill, and we certainly can't at the house. Would you join me at the Inn for supper after work tomorrow?"

Ian thought for a moment, drawing on the pipe he had just lit. "I don't see why not. About seven?"

"Perfect. I won't go back to the house now. Please say goodnight to the others for me."

Donald left, already preparing his thoughts to present to Ian at supper the next night. He wanted to toss his cap in the air, but it wasn't quite the right time. . . .

XIII

COMMUNICATION

Ian was indeed handsome as he passed the critical eye of Annie. She wondered about the important date for supper with Donald at the Inn, as did her father, but they were both pleased that he had been drawn away from home, if only for a short time. He made an impressive appearance in his good dark suit, white shirt and navy blue tie.

Donald had to look twice before he was sure it was Ian Maccrae striding toward him when Ian entered the Inn. "You're a handsome fellow, Ian. Like your daughter Annie, you don't always show off your good looks to their best advantage," Donald told him.

"You're making me blush, young man, so put a stop to it immediately!" Ian laughed as he spoke, "but it's nice to know."

"Well, if you accept the suggestion I'm about to make you'll have a lot of ladies running after you," said Donald with a grin.

"Suggestion?" For some reason the word alarmed him. "What suggestion?"

"Sit down and have a drink with me. Shall we talk before we eat, or would you rather wait?"

"If what you have to say will spoil my

appetite, we'd better eat first. If it's something good you have to suggest, I'm curious and would like to hear it now."

"So be it. I'm not sure how it will sit with you, but this is it . . ." One drink led to another and before the serious conversation and the excellent meal was over, they were two happy men, although Donald never got around to his intended invitation to Ian to come to America to manage his mill.

It was getting late and Annie was concerned. Da wasn't accustomed to late nights and she wondered where he was. Much later, she heard Ian and Donald coming up the path to the door, arms entwined and singing at the top of their lungs. She opened the door and ran down the path to meet them. "Hush! You'll wake up the neighbors! Da, I'm ashamed of you, coming home in this condition—and you, Donald—I never expected to see *you* like this."

For answer, he put his hands on her waist, lifted her off her feet and swung her around in a circle. "Ah, Annie, you will sing, too, when we tell you our news!"

She herded them inside, trying to dodge Donald's hands. "Da, it's off to bed with you, and Donald, goodnight!" she snapped.

"No so fast, daughter," said Ian loftily. "We have momentous things to talk about."

"Can't it wait until morning?" sighed Annie.

"No, my darling," Donald's response made her glance quickly at her father to see if he were too saturated with drink to notice the endearment he had used. She gasped as Ian winked at her. Then suddenly Donald was on his knees before her. "Your esteemed father

162

has given his approval to our marriage. Annie, my love, will you marry me?"

"Oh, Donald," she wailed, "Drink has made you reckless in your speech! I have told you and told you, I cannot, *will* not."

"I had forgotten," he teased. "Tell me why again."

She tried to communicate with a long, hard, meaningful look from Donald to her father, but either Donald actually didn't understand or pretended not to.

"I . . . will . . . *not* . . . leave father alone," she said at last, very slowly and distinctly. "All the girls will be gone, except Kate if she comes home, and I will not leave him."

Ian paced the floor with a very steady step before speaking his peace. "Now it's my turn, Donald," he began.

"I don't want to hear another word! If you aren't going to bed, I am." Annie rose and was about to leave the room.

Ian's voice grew stern. "Sit down, Annie. I am mindful and grateful that you have run this household—and *me*—all these years, but now you must be told that you cannot arrange my life for me, even though you are well-meaning." Annie's eyebrows shot up in surprise at her father's sober words. "I know this will come as something of a shock, but keep in mind that I am not an old man. I will be forty-five on my next birthday and have long looked forward to having a woman of my own —someone to share my home, my heart . . ." he paused, ". . . and my bed."

Annie put her hand to her heart and stepped back as if she had been struck. In a household where sex had never been discussed, it came as a blow to hear her father refer, however remotely, to his sexual needs. "Oh, Da!" She took his hands and tears spilled over them, "I didn't know . . . I thought I was the only one making a sacrifice . . ."

Donald came over and gently guided her to a chair. "Sit down, sweetheart. Your father has more to say."

"The rest of it can wait, Donald," said Ian. "I don't want to put yet another burden on Annie tonight."

But Annie's tears had ceased and now she gave a long, deep sigh. "You might as well tell me the rest." Her tear-stained face relaxed as she gave a little laugh. "Then I can have a breakdown all at once instead of in little pieces!"

Her laughter broke the tension and Ian continued. "I have long admired the Widow MacLaughlin."

"She knows this?" said Annie, taken again by surprise.

He nodded. "She returns my feelings. As you know, her youngest child, your good friend Jessica, is soon to be married. She will be alone."

"Why didn't you tell me, Da?"

"We both agreed that it would be wrong to bring another woman into my home while you were in charge of the household; she had no desire to dislodge you and yet, as my wife, this would be her rightful place."

Donald had been standing in back of Annie's chair with his hands on her shoulders. She took several deep breaths; then, putting her hands on his and looking up with undisguised love, she said, "In that case, I would be proud

164

to be your wife, Donald MacConnack!'' Ian came over and kissed Annie, gave Donald a hearty slap on the back and shook hands with him interminably, then left the young couple to themselves. They made good use of their first time alone as an affianced couple. And this time when Donald left, he abandoned all attempts at dignity, gave a skip and a jump and threw his hat in the air.

XIV

TWO WEDDINGS

The triple wedding of the Maccrae daughters was such a stupendous event, it filled a full page in the Glasgow *Herald*. Each month when Tommy posted a letter for Maggie, he brought her the newspaper; thus she knew about the celebrated event. She was sad at not having been there; Kate's name was missing, too, she noticed, and she wondered if it had been an oversight. There was mention of an extravagant reception to which, it seemed, all Paisley, Glasgow and Edinburgh had been invited. The reporter wrote of the aura of love that enveloped the assembled guests and the radiance of not only the three pretty brides, but their father and older sister as well. The two marriages to take place in the near future were not referred to, although after the wedding there was gossip in town of Ian's attention to the Widow MacLaughlin, as Mrs. MacLaughlin, her son and daughter intermingled with the Maccrae family. There was an increased feeling of closeness, although none but Donald and Annie knew they would soon all be related.

Donald had planned to leave the day following the weddings, but Annie's consent to be his bride changed his plans. It took two days for the Maccrae household, which now consisted only of Ian, Annie and Robbie, to settle down. The family had shrunk considerably, and yet the home was not sad or empty; Da and Annie were lighthearted. As for Robbie, she had seen small tokens of affection—a stolen touch of hands, an understanding glance—pass between Donald and her sister. She didn't take it too seriously, but was amused, thinking "Kate should see this."

When three brides and their spouses had returned from their respective honeymoons, they were all invited to a family supper at the Maccrae's. The long wooden table had to be extended to accommodate the three new husbands and Donald, plus three more. There was so much laughter and repartee among the girls that they didn't notice the extra chairs. But Scott did. "You have set too many places, Annie," he told her.

Ian answered quietly, "No, Scott, we are expecting guests."

Scott raised his eyebrows in surprise. A family party rarely included outsiders. Mary, Frances and Laurie were deeply touched at the fuss being made over their first visit after being wed. "It just shows," Laurie remarked, "how glad Annie and Da are to have us home."

"It almost makes me wish I hadn't left. They will miss us terribly," said Frances.

Mary gently disagreed. "I wouldn't say that, but it's a nice, warm feeling to be welcomed this way." The girls were gazing at the table which had been laid with their best tartan tablecloth, brought out only on special

168

occasions. The company china, glassware and family silver had already been set on it, giving the dining room a festive air.

"And Da and Annie are wearing the clothes they wore at our wedding; such a lovely thing for them to do!" Frances was becoming tearfully sentimental. Annie's dress of pale blue, a color she had never worn before the ceremony, had a jabot of fine white lace with ruffles at he wrists which was matched by the lace on Da's jabot. He also had wrist ruffles which dripped gracefully over the backs of his sturdy hands, and was wearing his kilt.

Having drunk their drop of whiskey—a generous drop—the men joined the ladies and the chatter had risen to a crescendo when a female voice broke through the din. "Hello in there! Is anybody home?" There was laughter in the question. "May we come in?"

Ian marched to the door, followed closely by Annie. The girls, eager to see who the newcomers were, expressed surprise to each other. "It's the MacLaughlins!" Mary didn't sound too pleased, but followed the others to join dutifully in their father's effusive welcome to the widow and her two children. Annie had greeted Gregory and was hugging Jessica, her best friend, more warmly than Mary felt was strictly necessary.

Mina MacLaughlin was a small, energetic woman of forty-two. Her stature was faintly reminiscent of Ian's beloved wife Dora, but there the resemblance ended. Mina had rust-colored hair, a slightly ruddy complexion and skin so smooth she had nary a wrinkle. Her handsome children, Gregory the eldest, and Jessica two years younger (the same age as

Annie) were proof that despite her long widowhood, she had raised her children well. Gregory, if he strained, could stretch to five feet nine inches; he had his late father's stocky build and ginger hair which would turn rusty as he aged. Jessica, though broad of shoulder, was slim and inches shorter than her brother. Her complexion was more pink than white and her hair was the color of cinnamon. It was through her whispered confidence that Annie participated vicariously in Jessica's romance. Jessica was still living at home, waiting for her fiancé to return from his last voyage with the Royal Navy.

The girls helped with the shawls and bonnets and Gregory's ever-present bagpipes. With a courteous hand, Ian guided the widow into the dining room. He seated her at his right with Gregory to her right, then Laurie and Malcolm, Robbie and, at the end, as always, Annie. At her right was Donald, then Jessica, Charles, Frances, Mary and Scott at Ian's left. Ian's eyes twinkled as he looked down the length of the extended table. "My, how the family has grown," he said. Mina MacLaughlin just smiled a mysterious smile.

Annie went into the kitchen and emerged with a huge tureen of fish chowder. She enlisted the aid of Jessica and Mary, who served the savory soup as Da ladled it out. Donald commented it was the best he had ever tasted, but Ian corrected him.

"It may be the best you have had so far, Donald, but you should taste the Widow MacLaughlin's. Ah, *that* is an experience." Under other circumstances Annie might have had hurt feelings, but now she was glad he had said it.

Mina modestly disclaimed that honor, saying nothing could taste better than Annie's. The Maccrae sisters cast meaningful glances at each other, wondering what these elaborate compliments were all about and, wondered Mary, why the MacLaughlins had been invited to their family party.

Laurie and Frances cleared the empty soup plates quickly. Then Robbie and her sisters marched in single file, bearing great platters of poached river salmon, quail, roast lamb, beans and slivered carrots, with covered trays of hot scones and freshly baked monk's bread. Ian carved and filled the plates while the girls served. With so many helpers, they were all able to partake of the meal at the same time. Silence descended as Ian said grace; then they all concentrated on the sumptuous feast before them until the light clatter of cutlery on bare china signalled that the table was to be cleared once more.

"Shall I serve the dessert, Annie?" Frances asked.

She looked at Ian who answered, "Not yet, Frances. I have some news to impart first." He had their rapt attention and waited until Donald, who had excused himself briefly, returned with several bottles of chilled champagne. "Our dear friend, Donald MacConnack, is leaving for America a week from tonight," Ian began. They made appropriate sounds of regret. "Wait, there is more." Everyone sat quietly, waiting. "He will take Annie Maccrae . . . ." he paused dramatically

171

"*MacConnack* with him!"

It took some seconds for his words to register, and when they did, he put up his hand to stem the babble of astonished comments. "Annie and Donald will be married on Wednesday morning. It will be a quiet wedding and . . ." he got no further. Everyone had sprung from his seat and surrounded Annie and Donald. Amid the congratulations and hugging they were teased about keeping their romance so secret. With a flourish, Ian popped the cork on the first bottle of champagne. He raised his glass as the others stood and joined him. "May you always be as happy as you are at this moment," he said gruffly. The glasses were upended and refilled. Then Mary lifted her voice above the others.

"Wait!" Her tone was commanding and they quieted. "Isn't Robbie going to Edinburgh University in September?" She was answered in the affirmative. "You will be all alone, Da!"

He tried to give her an answer, but a sisterly argument broke over his head. Robbie said, "Then I won't go to the University!"

Laurie spoke up. "Of course you will. We have a large house, Da, and if you come live with us, you will be close to Robbie, too."

Malcolm seconded her invitation. "We have asked Robbie to stay with us, but she said it would be better for her to board at one of the homes provided for the students. I want you to know you are both welcome in our home." All Ian could do was nod his thanks. Mary and Frances and their husbands had also invited Ian to share their home, but when Laurie and Malcolm made their offer they said no more. They still were not over the surprise that of all the Maccrae girls, Laurie had made the most prosperous marriage—until, that is, the announcement about Annie and Donald. Accepting the fact that Malcolm and Laurie had solved the dilemma, they clustered around Annie, admiring the antique ring come down through generations of MacConnacks and finally, from Donald's mother to him. With a sly wink at Mina, Ian stood once more and tapped his spoon on a glass to get their attention, but again he was forestalled by Mary.

"I would like to make a toast, Da, before you make a speech. May I?"

"Not yet, Mary," said Ian firmly. "We have more champagne and there'll be plenty for everyone to make a toast." He directed his next words to the MacLaughlin son and daughter and then to his own children. "I know you are wondering why the MacLaughlins have joined us tonight at our little—well, not so little—family party." All eyes were riveted on him, and he took a deep breath. "I am proud to announce that Mina MacLaughlin has done me the honor to accept my proposal of marriage."

For a split second there was total silence. Then the air was rent with shrieks of congratulations, the MacLaughlin family congratulating Ian and the Maccrae girls swarming around the Widow MacLaughlin. There were tears of happiness in the girls' eyes as they rained kisses on him. "You're such a sly puss, Da, you never told us one word!" "No wonder you wouldn't consent to live with us."

"Now, may I make my toast, Da?" Mary asked. He nodded in agreement over the embracing arms of his other daughters. "To the most deserving people I know—Da and Annie. And to the newest members of our family, Mina and her family, and Donald, who are wonderful additions!"

"Hear, Hear!" everyone cried. Gregory Mac-Laughlin then offered a toast. "To our new sisters!"

The others got up one by one. Each toast called for another glass of champagne and before everyone was finished, it was a very, very merry party indeed. Donald had his arm around Annie and Ian and Mina were holding hands.

The Widow MacLaughlin played the piano at all the church socials and now Laurie coaxed her to play. They all lifted their voices in song. Then Gregory brought out his bagpipes and Robbie performed a lively Highland fling.

As the party neared its end and the Mac-Laughlins were saying their farewells, Donald called for attention, his arm still around Annie. "I want to thank you for your good wishes and hope to see you all at the wedding. Annie will give you the particulars. I am proud to become a member of such a large loving family. Although I am taking Annie across the ocean to America, she will come back to visit often. My business is such that I make many trips across the ocean, and Annie will always be with me. Ian, thank you for having such a lovely daughter and entrusting her to my care." He turned to Annie. "Annie?"

She blushed and said, "I just want to tell you that our wedding will take place in the chapel at eleven o'clock Wednesday morning. We will not stay for a reception, as the ship leaves at two." Tears streamed down her cheeks as she continued, "I shall always remember this night, and will think of it often in my new home across the sea." Mina embraced her and kissed her on the cheek, then her sisters and brothers-in-law did likewise. They all shook hands with Donald.

When at last the door closed behind the MacLaughlins, bedlam broke loose. Annie's sisters wanted to know all the details of the romance that had been kept so secret, both hers and Ian's. Ian invited the men to join him in a pipe and left the girls to their chatter. There were smiles on every face as they said goodnight.

The night before the wedding Donald invited his future father-in-law and Mina, Robbie and Annie to dinner at the Inn. It was a quiet evening of conversation concerning everyone's plans for the future. Donald had accompanied Robbie to the University of Edinburgh. Although the university was reluctant to admit a female, particularly one who wanted to study engineering, Donald brought all his powers of persuasion to bear. He had brought along her drawings of the machinery Gunther had designed with her help, pointed out the improvements (all initialied) she had suggested, and at last she was permitted to register. Her course of study would concentrate on advanced mathematics and mastering German, the textbook language. Her future at the University would depend on how well she accomplished the first year. It was a challenge Robbie was ready and willing to accept. Not usually a tearful maiden, her eyes were moist as she thanked Donald fervently for his

175

support and for helping to finance her studies. "I don't know the proper words to tell you how grateful I am, but if you ever need me for anything, I will be there," she assured him.

"I am not completely altruistic, Robbie," Donald admitted. "In fact, I have a selfish interest in developing your brilliant mind. One day, I know the textile industry will benefit by it." A brotherly hug accompanied his words.

Robbie's admittance to the University was one of the first subjects they discussed, proudly and a little in awe of the "intelligent" young lady in their family. She turned the attention away from herself by asking, "When do you and Da plan to marry, Mrs. MacLaughlin?"

"We've talked a little bit about it. We would like to have the ceremony while Annie and Donald are still here," Mina replied.

"But we're leaving tomorrow after the wedding," Annie reminded her.

Ian took up as Mina started to falter. "We don't want to intrude on your special day, but . . ." even he had to reach for courage as he continued, "we've already had a *triple* wedding. How would you feel about our being married at the same time as you and Donald?"

Donald answered enthusiastically, "I think that's a tremendous idea! I know, dear," he turned to Annie, "that you want to see your father and Mina married. Am I not right?"

For answer, she rose and kissed her father and Mina. "I would be so proud to have a double wedding! We'll have to talk to our minister right away!"

"Yes," Mina replied, "and I'm afraid he'll think we're a rather weird clan. I hope he won't mind performing a double ceremony so soon after the triple one!" Then she added anxiously, "Please tell us honestly, do you mind?" She looked at Donald, who shook his head.

"I know Annie was concerned that we would miss your wedding. It's a marvelous solution."

"Good. We are planning to go away for a brief while, but that will depend on your plans, Robbie," said Ian.

"I'll tell you what I'd like to do, but remember, my plans are flexible until September." They waited while Robbie got her thoughts in order. "I want to teach our mill workers the intricacies of using the new machinery." She was thinking out loud. "That should take about a month. Then I will stay with Laurie and Malcolm until I find lodgings." By way of explanation she said, "At the University I was given a list of approved boarding houses in the vicinity."

"You plan to stay home *alone?*" said Mina, slightly shocked.

"Well, Mrs. MacLaughlin, someone should be here when Kate returns," said Robbie cheerfully, but she had her fingers crossed as she spoke.

"Of course. Robbie dear, I like the informality of your Americans. Why don't you call me Mina?"

"I'd like that, Mina." Robbie grinned.

"It's too bad Kate couldn't come with you," Mina continued. "Do you realize she will have missed *five* weddings?"

Donald added, "Accomplished with only *two* ceremonies!"

* * *

In a private moment before the wedding, Ian presented Mina, somewhat tentatively, with a sash in the Maccrae tartan. "Mina dear, I know you have worn your husband's plaid for many years. Will you accept this sash of the Maccrae clan as a symbol of my love?" he asked.

There was no hesitation as Mina, tears in her eyes, accepted the sash. "I am proud that you want me to wear it! I shall do so with great pride." Their grown children would have been surprised at the warmth of the kiss they subsequently exchanged. Love, respect and a need for each other were implicit in their embrace.

With the MacLaughlins and Maccraes and a few close friends from both families present, Annie and Donald walked down the aisle one week later, followed by Mina and Ian. When they reached the flower-laden altar they stood four abreast. The slight awkwardness that accompanied the bridegroom of the older couple giving away the bride of the younger was quickly gotten over. Annie looked lovely and fresh. She was wearing a dress Robbie had brought from America that had been quickly altered to fit her perfectly. It was ideal for the occasion, a delicate white batiste sprigged with violets. Laurie had arranged her auburn hair in a soft coiffure with a bridal wreath of white heather. She looked as virginal as she was, and only Mary was aware of the almost imperceptible apprehension in her eyes. But she was quickly reassured when Donald came alongside her, more handsome than she had ever seen him.

Mina, in a blue dress with a matching hat pinned to her topknot, wore the Maccrae sash over one shoulder, across her chest and fastened at the hip with a diamond brooch, her wedding gift from Ian.

After the simple but moving ceremony, hugs and kisses and a flurry of congratulations were kept to a minimum. Five carriages were lined up outside the white, small-steepled church, and Mr. and Mrs. Donald MacConnack climbed into the first, while Mr. and Mrs. Ian Maccrae got into the second. Both were decorated with flowers. Even the horses had garlands around their necks and the drivers each had a sprig of heather in his high hat. Family and friends filled the remaining carriages. When they dismounted a little distance from the pier, Gregory and his bag-pipes led the procession—first the newlyweds, then the other MacLaughlins, family and friends and a few whom nobody knew followed in high spirits. After more hugs, kisses and some tears, Annie and Donald were piped aboard by Gregory. Sodden handkerchiefs waved until the ship sailed out of sight.

The little section of deck outside their suite was theirs alone. Annie and Donald stood close together, not yet having entered the cabin. He was gentle as he turned her to him and held her tight against him. Annie's long suppressed passion flared as he lifted her in his arms and carried her over the threshold. For the first time they were alone together. Donald attempted to stand her on her feet, but she clung to him, clutching him to her as she rained kisses on his face. His senses were so inflamed he could no longer contain himself; he carried her over to the bed and she pulled him down next to her.

"Annie, my beautiful Annie, I love you so much! I don't want to hurt you but I can wait no longer," Donald whispered.

"I want you, Donald. Oh, my dear love, I've wanted you ever since we met," Annie murmured against his cheek.

In a frenzy she pulled at the buttons on her dress, and with Donald's help almost tore it off. He left her only long enough to shed his own clothes and when he returned, she lay naked on the bed, her skin white as milk with pink nipples standing high. Her eyes were glazed, her lips parted as she held out her arms to him and drew him to her. He tried to be gentle, but she would not have it and as his body molded itself to hers, she dug her nails into his shoulders. His mouth sought her breast, and her teeth left marks on his bare shoulder as they reached the zenith together, an explosion that left them limp. Annie's rapturous moans had become cries and now she lay, seeming almost lifeless except for the soft, dry sobs shaking her otherwise still form. Donald was wrung with remorse as he made an effort to soothe Annie's bruised body which was already showing bluish marks from the roughness of their uninhibited love-making. "My love, I am so sorry! Annie darling, I have hurt you and I did not want to," he groaned. "Please, dearest, forgive me!"

It was a while before Annie could summon the strength to speak. "Donald, I'm the one to ask forgiveness. I never thought . . . I never expected . . . I have dreamed about making love, and never thought it would happen, never thought it would be so glorious!" She was crying tears now. She reached over and kissed his cheek. "You are the culmination of all my dreams and it was exciting . . . and beautiful."

"You are exciting and beautiful, my love. I have never known anyone . . ." he stopped as he felt her eyes on him. "You must know I have known other women."

"I never thought about it," Annie admitted, "but of course, it would have to be."

"Never again—never! You are all the woman I'll ever want or need, and I intend to keep you happy. I'll have to keep myself in excellent condition." A grin formed on his mouth. She echoed it with a giggle and they once again exploded simultaneously, this time in wild laughter. The rest of the night they alternated between sweet love-making, and blissfully sleeping, encircled in each other's arms.

Their wedding night was one to be remembered—it had to be; it was the first and only time for the rest of the voyage that Mr. and Mrs. Donald MacConnack enjoyed connubial bliss. Annie was a very poor sailor. She spent all but the last two days on shipboard in bed, nursing the most severe case of seasickness the ship's doctor said he had ever tended.

XV

GUNTHER

At the end of the second week, Kate was hobbling about on a cane. Her recovery had been so rapid that the doctor wondered if he had misdiagnosed as a fracture something which was nothing more than a sprain. She was permitted mobility in her rooms but he told her not to try the stairs as yet. As he had promised, Gunther stopped by every evening. After visiting Katherine in her rooms with Birdy standing by, he would stay and have dinner with Amy, after which he would sip a cognac while she would play for him. "Donald would be so proud of you, Amy, the way you have taken charge of the household," he said one evening. "I keep looking for the little girl I knew and in her place I find an excellent hostess and a young lady who is growing into beautiful womanhood."

Amy cherished that conversation, although it was sometimes hard to hold onto as she watched Gunther, arm around Kate's slender waist, helping her to walk. She could not misunderstand the tenderness with which he catered to her helplessness . . . pseudo-helplessness, Amy was sure. Eventually, Amy would excuse herself on the vague pretext of being needed in some other part of the house, too annoyed to remain.

The last time she felt compelled to leave, Gunther seized the opportunity her absence afforded him. Gently helping Kate into her chair, he lowered himself to one knee. "I adore you, Katherine! Will you marry me?" he asked, flushed with ardor and excitement.

She had anticipated his proposal and had prepared her reply. "Gunther, you are a fine person and I am honored that you have asked me to be your wife. I am very fond of you, but my heart belongs to another."

His face paled. "I did not know—forgive me. Who is the fortunate man? Are . . . are you planning to be married?"

"Definitely!" Kate said briskly, ignoring his first question. "I'm not sure exactly when, but in the near future."

Gunther did not stay for dinner.

Amy permitted Katherine free access to the servants; the first few days of her enforced stay in bed she kept them running, demanding attention far exceeding her needs. When the doctor gave his consent for her to walk about in her rooms, Amy expected the demands would lessen. Instead, Katherine assumed the proprietary air of mistress of the house, countermanding many of the instructions given by Amy. She had one of the servants take a note to Amy's dressmaker and ordered a peach silk robe trimmed with ostrich feathers, a request Mrs. Oakley was hard put to fill, although she managed. One early evening when she was sitting in all her pale peach glory, her hair loose and the ostrich feathers softly curling around her face, Birdy announced that she had a caller.

"Who is it?" asked Kate.

"A . . . a *person* from the mill. He said he had a gift for you from the other workers." Birdy's tone was disapproving. Having a "mill person" in a lady's room was definitely not acceptable behaviour. "I don't think Miss Amy would approve," she said firmly.

Sitting in a chair made it difficult to draw herself up to the commanding position she would have liked to assume, in spite of which Kate sat up as straight as she could and snapped, "Do as you're told, Birdy. Bring the 'person' to me!"

Birdly left in a huff; moments later, a knock on door heralded her return. "Come in," Kate lilted. Then, "Rory!" she cried. "How good of you to come!"

Rory shifted a large bouquet from one hand to the other while Birdy stood in the door at strict attention. "We all hope you are feeling better and wanted you to have the flowers as a token of our esteem," he mumbled shyly.

"What a lovely gesture!" Kate gushed. "They're truly beautiful. Please thank everyone for me. You must leave their names —I will write a note to each one." She said peremptorily to Birdy, "Put them in vases." Birdy, shaking her head in disapproval, snatched the flowers and stalked out.

"They all signed their names to the card." Rory handed it to Kate and she glanced at it.

"How sweet. Put it on my desk, Rory, and sit down."

He sat down stiffly. "You look beautiful, Miss Katherine," he said. "Are you feeling better?"

"I'm fine, thank you. But I am going mad penned up in these rooms. The doctor doesn't want me to walk up and down the stairs as yet. I don't know how much longer I can stand it."

"That's the only reason you must stay here?" he asked. She nodded pathetically. "Would you like to go downstairs now?"

"If only I could!"

"No sooner said than done." Without further ado Rory lifted her out of the chair and started for the door where they met Birdy coming back.

She lost her usual reserved demeanor. "What are you *doing? Miss Katherine . . .*" she gasped.

"Hush, Birdy. Mr. Sullivan is going to carry me downstairs so I can see how the other part of the world lives," said Kate with a broad smile.

"You mustn't . . . Oh, I wish Miss Amy was here!"

"We will go into the conservatory. Bring the gentleman a decanter of Mr. Donald's Irish whiskey," (Rory grinned) "and I will have sherry."

Birdy's stiff back leading them down the stairs to the conservatory said more than mere words could have.

Rory held her in his brawny arms as gently as he would a child. "You are so strong, Rory! Your arms are like steel," Kate said softly. She touched one muscular arm, knowing full well what would happen. She was gratified when she felt his muscles tense. He carefully concentrated on each step to fight down the desire that was consuming him. He placed her on a chaise longue and turned his back, ostensibly to sit in a chair on the other side of the conservatory, then stopped as though to admire a large rubber plant on the way. He had barely composed himself when Kate said, "Come sit by me." He sat at the far end of the chaise, trying to ignore the glimpse of bare ankle showing beneath her robe. "Tell me about the mill and what's going on," Kate continued.

Birdy brought in two crystal decanters and glasses. Kate poured whiskey for Rory and wine for herself. "I don't think the doctor would want you to have wine, Miss Katherine," Birdy said through pursed lips.

"It's quite all right, Birdy. Don't fret so! Now, you must have something to do. I'll call you if we need anything else." Birdy took one step, faltered, turned back and then at a motion from Kate, turned on her heel and left, muttering to herself that she was glad Bessie wasn't present to see such behaviour.

Kate and Rory spent an hour together, laughing at the stories he told her about the people at the mill. He told her of their parties and dances and the gaiety that was predominant in their get-togethers every Saturday night at McCarthy's saloon. "Oh, Rory, how I would love to go there some time," cried Kate.

"It wouldn't be right for such a lovely lady to go to a saloon, Miss Kate, but I am sorry. I think you would enjoy it as much as the others."

"I don't like that kind of talk, Rory," Kate pouted. "I am not really a lady, except," and she winked, "on the outside when I have to be. I think there must be some wild Irish blood coursing through my veins." She then offered him another drink, which he declined, saying, "I have to carry you up the stairs again and another drink might make me miss my step."

This caused more laughter. Meanwhile, Kate had managed to pour a drop of whiskey in her glass when she had finished her sherry. "I can just see us tumbling down the steps! Birdy would have a conniption fit!"

Amy and Gunther, returning from dinner at the Horton Smythes', were greeted with loud laughter as Birdy, who had been waiting for them, started to whisper to Amy about what was going on. "I'll find out for myself, Birdy," Amy told her. Gunther followed as she walked quietly into the conservatory at the same moment Rory picked Kate up in his arms.

Not until Gunther gave a rather startled greeting did Amy recognize Rory Sullivan. She had met him at the mill party. "Kate . . . what are you doing down here?" she asked.

"Don't look so alarmed. I finally found a gallant gentleman who took pity on my prisoner status. You have no idea how grateful I am. I had almost forgotten what it looks like down here," said Kate gaily. Rory stood there, still holding Kate, not knowing what he should do.

"I'm sorry, ma'am, if I have done the wrong thing," he mumbled, "but Miss Katherine was so forlorn all by herself upstairs, that I offered to carry her down. We were just about to go up again. It's time for me to leave."

Gunther answered curtly, "It *is* late. I'll take Miss Katherine upstairs myself."

"Oh, no, Gunther, I'll trust myself only to this strong man here," Kate teased. She put her arm around Rory's neck. Unsure of how to proceed, Rory hesitated, a question in his eyes as he looked first at Amy, then Gunther. Amy motioned him to go ahead. Kate carried on all the way upstairs, her teasing laughter trailing behind them. Amy waited until Rory was on his way downstairs before ascending. "Gunther, will you see Mr. Sullivan to the door?" she asked frostily. Rory said a flustered goodnight, feeling guilty and not knowing why, except that he knew he was out of his class. But he dismissed that thought as he whistled softly to himself, still feeling the warmth of Kate's body and the heady perfume of her hair as he held her close.

Gunther, disgusted at the scene he had witnessed, was about to leave when Amy called to him. "Kate would like you to come up for a moment."

He reluctantly obliged. When he had entered Kate's sitting room, she said, "Amy, Gunther, I don't think I have anything to apologize for, but if *you* think so, please accept this as one. I've wanted desperately to get out of these rooms and when I said so, Rory offered to carry me downstairs. It's the first time in months that I've been able to share laughter with anyone. He is very humorous and I feel so well that I'm sure that now I'll be able to get downstairs by myself."

"Don't try it until you see the doctor, Kate." Amy was honestly concerned. "And I'm sure there was no impropriety intended."

"In the future," Gunther added stiffly, "if

you have to be carried anywhere, I'll do it." Amy looked at him quickly and he added, "I'm sure Donald would prefer that to having Rory do it."

Kate glanced at him quizzically. Had he guessed her secret plans concerning Donald? She couldn't be sure if there was a hidden meaning in his words. He turned to Amy. "Don't you think so?" he asked.

"I suppose so," she said slowly. "We'll see what the doctor has to say tomorrow. Perhaps you are right, Kate. Perhaps your leg is strong enough to walk downstairs by yourself."

"And up! I'm sure I can do it," said Kate. "Now, I have something more to say before I go to sleep. If you look around, you will see the beautiful flowers Rory brought to me. *All* the mill workers sent them and I'm grateful. Gunther, I don't want you to say one word of this—this incident to anyone, particularly not to Donald. That goes for you, too, Amy. Rory did nothing wrong, just showed his concern for me in the best way he knew, and if you must know, I quite liked it." She saw the quick glance that passed between Amy and Gunther and covered her mouth to hide a theatrical yawn. "Goodnight," she sighed. They were dismissed. Completely nonplussed by her change of attitude, Gunther and Amy left as Kate stood leaning on her cane. "Be sure to close the door," she called after them.

Gunther led the way. Amy saw the way his shoulders were shaking, and she could see that he had his hand over his mouth. She had been rather amused at Kate's highhandedness, but now her heart ached to see Gunther's reaction. He walked into the drawing room and she was uncertain about following him. Perhaps she should let him be alone with his grief . . . As she entered, he turned and closed the door and burst into the loudest guffaws she had ever heard from him. His laughter was so contagious she found herself joining him. "I thought you were crying," she said at last.

"Oh, my sweet, darling little Amy! I know I shouldn't poke fun at Kate but she was *so* funny." He laughed until he threw himself into a chair, exhausted. "I'm not insane, really, dear Amy, but it's the first time I actually saw Kate playing the role of siren." He sighed. "I thank God I did. I almost fell into her web. I have been noticing it more and more and tried to convince myself I was being unfair because she didn't feel well. I am so relieved, I cannot tell you." He took her hand in his. "There's more I cannot tell you now, but we have a lot of talking to do, serious talking. I just want you to know this; the evenings I spend with you are the only reasons I continue to visit."

Amy's eyes were shining through her tears. "And evenings with you are the happiest of my life. You will continue to come?" she asked anxiously.

"Nothing could keep me away. I'll see you tomorrow night." Taking her chin in his hands he turned her face to his and kissed her on the mouth. "This time it was no accident. I suppose I shouldn't have done it, but I couldn't resist it," he told her, his voice suddenly serious.

"I'm glad." Amy closed her eyes in ecstasy, as Gunther dropped a light kiss on her forehead and left.

XVI

SURPRISE!

From then on, Gunther duly paid his official respects to Kate and spent his evenings with Amy. Katherine did not mind being ignored; after all, when you reject a proposal of marriage you can't expect any other behaviour, she reasoned. Besides, she had Rory to keep her company while she waited for Donald to return.

Once a week she invited him to call and as her injury healed they walked, slowly at first, then more vigorously as the weeks passed. Annoyed that Donald had delayed his return, she became even more daring in her flirtation with the handsome mill-hand. One day Amy received a letter which she read to Kate. Donald had mailed it just before leaving Scotland and said he would be home in three weeks. Amy wondered why had had prolonged his stay; Kate was annoyed. "He certainly doesn't miss us, does he?" she snapped, and didn't wait for a reply.

When Rory called on her that week, she had made a daring decision. "Do you still have parties at the pub . . . I mean McCarthy's, on Saturdays?" she asked, eyes sparkling.

"Yes, Miss Katherine . . . " she pointed a

finger at him, shaking her head. "I mean yes, Kate, we do. Why do you ask?"

Kate fluttered her long lashes. "I have never asked you if you have a special lady friend. Do you?"

Rory pursed his lips and cocked his head to one side, evidence that he was thinking of the proper answer. Slowly he said, "Not really. I don't take anyone to the parties. I guess Rosie is the one I dance with most."

"Does she meet you there?"

"No, she works there."

Kate digested this information for a brief moment. So Rosie was a barmaid. "Would you take me this Saturday?"

"Oh, Miss . . . I mean, Kate, I don't think that's any place for you. It gets pretty . . . noisy, and sometimes," he added honestly, "a little rough. You know, some men drink too much and," he laughed, "they're all fighting Irishmen."

"With you there to protect me, I wouldn't worry about that," Kate said demurely.

"You really want to come?" She nodded emphatically, clinging to his arm. There was no way he could resist her. "What will Miss MacConnack say?" he asked.

"I don't have to ask her. She's nothing to me," Kate said airily. She was, however, having second thoughts about the matter, and added, "She has dinner every Saturday with Gunther. I'll wait until they've left and then I'll meet you just a little way from the house." She couldn't take a chance that Donald would find out.

Against his better judgment, Rory said he would be at the meeting place at eight o'clock.

Her nearness made it impossible to deny her anything, but after leaving her, he too had some serious doubts. Not only could she get in trouble with the MacConnacks, but his job as foreman at the factory might be jeopardized. And yet, the thought of holding her in his arms as they danced overwhelmed him and the little warning bell that had gone off in his brain was ignored.

Katherine spent the week trying to solve the age old problem, "What shall I wear?" All her new clothes were much too grand and she didn't want to seem that way; she wanted to appear one with the people she would be meeting. She finally was inspired to ask one of the maids, tipping the girl generously to keep it confidential, to buy her a simple outfit that would be proper for the occasion. The maid asked no questions, but her mind was busy.

When Rory met Kate that night, she was enveloped in a full-length woolen shawl. He couldn't believe his eyes when they got to McCarthy's and she unwrapped herself, to reveal a rose colored V-necked blouse tucked into a black skirt with rose colored stripes and a flounce at the bottom. She wore a black satin ribbon around her neck, tied in a tiny bow. In a burst of admiring enthusiasm Rory put his hands on her waist, lifted her and kissed her. He was immediately abashed and begged her pardon. "I'm sorry, I just couldn't help myself! Somewhere along the line of your ancestry there must have been an Irishman!"

"Rory, you make my heart sing." She stroked his face. He put a protective arm around her shoulders and led her to a table, then excused himself and went to the bar to order drinks. Kate took advantage of the time to inspect her surroundings. It was not as much of a surprise as she had anticipated. Although she was not supposed to know about the pubs in Glasgow, she did, and McCarthy's saloon was not too different. The worn, small octagonal tiles on the floor were bordered in brown; the bare, oak tables and chairs were placed at a fair distance from each other; a lamp with a dark green shade hung over each. She looked for a dart board but there was none. The only decoration Kate could see was a large paper rose fastened with green net high on the mirror in back of the bar; there, too, stood the barmaid with her back to the room. Kate knew this must be Rosie, she was watching her in the mirror. A few men were standing at the bar. Kate envied their casual freedom and promised herself that one day she too would stand with her foot on the shiny brass rail.

"Rosie," Rory spoke to the barmaid's back, "let me have a pitcher of beer." He was filling two plates with the free food laid out on the bar and did not at first notice how long she took to turn around. Finally he repeated his order. "A pitcher of beer, Rosie."

She pulled at the long pump handle of the beer keg, filled a pitcher and slapped it down hard, slopping the contents over. Rory understood the message. "Don't be mad, Rosie. She's a very special lady and wants to have a good time," he told her with one of his dazzling grins.

"You mean your society woman is slumming, that's what she's doing! She should stay where she belongs, and that's not here," Rosie said much too loudly.

"Keep your voice down! She doesn't feel that way at all. She loves to dance and hear laughter and they don't do that at the big house."

"Sure! Me heart bleeds for her, poor thing. Well, I hope she gets an eyeful of how the *working* people play."

Rory protested further. "She works. She's usually at the mill every day."

"And now I know why!" Jealousy flashed in Rosie's eyes as she looked him up and down. "Go back to your fancy friend, I'll bring the beer." She wanted a closer look and when she got it, her heart sank. She never had a rival for Rory's attentions before and Kate's beauty made her feel like a slovenly drudge. "I'm sorry, Miss," she simpered, "we're all out of champagne."

Kate noticed the sarcasm and answered sweetly, "Oh, I don't want champagne, I want what you have."

Kate had never seen Rory's hair-trigger temper but Rosie had, and one warning look from him was enough to send her flouncing off to the bar muttering to herself. "I hope she chokes on that beer, the hussy!"

Rory was not only angry, but bewildered at Rosie's hostility to Kate. There had never been anything between him and Rosie. As far as he was concerned, they were just good friends and dancing partners. He dismissed her from his mind and turned his attention to Kate, who watched him pour the beer expertly. She was delighted at the marvelous head of foam in the beer mug. "You're wonderful, Rory! You didn't spill a drop. Can I drink that foamy stuff?" He nodded and as she did, Rosie, behind the bar again, waited hopefully, hands on hips, for her to choke. "It's delicious—so cold and refreshing," Kate said when she had finished. He filled her glass again and then his own and they clinked them together.

"I hope you enjoy yourself tonight, Kate," he said.

Again Kate held up her glass. She wanted to make a toast. "May this be the first of many times at McCarthy's . . . with you."

"Glory be to God, I would like that!"

Kate hadn't noticed the three-piece band that was setting up at the other end of the saloon, composed of a piano, a fiddle and a banjo. When the music struck up, excitement heightened in Kate's eyes as Rory took her by the hand and guided her to the space provided for dancing. As he placed his hand on her waist, one of the men from the bar called out, "Hey, Rory, how about introducing your lady friend?" Before he had a chance to answer, Kate said she would like to meet his friends. She had seen Rosie talking to this man and knew she had put him up to it. "I don't want them to think I'm a snob." Reluctantly Rory danced her over to meet the man called Gerry and danced her away again as soon as the introduction had been accomplished.

He and Kate danced as if made for each other. Only a few recognized Kate and, taking the cue from her, pretended they didn't. But they were friendly and accepted her as Rory's ladyfriend for the evening. Rory was very popular and between dances some of his friends stopped at their table and at his invitation had a beer with them. Kate was more comfortable than she had been in all her time in America. There was only one bad moment. Gerry, the man at the bar, took advantage of the previous introduction and asked her to dance. Rory tried to catch her eye before she answered but it was too late. "Do you mind, Rory?" she asked, placing her hand over his. She was on her feet before he could voice an objection, and Gerry whirled her away. This was a different kind of dancing, and she had all she could do to keep her balance. He pulled her hand behind her waist then, throwing her away from him, unrolled her like a toy at the end of a ribbon. Rory caught her and brought her back to the table.

"I tried to warn you, Kate. Gerry is not really one of us. He doesn't work at the mill nor does he live around here. Every once in a while he wanders in. He's a roughneck and always starts trouble." Gerry stood in the middle of the floor, scowling, jaw set and shoulders back. He spelled trouble with a capital "T"; the other dancers closed ranks around him and by the time he had pushed his way through them, Rory had wrapped Kate in her shawl and spirited her outside the saloon. There was just enough light for him to see that her hair had come loose. Kate was enraptured as he tenderly smoothed the tendrils back from her face and replaced the pins. "I am so sorry, Kate. I wanted to take such good care of you and instead . . ." his voice trailed off.

"Rory, dear Rory, it was all my fault. I was too eager to have your friends like me. I hope I didn't spoil the evening; please invite me again."

"Ah, Macushla, I would be happy to have you with me always." Her upturned face was a temptation he couldn't resist and he bent and kissed her lightly; a kiss which she returned. Then with a wave of her hand, she ran off before they arrived at the house. He waited until she had vanished inside.

Amy and Gunther were in the conservatory and Kate's luck held. She tiptoed up the stairs with nary a twinge from the injured leg. She meant it sincerely when she had told Rory her heart was singing. He was such a *man* and had such a wonderful sense of humor and fun, yet could be so tender, so gentle.

She called Birdy to fix her bath, then dismissed her. After she had bathed, with her head still in the clouds, she tumbled into bed; her last thoughts were, if only Donald were like Rory—or was it the other way around? She laughed to herself and fell asleep, happier than she had been in a long time.

That lighthearted feeling persisted and changed her disposition. She said "please" and "thank you" and "May I" to everyone and everything. And whenever she could, she met Rory secretly. Kate had counted the days to the following Saturday when they went again to McCarthy's. She wore the same clothes and was gratified to see that the maid had chosen well; all the other girls were similarly dressed; in addition to their "Sunday best" they obviously had a "Saturday night best." The second party was even better than the first. There were no awkward moments, and this time even Rosie accepted her, albeit grudgingly.

They held hands walking home that night.

"We're going to put in extra time this week, Kate, so I won't be able to see you until Saturday—that is, if you want to go to McCarthy's again," Rory said. Kate pulled him over to a low wall that ran along the side of the road.

"Sit here with me for a little while, I want to talk to you."

"That sounds serious," said Rory, a twinkle in his eyes.

"It is." Kate paused for a moment, then took his hand in both of hers. "I'm not going to see you again after Donald returns." His head jerked back as if she had hit him. "You must understand, please," she begged.

Tears welled in her eyes as she continued, "I have never, in all my life, met anyone I admired more or whose company I enjoyed more . . . but while I am here under his roof, Donald is—is a kind of guardian."

"Dear heart, that is a terrible blow," Rory muttered. "I thought when you said you didn't have to ask Miss Amy . . ."

Slowly and sadly Kate shook her head. "I knew she wouldn't tattle on me if she found out, but with Donald here, that's another matter. You see, Rory, I want to stay in America. I haven't quite figured out how, but somehow the MacConnack family may be the answer. Can you understand?" It was a necessary lie, but one she hated telling. Rory was silent for what seemed a long time. Finally, he said, "I am grateful, Kate, that you have given me so much of yourself. While my dreams seemed to be impossible and I knew it, I dreamed them anyway."

"I know, Rory, I really *do* know." She held her arms out to him and he folded her to his breast with a tenderness she had not known before. He kissed her eyelids, her chin, the tip of her nose and finally, a long, passionate kiss on her lips which she returned equally passionately.

Rory left quickly, and Kate's heart was breaking as she realized that Rory was the only man she would ever love. She felt she had died a little over their goodbye, but she convinced herself she would just have to suffer. She'd get over it in time. Too long had she planned on becoming Mrs. Donald MacConnack to let her emotions take possession of her. Donald had wealth and position to offer and she was determined to attain them for herself.

Until Thursday of the following week, Kate remained in semi-seclusion, purging her heart and mind of Rory Sullivan and preparing to devote all her love and fidelity to Donald.

Gunther went to the ship to meet Donald while Amy and Katherine waited at home for his arrival. Kate's dress and manner were demure and her face pale, which made Amy wonder what role she was going to play this time. She didn't need the scent to know Kate's pallor had been enhanced by talcum powder. But secure in Gunther's love, she could afford to be amused by Kate's performance.

As the carriage came to a halt in the drive, Donald alighted and both girls ran to him. With an arm around each, he escorted them back to the house. Amy gave him a hug, and Kate fussed over him, chattering as if she hadn't spoken a word since he had left almost eight weeks before. "Donald, I missed you terribly! I thought you were never coming back. Why did you stay away so long?" she pouted prettily as she fondled the hand that still rested on her shoulder.

"My dear Katherine, if you will be still for just one moment, you will find out," said Donald, a smile tugging at the corners of his mouth. His words sounded promising and Kate allowed herself to be guided into the drawing room. He called to Amy, who had lagged behind with Gunther. "Come in here, dear, I have a surprise for you both." When Amy and Gunther had entered, he directed, "Amy, sit over here." He pointed to a chair at the side. The surprise was really for Kate's benefit. "Now, close your eyes until I say 'ready.' No peeking, Kate, this is a surprise I want you to appreciate." She was truly excited. Would he go to all this trouble to present a ring? Whatever it was, it had to be something of great significance.

"Ready!" Donald sang out.

Amy and Kate opened their eyes, and for a moment there was stunned silence. A tired but glowing Annie came forward as Kate leaped up to meet her, arms outstretched. "*Annie!* I don't believe my eyes! How wonderful to see you!" Her joy was sincere as she embraced her sister and cried from sheer happiness. Annie stroked her hair and quieted her. At last Kate turned to Donald. "Well, that certainly was a surprise, a tremendous one, and I thank you. But," she turned back to her sister, "What are you doing here? I hope," she added suspiciously, "you didn't come to bring me home!"

Annie shook her head, and Donald came over to them, bringing Amy with him. "I think introductions are in order. Kate, Amy, it is my great pleasure to present my wife, Mrs. Donald MacConnack."

Kate's indrawn breath was audible. She paled and held on to the back of her chair to steady herself; it was as if her knees had turned to water. Only her iron self-discipline kept her from fainting. With great effort she found her voice, although it was weak and piping. "Your wife?" She stared from Donald to Annie. "Annie, you and Donald . . . ?"

"I wish you could have been there, Kate dear," Annie replied softly. "We were married just before the ship sailed."

"It was a double wedding ceremony, Kate," Donald added. "Your father married the Widow MacLaughlin at the same time."

"Da? Oh my God!" Her father's marriage, while a surprise, wasn't a blow, but the news seemed to intensify the shock she had just received.

Gunther watched Kate closely and couldn't help admiring her strength. But now her smile had become fixed and he knew she needed some assistance. "Why don't we sit down? I'm sure you're tired, Annie, after your long voyage."

"Yes, I am. As my husband will tell you," she cast a loving glance Donald's way, "I am a terrible sailor. I was sick all the way over."

"Poor dear!" Amy kissed her cheek. "I'm so happy to have you as my sister! I hope when you've rested you'll tell us how this all came about. It truly is a magnificent surprise. So much so that we forgot to congratulate you on your beautiful bride, Donald. I'm happy for you, dear," she said as she kissed him.

Katherine sat down rather abruptly to conceal the trembling she couldn't control. She clasped her hands together tightly and her breathing began to return to normal, then said, in a semblance of her normal voice, "Donald, if you have any other surprises, you had better reveal them in easy stages. God knows, Annie, I never expected to see you here and certainly not as Don . . . as a bride." She attempted to cover up her near-mistake by saying quickly, "You do look tired, dear. I'll take you upstairs." Defiantly she said to Donald, "She can rest in the room Robbie had."

"Oh, no, Kate! My wife will occupy my rooms with me until we have set up a proper place for us. I didn't want to spoil the surprise or I would have written ahead to have rooms ready for us. Anyway, Annie, you should choose the decor, don't you think so?"

"I'm so tired and happy, right now all I can think of is a comfortable bed." She kissed Kate. "I'm very, *very* glad to see you, dear! You've been missed. We have a lot to talk about, but it will have to wait until tomorrow." She kissed Amy and gave a peck on the cheek to Gunther who had been standing by, still intently watching Katherine. Donald, with his arm around Annie, supported her up the stairs to what had formerly been his bachelor suite.

Without a glance at Amy, Kate pulled the bellcord and summoned Jeffrey. "We didn't toast the bride and groom," she said. "Bring some champagne for us and take some up to Mr. Donald—with two glasses."

"Yes, bring the champagne," Amy directed,

"and see if there is some soup for Mrs. MacConnack." The butler raised his eyebrows. "Yes, that's right," she continued, "my brother has brought us a beautiful bride. She had a bad crossing, so she'll want something very light. Bring Mr. Donald something heartier—I don't think he'll be down for dinner."

When Jeffrey had returned, Gunther poured the champagne and proposed a toast. "To the beautiful bride and stalwart groom; may they have a long and happy life." He turned to Kate. "Annie really is beautiful. How many Maccrae daughters are there?"

"There are seven of us," Kate murmured.

"All beautiful?"

Kate shrugged carelessly. "Some more than others." She drank most of the champagne, played with her food at dinner and, annoyed at Amy and Gunther's running conversation as they discussed the future with a new mistress in the house, excused herself when they went into the library for coffee. She felt cold and numb and a little sick as she undressed and quickly got into bed. Her pillow was soon wet with tears of hate and guilt at the dreadful thoughts she was harboring against her own sister; how had Annie gotten Donald to marry her? Did Da suggest it because he wanted to marry Mina? Donald loves *me*, she wailed to herself. Why did he marry *her*? And why did Da marry that rusty-haired old widow? Round and round her brain ran until she came to the conclusion that despite his marriage, she would always come first with Donald. "He is probably fond of Annie but he can't resist me," she told herself, then turned her pillow to the dry side and promptly fell asleep, assuring herself that there would be no difference in her relationship with Donald. But she didn't attempt to define that relationship, even to herself.

When Jeffrey had announced to the cook and the kitchen staff that Mr. Donald had brought home a bride, each tried to outdo the other to make the dinner trays attractive. With a discreet knock at the door of Donald's suite, Jeffrey brought the champagne. Birdy came in to help Annie unpack, but when she saw how weak and tired she was, her maternal instinct came to the fore, and she quickly helped her into a nightgown and robe. Meanwhile, Jeffrey had laid the table. There was clear soup and tiny sandwiches, and thick slices of roast beef for Donald. A bud vase containing a single rose had a card attached; "Welcome, Mrs. Donald," signed by the staff. Annie smiled and said a simple "Thank you;" it was the most she could manage. The Scots are a stoic people and Annie personified their virtue of endurance. She hid her bone weariness and drank the champagne, sipped at the soup and nibbled at the sandwiches, while Donald ate heartily. He looked at her closely as he poured the last of the wine. "Sweetheart, you look exhausted. Let me help you to bed."

"If I sleep, dear, even for just a little time, I'll feel fine," she assured him. "I'll not deny you this first night in our home."

Donald tenderly kissed her forehead. "You sleep as long as you like, my love. I have every intention of making up for the nights we've lost, but not tonight." He stroked her hair softly until she slept. When he got into bed beside her, she turned toward him and slept peacefully in his arms all night.

PART THREE

XVII

ANNIE

Before she set sail for America, Annie had never been sick a day in her life, but a whole month passed before she had regained enough strength to come down to dinner every night. She had asked Amy and Katherine not to mention to Donald that she spent most of her day in bed. He was very anxious about her health and when she didn't respond quickly enough to Dr. Wilson's visits, he took her into New York City to visit a doctor who specialized in difficult diagnoses. While she was dressing, Dr. Thompson came out to relieve Donald's anxiety. "Nothing to worry about, Mr. MacConnack . . . Ah, here she is!"

Annie was beaming. "I feel like such a simpleton, Donald. I was so sick on the ship it didn't occur to me it could be . . ."

"Darling, what is it? Tell me!"

"We," she whispered, "are going to have a baby!"

Donald sat down with a thud. "Oh, my God!" He put his head in his hands. "I was so afraid —I thought . . . why didn't I think of that?"

The doctor said jokingly, "Well, it seems you did." They laughed self-consciously and then, ignoring the presence of the doctor, came together in a tearful embrace.

"I will bring my wife to see you next week, doctor," said Donald when he had recovered. "She must be very well taken care of."

The doctor wagged his head. "No, no, no. You can bring her in next month if you wish, but I think it would be best if you find a local doctor." He turned to Annie. "Mrs. MacConnack, after next month you may not feel like traveling to the city, particularly if the nausea continues. When it bothers you most, eat some dry bread or crackers, but be sure you eat enough food to keep up your strength. Have your cook take a large piece of beef and boil it in just a little water and drink the broth. Have at least one glass every day. Remember, to have a healthy baby you must stay well." Her face turned a sickly green at the thought of food, but still she smiled.

"I am embarrassed that I didn't know why I was sick, especially in the morning. I am the eldest of seven girls and I was present at the last few births."

"Your mother must have been a very strong lady," said the doctor.

"No, she wasn't. She died soon after the last was born," Annie murmured.

Dr. Thompson caught the little flicker of fear in her eyes. "I'm sorry. But if you take proper care of yourself, you will be fine. You look delicate but you're structured to carry children well."

Donald shook hands with the doctor. "Thank you, Dr. Thompson, thank you very much." He put his arm around Annie and tenderly supported her out of the office.

Dr. Thompson turned to his nurse. "I don't know why they always thank *me*. *I* didn't have anything to do with it. I just hope that young man doesn't treat her like an invalid." He completed his notes on Annie's case. "Keep that in the active file; Mr. MacConnack won't be satisfied with another doctor, not yet."

Annie, seated at the foot of the long dining table as mistress of the house, had Amy on one side and Katherine on the other. Donald was at the head of the table. At his request, Amy had ordered a gala dinner and very quietly instructed Annie as to how to proceed in future. Kate made no effort to help and was, Donald noticed, more than usually overbearing in demands of the servants. Before dessert and coffee was served, Donald rose and lifted his glass. "I have a very important announcement to make, and a toast: To my beloved wife, who is soon to make me a father!" Amy and Katherine drank, saying, "To Annie." Then forgetting the formality, Amy hugged Annie, then ran to her brother and hugged and kissed him. Kate kissed Annie grudgingly and said so no one else could hear, "you certainly didn't waste any time." She then rather acidly congratulated Donald, after which they all rose to go into the drawing room. Kate, though she had hardly touched her food, announced that she had eaten too much and needed to take a walk. As she was leaving, she met Gunther at the door. "Oh, Gunther," she cooed, "I haven't seen you in such a long time. How are you, dear?" She reached up and gave him a peck on the cheek. "If I had known you were coming, I wouldn't have planned to go out." He was surprised at the warmth of her greeting, since she had barely spoken to him over the past weeks. "Wait 'til you hear Donald's news!" she chirped, gave an airy wave of her hand, and left.

Once outside, Katherine walked with long, rapid strides as she tried to rid herself of her anger at Donald. Not only had he actually married Annie, but had immediately begotten a child! Kate took it as a personal affront. Though she had no particular destination in mind, she unconsciously walked along the path that would take her to McCarthy's. Rory had rooms over the saloon and they had spent many happy evenings walking through the little park nearby; and there he was, leaning against a tree, smoking his pipe! His face lit up with joy when suddenly she came into view.

"I spoke to the Little People and they must have conjured you up for me!" he cried, touching her face tenderly. "I was afraid you were only a vision, but you're real, dear heart." He held her close. "What is this? Tears? Is something wrong, Macushla?"

Kate sniffled sorrowfully. "I missed you so much, Rory dear. I just couldn't stand being away from you." It wasn't a lie—she *had* missed him. Although she had made her mind up not to see him again, having his arms around her was exactly what she needed. And he didn't have a pregnant wife at home!

"Did Mr. MacConnack come home?" Rory asked. She nodded. "Does he know you're here?"

Kate tossed her head. "It doesn't matter. He not only came home, but he brought a bride with him. He's not going to worry about *me*."

214

"A bride?" Rory repeated. "Well, that must have been a surprise to everyone. Do you like her?" he asked in all innocence.

"I love her," said Kate truthfully, "but she's not the proper wife for him."

Rory was puzzled at her answer. "You say you love her. How long have you known her?"

"All my life," Kate sighed. "Annie is my oldest sister, the one who raised us after my mother died."

"And you didn't know about the marriage?" She shook her head. "That *must* have been quite a surprise! I'm sure, though, you're glad to have her with you."

"Not really. I'm not quite sure what will happen to me now. I don't think I'll be able to make my home there much longer. Oh," she said impatiently, "I don't even want to think about it! I wish there were some place we could just sit and talk and love each other."

If Rosie had angled for an invitation to go to his flat, he would have known exactly what she had in mind, but with Kate, he took her literally. After all, Rosie wasn't a lady!

"There is a back entrance to my rooms with steps leading up," he told her. "We can sit on the steps, and then you must go home before you are missed. I don't want you to get into any trouble, my dearest, with your sister."

Kate knew he was right. They sat decorously on the steps for a while and he kissed her and soothed her and did all the right things that came straight from his worshipful heart. Time passed all too swiftly. Finally Rory said, "I'll walk you home, Kate—right to the door, if I may."

"Not yet, Rory. The family has had enough

surprises for one week . . . I'm not ready to add another just yet.'' Kate hated to leave him, but he didn't quite fit in with her sketchy plans for the future.

That night Katherine sat up very late trying to find her way out of the maze she had woven for herself. She spent a good deal of time thinking about Gunther. He had asked her to marry him and had only turned to Amy when Kate had rejected his proposal. If she used her wiles on him, she was sure she wouldn't have any trouble getting him back. He wasn't Donald, but he was probably second best. He had a good reputation, he was well educated, and had an excellent job; his European manners made him truly gallant, and he was good looking. He also seemed to have modest wealth, Kate's chief requirement for a prospective husband. She settled on Gunther as a compromise and spent the next hour crying her eyes out for Rory. She shocked herself with the conclusion she finally arrived at —Gunther would be her husband, and Rory her lover. With her problem resolved, at least in her mind, Katherine slept.

Amy was well aware of Kate's intentions. As she wrote to Robbie, ''I could probably put a stop to it, but because I know he was in love with her at one time, or thought he was, I think it is best if I say nothing. It is a test and perhaps I'm not being fair to my love, but if she can take him away from me, it's better to know now. From what I have observed, he seems confused and sometimes irritated by her attention.''

One night when Gunther came to take Amy

to a dinner party, he waited in the drawing room. Annie still had not come downstairs and Katherine, who had been watching for him, poured him a glass of sherry, then pulled a small footstool over and sat at his feet. She adroitly brought the conversation around to his latest improvements in the machinery at the mill. They were deep in conversation when Kate heard Amy's footsteps in the hall. She put her hand on Gunther's to emphasize a rather innocuous remark. Assuming maidenly confusion, she pulled it away quickly as Amy joined them. Gunther frowned, Amy smiled her greeting, pretending not to notice Kate's gesture, and Kate, somewhat miffed, went upstairs to bring Annie down for dinner.

When they returned from the dinner party later that night, Gunther said to Amy, "We need to have a serious talk, darling, somewhere where we won't be disturbed."

"Let's go into the conservatory." She took him by the hand and drew him close as they walked in. "Will you have some brandy?"

"Yes, that would be good."

After the brandy and Amy's demi-tasse had been brought in by Jeffrey, they sat together. "You know I love you, Amy," he kissed the palm of her hand, "and I'm sure you love me." She kissed his cheek in answer. "I intend to speak to Donald but I must ask you before I do. I want to marry you, and I'd like to announce our engagement right away. Would you consider it?"

"I *do* love you Gunther, and I've been waiting for you to ask, but I'm curious. Why now?"

Rather than answering her question, he said,

"I know you can't be married until your seventeenth birthday, but that's not too far off. We should, according to convention, be engaged for six months. That means we would have to wait until March and honestly, if you and Donald will consent, I'd rather not wait that long. Right after your birthday would be perfect."

"I think so, too, darling," Amy paused. "Does this have anything to do with Katherine?"

"I suppose so, in a way. I don't know what she has in mind, but she—I guess I sound immodest, but really, Amy, she annoys me by gushing and fluttering over me! If we announce our betrothal I won't have to put up with that. But more important than that, I can't wait to have you all to myself, my very own wife."

"Of course I have noticed how Katherine flatters you at every opportunity, and as uncomfortable as it is for you, I must confess I'm glad you find her annoying. Besides, I would like to be Mrs. Crismann, very, very much!" There was a pause for a long embrace. When Amy could speak again, she began, "But . . ."

"Don't *say* that!" he exclaimed.

"All right, I won't say 'but' . . . *but*" he put his hand to his head and she giggled, "there is one small condition."

"You want me to walk across the floor on my hands!" Gunther teased.

"All right, I will—this minute, if you insist!"

Amy went into gales of laughter and he joined her. It was part of their attraction for each other that they could have silly fun. This time it was all out of proportion to the joke;

they were both giddy over the fact that they had agreed to be betrothed.

"Let me continue. Seriously Gunther, it's Annie. Donald doesn't know that she still is not well. Because she is *enciente*," he raised an eyebrow in approval of her choice of the French word, "she has put on weight and looks healthier than she did, but she has little strength. As you know, I have been instructing her in her duties as mistress of this house. She makes an effort but it's only half-hearted. You see," she explained, "she ran her father's home and raised her six sisters. She is having a difficult time adjusting to a different way of life and, frankly, I don't think she wants to."

"Does that mean you can't have your own home?"

"No. She will learn and perhaps if she knows we plan to marry in . . . January?" he took her face in both hands and almost smothered her with kisses, "she will make more of an effort," Amy added when she could breathe again.

"Where does Katherine fit in?"

"If it's up to Donald, nowhere. Kate doesn't pay much attention to Annie and when she does, it's usually to point out that she's doing something wrong. But she does love her, and after being mean to Annie, she overwhelms her with attention. The two next oldest girls to Annie, Mary and Kate, have always felt a little resentment because Annie ran their home and was second in authority only to their father. Annie told me this one day when she was making an excuse for Kate's erratic behaviour. She says she doesn't mind. But Donald minds very much and has decided it's time for Kate to return to Scotland."

"Does Kate know this?"

"Not yet. Donald plans to talk to her over the weekend."

"If you'd like, I'll call for you early. If Kate makes a scene, it could be very unpleasant for you," Gunther suggested.

"No, dear, I'll have to be here; there's no telling what she might do. You can help, however. Would you mind very much if we have dinner here on Saturday instead of going to the Whittakers? It's still early—I don't think they'll mind too much if we cancel our date."

"Of course they won't. What do you plan for Saturday?"

"How would it be—tell me if this sounds plausible—if we have a dinner party at home to celebrate our engagement—just the family? We can have a formal party at a later date. Then, on Sunday, Donald can talk with Katherine. I believe she'll be more than willing to go home to Scotland, particularly under the circumstances."

"That sounds good, if Donald doesn't object to our marriage."

"He's so happy, he wouldn't object to anything!" Amy laughed.

And she was right. Donald was simply ecstatic over the engagement and gave his approval then and there for their early marriage. "By that time, Amy, Annie will be able to take charge of the household. The young heir isn't due until March and Mrs. Wheeler will help her as much as need be. I plan to have a nurse here for the last two months, too. So you see, little sister, you're free as a bird to make your plans."

220

"And Katherine?" Amy asked later, when she and Donald were alone.

He sighed deeply. "If she were a different kind of woman, she could be of much help to Annie. As it is, all I can see ahead is trouble as long as she's with us. No, I'll go through with her scheduled departure. I'll reserve her passage tomorrow. There's a ship that's sailing in three weeks, I believe."

Amy, relieved by his decision, felt like a fledgling bird about to try her wings.

XVIII

KATE DEPARTS

On Saturday night at Annie's request, Donald waited for her at the foot of the winding staircase. It took all her strength and great determination to descend without help, but his extravagant praise was her reward.

"You are a vision of loveliness, my darling!" he breathed. With relief, she grasped the hand he held out to her. Drawing her closer, he took both her hands in his. "Here, let me look at you," he said. His eyes adored her as he continued, "I am so very blessed to have such a gracious and beautiful lady as mistress of the manor!"

Exertion had brought a slight flush to Annie's otherwise pallid complexion and Amy had outdone herself, convincing her dressmaker of the urgency of making a gown for this gala evening; Amy had supplied the measurements and selected the material. Her taste was superb. The pale rose satin enhanced her coloring. The dress was worn off the shoulders with a trim of ecru lace which set off her alabaster skin. Birdy had originally done her hair with four fat curls in the back, to which Annie objected strenuously, saying, "No, Birdy, that is much too young for me. No

curls hanging down my back." So Birdy had
gathered up the offending curls and with a
deft twist of the wrist, lifted them up to the top
of Annie's head and fastened them with two
satin roses which matched her dress.

Donald proudly drew her arm through his
and they joined the others in the drawing
room. Kate went to her immediately, put her
hands on her sister's tiny waist and kissed her.
"Annie, I never saw you look so beautiful!" In
all sincerity she added, "I am truly envious."

Annie squeezed her hand. "That is something you will never have to be. None of our
sisters can match your beauty." Kate silently
agreed with her, although seeing Donald's
pride in his wife sharpened the edge of her
temper.

A short while later, Kate was about to have
her third sherry when Annie softly reproved
her. "Kate, don't you think you've had
enough?" But Kate paid no heed and with an
insolent look turned her back and walked
away. None of this was lost on Donald.

When dinner was announced, Gunther
offered his arm to Annie, but "Forgive me, old
chap," Donald said. "This is the first dinner
party my wife has planned and *I* would like to
escort her to her rightful place as mistress of
the MacConnack Manor."

Annie was nervous but proud as she looked
down the long damask-covered table. It was no
longer than the one at home in Paisley, but
very different in its formal setting. This
accomplishment had been a struggle for
Annie. She had spent the past week with Amy
and Mrs. Wheeler standing by, going over the
menus of dinners past. Many of the unfamiliar

dishes had to be explained to her but her choices won their approval. Annie would have liked to do the cooking herself as she had at home but the cook wouldn't even have her in the kitchen, except for a brief visit. Annie herself had selected the crystal, the silver and the very special, fragile Limoges china, as well as the satiny white cloth on which it was set. She had seated Amy at Donald's right, Gunther next to her, and on the opposite side, looking rather alone, Kate was placed. She thought fleetingly how strange it was that Kate, the most popular of the sisters, was the only one— if you didn't count Maggie—who did not have a partner.

Annie was gratified with the evident success of her first dinner party. Katherine asked, not quite convinced, "You did this all by yourself?" Smiling, Annie nodded and Kate added, "Very good." But some demon within her wouldn't let the compliment stand and she finished in mock surprise, "I suppose you'll prove a credit to Donald after all!" Annie's smile vanished and Amy, usually a placid young lady, could have driven the carving knife into Kate's heart, but no one else paid any attention.

When dinner was over, Annie asked, "Shall we have coffee in the drawing room?" As they started to rise, Donald spoke.

"If you don't mind, dear, I have something to say before we go inside."

Self-consciously, Annie almost whispered, "Of course, Donald." She glanced at Amy. Had she made a mistake? But Amy smiled reassuringly as Jeffrey brought in a bottle of chilled champagne.

"On this happy occasion, I am proud to announce that Amy and Gunther have asked me to tell you of their betrothal. They will become Mr. and Mrs. Crismann in January, immediately after Amy's seventeenth birthday."

Annie was delighted and with the others raised her glass. Kate barely sipped at hers.

Gunther kissed Amy, then rose. "Thank you," he said, then opened a velvet ring box and asked Amy told hold out her left hand; he placed a Tiffany-set diamond ring on her third finger. The size of the stone made even Donald gasp. "Amy, dearest, with this ring I give you my heart and," he continued quickly, "there is something I have not mentioned concerning my family. In truth, we shall be Baron and Baroness Crismann and as such, you will share with me many prosperous lands in Germany."

During the stunned silence that greeted this revelation, he added, "I don't use my title here in democratic America, but, Little Amy, you will indeed be a baroness."

Amy was so excited she felt faint. Donald and Annie, momentarily awed by this news, were silent until at last Donald said, "Does this mean we have to kneel in your presence?" Laughter broke the tension for all but Katherine, who pushed her chair away from the table without a word and ran out of the house. Her face was flushed with anger and she knew she had to find something to throw or she would explode. A baroness! That little snip a baroness! She ended up at the duckpond where a family of ducks floated peacefully on the surface—until the poor mother duck was forced to shelter her little ones as stones rained on them. Kate's rage was not appeased and in a frenzy she stalked back and forth along the water's edge, heedless of the damage being done to her kid slippers.

"Baron, indeed! And to think I could have had him like that!" She snapped her fingers. "How could he even *look* at that dull, stupid child? All she can do is play the piano! She won't keep him long—he'll get tired of her and look for a real woman!" Tears of jealousy and rage finally flowed and she threw herself down on the grass, buried her face in it and screamed as if she were in mortal pain. She cried until there were no tears left. Then a sudden thought popped into her head. "I'll go see Rory—he'll comfort me." But no, she couldn't do that now. Everyone would be wondering where she was. She'd have to go back before someone came in search of her. She washed her face in the pond water, then sat crosslegged in the grass rocking back and forth, back and forth, until some semblance of reason set in. "Maybe," she thought, "this is for the best. When Amy gets married she will move out of Donald's house. Annie's baby will soon be due and I will take over as mistress of the house. Annie will never learn how to run a formal household and, yes, Donald will have to depend on me for all things." She emphasized to herself, as she said it aloud, "All things."

She smoothed her hair, brushed the grass off her dress, and returned to the house still muttering to herself, "So Gunther is a baron. Who cares? He doesn't use his title . . . not even Donald knew about it. It would be farcical to call Amy, Baroness!" She was in a better humor when she entered the house, to find Annie, Donald, Amy and Gunther engaged in joyous conversation. She stood at the entrance to the drawing room, and was forced to cough once or twice before anyone noticed she was there.

"My sincere apologies, everybody, I was suddenly taken ill and had to get out in the air," she said brightly. "Amy, dear little Amy, I am so happy for you! Gunther, may you both be as happy as you deserve to be." The double meaning was not lost on Gunther, who caught Donald's eye as he accepted her good wishes. Amy thanked her graciously, but Annie was secretly shocked at Kate's rude behaviour in dashing away as she had. "We were just going to retire, Kate. It has been an exciting evening," she said rather coolly. Pretending not to notice Annie's tone, Katherine took her arm and they preceded Donald up the staircase. "I am so proud of you, Annie," she gushed. "Your dinner party was truly remarkable." But Annie's head was aching and she had nothing to say in return. Kate's unpredictable actions had become more than she could handle at this stage of her life. "When I get my strength back," she promised herself, "I'll have a lot to say to Kate; her bad manners are a reflection on Da and me." But now wasn't the time. All Annie wanted to do was crawl into bed and fall quickly asleep. Her long promised, long awaited night of love with her husband had not yet taken place. Donald understood that it was more than her delicate condition could tolerate. Though they adored each other, a warm kiss and embrace was all that passed between them, and he understood, even to the extent of arranging for them to have separate rooms.

Sunday morning, as was his custom, he went to Annie's boudoir. He was surprised to see her still in bed. As he bent down and kissed her, he asked, "Aren't you coming down to breakfast?"

"Not this morning, dear. I think I'll stay in bed today," she murmured.

"Are you ill? Shall I call the doctor?" Donald asked anxiously.

Annie hastened to reassure him. "No, no, darling, I'm just tired. Last night was a bit exhausting; the news of Amy and Gunther and then Katherine's . . ."

"Don't talk about it, sweetheart. By now, we all know Kate pretty well. In fact, I'm going to have a talk with her today," Donald informed her.

Annie pulled herself up on her pillows. "About what?"

"It's time for her to go home, dear. If she were of any help to you whatsoever, she could stay as long as she likes, but she's not. She's a troublemaker, Annie." The minute the words were out of his mouth he knew he had made a grave mistake. He had forgotten how protective Annie was of all her sisters.

Annie was trembling with agitation. "You break my heart, Donald. I know Kate has always been somewhat of a problem. She's probably the only dynamic member of the family—but she wouldn't hurt anyone deliberately, especially me. Please, let me speak to her." Annie was crying now. "Promise you won't say anything to her until I do!"

Donald, crushed, sat on the bed and put his arm around her. "Don't cry, love. Hush . . . Of course I won't say anything if you don't want me to. I thought perhaps it would be better for you if . . ."

"Oh, no, Donald." Annie had stopped crying, but she was still nervously excited as she tried to explain. "It's probably my fault—she was so glad to see me and I have been no company for her at all. I've been pampering myself but," she said too eagerly, "I will get up now and come down to breakfast." The effort to swing her legs out of bed took more strength than she had. "Give me a few moments, dear, and I'll be fine," she whispered as Donald leaped up to support her, then sat down on the bed again and took her in his arms.

"Annie, Annie, have you forgotten you are trying to move *two* of you?"

She rested her head on his chest and sighed deeply. "I'm sorry—I didn't forget, but I thought I could do it. I would so like to see Kate . . ."

He fluffed up her pillows and placed her, half reclining, against them. "How would you like it if I send Kate up to have breakfast with you here?"

"Oh, I would like that! Will you ask her?" she said eagerly.

On the way downstairs, Donald decided to try a new approach with his troublesome sister-in-law. He would smile instead of frown whenever he looked in her direction. He would make a major effort to avoid showing his annoyance.

Kate was standing at the buffet trying to make a choice of breakfast food.

"Oh, Kate, I'm glad you haven't eaten as yet," Donald said with forced cheerfulness. She was so engrossed in coddled eggs as opposed to wheat cakes that he startled her. She whirled around, empty plate in hand, and was thrilled to find him smiling at her. So he wasn't angry with her after all! But how could he be, when deep down inside he loved her?

"Good morning, Donald. I thought I had missed having breakfast with everyone," she said, returning his smile.

"No, but I would like to ask a favor of you." He had joined her at the buffet and affected a conspiratorial air.

"Anything—you know you can ask *anything* of me. What can I do for you?"

"Well," he said as he looked at her intently, "Annie wanted desperately to come down to have breakfast with you this morning, but she is feeling poorly and just does not have the strength to dress and come downstairs. Would you ask Mrs. Wheeler to set a table upstairs for you and bring a tray to Annie?"

Kate lowered her eyes so he wouldn't see the disappointment reflected there; she had thought they would be alone at breakfast. But she said, "That's a lovely idea. If I had known Annie wanted company, I would have spent more time with her. I'll find Mrs. Wheeler now."

"Don't tell her I suggested it, Kate. This is just between us," Donald added, hoping that Kate, with her love of melodramatics, would enjoy playing yet another part. He could feel her sweet, warm breath as she raised her face to him; she put her hand on his arm. "It will be our little secret, Donald." She almost danced

231

out of the room, sure that beneath his stern demeanor, he did find her attractive. Meanwhile, Donald said a silent prayer that he wasn't making a bad situation worse by his little white lie.

As Kate and Annie breakfasted, Annie chattered more about home and the family than she had since arriving. She went into great detail about the weddings, ending with, "We were so sorry that you and Maggie were not there." Then they talked about Maggie, wondering where and how she was. Time passed quickly and Annie had responded brightly to Kate's presence. Birdy was greeted warmly when she came in to prepare Annie for her morning nap.

Kate breakfasted with Annie in her room every morning for the next week. Donald was grateful to Kate as he saw Annie start to take an interest in life again. Kate would leave her after breakfast and in the afternoon would return. One day she brought along a cribbage board. "See what I have! I thought you might like to play this afternoon," she said.

Annie was enthusiastic. "I haven't played in years—you will have to refresh my memory." They played every afternoon thereafter, and before the week was out, Annie felt well enough to sit at the table rather than remaining in bed. Kate enjoyed the afternoons with her sister, but much more than that, enjoyed the time spent alone with Donald. Amy was so starry-eyed and busy planning her wedding that she was seldom in evidence.

On Monday of the third week after the dinner party Annie expressed a desire to have dinner again with the family. Donald held her arm as she walked down the stairs; he threw a look of gratitude to Kate as he seated her in her rightful place at the foot of the table. Although Annie only picked at her food, she stayed through dinner and spent an hour with Donald and Katherine in the drawing room where they had coffee; Amy and Gunther were out for the evening. "Darling," he said, "your games of cribbage seem to have done you a lot of good. How would you like to learn to play chess?"

"Oh, dear," she laughed, "I can barely struggle through cribbage! I have never mastered chess, but Kate is very good at it." She turned to her sister. "Why don't you take my place?"

"Thank you, Annie, if Donald doesn't mind, I will."

Only Kate was aware of the double meaning in her words.

Donald asked Jeffrey to set up the chess board, then turned to Annie and said, "I'll take you upstairs, dear."

"No, that won't be necessary. Just call Birdy —she will help me upstairs." Annie said goodnight to Kate and kissed Donald, then walked slowly and with Birdy's help managed the stairs.

"I'll look in on her before I go to bed," Donald said as if to himself. It was no secret that he and Annie did not share a bed. Kate said nothing.

Both she and Donald were good chess players, and sat for the next few hours in deep silence as they worked out the moves. When at last Donald looked at his pocket watch, Kate

233

straightened her back, stiff from having been bent over the board for so long, clasped her hands above her head and leaned back in her chair. Almost without his volition, Donald's gaze fastened on her round, firm breasts delineated so clearly under her white silk dinner dress, and she saw the glow in his eyes before he abruptly turned away; he hated himself for the stirrings he had felt and, saying a quick goodnight, left her alone. Retiring to the library, Donald picked up his newspaper after pouring himself a glass of brandy and sat down to read, but Kate's tantalizing face and figure kept swimming between him and the print. In disgust he threw the paper on the floor, then turned down the lamp and went upstairs. On his way to his room he stopped in to check on Annie and found her peacefully asleep. He stroked her hair lightly, then quietly left, closing the door after him. He loved her so much and yet somehow there was no desire left. Instinctively, he feared that despite the fact that their marriage had been consummated and a child was on the way, they might never again live as husband and wife. He slammed the door of his room and shook his head vigorously to clear his head of the thoughts that came unbidden.

Kate was a terrible temptation.

Amy was caught up in a social whirl. She dined at home two or three times a week but since her engagement to Gunther, they were invited out often. When she was at home it seemed to her that Kate was sweet and thoughtful, Annie was stronger, and the time they all spent together was more than congenial, it was positively jovial.

A pattern was established; dinner at seven, with or without Amy. Then Kate and Donald would sit down to their nightly game of chess. There was laughter before and after the game, and eventually, a nightcap before retiring. At first Annie was delighted that her husband and sister were getting along so well that there seemed no necessity for the threatened talk with Kate. But as time wore on, she began to resent the laughter that seemed to burst out spontaneously as soon as she left with Birdy. She began to wonder if they were laughing at her, and before long she was convinced they thought she was a fool for being unable and unwilling to learn the game. Once she even called out, "What is so funny?" There was no answer because she didn't say it aloud, although she thought she did.

One night, after Birdy had tucked her in, Annie couldn't sleep. She wanted desperately to talk but there was no one she could confide in. With some effort she got out of bed, walked over to her vanity table and sat before the mirror, talking to her reflection. "I know Donald loves me, but . . ." she hesitated, not wanting to say the words even to herself, "I . . . don't *trust* Katherine. Not having a man of her own has never stopped her from flirting or . . . or . . ." Again she could not face her own fears. "If I don't do something, she'll turn Donald against me." She started to cry and threw herself onto the bed sobbing. "Then what will I and my poor little baby do?" She worked herself into such a state that Bessie, who was turning down the master's bed, heard her and came running. She tried to quiet her with no success and ran down the stairs calling, "Mr. Donald, come! Mrs. Donald is very upset!"

He raced up to her bedroom with Kate close behind. Gently he turned her toward him and held her in his arms. "What is it, my love, does something hurt?" he asked, worried. Annie had started to calm down when she looked up and saw Kate standing in the doorway beside Bessie who was wringing out a cold cloth. Katherine took it from her and attempted to place it on Annie's forehead. Donald felt her recoil and took the compress from Kate.

"Send them away, Donald!" Annie's voice was unnaturally shrill. Bessie immediately backed out. With a question in her eyes, Kate obeyed the slight motion of his head and also withdrew, wondering if this display of Annie's was simply the hysteria of a frail pregnant woman, or did she suspect what was happening? Had Annie recognized as Kate did Donald's unconscious response to her insidious seduction?

Kate spent the next hour undressing and carefully grooming herself. She had selected her peach nightdress and ostrich-trimmed robe, let her hair flow loosely over her shoulders and used just a touch of the perfume Amy had given her. If Annie *did* suspect, Kate could see no reason for her flying to pieces. Annie should be grateful that Kate's charms kept Donald close to home, rather than seeking unsavory female companionship elsewhere.

She walked quietly down the long corridor to the other wing. Annie's door was ajar and she could see Birdy sitting by the bed in a comfortable chair. She looked up as Kate opened the door a little further and put her finger to her lips, then pointed to Annie who was in a deep sleep. Closing the door, Kate then tiptoed to the door of Donald's room. It was closed, but she turned the knob and slid in silently. He did not hear her. He had started to prepare for bed and had suddenly been overwhelmed with emotion. When Kate entered, he was sitting on the edge of his bed, head in hands. Before he knew she was there, Kate was on her knees in front of him. His first reaction was panic, but she put her hands on his bare chest saying in a soft, liquid voice, "Ah, Donald, don't feel so bad. Annie will be all right." He wanted to rip her hands off his body but couldn't find the strength.

"You shouldn't be here, Kate," he muttered indecisively, raising her to her feet. Kate leaned forward, pressing her thinly clad body against his. "My God, what are you doing to me!" he moaned as he held her tightly in his arms.

"Darling Donald, you have needs that are unfulfilled," Kate whispered. "You need a vital woman and Annie is incapable of being a proper wife to you."

Despite all her calculations, even arousing him as she had, she had made a mistake. He threw her roughly on the bed where she lay with her eyes closed, awaiting him. Instead, he gabbed her by the wrists and yanked her up. "Go back to your room, Kate, and never come in here again! You have absolutely no moral sense or sensitivity to anyone else. Your own sister—how could you?" His voice was low but there was no mistaking the

237

rage he felt; but he was angrier at himself than he was at her; as she cowered before him, his fists were clenched and his face was red with fury. "Get out!" His whisper was a shout.

Kate was shocked and frightened by his outburst. She tried to scuttle past him but he stayed her flight just as she reached the door. He opened it and looked into the corridor before allowing her to leave, almost shoving her out.

Kate's robe streamed behind her as she fled to her own room. She closed the door behind her and leaned against it, panting. When her breathing had returned to normal, she started to pace, hand to head. "What in God's name possessed me?" she asked herself. "I had everything timed so perfectly, and I couldn't wait. I thought tonight would be the perfect time . . ."

She sat on the chaise and decided she would have to make amends—but how? She tried to get her thoughts in order but couldn't concentrate. "Donald is such a cold fish, no wonder he can live as he does with Annie!" She got up and walked to the mirror, examining herself. "How could he not want me?" The only answer she could find was that she had been mistaken about him. He was bloodless, had no passion.

She was suddenly exhausted and determined to put off thinking about it, but she lost her desire to sleep as soon as she lay down and a rush of longing came over her. "Rory, oh God, I need you," she cried out. "It is so hard to be away from you! And I'm farther away than ever from finding a wealthy husband." It was the first time Kate had wavered in her desire to be mistress of a vast estate and equally vast fortune. She ached to have Rory's arms around her.

The little sleep Kate had that night was restless. Donald didn't sleep at all. Annie slept the sleep of exhaustion and awakened the next morning still tired and feeling ill.

The next few days were uncomfortable and very frustrating for Kate. Annie refused to see her and as often as she tried to waylay Donald at breakfast, somehow she always missed him. Amy lived in her own world and while always her sweet self, seemed to notice nothing amiss. For three days it was like living in a ghost house. On the fourth day, a Thursday, Kate decided to do something about the situation. Taking her cribbage board, she tapped on Annie's bedroom door. Birdy answered and told her Mrs. Donald didn't want to see anyone, but Kate brushed past and confronted her sister. Annie had heard the commotion and was sitting upright, clutching her bedcovers. "I don't want to have any visitors," she faltered.

"I'm not a visitor," Kate snapped. "I'm your sister and I want to know what is wrong with you. Why don't you get out of that bed and behave like a normal person?" she all but shouted.

Annie began to tremble and Birdy tried to intervene, "Please, Miss Katherine, you're upsetting her!"

"You have no right to talk to me like that, Kate! If my husband were here you wouldn't dare," said Annie feebly.

"Your *husband?*" Kate repeated. "Why, you

239

are not even a good companion to him, let alone a wife! Get up on your feet and start thinking about him for a change!" She could see that Annie was working up to a fit of hysteria and she softened her tone. "I say this for your own good, dear. Just because you're going to have a baby doesn't mean you must become a chronic invalid. Let me help you get up." She moved as if to assist her and Annie let out a weak cry.

"Birdy, make her go away." She pulled the covers over her head as Birdy almost forcibly guided Kate to the door.

"I'm going," Kate called over her shoulder. "I find your self-pity *disgusting*, Annie. I won't try to help you again, don't worry. And don't blame me if your precious husband seeks out other women!"

When Donald came to see Annie before dinner that evening, Birdy tried to catch his eye but he was unaware of her furtive gestures. He came in with a firm step, striding over to the bed and bent down to kiss Annie. Her eyes were open but seemed unseeing and she did not acknowledge his presence.

"Annie? Aren't we going to have dinner together tonight?" he asked.

She lay as if in a trance. "What is it, love, what's wrong?" He was beginning to be anxious.

Annie stared straight ahead. "Nothing."

"Well, then," he said, pretending he wasn't alarmed, "*I* am very hungry. Birdy, set up the table for me and bring a tray for Mrs. Donald. I'll feed you, darling. You don't have to eat much, just a little bit. Try for me."

She slewed her eyes around to him. "I don't want anything. Go downstairs and have your meal where you can have company, someone to talk to. Please, let me alone. I want to sleep." Her voice sounded dead, without expression.

He looked up with a question in his eyes at Birdy who was beckoning to him. She walked into the corridor and told him about what had transpired between Annie and Kate that day.

Donald kept his temper in check and squeezed Birdy's arm in thanks, then took another look at Annie who had her back to him and was, ostensibly, asleep. His teeth were clenched in anger as he went downstairs; he avoided the dining room where he could see Amy and Katherine sitting in silence. Ringing for Jeffrey, he told him to bring his dinner into the library. He poured himself a stiff drink of brandy and would have had a second but he had a lot to think about. He must get rid of Kate, should have done so weeks ago, but without upsetting Annie—or would she perhaps be glad to see her go?

It was two days before Donald felt Annie's state of mind had improved to the point that he decided to risk bringing up the subject of Kate. Although common sense told him that he should give his wife more time to completely recover from her brief, deep depression, he couldn't chance having Katherine in the house for an indefinite period.

When Donald had put her out of his room, it was an act of desperation; throughout his enforced celibacy he had kept his passions at a low ebb, but Kate had deliberately inflamed him until only his rigid self-discipline kept him from using her to satisfy desires that were no longer dormant. Twice in the past few days she had stopped him, putting a hand on his arm as she attempted to ask his forgiveness. Each time he shook her off, but his arm burned at the memory of her touch. He was convinced that, in spite of his revulsion and self-disgust, he could not hold out much longer. The only solution was to put as much distance between Kate and himself as possible, before the rift she had created between husband and wife became a chasm.

Now Annie sat across the table from him in her room. "You look well and beautiful, dearest. Are you feeling stronger?" he asked hopefully.

"Thank you, Donald. Yes, I am. In fact, I may come down to dinner tonight." Her voice was polite, yet distant.

"Oh, Annie!" This was more than he had anticipated. "Perhaps you would do better to wait a few days!"

She eyed him suspiciously. "Don't you want me to have dinner with you?"

"You know I do, but . . ."

"It's because of Kate, isn't it?"

Again he was taken aback; he'd never known gentle Annie to be so direct. It strengthened his determination to get to the heart of the matter. She waited patiently for his answer.

"Well, yes, and no," he said after a lengthy pause.

"I don't understand. 'Yes and no'. What does that mean?"

"All right, dear, I'll make it perfectly clear. I had to be sure you would be strong enough to listen to what I have to say. It *is* about Kate."

Annie's heart thudded painfully but she said nothing. "It's time for her to go home," said Donald. Annie's eyes opened wide; she had expected a defense of her sister. He continued, "She should have gone long ago, when we first discussed it; she upsets you and irritates me and everyone else in the household. Her work is finished here and . . ."

Annie put up her hand to stop him, and said, "You don't have to go on. I know all the problems Kate has caused; and a lot of it is my fault for not letting you proceed. I agree with you absolutely. It's time for Katherine to go home."

Donald breathed a heartfelt sigh of relief. "You are a never-ending surprise, darling. I was afraid to approach the subject for fear of making you even more unhappy. Thank you for agreeing with me." He got up and put his arms around her. "Thank you, darling. I love you." She allowed him to kiss her warmly but was less ardent when she returned the kiss. "Now do you understand why I thought it was best for you not to come downstairs for today?"

She nodded. "Of course, you are right. When do you plan to speak to her . . . or did you want me to do it?"

"No, dear. I'll take care of that."

"Let me know what happens, Donald, and I will want to see her after you speak with her."

"I will talk to her today after I have contacted the shipping company." He used the napkin to pat his mouth. "Have you enjoyed your lunch, dear?"

She was glad he had not noticed that she had barely touched her food. "Will you send Birdy to me? You go ahead, dear, I'll sit here until she comes."

"What can I do for you, Mrs. Donald? Would you like to rest in bed for awhile?" Birdy asked as soon as she arrived.

"No, I think I shall sit at the window and work on my embroidery," Annie told her. Birdy was delighted at the request, and arranged a chair and a small table for her to lean her elbow on while plying the needle with its bright colored threads through the piece of hand-loomed linen that would eventually be the cover of a small pillow. "That's very pretty!"

"Thank you, Birdy. Now I'd like to be alone for a little while. Take some time for yourself and come back about . . ." she looked at the china clock on the mantel over the fireplace. "Oh, I don't know, I'll ring for you about four o'clock."

"That's a long time for you to be by yourself, Mrs. Donald."

"Perhaps I won't be. Mr. MacConnack may get back from the city early. Don't worry, Birdy. I'll call if I need anything," she said, smiling.

"All right, if you're sure you don't want me to stay . . ." Birdy's voice trailed off. She didn't know whether to rejoice because of Annie's sudden independence or to worry about it. When Annie insisted that she would be fine, Birdy reluctantly left her alone.

It was good to be busy again, Annie thought, but it wasn't enough. As she bent her head above the fabric stretched taut by the hoops, the work was so mechanical that her thoughts were free to roam. Tears brimmed over as she thought about Kate's dreadful words to her about Donald. She berated herself for not being able to handle the situation, or not having brought Kate up properly. It was shameful to have her own sister put out of the house. If Annie herself had been the only one involved it wouldn't have been so bad but, Annie rationalized, Kate must have been obnoxious to make Donald angry enough to send her home to Scotland. But then, she should have allowed Donald to send her home five months ago, and furthermore, Katherine would have her pick of several young men who were eagerly awaiting her return to Paisley. As Annie's resolve reasserted itself, she put aside her needlework and closed her eyes. She was tired, so tired . . .

By three o'clock Donald still had not returned. At Birdy's insistence, Annie lay down. "If Mr. Donald returns before I get up, ask him to wake me. I feel very well," she said as Birdy started to protest, "and I am most anxious for news he will bring." Reluctantly, Birdy promised she would.

It was almost six when Donald finally arrived. Annie had napped, bathed and was freshly robed. Birdy was supervising the maid who was setting the table in Annie's room for dinner as he walked in, congratulating himself that he had made the right decision.

"You look beautiful, sweetheart. Did you rest this afternoon?" Donald said, kissing Annie's cheek.

"Yes, I did but now I am most anxious to know . . ."

For answer he handed her an envelope

which held the reservation for a cabin on a ship leaving the following Saturday. She turned it over thoughtfully. "How . . ." she paused, "how do you plan to tell her?"

"Don't fret, darling. I am sure she knows there is no reason for her to stay any longer. I don't anticipate a problem."

Annie did, but she said nothing.

Donald was finishing his breakfast the next morning when Kate joined him and blurted out, "I *am* glad to see you, Donald. I know I was impatient with Annie and made her angry, but it was only because I see how lonely you are. I thought . . ."

He put up his hand to stop her. "Further explanation is not necessary, Kate. Annie is fine." He rose. "I am going into the library now. When you have finished your breakfast, will you join me?"

Kate's eyes widened in surprise at the unexpected invitation. "Of course. I won't be long."

"We have a lot to talk about, you and I," he added, then excused himself. As Kate watched him leave the room, her hopes rose. He wanted to speak to her where no one could hear; perhaps he had realized at last how important she was to him. Kate's imagination took flight; she could see herself so clearly as mistress of the house, taking care of "poor Annie" and spending her nights in Donald's bed. He wasn't really such a "cold fish" as she'd accused him of being in her anger. Kate felt a surge of power and walked into the library fully confident that he could no longer resist her.

"Sit down, Katherine," Donald said, pointing to a chair at the other side of the desk, behind which he sat. "I want very much for you to understand what I am going to say, and trust you will cooperate gracefully," he began.

Kate heard what she wanted to hear and misunderstood his intentions. "Anything, Donald, you know that! I am sure we can work everything out together."

"Good. I have something for you." He handed her an envelope.

"Oh?" She studied it curiously. What could it possibly contain?

Donald sat quietly for a few moments. Then, when Kate still had not moved, said, "Open it, Kate."

She snapped out of her daydream and hastily ripped open the envelope. "What is this . . . ?" she asked, staring at the paper in her hand.

"A reservation for your return to Scotland."

Kate was truly bewildered by this turn of events. "I don't understand. I'm not going home. What made you think I wanted to go back?" she protested.

"Your stay here has been much too prolonged. Among others, your father very much wants to see you . . ."

She spoke at the same time, " . . . and now of all times, with poor dear Annie needing her family around her . . ."

"Stop right there, Kate," said Donald firmly. "I would like your departure to be an amicable one, but if you insist, I can give you many reasons why I want you to leave. I'd prefer, however, not to go into them."

Kate's voice was shrill. "How *dare* you speak to me like that! You're afraid of me, that's what; more than that, you're afraid of your own feelings for me. If Annie ever finds out you want to get rid of me and *why . . ."*

"Annie and I are in full agreement. I have nothing further to say. Your ship sails next Saturday."

She jumped to her feet, her face scarlet with humiliation and temper. "*This* is what I think of your little scheme!" She tore the reservation into little pieces and flung them at him. "I have no intention of going home now or ever, and there's no way you can make me. Annie *never* would let you do this to me. I'm going upstairs right now and tell her what you've done!"

"Katherine!" Donald's voice was stern and deadly. "Stay away from Annie. She is not well and you upset her. I warn you, if you do not do as I say, you'll find yourself out on the street tomorrow, bag and baggage."

"Don't you dare touch my things! When I leave here—*if* I do—it won't be to go home to dreary old Paisley! Cancel the reservation!" She stamped out of the room, not stopping to get a wrap and ran, tripping and stumbling, her arrogance dissipating in her flight, until once again she found herself at the duck pond. But this time no stones were thrown. She stood with her face to the morning sky, her hands clasped in anguish. "What do I do now?" she whispered. Slowly she sank to the ground and sat quiet as a statue, eyes wide with fear. She moaned aloud, drowning in self-pity, "Where will I go? No one wants me." She hugged herself as she started to shiver. The thought that suddenly struck her was like a bolt of lightning, "Rory! Oh, my dear God, Rory wants me!"

* * *

By the time Kate reached the steps to Rory's flat, she was very cold, her hair had come undone, her eyes were red and her face tear-stained. She didn't call or knock on his door but leaned against it beating it with her fists.

On Sunday morning Rory slept late after Saturday night shenanigans, so it was several minutes before the thumping on his door penetrated his consciousness. Hair tousled, eyes drowsy, he threw on a robe to hide his naked-ness and finally opened the door, blinking in the strong sunlight.

"Kate! Oh, my darlin', what is it?" He caught her as she collapsed against him. His arms trembled as he picked her up and carried her to his bed, still warm from his body.

"Rory, darling Rory, I am so unhappy. I'm so glad you're here!" she sobbed.

"You're shivering. Why are you out in the cold without a wrap?" He tucked the bedclothes around her.

"Don't cry, dear heart. I'm here. Hush, my love." As she began to calm down, he asked, "Has someone hurt you?"

Kate started to cry again. "Yes, oh, yes! Hold me Rory, hold me close . . ."

There was only one way he could do that; he slipped into bed beside her and gently caressed her. "Rest, my beauty. Later you'll tell me who hurt you and I'll kill him," he promised grimly.

His words thrilled her. "I'm tired, but I can't rest comfortably with all my clothes on," Kate told him. She raised one leg so he could unbutton her shoe. Muttering that he was a clumsy fool, he quickly undid one, then the other. As he pulled them off, she tucked her feet back under the covers which she pulled up to her chin, wriggled a little, then said, "Rory, pull."

"What do you want me to pull?" he asked, perplexed.

She thrust her legs out from under the covers again. "Pull the ruffles."

He took one look, gulped and with his head turned in the other direction, did as he was told. Her frilly lace-trimmed drawers came off in his hands. "I—I think I'd better make some tea," he said as he beat a hasty retreat.

When he came back a few minutes later, Kate had drawn the covers up under her armpits. Rory saw immediately that she was naked, at least on top. "Kate, Kate, darlin', you'd tempt the devil in any man!" He was breathing heavily. "I'll drink my tea in the kitchen."

"Don't leave me, Rory, please don't leave me." She began to cry again softly.

"I don't want to leave you, but this is a dangerous thing we're doing; neither of us with clothes on." He sat down gingerly alongside her on the bed and took her hand. "Why are you so upset? Can you talk about it now?"

Kate struggled to restrain her sobs. "I'm being sent home, put out of the house. Donald made reservations on a ship that sails next week. He says Annie wants me to go home, too. She needs me, and he *made* her say that!"

"Why, my darlin'? Why do they want you to leave?" Rory asked.

The lie tripped off her tongue as easily as truth. "Donald found out I've been coming to the saloon with you. His horrid little sister, Amy, spied on me and then she told him."

Rory thought about this for a moment. "Are you sure that's what happened? That's a strong accusation to make against Miss MacConnack."

"Would I say such a thing if it weren't true?" cried Kate, the picture of beautiful righteous indignation. "She's always hated me and she's such a goody-good, everybody believes her; it doesn't matter what I say." The covers fell away from her as she reached up and put her arms around him. "Nobody wants me. I'm so alone!"

It was more than Rory could stand. "Macushla, I want you more than anything in this whole, wide world!" His robe came off and joined Kate's clothing on the floor where she'd flung them as he climbed into bed, pressing his hard, naked body against the yielding softness of hers.

Kate did not realize until that very moment how strong was her desire for Rory. His passion fed her own, fanning it into an all-consuming flame which sent fire coursing through her blood. They had lusted for each other from the time they had first met. Now the melding of their bodies built to a crescendo, after which they lay, exhausted and ecstatic, in each other's arms.

For all Kate's apparent boldness, she had never been with a man before, but this passionate coming together of their hungry bodies seemed natural and foreordained. Her heart fluttered as she came out of a half-sleep. Rory's warm mouth was dropping light kisses on her eyelids, the tip of her nose and under her chin. His hand was cupped around her breast as his mouth sought the soft, firm mound. Fully awake now, she was suddenly conscious of his nakedness. Her eyes, which had opened at his touch, now closed tightly and she bit her lip.

"I love you so much, Macushla," Rory breathed. "Look at me and tell me you love me, too." His hands caressed her as he spoke. She had been lying on her back and he turned her toward him, tilting her face to his.

"I do love you, darling Rory, but . . . I'm . . ." she faltered, "I've never seen a man . . . like this . . . before . . ."

He adored the innocence which belied her bold manner. "Don't be afraid, dearest. Give me your hand." He guided her tentative hand to all the contours of his warm, muscular body. At first he had to exert a little effort, but as the exploration proceeded the heat of passion enveloped them again. She ran her hands through his hair, then spontaneously they moved down his back until she reached his taut flanks and pressed him to her; once again they came together in the act of love.

"You are beautiful, Rory," she said when they lay together afterward.

"Men aren't beautiful, Kate. You are!"

"Your body is beautiful," Kate purred. She no longer needed his guiding hand as she traced his muscles, then ran her fingers through the dark crisp hair on his chest.

"Kate, Kate, angel," he kissed the top of her head, "no more, not now, darlin'." He glanced at the clock on the wall. "It's three o'clock and your family will be looking for you."

252

"Let them, I don't care!" she cried.

"If they come here and find us together, we will both be in real trouble," Rory told her. "Come, love, get dressed." He got up and fetched a towel which he handed to her. Only then did she realize she had stained the sheet.

"Oh, Rory," she gasped in embarrassed dismay, "what have I done?"

"Don't fret, darlin'. It means you have given me your virginity," he said tenderly.

When they were both washed and dressed, Kate asked, "Do I look different?"

"More beautiful than ever I've seen you. Katherine Maccrae, do you know what this means?"

"I only know I love you, Rory, and this was the most terrible and wonderful day of my life!"

Rory took her by the hand and sat her down at the table, then brought out a bottle of wine. "We must talk for a bit, Katherine." She nodded and sipped the wine he had poured. "I love you more than life itself but," he sighed heavily, "I have nothing to offer you. You are a lady and have every luxury at your fingertips. I don't expect to work at the silk factory for much longer—I've made some plans that will make for a comfortable life, but not what you are accustomed to . . ."

"Rory—oh my love, are you asking me to marry you?" she whispered. He lowered his eyes, suddenly shy. "I don't live at home the way I have been living here. All this luxury was a temporary thing at best. I must admit I had hoped . . . well, never mind. I work as a weaver at home. Whatever you have, if you are asking me to share it, the answer is, I would be the happiest girl in the whole world!"

Rory could hardly believe his ears. He picked her up in his arms and danced around the room with her, almost suffocating her with his kisses. "I've wanted to ask you for so long but didn't dare to think you would even listen." He put her on her feet. "Now, my bride-to-be, I will take you home and we will announce that fact. We will be married as soon as possible, and no one will dare be mean to you ever again or they'll have me to deal with!"

Now that she had committed herself, Katherine's mind was working fast. "No, Rory, I don't think that's a good idea. I'll go home and I won't say anything yet. I'll tell Annie as soon as she's feeling better and then I'll come to you and we can be married. I'm afraid Donald might discharge you if he knows about it now."

Reluctantly Rory had to admit she was right. "I'm not quite ready to leave the mill yet. I thought I'd stay until the end of the month."

There was a long silence. Finally Kate came up with a question. "Can you tell me what your plans are, or would you rather not talk about it?"

"If you're going to be my missus, you have every right to know, although I haven't told this to anyone. Pat McCarthy is planning to retire to Ireland. He has offered to sell me the place."

"Rory, that's just wonderful!" said Kate. "Can you afford to buy it?"

"Yes, I've saved most of my wages, except for expenses, and I can give him a substantial amount as a down payment and pay him the rest out of the profits. He has made a lot of money here and says that anything I can send will be fine with him."

"I have some money. I've saved my salary, too! It hasn't cost me anything to live since I've been here. Even my clothes were paid for," she said excitedly.

"Oh, no, Kate dear, I'm the man of the family," he grinned, "at least I will be when we're married, and I'll take care of the finances. You keep your money."

"I love you Rory Sullivan, I really do," she sighed, sliding her hands under his shirt.

"Don't *do* that, Kate—I can't think when you touch me and I need my wits about me now."

There was another long silence. Again it was Kate who spoke. "What do you think about this . . . I'll have my trunk picked up on Tuesday and brought here. I'm sure nobody will notice it's a day too soon. When you go into the factory on Monday—that's tomorrow —you must tell them you're leaving. I think they ask two weeks notice, don't they?" He nodded. "Well, they won't get it, that's all. One week from today, we can be married!"

"It's not quite that simple. The banns have to be published."

"That's Catholic!" said Kate, surprised.

"Of course. Dear heart, I forgot—you're a Protestant."

"Presbyterian! Oh, dear! What do we do about that?"

"Well," his grin was mischievous, "There is one way we could get married in a hurry . . ."

"Where? How? Please, Rory . . ."

"In a little town north of here, I have a very good friend. He has been trying to talk me into

255

settling down for a long time. I think he might do it."

"Wonderful! What's his name?"

"Father Mulligan."

"A priest!" Kate gasped. With his head cocked to one side, his eyes held a question, which Kate anticipated. "I'm not very religious, love, but my family would be horrified. Oh, well, they'll be horrified anyway! When can you find out?"

"I'll see you home and if I leave right away, I can probably see him before nightfall," Rory told her.

"It's a lovely day—I can see myself home. Go now and hurry back. But how will I know?" she almost wailed in her impatience.

"If you can get out about nine o'clock, I'll be on the path near the house."

Kate flew into his arms. "I'll be there!"

But when they met that night, Rory's news was somewhat disappointing. Father Mulligan had said that he could have managed a shortcut if Kate were a Catholic, but unless she converted, he couldn't perform the ceremony. He had stepped out of his role as a man of the cloth for a brief moment. "You can be married in a civil ceremony if you go as far as Albany. I have a friend there and while I won't contact him, you may use my name. However, my boy, I will expect your bride to take religious instruction and eventually convert to the Catholic religion, and *then* I will perform the ceremony."

Rory had promised. He would have promised him the world, as Kate did when he told her. If becoming a Catholic would ensure

256

her marriage, she would do it without a qualm.

When Donald was told on Tuesday Katherine's trunks had been picked up, he was greatly relieved. He hardly saw her at all during the ensuing days and was satisfied by her subdued manner. Apparently she had resigned herself at last to the inevitability of her fate. She spent a lot of time in her room, even taking her meals there, ostensibly getting ready for her journey. She also avoided Annie.

On Saturday, the day of Kate's scheduled departure, Donald sent Jeffrey to see to Kate's hand luggage, but the room was empty. The closets and drawers were bare, the baggage gone, as was Kate. On her pillow she had left a note addressed to Donald: "I am addressing this to you and I trust you will impart the contents to Annie with less shock than if I left this directly for her attention. I am not going back to Scotland and will be in touch with you both in a little while. I will not disappear as Maggie did because my future is now assured and I look forward to it happily.'"

At the very moment a stunned Donald was reading the note, Katherine Maccrae and Rory Sullivan were united in marriage.

XIX

SULLIVAN'S SALOON

Four weeks later, an envelope addressed to Mr. and Mrs. Donald MacConnack was hand-delivered. Fortunately Jeffrey was standing by as Annie stood in the great hall and opened it. She recognized the handwriting immediately but the contents shocked her and Jeffrey caught her as she collapsed in a swoon. He called for Birdy, who revived her.

"What is it? Is it bad news?" she asked worriedly, glancing at the envelope and note on the floor.

"Oh, Birdy, I don't know what it is, bad news or good!" said Annie. "My sister Kate ran off— you know that—and now she's gotten married! Will you please ask Jeffrey to bring the trap around? I have to talk to my husband!" She began to struggle to her feet, but Birdy put her hands on her hips and pursed her lips. "I'm sorry, Mrs. Donald, but I can't let you do that. Even without the shock you just had, you are not in any condition to go off to the mill. If it is urgent that you see him, I'll have Jeffrey send one of the stable boys with a message for him to come home."

"He'll be frightened if he's summoned home

in the middle of the day—he'll think I'm ill," said Annie, wringing her hands.

"Then you must write a note and tell him what's happened. Please, you must be calm; let me take you upstairs, Mrs. Donald. You can write the note and then rest."

Annie had to go along with her suggestion; the little strength she had stored up for the day was exhausted by her emotional reaction to Kate's announcement. Her message was brief: "I have heard from Kate. I must talk to you."

Mike the stable boy had driven the trap to the mill and delivered the note to Donald, who left immediately. He snatched the reins out of his hands and drove home at such a reckless pace that Mike prayed as he clung to the seat.

Birdy was waiting for him as he raced into the house; she put her finger to her lips. "She just fell asleep, Mr. MacConnack. She's all right, but the note from her sister upset her something fierce!"

"Where is it?" he asked. Birdy pointed to the table in the hall where she had replaced the note in its envelope when Annie dropped it. He tore the envelope in his haste to get the note, and gasped, "Oh, my God!" It was an invitation to attend the wedding reception of Mr. and Mrs. Rory Sullivan. It was also an announcement of the opening night of Sullivan's Saloon, formerly McCarthy's. At the end, Kate had written, "I hope you will come and share in our happiness. Love, Kate S." He read and reread the words. "How *could* she? My poor Annie, no wonder she was upset! Is this her revenge on us for forcing her to leave? Rory Sullivan—my God!"

He went upstairs and sat beside his wife holding her hand until she stirred, his thought in turmoil. It took a few seconds for her eyes to focus.

"Donald," she moaned, "did you read it?"

"Yes, darling, I did. Look dear, I have had a few minutes to think about it and it may not be all bad news. Though I was furious when he quit without notice, Rory Sullivan is a good man and obviously an ambitious one, though certainly not the one either of us would have chosen for her. But Katherine is a wild kind of rebel. I think it might be a good match for her."

Annie sighed. "I can only hope you're right." She paused. Then, "I'd like to accept the invitation," she said tentatively, fearing his response.

"Of course we'll go, at least to pay our respects and acknowledge her new status." Annie, relieved, sat up and with his support gained her feet. "Do you feel strong enough to come down to dinner?" he asked. She nodded. "Shall I wait for you?"

Annie shook her head. "Sweetheart, you baby me so much, I am getting too dependent on you. I'm beginning to realize that Kate was right about that. Don't wait. I'll join you downstairs. Perhaps I'll even have a glass of sherry. It's funny—I was horrified at first, but now I think I'm almost glad!"

"You know, I honestly think I am, too," said Donald, smiling. "Call me if you need me."

Amy met him at the foot of the staircase, a piece of note paper in her hand. Apparently she too had received an invitation. "Did you get one of these, Donald? Did you *read* it? Can

261

you *believe* it?" Her voice was high with astonishment.

"Yes, Annie notified me the moment she received it. That's why I'm home early."

"How did she take the news?"

"She's over the first shock and became reconciled to the idea quite rapidly. After all, it's a *fait accompli*—what else is there to do but accept it? I didn't realize Kate was so desperate to stay in America that she'd marry someone like Sullivan."

Amy looked thoughtful. "I'm not so sure that's the whole story, Donald. Nobody is supposed to know about it, but I happen to know she went out with him at least once a week. I have a feeling they are in love, but Kate would have given him up in a flash in exchange for position and money. When that prospect vanished, it left her free to marry Rory."

"Perhaps you're right. Who knows? Will you attend the reception at the . . ." he grinned "saloon?"

She laughed lightly. "Don't be mean. I'll have to see what Gunther says. You know, she *has* been rude to us. He has no patience with her and I'm not sure that I want to coax him. I'll talk to him tonight . . ." She looked at the invitation again. "There won't be time to respond to this—I just realized it's tomorrow night!"

"It will be best, I think, if we just show up at the appointed time. I'll make your excuses if you decide not to go." Amy thanked him with a kiss and left to dress for dinner. Shortly thereafter she and Annie came down together.

Gunther joined them as they were having

drinks in the drawing room. Out of respect for Annie, he concealed the contempt he felt for Kate's action. Donald tried to switch the conversation to other subjects but the talk was all of Kate and Rory. It wasn't until Annie had retired to her room after dinner that Gunther reluctantly agreed to attend the reception. "Not for Kate's sake, dear, but for Annie's. We won't have to stay long," Amy assured him.

The next evening, Annie, Donald, Amy and Gunther arrived at Sullivan's Saloon at the appointed time. Donald was worried. The short walk from the carriage to the entrance of the saloon should not have made Annie tremble so; he hoped it was only in anticipation of the meeting that was about to take place, and not evidence of her worsening health. Dr. Thompson said she and the baby were both doing as well as could be expected, but he had also warned her against overexerting herself.

Inside, Kate Maccrae Sullivan was trembling, too. In the short space of time since Rory had taken over the saloon, there had not been time to make any of the renovations she and Rory had planned. There was still sawdust on the floor and the same gaslight fixtures hung over the long, mahogany bar. Kate had, however, put red and white checked tablecloths on the individual tables and polished the floor, the brass, the glasses—everything she could lay her hands on. It was the most she could accomplish in such a short time. When the MacConnacks entered and Kate saw her sister looking pale and apprehensive, she ran over and embraced Annie in tears, asking for-giveness for all the trouble she had caused and for eloping.

"I was afraid you'd try to stop me, or Donald would, if I had told you. I love Rory more than life itself and I know we'll be happy! It's a merry life here, and I'm going to take an active part in it." With her arm around her sister's thickening waist, she led her over to one of the tables, then motioned to a waiter to add another table so that Donald, Amy and Gunther, who were following and whom Kate had finally acknowledged, could be seated. Kate felt a certain stiffness with Donald, Amy and Gunther, but they all dutifully offered their wishes for happiness. When Rory appeared, looking strong, handsome and confi-dent, he too was congratulated by all and kissed by Annie.

"Welcome to our family, Rory," she said a little breathlessly. "Our home is always open to you and Kate and we trust you will visit us often." Donald, after a moment's hesitation, shook Rory's hand and seconded the invitation, albeit somewhat coolly. For all his apparent self-confidence, Rory's eyes took on the look of a puppy who had been petted instead of being punished as he had antici-pated.

Kate had ordered several cases of champagne for the occasion and even Gunther volunteered a toast to Mr. and Mrs. Rory Sullivan, realizing he would no longer have to worry about Kate smothering him with attention whenever he visited Amy. As his relief mounted, he drank more champagne and his enthusiasm grew proportionately.

Now regular customers and many of Rory's friends started to drift in. They drank the unaccustomed champagne ("On the house," said Rory expansively) and offered toasts to the happiness of the marriage and the success of Sullivan's Saloon. But it wasn't until Donald and the others left that the celebration really took off. Rory announced that *all* drinks were on the house, and the beer and whiskey flowed. By closing time, Kate was delirious with joy and giddy with drink. Rory had to carry her upstairs to bed, but neither could remember how they got there the following morning, or even if they had made love.

It soon became evident to Kate that living in Rory's three rooms was going to be a problem.

The next few weeks were busy ones as she took it upon herself, with the help of the local carpenter, to break through walls and enlarge the space she and Rory would occupy. It wasn't nearly as grand as her rooms in the MacConnack mansion, but it was a modest effort to improve the style and manner in which they lived. Rory was glad of the saloon downstairs, which he could escape to when Kate's efforts at redecoration overwhelmed him. But eventually he not only got used to it, he liked it.

Kate had never been so happy. She knew now the satisfaction her father had felt each time he added a room to his home. She drew up plans, supervised, approved or disapproved all construction and decoration. When it was completed, Rory was so proud of his large remodelled flat that he often invited his friends to visit and admire.

Having completed her first project, Kate next turned her attention to the saloon and made some improvements, although she was restricted somewhat by Rory who wanted to keep the saloon looking like a saloon. "No pink cushions on the chairs and no fancy aprons on the barkeep," he teased.

Kate's energy since becoming Rory's wife was so high that she just had to keep moving. Now she grabbed him by the shoulders and whirled him around the tiny dance floor, saying as they tripped and almost fell, "See, now you *know* it is too small. Please, Rory, I promise no pink decorations but I do think we should make the dance floor bigger."

He threw his hands up in resignation. "Whatever you want, my darlin', but I mean it when I say *nothing pink.*" She danced away from him, threw him a kiss and ran to locate the carpenter.

The dance floor was enlarged, more tables moved in and, although Rory didn't notice, there was just a touch of pink in the new globes on the gas fixtures. That accomplished, Kate insisted on learning to tend bar, over Rory's objections. "When we're busy, darling," she argued, "we all have to help."

"That's no place for you, Kate," Rory blustered. "Ladies don't belong behind a bar."

"I'm not a lady!" She winked at him wickedly. "I'm Mrs. Rory Sullivan!"

Kate tended bar, waited tables, sang and danced for the customers and they loved her. Sometimes Rory thought the men loved her a little too much; fights kept breaking out over who would have the next dance with her.

As for Kate, she lived in a never-ending state of excitement.

XX

A WEDDING AND A BIRTH

On January 16, 1882, fifteen days after her seventeenth birthday, Amy and Gunther were married. Robbie, deep in her studies at the University of Edinburgh, much to her regret had declined Amy's invitation to be maid of honor. Annie, though six months pregnant, took her place. She wore a mauve moire dress tiered with ruffles, with a matching tricorne hat. The ruffles hid the little bulge that would hardly have been noticeable anyway.

Amy wore the white satin gown which had come down through several generations of brides on her mother's side. Her mother had been the last to wear it. The high lace collar was boned and tiny satin-covered buttons marched down the back of the dress to her tiny waist. She wore many petticoats under the full skirt from which white satin pumps peeped out when she walked. Her bridal veil, also an heirloom, was the *piece de resistance*. Lace, handmade by French nuns a hundred years ago, had been embroidered by the artisans of Florence with seed pearls all the way down to the border of the twelve-foot train. Because of the weight of the veil, it was anchored to her Victorian styled pompadour with small pearl-headed pins. Two of her bridesmaids were assigned to keep it straight as she walked down the aisle. Amy was radiant, the perfect bride, ready to take her place in society with the perfect bridegroom.

Donald gave his sister away and J. Horton Smythe was Gunther's best man. They were all handsome in their cutaways, but Amy saw only Gunther as she slowly drifted down the aisle on her brother's arm. It was a grand wedding; six bridesmaids in palest pink; Annie, a lovely matron of honor; a tiny flower girl who strewed rose petals before the bride; and a ring-bearer matching in size. The little-used ballroom of the MacConnack mansion was thrown open and the reception lasted into the early hours of the morning.

After much coaxing, Kate had convinced Rory that out of courtesy they would have to attend. "After all, dear, Amy and Gunther accepted *our* invitation," she reminded him. He agreed, on the condition that he would not have to stay more than an hour at the reception. She, however, could stay as long as she liked. Kate engaged Mrs. Oakley, Amy's dressmaker, to make a violet velvet dress with ecru lace at the deep vee neckline, and for the first time in her life, had her hair dressed professionally. She insisted that Rory have an evening suit tailored for him. "We will have to attend these grand functions occasionally, darling, and you must have a suit that is made just for you. I want to show everyone how handsome you are," she'd told him. When they stood in front of the large mirror in the saloon, he had to agree they made a good-looking couple. It also renewed his feeling of guilt for having taken Kate away from this kind of life. It wasn't until they returned home and Kate tore her dress off and threw it on a chair, saying, "Thank God that's over; you'll never know how grateful I am that you saved me from their boring company!" that he was reassured Kate was where she truly belonged —with him.

Amy and Gunther spent a brief week in the city of New York, postponing their honeymoon until the weather was more conducive to a visit to his parents in Germany. Amy was anxious to get back to start decorating her new home, a neighboring estate which had been Donald's wedding gift to them. A good part of the stay in the city was spent interviewing fashionable decorators, one of whom she chose to come to Tarrytown the following week. The newlyweds stayed with Donald and Annie until the house was finished. It was a good plan for all concerned, as Amy was a great help to Annie in the ensuing months. As the time for the baby's birth neared, her health deteriorated.

On the 26th of March, 1882, Donald Ian MacConnack Junior was born, healthy, crying and hungry. Since Annie couldn't nurse him, a wetnurse was called in. Amy and Gunther moved into their own home on the 27th, giving up the suite originally used by Robbie and Kate and making room for the nurses who were needed around the clock. Annie's strength had ebbed so low that her life was despaired of. Donald spent most of every day at home; only when she slept would he leave and spend a few hours at the factory.

Dr. Thompson had selected the nurses and had also recommended a local doctor who stopped by twice a day that first month. Annie not only had no strength, she seemed to have no interest in living. The nurses almost force-fed her, urging her to build up her strength and reminding her about her handsome son and her worried husband. It was some time before even Donald could get a weak smile from her. Annie lingered in this condition for two months and might have died without the professional attention she received. However, during the third month she asked for the first time if she could see her son. It was a good sign, and Donald brought him in saying jokingly, "Our young man has been asking for his mama."

He laid the baby in her arms and a flicker of maternal pride in this cherub of a child began to stir within her. She saw him more often as time went on and when he was four months old, two of Annie's nurses were dismissed. She kept Emma, the one she liked best and who shared her suite with her. There was no thought of Donald moving in. Mrs. Wheeler had run the house competently while Annie was ill, and she elected to have the house-keeper continue to do so. She rested most of the day and occasionally took a walk with Donald in the evening. They would come in to dinner, at which she pecked to satisfy her husband, and thence she was off to bed.

Donald waited patiently and anxiously for his loving Annie to return but it never happened. She withdrew further into herself.

Not even Junior excited her interest. She would play with him when he was brought to her and feel relieved when he was taken away by his nursemaid.

Amy and Gunther were finally about to set off on their long-delayed honeymoon, and asked Donald and Annie to dinner the night before they departed. Although Annie was technically well enough to accept the invitation, she had no desire to leave the security of her own home. For the first time Donald urged her to accompany him, and eventually she agreed. Perhaps, he thought, he should have made more demands on her and she would have risen to meet them. As it was, he felt that this illness of Annie's was somehow his fault, although Dr. Wilson had told him that such melancholy was not uncommon after the birth of a child, and that she would recover.

While he projected his conviction to Donald, the doctor wasn't sure that Annie *would* recover. He knew her problem was more than that which so often accompanied childbirth. He had tried unsuccessfully to get her to talk about herself, but she said she had no problems; she just couldn't get her strength back.

But Annie herself knew what was wrong and cried in secret all the time. She felt alone, with no one close to her to talk to. She loved Donald, but he didn't fit her family image; Amy was almost a stranger—a dear one, but a stranger nevertheless; and Kate, her only tie to her homeland, had moved out of that sphere when she married Rory, an Irish saloon owner. Annie was pining for her family, for being in charge of Da and six girls, good and bad, for the household that was hers alone, and for Scotland, her homeland. She wanted the impossible—to go back in time.

Amy and Gunther sailed to Europe the first week in July. They spent an idyllic month with his parents. Amy found the mother and father she had never known, and they, the daughter they had been denied. Although they all knew it would never take place, the young people extracted promises that Gunther's parents would visit them one day in America.

Another month was devoted to traveling through Austria, where they spent much time in romantic Vienna; France, where they stopped such a short time that they promised themselves a longer trip in the near future; and finally to England and thence to the high point of their journey, Edinburgh, Scotland.

They arrived on a bright blue morning to find Robbie waiting for them. As they approached, she made a deep curtsey. "M'lord and lady," she said reverently. Amy was about to be angry at this humble reception until she saw that Robbie was laughing.

"Get up, you silly goose!" she cried.

Robbie sprang to her feet and embraced her, then Gunther and then Amy again. "You both look so wonderful!"

"We've missed you, Robbie," Gunther said, "but I must tell you Donald is very proud of you. He has had a report from the University, at his request, of your progress."

"I'm glad he's satisfied. I've never struggled so hard nor enjoyed anything as much as I do my studies," she told them. With great pride she took them to her very own flat after they had settled in at the Edinburgh Hotel.

"You live here alone?" Amy asked, slightly scandalized.

"Well," Robbie laughed, "yes and no." As she brought out tea and scones, she explained, "I have these two rooms and a little space to fix my meals. However, there are nine other students in the house. Mrs. Craig, the lady who owns the house, also provides board, but I prefer to eat here."

Gunther was curious. "I know you're very independent, Robbie, but wouldn't you be better off if you made friends with your housemates?"

"I've made friends, Gunther, but," and she lapsed into perfect German as she explained and later translated for Amy, "there are six female students in the entire university. I am the only pre-engineering student; therefore I would be eating with men all the time."

"You wouldn't like that?" Amy asked mischievously.

Robbie answered seriously, "Too distracting. For one thing, I'm a kind of freak to them. They can't understand why a woman would want to be an engineer. For another," she answered a little smugly, "I am already promised."

Amy and Gunther both jumped up. "Who? When are you getting married? Why haven't you told us?"

"No, no, my dears, you misunderstand me. Not for a while yet . . . I thought you realized that J.H. and I were very close."

Amy sat down with a thud. "Of course, but I . . ."

"Me, too," Gunther said. "But we thought you were just friends."

"That's true. However, he's been here to see me. You know he's at Oxford, and we correspond a lot. I hope you plan to stay at least a week because he's coming for a weekend." She changed the subject. "Enough about me! I want to hear all about the wedding and what you've been doing—but first, tell me about Annie."

Their faces fell and Robbie's secret fears were confirmed. "She's not very well, dear," Gunther said, "but Amy knows more about her than I do, so I'm going to leave you girls to talk. If it's all right with you, Laurie has invited us for dinner at eight o'clock."

"Fine. I don't see nearly enough of the family," Robbie said.

"Shall I pick you up here, Amy?" Gunther asked. They decided Robbie would walk Amy to the hotel, return to her lodgings, and meet Gunther and Amy there later.

After Gunther left, the two girls talked for hours. Robbie knew something of Annie's disastrous voyage and that she had become with child almost immediately. She also knew about the son born to her and Donald, but not too much more about Annie's health or the baby's; Annie's letters were very brief and noncommittal.

"The doctors—and there have been several —can't find out why Annie doesn't regain her strength. Dr. Thompson, the one she likes best, seems to think that for some unknown reason, she has lost the will to get better," Amy sighed.

"Oh, Amy, that's terrible! Do you have any idea why? You don't think she and Donald . . ."

Amy shook her head decidedly. "No, nothing like that. They adore each other and he worries about her all the time. He's changed . . . Donald was always serious but now he's even more so. Annie doesn't like to leave the house, so he stays with her when he's not working."

"I know Kate left and got married; couldn't she be of some help?"

"I think Kate's behavior upset Annie very much. They've made up, but things will never be the same between them. Are you sure you want to hear?" Robbie nodded and Amy proceeded to tell her about what had transpired, including what pertained to herself and Gunther. "Have I shocked you?" she asked when she had finished.

"Nothing Kate does shocks me. I'm surprised, yes, but shocked, no. You see, Amy, I knew when Donald and Annie married that it was going to devastate Kate. Although she never said so in so many words, she fully intended to become Mrs. Donald MacConnack."

"And when she found that was impossible, she settled on Gunther . . ."

"And when that was impossible, she married Rory. Poor Rory—third best!" sighed Robbie.

"I don't quite agree with you, Robbie. Rory Sullivan is completely rugged and masculine and, though unpolished, very attractive. While she appears to have wrapped him around her little finger, he is a very strong man and, I think, just what she needs. From the little I have seen of them they are very happy together. My theory is that she loved him but wanted the wealth and position Donald or

277

Gunther could have offered. I think she was relieved to have the decision made for her."

"Do you think I should go back with you and see if I can help Annie?" Robbie asked.

"No, she would know you were sacrificing your education and it would distress her. I think after this first year she will begin to pick up again. It's just taking her a long time to adjust to a new way of life and to being a mother."

Amy looked at her watch; it was after four. "I think it's time for me to go. Perhaps I can take a short nap before I dress for dinner."

They walked slowly back to the hotel. As Amy had indicated the points of interest on the way to Tarrytown, so Robbie did now as they walked through Edinburgh's streets. "There's so much more to see, Amy, but we'll keep it for another time," she said, giving Amy a brief hug. "See you in about three hours."

Robbie took long strides on the way back to her rooms. Today was the first one she had not spent in study and she knew she ought to get to her books for an hour or two. But she did not study. Instead she gazed into space, her mind's eye filled with images of Annie and Kate . . . .

PART FOUR

XXI

MAGGIE

When Maggie left the ship with Ellen Colton, she had no idea of the situation she was walking into. Ellen's family were wealthy shipowners and members of high society. The carriage stopped in front of a four-story brownstone on Fifth Avenue, which Maggie would learn later was the most fashionable residential district in the city of New York. After she had handed the sleeping baby to a nursemaid in a starched, white uniform, Ellen took her by the hand and led her into a spacious entrance hall where a butler relieved them of their outer clothing. "Edward, Miss Anderson will be staying with us," Ellen said. "Will you see that the front suite on the third floor is prepared for her? And please let me know which one of the maids will be assigned to her."

"I will see to it immediately, Mrs. Colton. I think Emily would be a good choice," said the butler.

"If you think she's ready, Edward." Ellen turned to Maggie, who was dumbfounded at the idea of a maid of her own. "Emily is my personal maid's daughter and she has been training her," she explained.

Maggie, like her sisters in Tarrytown, soon got used to dealing with servants and, like them, she revelled in the beauty of her bedroom, sitting room and bath. Her rooms looked out on Fifth Avenue and six extravagantly draped windows made the rooms bright and cheerful. Maggie wasn't homesick—she had little reason to be. Her sitting room, also on the Avenue side, gave her a place to be alone when she wished, and to indulge in her favorite pastime, sketching. She and Ellen walked together often and on one of their expeditions Maggie found an art shop where she bought drawing paper and pencils. When Ellen retired to take a nap each afternoon, Maggie spent the time sketching.

It was arranged that John would be home to celebrate his son's first Christmas. Mrs. and Mrs. Twombley, Ellen's parents, came laden with toys and gifts; John brought exotica which he had picked up in several of the countries his ship had visited. Maggie, a little at a loss amidst such splendid gifts, offered the only thing she could. She had drawn a miniature portrait of the baby for his grandmother and grandfather, and a larger one for Ellen and John, and had bought wind chimes to hang in the baby's room.

Since her return from Europe, Ellen confined her entertaining to afternoon, when she would have her friends in to tea; Maggie met them all. She had now passed her fifteenth birthday (which had been unobserved, as she had told no one.) Her youthful gaiety and the slight sense of mischief she projected made her a general favorite. Her *joie de vivre* proved infectious to Ellen, and she had few moments to be lonely for John.

One afternoon coming in from their daily walk, Ellen said, "Let's have tea in the library, Maggie. There's something I have to discuss with you."

She sounded so serious that Maggie was alarmed. "Is anything wrong?" she faltered.

Ellen's laughter trilled. "Of course not, but it is something we have to discuss seriously."

Maggie sat primly and poured tea at Ellen's request.

"You do that very well, Maggie. You learn quickly and I'm proud of you," Ellen said approvingly.

Maggie blushed. "I've had an excellent teacher in you, Ellen. I've never aspired to such a position in life, but thanks to you, I am enjoying every moment."

Ellen smiled, then said briskly, "Now to the business at hand." Maggie's eyes were wide with attention. "Every year John and I give a Spring Ball the first week in June. It is a very festive affair, the first major social event of the summer and the last before we go to our summer home on the Jersey shore."

"You have another home?" asked Maggie, amazed. What could anyone possibly want with a second home when they had a beautiful place like this?

"A lovely one with our own beach and a veranda that faces the ocean. I really look forward every summer to leaving the city. This time it will be even better. Little John will love it and so, my dear, will you. He will need someone very young and sprightly to play with."

Maggie lowered her lashes. Maggie had never mentioned how old she was, and it was the first time Ellen had alluded to her extreme youth. She managed not to gulp but her complexion changed to a warm pink.

"Don't worry, dear—whatever your age, you're quite old enough to do the things I've planned."

"Thank you for not asking questions. I do have some secrets which I shall tell you one day. Meanwhile, as you say, I'm sure I'm old enough . . ." she paused, puzzled, "for what?"

"For some more sophisticated clothes. And the first thing on the list, because it will take the longest to make, is a ballgown."

"For *me?*" Maggie's voice squeaked in surprise.

"*Oui.* Do you know what that means?" Ellen asked, smiling.

Maggie nodded eagerly. "I've picked up a little French—but I want to know why I need a ballgown?"

"Because, my dear, you can't go to the ball without one and I intend you to be there."

"How wonderful!" breathed Maggie ecstatically. Then she added, "I'll get one on the condition that I pay for it. I haven't touched one cent of the money I earned from the . . ." she made a face "Hendersons."

Ellen dismissed the subject of money with an airy wave of her hand. "We'll talk about that later. Madame Landré, my dressmaker, will be here tomorrow and we'll decide what we want her to make for us."

"But it's almost six months till June—does it

284

take that long to have a gown made?" Maggie asked.

"No-o-o," Ellen drew the syllable out, "but she will have to make two, one for each of us, and she is very much in demand. If we make our selection now, we'll be sure she can accommodate us."

Maggie smiled and shrugged. "That's fine with me, Ellen. Did you say she's coming here?"

"Yes. The rooms behind yours are sewing rooms. We have a dressmaker's dummy in there and all the things Madame needs."

"What time will she be here?" Maggie wanted to know.

"In the early afternoon. Instead of going for a walk tomorrow, we'll spend that time looking at her fashion books and deciding on fabrics and colors. After that she will come in the mornings for fittings and so forth."

Maggie was enchanted. A ballgown made especially for her! How she wished she could share her excitement with her sisters!

Lily Landré, an attractive Frenchwoman in her early forties, came to the house the following day with pictures and suggestions.

"I don't know, Madame—I don't see anything that I particularly like," said Ellen with a frown. "What about you, Maggie?"

After a momentary pause, Maggie blurted out, "I hope you'll forgive me for doing this, but I know just exactly what I would like. May I show you? I'll be back in a minute!" She jumped up and dashed to her room, returning with her drawing pad.

Ellen and Mme. Landre exchanged startled

glances over Maggie's bent head as she turned page after page of dresses and gowns she had sketched. She finally found the page she was looking for. "*This* is what I would like." She looked shyly at the dressmaker. "It's fairly simple except for the trim. Do you think you could make it?"

"That is magnificent," Mme. Landré exclaimed. "It would be a pleasure to work on such a lovely design—but the signature—what is it?" She was looking at a sketch of a very simple Grecian style dress with crossbands under the bosom, softly draped sleeves and a band around the waist. In the lower right hand corner of the page was a funny little squiggle.

"That's my little fat fish," Maggie said unable to come up with a better description. "I sign all my sketches that way. Now on this dress, which I would like in pale blue," she continued quickly, "I would have the bands embroidered in white, wear white gloves and a white plume in my hair. As for shoes . . ." She thought for a moment. "Blue silk!" She sat back, satisfied with the word picture she had created to enhance her sketch.

Ellen's laugh trilled and Lily Landre joined in her laughter. "I have never known anyone who could describe so clearly, without a pattern, exactly what a gown would look like. My dear child," Madame continued, "you are wasting a precious talent. May we see your other sketches?"

"Of course! Let me show you the one I'd like for you, Ellen," said Maggie eagerly, hastening to add that this was her personal taste and if Ellen didn't like it, that was quite all right.

Both Madame and Ellen agreed that Maggie's choice was perfect. "It has the little fish worked into the trim," said Mme. Landre. "Is it to be embroidered?"

"No, but it *would* take a lot of work. The dress is supposed to be a deep ivory satin. The band above the off-the-shoulder flounce has the little fish worked in bronze beads. That may be difficult."

"*Mais non!*" Madame was excited. "It is exquisite! My little Madeleine does very fine bead work. Oh, Madame Colton, it is perfect for you!" She scolded Maggie lightly. "Why do you keep these sketches hidden? When people discover these are your own designs, after the ball is over you will have people knocking at your door, begging you to design something for them!"

Maggie blushed and stammered, "You . . . you are very kind; I am flattered that you think so well of my sketches."

"You could at least have shown them to me," Ellen reproached her.

Maggie shrugged. "I never thought about showing them to anyone. This is what I do when I spend time in my room, that's all."

"You're a never-ending surprise, Maggie," said Ellen, shaking her head. "Tell me, is the little fish your personal mark? I notice you have it, in one form or another, on each page in the book."

"I guess so. I didn't intend it to be a fish, but it *does* look like a little fat fish with a curled tail, doesn't it?" What she didn't say was that she had adapted the basic figure of the paisley design with which she was so familiar, and for her own satisfaction had used it as a signature. It was a part of her heritage, one she would never forget.

XXII

MISS MERMAID

Ellen's mother invited Ellen and Maggie to tea one afternoon shortly after the ball and when they were comfortably seated, she said to Ellen, "Do you know that you and this young lady have become the center of much speculation among our mutual friends?"

"Whatever for?" Ellen asked, although she thought she knew the answer.

"They insist you have found a new designer and you are keeping it a secret," said Mrs. Twombley.

Ellen and Maggie looked at each other and burst into giggles. "Well," Ellen drawled, "that is not strictly true. But I have found a new designer, and I will be more than happy to reveal the name."

Maggie embarrassed, pleaded, "Oh, Ellen, no!"

Mrs. Twombley, puzzled at the byplay, asked, "Whyever not? Who is it?"

"Maggie!" Ellen announced proudly.

"Maggie? *Our* Maggie? *This* Maggie? This child?" gasped her mother.

Maggie protested, "Oh, Mrs. Twombley, I'm not really a designer. I have always sketched. I do it for my own amusement."

"Of course—the miniature you gave us of Little John, and the one you gave Ellen and John! So you create costumes, too! This is wonderful! Maggie, my dear, if the rest of your designs are as good as the gowns you and Ellen wore at the ball and if you want a profession, all you have to do is let me spread the word to my friends."

Ellen was excited. "What do you think, Maggie? I know you've been restless. Walking with me and playing with the baby is hardly enough to keep you fully occupied. Of course, there are several young men who would be glad to keep you busy . . ."

"No Ellen, I'm not ready for that," Maggie said quickly. "I suppose I am ambitious—I have a lot of ideas for ladies' clothing, but I can sketch and that's absolutely all. I don't sew . . ."

"Then who executed your designs?" Mrs. Twombley asked.

"Madame Landré," Maggie told her.

Ellen took it from there. "She was high in her praise. She told us Maggie would have people knocking on her door after they saw the dresses we wore." Ellen's mind was working fast. Turning to Maggie, she said, "We could give you the whole third floor for a studio. Mother, I think you *should* pass the word along!"

"Wait, please, Ellen," Maggie protested. "You're going too fast. Please think about this. You forget, that means people coming in and out of your home. Why, it would turn it all topsy-turvy! I thank you both for your interest and praise, but I must have some time to think about it, too—although I admit," she added quietly, "I love the idea."

Mrs. Twombley agreed that she wouldn't say anything until Maggie made a decision.

After a week of meetings with Madame Landré, it was decided they would set up business together. Maggie would design and Mme. Landre would see to the execution of her ideas. While Maggie and the Coltons were at their summer home, the sewing room on the third floor was converted according to Maggie's instructions with mirrors, chairs, a drawing table and a tall stool, and a six-inch platform that would be used for fittings. The actual sewing would be done at Lily Landré's flat which was large enough to accommodate two seamstresses in addition to herself.

Over the summer, Ellen took charge of writing announcements to Madame's customers and all Ellen's and her mother's friends. All Maggie had to do was sign them. But she couldn't come up with a suitable name for herself. She didn't want to use the pseudonym Anderson, and she didn't want to be known as just plain Maggie. They decided to let the name go for awhile. When the Coltons and Maggie returned to the city, Madame established an office in the sewing room where she would consult with her customers over the fashions in Maggie's book. When necessary, Maggie would join them to make suggestions or alter a style to make it more becoming to the client.

The venture was an immediate success. Everyone, it seemed, was talking about the "new young designer's" clothes and their list of customers was growing faster than Maggie and Lily could keep up with them. They faced the choice of limiting the number of women they serviced, or expanding their operation and neither were quite sure how to handle that.

At Ellen's suggestion, her father set up a meeting with the three of them. As the owner and president of his own shipping company, Mr. Twombley had access to all the necessary advice and business acumen needed to steer them in the right direction. He admired Maggie, "that little slip of a girl" and was pleased that Ellen was taking such an interest in the project that she no longer pined during her husband's long absences. The upshot of the meeting with Mr. Twombley, his attorneys and accountants, was the purchase of a house, underwritten by Ellen and John, on Avenue A and 58th Street, near the East River. It was the last in a series of brownstones that had been built to house the very rich, but the neighborhood did not improve fast enough to suit most of those who had bought homes there and they were being sold at a price that was more than reasonable. There were coal sheds and breweries to contend with, but the house they decided on had property, which they landscaped; and it was bright and cheerful with a good view of the river and the Long Island countryside beyond.

It was necessary to come up with a name for their corporation. Studying her "little fat fish," Maggie was inspired to combine it with her initials and decided on Miss MerMaid. Ellen and Lily loved it.

"It is certainly better than Miss Fat Fish,". Ellen remarked dryly.

But soon Ellen had mixed emotions over the success of the enterprise she had encouraged. Maggie moved out of the Colton home and into the new house with Madame Landré. She and Lily had more than enough room to use for living space and plenty of space to accommodate six additional seamstresses and their sewing machines.

Money flowed in and Ellen was paid off in the first two years. Miss MerMaid had grown to such proportions that when the house next to them was offered for sale, they bought it immediately. Shortly afterwards, Maggie moved into the new house, leaving the other to Lily and her dressmakers. In her new home she had a bookkeeper and a social secretary who also acted as a companion and chaperone.

Each time the Coltons moved to the Jersey shore for the summer, John was given a two-month vacation during which he renewed his loving relationship with his wife and son. The days were filled with fun, the nights with festivities, as they entertained frequently.

Maggie spent each summer with them. After an early breakfast, she would work on her sketches from nine to twelve on the terrace overlooking the beach. The pale sand and blue ocean were an inspiration which she used to good advantage. Before lunch she took a quick dip, then went back to work for another hour, managing her time so she could have at least an hour with Little John. They played in the sand at the edge of the surf, building castles and forts; the baby worked as industriously to destroy them as Maggie did to build them. He was a happy child and when his papa was at home, Maggie gave the Coltons much time to be together.

To the small, exclusive, coterie of summer dwellers at the shore, Ellen Colton's dinner party was the opening of the season. Her first dinner this particular year was to officially introduce Maggie, though she was already known to many of the ladies who were wearing her Miss MerMaid fashions. Among the guests was Mortimer Sheldon, a leather manufaturer from Massachusetts. He was a childless widower, his wife having died five years earlier. When his eyes first lit on Maggie, his heart beat wildly; he had found the perfect mate. Her diminutive stature, rose-gold hair and delicate features represented the child he never had; her petite, shapely body—a pocket-Venus, he called her—made her a desirable second wife.

Mortimer had little opportunity to get close to her on that first occasion as she was surrounded most of the evening by others equally eager to welcome her. He left early, his mind awhirl with plans to make her his very own.

The following morning, Maggie received a huge bouquet of roses tied with a green satin ribbon. A card was pinned to the ribbon with a diamond brooch: "Please accept this as a token of my deepest admiration," she read, astonished, The card was signed "Mortimer Sheldon" and hard as she tried, she could not remember him.

Four o'clock was the accepted time for

callers and Ellen's home became the only place to be at teatime (although there were stronger libations for those who wanted them). Mortimer was the first to call that day, carrying another tremendous bouquet. When he was announced, Maggie came forward to meet him, took the flowers and asked the maid to put them in water. As she extended her hand he held it too long and kissed it greedily. Inwardly she recoiled from this unprepossessing *old* man. He was approaching fifty and the passing years and his unstinting devotion to business had not been kind to him. His eyes had puffy, dark bags under them, his whole being had sagged and his mouth on her hand felt loose-lipped and wet. Although he didn't resemble the man in the least, a picture of Dr. Henderson flashed in Maggie's mind's eye. A few years ago, Maggie would have run from him; but now she called on her newly acquired sophistication to handle the situation.

"Mr. Sheldon," (she withdrew her hand, wishing she could wipe if off) "thank you for the flowers, but I cannot accept the gift you attached to them." She reached into a pocket of her dress and held out the diamond pin.

He pushed her hand away. "My dear, this is just a token of my affection. There is much more I will give you when we get to know each other better."

"Again I thank you," Maggie said firmly, "but believe me when I say I will *not* accept gifts of jewelry or anything of great value. Flowers if you insist, although I prefer not to receive anything."

Mortimer, delighted by her maidenly reserve, said, "I am a very wealthy man, my dear, and it gives me pleasure to lay treasures at your feet."

Exasperated, Maggie was about to answer when another caller was announced. She thrust the brooch into his hand and with relief moved away to greet the newcomer. She managed to dodge Mortimer's attentions for the rest of the afternoon and was satisfied that she had discouraged this insistent man.

She had not.

Mortimer was obsessed with her extreme youth and enchanting prettiness and called every afternoon, always with flowers and candy, as she had decreed, but also with an expensive trinket hidden among them. A week later he caught her as she tried to skirt him to receive Mark Walden, a young law student who was also smitten with Maggie, but secretly.

"Maggie!" Mortimer grabbed her hand and literally pulled her to the other end of the terrace. "I love you, Maggie. I want you for my wife. Marry me!" He had his hands on her shoulders, trying to draw her close, slobbering wet kisses on her face. With all her strength she wrenched out of his grasp, brought her hand back and slapped him with as much force as she could muster. Ellen, who had witnessed the whole thing, called for John and came running, ostensibly to Maggie's aid, but it wasn't necessary. Mortimer was rubbing his cheek, stunned at the unexpected blow.

John, firmly guiding Mortimer to the door, was angry, but he also felt sorry for the older man. "What in the world is wrong with you, Morty? I told you to leave Maggie alone!" he said.

"I wouldn't hurt her, John. I *love* her," Mortimer whined. "I can do so much for her."

"Why can't you understand that she doesn't want this? She has worked hard to become wealthy in her own right."

"She's only a child! She doesn't know what she wants. I can show her the world," Mortimer persisted.

John took a deep breath and said, "We've been friends for a long time, Morty, and I'm sorry to say this, but I must ask you not to come here again."

"You're being cruel, but I'll be patient. You will see, she'll come to me one day," Mortimer babbled.

"And no more gifts."

"Not even flowers?"

John had him out of the house by this time and said as he handed him his hat, "Not even flowers. Stay away from her!"

Scowling, John turned his back on his former friend.

"Are you all right, Maggie?" John asked softly, having completed his mission. She nodded. "He won't bother you again."

"Thank you, John," said Maggie. "That's the second time you have rescued me from the unwanted advances of a lascivious man!" He raised his eyebrows in question. "Dr. Henderson." He smiled as he acknowledged her statement. He had forgotten about the doctor.

Three weeks before the summer house was to be closed for the winter, Ellen and John gave a beach party that was to continue through dinner and end with a gala ball. It was the last affair of the season and invitations were much sought after.

Judge Walden, Mrs. Walden and their son Mark were seated at the breakfast table when their mail was brought to them. The Judge held up a large square white envelope addressed to him and Mrs. Walden. "Well, Mother, I think this is what you have been waiting for," he said, smiling. There was another for Mr. Mark Walden. He had waited for it much more anxiously than his mother had. He tore open the envelope and with an ear-to-ear grin said, "Yes, this is it—my invitation to the Colton party."

His mother, reading her invitation, nodded and smiled her satisfaction. Judge Walden, watching them, said, "I'm glad it finally came. Now maybe you'll both be fit to live with."

"Now, Father," his wife chided, "you know you look forward to the party, too." He nodded in agreement and, although hesitant to do so, he decided to speak his mind.

"Mark, I know you are enamoured of this young Maggie person. She is indeed a prize." Surprised, Mark waited, not sure he wanted to hear the rest. "However," his father said in his most judicial voice, "you must be sensible. She has many admirers and from what I hear, she prizes her independence and is not ready to make a commitment." Mark wondered where this was leading. "Take my advice and don't press her. Be attentive, thoughtful and always respectful, but put aside all thoughts of marriage. First," he said quickly as Mark was about to protest, "you're not ready for it, either. You have just graduated from law school and your first year with the law firm

298

with which you will be affiliated will be a hard one, requiring much concentration and work. You will not have time for socializing and certainly for nothing as serious as marriage, or even an engagement.''

"Father," Mrs. Walden said sharply, "that's a terrible thing to say to a young man in love!"

Mark spoke up. "Please, folks, there is nothing to argue about. True, I am in love and have already spoken to Maggie about it." He looked crestfallen. "She is not in love with me, or anyone—and as you said, her life is wrapped up in her career. She asked me to remain her friend. I plan to do so. As for my work, Father, you must have faith in my integrity."

His father frowned. "I do, son, but I know love does strange things to people. I'm glad we had this talk."

He rose as did Mark and his rather unhappy mother, who said sadly, "I'm disappointed, I must admit. I was sure Maggie favored you. She doesn't know what she's missing."

Mark laughed out loud, his white teeth gleaming against the coat of tan he had acquired that summer. "Mother, you are the most prejudiced person I know, and I love you for it." He kissed her and went to the bath-house in back of their estate to change for his morning dip in the ocean.

When Peter and Penny Meredith returned from the city, their mail had not yet been read. A little frown formed on Penny's brow as she read the Coltons' invitation. It took her only a few moments to decide what she must do. She wrote a note to Ellen and dispatched it with one of her servants who waited, at Ellen's request, while she answered it. "Dear Penny, Of course your guest is welcome. Aside from the fact that we want you and Peter to be with us, bringing one whom you describe as a darling young man is just what we need to add to the party. Come early and bring your bathing costumes. We looked forward to seeing you and meeting your guest."

XXIII

MARCEL MENNON

On the day of the Colton's beach party, the guests drifted in all afternoon, dressed in casual attire. For the first half-hour Ellen, John and Maggie received the guests and guided them to the bathhouses or directed them to the tennis courts. There was picnic-style lunch on the beach or less informal al fresco dining at small tables set on the veranda.

The ladies waited to see what kind of bathing dresses the hostesses would wear and they weren't disappointed. Ellen was in a bright blue knee-length costume with elbow length sleeves and a deep U-neck. With it she wore a polka-dot cap. Her bloomers, more daring than most, ended just above the calf of her leg, and she wore matching stockings. Maggie was in lavender, completely covered from chin to toes in a one-piece suit that was tight all the way down. She had draped a deep violet skirt from her waist to just above her knees. Instead of a cap, she had wound a violet turban over her hair. Of course, the immediately recognizable MerMaid insignia was embroidered on each dress. The moment they emerged from the cabana, they were surrounded by the women guests.

"You didn't tell us you were designing bathing clothes, Maggie! I *must* have one for my trip to the South of France this year"—or Italy, or Spain—was the tenor of the remarks.

John Colton finally rescued them from their admirers.

Free at last, Maggie ran down the beach to ride the waves. The day was bright and beautiful and the ocean was calm. Giggling, she hugged the amusing secret of her "sophisticated bathing dress" to herself—her delicate complexion burned at the slightest hint of sun and the only way she could enjoy the beach and the water was to cover herself completely from head to toe. Thence her highly original design. As she headed for a fair-sized wave coming in she laughed aloud as she attempted to leap over it. But her timing was off and she found herself engulfed by water, being turned this way and that, trying to get to the surface gasping and fighting for air. Suddenly a strong pair of arms scooped her up, carried her to the beach, stood her on her feet and reaching for her hands, held them high over her head as she choked and coughed. "I'm all right, thank you," she spluttered. She shook her head to get the water out of her eyes and ears and looked up. A tall stranger was standing there, but she couldn't quite focus on his features.

"You are sure? You must be more careful," he scolded in an accent which Maggie recognized as French. "You are too . . . too . . ." he searched for the proper word in English and could only remember the French, "*petite*, you know?"

She nodded. "I *do* know—but I don't know *you*. First let me thank you and then," she extended her hand, "I am Maggie and I must tell you, you are more than welcome. I just might not be standing here otherwise!"

"Do you swim?" the stranger asked. He had taken her hand in a strong grip and didn't show any sign of letting go.

"I thought so, but now I'm not too sure," she laughed.

"I am a strong swimmer. Come with me."

Her vision had cleared by now, and she looked up into his face. Standing before her was a young man with a mop of dark blonde curly hair, expressive, liquid brown eyes, and a physique that emphasized his striking resemblance to representations Maggie had seen of the Greek god, Apollo. He held out his hand and hers trembled as she placed it in his. "You didn't tell me *your* name," she said as she trotted alongside him, pulled along by his grasp on her hand.

"Marcel Mennon," he called back as he ran into the ocean, forcing her to run with him. "I am staying with the Merediths." They ducked under a wavelet and as they came through it together he said, "I would bow, Mademoiselle Maggie, but if I did, I might drown and if I drowned, what would you do?"

She let out a whoop of laughter and swallowed a mouthful of water. Once again he held her above the water, his arms around her waist in a tight embrace. As she spluttered and coughed and finally caught her breath, she still found it hard to breathe normally; he kept her close. "You see? I obviously cannot allow you to swim alone. Lie back in the water."

303

"I will not!" She pouted and played the coquette. She couldn't believe her own behaviour. She had never flirted with anyone before; never had met anyone who interested her enough to inspire her to make the attempt.

"Do not be naughty." He placed her weightless body back down in the water. She had no choice and though he admonished her not to laugh, she couldn't help herself. He lifted her out of the water again.

Flustered, Maggie said, "I think I'd better swim back the rest of the way . . . Oh, my goodness, look!" She pointed to the beach as she came to shallow water and could stand. Mark Walden was dashing madly toward them and Mortimer Sheldon, who had been reluctantly reinstated into the Coltons' good graces, was standing at the edge of the water, wringing his hands. Word had quickly circulated that "Maggie is drowning," or "a young man is trying to drown Maggie!"

Mark let out a shout and the others followed him to the water's edge.

"I'm all right, Mark—we were just having fun!" Maggie cried. Chagrined, he sloshed back, looking anxiously at Marcel whom he had never seen before, then at Maggie. She stifled a giggle as she saw the comic figure of Mortimer Sheldon in a droopy woolen suit, looking for all the world like an elderly buffoon.

John and Ellen came down to see what the fuss was about and Peter Meredith joined them. He groaned as he saw Marcel and Maggie coming out of the water together. "Oh, Lord, that's my guest! I haven't even had time to introduce him, and he's already in trouble."

304

"They don't look as if they're in trouble to me," Ellen laughed. "I've seldom seen Maggie look so carefree and full of fun."

"It's all right, folks," Maggie called out. "Sorry if we worried you. We were just playing a game." She took Marcel by the hand. "We have a newcomer in our midst, the guest of Peter and Penny Meredith—Marcel Mennon." A cheer went up and Peter and John introduced him to those nearest. Mark and Morty walked disconsolately away and consoled themselves with mint juleps, as Ellen threw a large towel around Maggie's shoulders and shooed her to the house to change before she caught a chill.

When Maggie came back she was wearing a pale blue dress and a wide-brimmed leghorn hat with violets nestled under the brim. She sat on the veranda and the butler brought her an iced lemonade. Meanwhile, Marcel had changed, too. He had carelessly slung his white flannel jacket edged not in the usual navy blue but in brown, over his left shoulder. He wore a white shirt open at the neck, and Maggie thought she had never seen a more handsome man in her entire life.

As he came toward her, Maggie's heart rejoiced. She had never seen anyone like him; he delighted her artist's eye. The attraction between them was immediate and strong.

Others joined them, and the afternoon came to an end. The Merediths took Marcel with them when they returned to their own home for dinner and to dress for the ball. Those of the guests who lived nearby went home, too. Those who were staying with the Coltons retired to their rooms and came down in time to partake of the buffet which had been set up in the dining room. The ball didn't start until nine, giving all an opportunity to rest and bathe and dress.

Marcel returned early; Maggie was eagerly waiting for him. As the guests started to straggle into the ballroom, they went out on the terrace, the only place they could be alone. They walked slowly, hand in hand, the soft glow of Japanese lanterns casting flickering shadows on these two vital young people who were rapidly falling in love.

"You must come to Paris, Maggie. I want to show you my world," he whispered into her ear.

"That sounds heavenly," she sighed, "but my work keeps me here."

"We shall see, *cherie*, we shall see."

Maggie was thrilled by the implication of his words. They had reached the end of the terrace and turned to face each other. Maggie's heart was beating so hard she had difficulty breathing; he was like a magnet drawing her closer by sheer animal sensuality. Marcel bent and placed a light kiss, not on her mouth, but just under her ear; she was afraid she might swoon. "Hello, you two—come inside before you catch cold," Ellen called. Maggie blinked as she came back to reality.

Marcel placed his hands on Maggie's bare, trembling shoulders. "Forgive me—you *are* cold." Maggie shook her head as he continued, "I am so warm with love for you, I didn't realize . . ." he kissed her hand; then, holding it tight in his, led her back to the ballroom where a waltz was playing. "Dance with me so I can hold you close," he ordered. He held out his arms and she melted into them. He didn't place his hand on her waist but put his arm around it and held her much more tightly than convention allowed. Maggie, entranced, did not protest. When the dance finished she handed him her dance card. He filled in every space and handed it back with a grin and a wink. In spite of herself, she laughed and returned his wink.

Watching them together, Mortimer Sheldon knew he had lost. Mark Waldon also saw his hopes dashed for any future with Maggie. They both left early.

As the last guest was reluctantly departing, Marcel, ever the gallant, made his proper adieux; he kissed Ellen's hand, shook hands with John and let his eyes pour love into Maggie's; their hearts embraced though they did not touch. Forever after Maggie remembered this day and evening as though it were a beautiful dream.

Marcel had two weeks before his ship sailed to France. He and Maggie spent every possible minute together. The first week they played tennis, swam and walked along the shore. Sometimes they talked and sometimes no words were needed between them.

The second week, Maggie returned to the city and cancelled all appointments. They went to dinner at Delmonico's and to the theatre to see the incomparable Maurice Barrymore. For that week, she lived in a flurry of flowers, champagne, supper clubs and theatre such as she had no idea existed. Marcel, though a visitor from another country, knew more about the world of entertainment in the great city of New York than Ellen or John Colton, who were native-born.

Too soon their time together had passed. The day Marcel left, Maggie went to the ship with him. She stood on the pier and tried to find him among the passengers lining the rails. Suddenly her eye was caught by a cap wildly waved from the main deck. She waved back with her handkerchief and not finding that sufficient, untied the scarf she had knotted around her neck. It was bright red and she had chosen it for just such a purpose. Marcel threw kisses which she caught and returned. As far as they were concerned, they were the only two people in the world. Maggie stood and waved until she could no longer see the ship. She whirled to find John and Ellen at her elbow. They had come, with the Merediths, to wish Marcel *bon voyage.* "We're in love!" Maggie cried. "Madly in love!"

"If it were anyone but you, Maggie," Penny pouted, "my feelings would be very bruised. Marcel didn't even know we were here most of the time."

"I know, I know!" she exulted. "Isn't he the most wonderful, the most . . ." she stopped short and looked from one to the other, blushing. "Don't pay any attention to me—I'm just overexcited."

Ellen hugged her. "This looks very serious, young lady—and I'm so glad! Marcel is a charming and highly eligible young man."

There was no point in answering. Aside from the feeling of love which had enveloped both young people, nothing had been declared, no promises made, except that Marcel vowed he would be back very soon.

Etienne Mennon, Marcel's father, owned the famous vineyards that produced Mennon champagnes and wines. As soon as Marcel arrived home, he had a case of their finest champagne sent to Peter and Penny Meredith, with a special, hand-painted bottle in the case for Maggie.

Maggie's concentration on her work was very deep and rarely could outside thoughts intrude; but now she would be industriously sketching out her ideas for new styles and suddenly the pencil would fall from her hand and she would gaze off into space as Marcel's face, unbidden, would swim into her vision . . .

When Marcel met Maggie he was not quite twenty-one years old. On his twenty-first birthday his father retired and turned the ownership of the Mennon Company over to his only son. Marcel delegated authority to an older man who, as acting president, ran the company very well. Marcel would make it a point to appear in the office every morning and stay for an hour or two, then dash off to lunch and from lunch go on to the salons of his many friends. He was handsome, wealthy and popular with women, from the high social strata of his parents to the little *soubrettes* in the cabarets. He was a good fellow, well liked for his easy disposition and his generosity in freely supplying them with the best champagne in France. Although he made an effort to appear as a businessman, he lived the life of a dilettant. There was more distance between Marcel and Maggie than the Atlantic Ocean.

XXIV

COURTSHIP

Ellen invited Marcel for the Thanksgiving holiday. He arrived early in the week and stayed a week longer. He and Maggie spent every day together. Again, the time flew far too fast.

Instead of the usual *bon voyage* party the night before he was to return to France, Maggie invited him to her home for an intimate dinner. Her housekeeper, Letty, was thrilled that Miss Maggie was going to entertain a gentleman. To make it a very special dinner, she baked squabs and served them on a bed of wild rice. For the first time Maggie brought out the rose-sprinkled Haviland china which had been a housewarming gift from Ellen and John. The silverware and crystal sparkled, as did the star-shaped crystal candelabra over a table covering of lace on a rose linen cloth. A low bowl of tiny roses was in the center of the table between the candles. All the romance in Letty's soul had gone into this labor of love for her Miss Maggie, who was lavish in her praise.

"Just one more thing, Letty," she said. "The ice-bucket on a pedestal."

"I have it ready, Miss Maggie." Letty

brought it out, polished to a bright sheen. She had chopped a cake of ice for half an hour to get the right size pieces in which to bury a bottle of champagne.

Maggie dressed with greater than usual care, selecting one of her own designs, a rose peau de soie, with a deep, softly draped square neck and a triple flounce from her knees to her matching satin pumps. Her hair was combed back into a simple chignon at the nape of her neck. She wore delicate rose pearl earrings and a choker to match. Her efforts were well rewarded when Marcel arrived.

"Ah, Maggie, you are so beautiful!" He held her at arm's length, made her turn around and kissed both her hands. "*Tres chic.*" He put his thumb and forefinger together. "You belong in Paris."

They sipped champagne until Letty, in a neat black uniform and dainty white apron and cap, announced dinner. Their voices were low as they ate and spoke of the enjoyment of the past weeks. Before they had coffee, Maggie took Marcel on a tour of her work place. She showed him her design studio and took him through the sample sewing rooms. He was very impressed. "I had no idea you had such an extensive operation, Maggie!"

"This is the lesser part of it," she said, laughing. "Lily Landré takes care of the manufacturing and most of it is done in her house, which is next door to this."

They returned to the living room. Letty brought in demi-tasse and cognac. Marcel seemed very subdued and was quiet and withdrawn for a long time, deep in thought. "You're very quiet, Marcel. Is anything wrong?" Maggie asked anxiously. They were seated on a velvet-covered settee in front of the large bay window she had had installed to give a view of the river. The ugly buildings surrounding her property disappeared into the magic of the starlit night.

"No," he answered quietly, "not wrong—but I do have a question." Maggie waited, not sure what to expect. She had never seen him so serious before. "Would it be difficult for you to leave all this?" he said after a pause.

She put her hand on his. "Please try to understand, dear. This is my life. It all started with two ball gowns I designed, with no thought of going into business. I can thank Ellen Colton and her family, and Lily, for literally pushing me into a lucrative career. Why do you ask?"

"You know I love you, *cherie*. I think of no one but you." He kissed her hand and drew her close.

"I love you, too, Marcel—but before you ask, I could not give this up, and I know your business is just as important to you. I have never been in love before—it just seems unfair that we should have to be so far apart," she sighed.

"There must be some way . . ." his voice trailed off. He could not think of a solution, either. "I have known many women, but never one I wanted to be with for the rest of my life. Think about it, beloved—we have to find an answer."

But no answer was forthcoming. Before Marcel left he presented Maggie with a diamond-studded monogram pin—with his initials, not hers. "This gift is to remind you of

313

me. Please wear it always," he said as they passionately embraced.

The next few months were busy ones and only their letters kept them in communication with each other. Marcel visited New York once more for two weeks in March, pressing his suit even more ardently than before. Maggie had to force herself to resist his charm and her love for him. Each day it became more difficult to refuse his constant proposals of marriage. It was with a breaking heart that she saw him off once more.

Despite Maggie's lovelorn state, the months passed swiftly and Maggie and Lily were soon finishing the last of the seasonal wardrobe rush and looking forward to vacations. It was no longer possible to take the whole summer for themselves. This year they decided they would spell each other. Maggie was going to Ellen's country house after Lily returned from a visit with her family in France, something she had not dared to dream of before the advent of Miss MerMaid. Maggie's vacation would begin on the fifteenth of July, but she planned on spending weekends and holidays with the Coltons until then.

Ellen's Fourth of July party was in full swing as Maggie and Mark Walden were coming out of the ocean. Suddenly she heard her name called.

"Maggie . . . Maggie!" She whirled at the voice she knew so well even though she hadn't heard it in several months. Abandoning all convention, she flew up the beach and into Marcel's outstretched arms. He held her tight

314

with no thought of what her wet bathing dress would do to his immaculate white suit. Their murmurings were love-laden and emotional between the kisses they rained on each other; "I've missed you so much!" "My darling, it's seemed like forever!" Maggie's heart and mind were aflame as was Marcel's desire. She was limp in his arms as he swept her off her feet and carried her up the beach. She kissed him with a passion she did not know she possessed. As he placed her in a chair in the terrace, there was a spattering of applause from the assembled guests. But it was as though the two of them were alone in the universe. Maggie reached up and pulled his face down to meet hers and gave him another long, lingering kiss. The applause was louder this time. With nary a blush between them they took a bow and kissed lightly again, then Maggie said breathlessly, "Marcel, my love, have a swim while I get dressed! I'll see you on the veranda in thirty minutes."

He arrived on the veranda at the same time she did, both glowing with youth, health and love. They sipped iced drinks and spoke all those tender words lovers say to each other while the other guests left them discreetly alone.

"I have something for you, my sweet," Marcel said as he brought out a velvet box. He opened it to display an exquisite diamond ring in an antique setting. "My darling, this is a family heirloom, passed down through generations to every Mennon bride-to-be. Will you wear it?"

Maggie could no longer resist. "It is the most beautiful ring I have ever seen," she breathed.

"Yes, dearest, I will be proud to wear it and I will cherish it always!" She held out her left hand. He put the ring on her third finger, kissed it, then turned her hand palm up and placed another burning kiss there.

"I have something else for you," he said. "Before I left France, I had a long talk with my parents. My mother gave me the ring along with this note for you." He gave her an envelope which contained a brief, but heart-warming message: "We look forward to knowing our son's dear one. Will you come back with him and spend some time with us? We await you with open hearts and arms."

Marcel held his breath while she read the note. When she looked up, there were tears in her eyes. "What a lovely, warm person your mother must be!" Maggie paused for a long moment. "Lily will be back on the fifteenth and I will be free for a month." She smiled radiantly and continued.

"Yes, Marcel, I would love to know your mother and father. When are you planning to leave?"

Marcel took her in his arms. "You make me so happy, *cherie*," he whispered with his mouth close to her ear. "The next ship is leaving New York for France on the twentieth. Can you be ready?"

"Yes, of course—but I will have much to do before then. I'll have to return to the city tomorrow and begin making preparations. Sweetheart, if you want to stay here I won't mind."

"No, no," Marcel protested. "I want to be where you are."

"You could stay at the Coltons'," Maggie

mused aloud, "but I have a better idea—I will move into Lily's place and you shall stay in mine."

Slyly he suggested, knowing the answer, "Perhaps we could *both* stay in your home?"

"You know better than that," said Maggie, blushing. She didn't admit even to herself how tempting the idea was. Though the physical attraction between them was almost overpowering, Marcel respected Maggie's virginity and had never taken advantage of her youth and inexperience.

That night, the Coltons' party turned into a celebration of the betrothal of Maggie and Marcel. At long last, tired and dizzy from too many toasts, they said a lingering goodnight, and Maggie retired to her room, too excited to sleep. The letter from Marcel's mother had awakened thoughts of her own family and before going to bed, Maggie wrote to them of her engagement. "I will be in Europe until the end of August and hope to spend some time with you if you will have me. I love you all!"

But the next morning she tore the letter to shreds. It still wasn't the right time. She didn't understand her own reluctance to see her family again. Perhaps, she mused, she feared that both she and they would be so changed that they would seem like strangers, and that she couldn't bear . . .

The next two weeks were busy ones. Maggie hardly had time to confer with Lily, making arrangements for her absence. Before the day of her departure, Lily said she had something of importance to discuss. "Can you forego one luncheon with Marcel and have it with me instead?" she asked. Realizing her neglect of the older woman, Maggie readily accepted her invitation.

At first they talked about Lily's visit with her family and how much she had enjoyed being with them. Then she finally came to the reason for her invitation. "Maggie, I would like to suggest that we open a salon in Paris. I'm sure you have noticed that twice a year even our best customers go there to shop. Everyone wants to wear a Worth gown, but it is only because the label guarantees it is a Paris original that makes it important."

"You mean it isn't Monsieur Worth's design?"

"No, no, no!" Lily shrugged her shoulders, in typically French fashion. "I don't mean that. His clothes are exquisite, but no more so than ours. We could give him competition. The field is wide open—Miss MerMaid could become an international house of fashion!"

Maggie took a deep breath. "Good heavens! It never occurred to me that we could become international. I have to think about this. I plan to spend some time in Paris . . . Lily, do you really think we could compete with the House of Worth?" Lily nodded again vigorously. "That's very exciting, Lily! Before I leave, give me some idea where I should look for a proper address for a studio. You know," her eyes were sparkling, "I think it just might be worth a try!"

"I *know* we can do it!" Lily was exuberant at Maggie's acceptance of her suggestion and brought out a bottle of champagne to celebrate; "Mennon Champagne," she pointed out. "The finest there is."

They agreed not to mention the possibility of

a Paris salon to anyone until Maggie returned. "Particularly," Maggie urged, "don't say anything to Marcel. I know I shouldn't keep secrets from him, but he will pressure me to stay whether I think it is right or not."

Lily knew the way of lovers and solemnly agreed not to breathe a word to anyone, not even Maggie's fiancé.

XXV

CHATEAU MENNON

Maggie's luxurious trip to Europe was the complete opposite in every way of her voyage to America. July was the best time to make a crossing, and the steamship made good time. Except that she and Marcel did not consummate their love, it could have been a honeymoon. They mingled with the other first class passengers on occasion, playing shuffleboard and other deck games, but the evenings were theirs for romance.

As they stood on the deck one evening and looked over the black water, Marcel pointed to the golden path of light made by the moon. "I ordered that for you, Maggie dear. Do I get a thank you?"

She reached up with her hands on his shoulders, stood on tiptoe and kissed him. "Thank you, my love, it is quite beautiful— but if I didn't love you so much, I would say that you are taking credit for that over which you have no control," she teased.

"If you love me as much as you say, you would believe *everything* I tell you." He was only half-jesting. "You know," he caressed her face with the back of his hand, "I don't think you love me fully and completely." They were alone on deck and he pulled two deck chairs close together. Maggie stretched out in one, mesmerized by the gentle motion of the ship and Marcel's soothing voice, but now she pulled herself into a sitting position. "That's a terrible thing to say! You know how much I love you!"

He leaned toward her and gently laid one hand on her breast. She recoiled ever so slightly, but Marcel was aware of the motion. "Not enough. You won't even let me touch you. I find it hard to remember your Scotch Presbyterian background."

Maggie laughed. "It's true. I was raised in a strictly moral home. Familiarity before marriage is not permitted," she added primly. "But when you touch me or hold me too close, it is hard for me to hold on to the values I have been taught." She couldn't admit to Marcel that the implication of being possessed brought vividly to mind Dr. Henderson and Mortimer Sheldon. She wanted to give herself to Marcel, but was afraid of the act itself. She had no idea what was expected of her, or more, what to expect.

With a sigh, Marcel answered, "In that case, my dearest, I think we should be married very soon. You would not deny your favors to your husband, would you?"

Maggie's brow wrinkled in a little frown. "Marcel, I have told you over and over, I am not ready for marriage just yet. I am enjoying our courtship—give me more time, please," she entreated.

"As you wish . . ." He rose from his chair, turned on his heel and left her. When he didn't return after half an hour, she went in search of him and found him at the bar. He bowed deeply and almost fell on his face. "My beautiful fiancée, I love you!" he said, slurring his words.

The bartender leaned over and whispered to Maggie, "He's had a little too much to drink—says he's drowning his sorrows."

Maggie flushed. "We had a slight disagreement," she said stiffly. He nodded, knowing the way of a lover's quarrel. "Can you get someone to take him to his cabin?" she asked.

The bartender snapped his fingers and two of the stewards came over and supported Marcel, one on each side, each holding an arm. He went peacefully, blowing kisses to Maggie. Though she was embarrassed, she could not be angry—he looked adorable with his hair falling in his eyes and his knees a little wobbly. And his condition was really all her fault. She would have to give more of herself, or she would lose him, and without Marcel, she didn't know how she'd exist.

A contrite Marcel knocked timidly on her door the next morning. He was hiding behind a large bouquet of flowers and, like a little boy, peeked out from behind them when she opened the door.

Maggie threw her arms around him, knocking the bouquet to the floor. "I'm so sorry! Will you forgive me, darling?" she cried.

He was absolutely nonplussed. "That's what *I'm* supposed to say. I behaved very badly." He couldn't say any more—Maggie's lips were pressed to his, which ended the entire unhappy episode. The rest of the voyage was peaceful. Maggie learned to accept and enjoy

323

his caresses, and he didn't ask for more than that—at least, not now.

They were met at Marseilles by the Mennons' coach and four. After a long ride through beautiful countryside, it was dusk when they entered the Champagne District. Maggie's nervousness increased as they neared the Chateau Mennon. Despite the warmth of Mme. Mennon's note, Maggie envisioned Marcel's mother as a courteously aloof aristocrat, tightly corsetted, with hair stiffly piled high.

They entered a long drive bordered by tall trees which stood like sentinels and rode for almost a half hour before the Chateau came into sight. Maggie let out an exclamation. "Oh, Marcel, it is truly a castle!" There were turrets at each end and elaborate scalloped stonework everywhere on the huge, impressive building.

She clung to Marcel's hand as he helped her out of the carriage and led her up to the terrace to meet his parents, who were waiting for them. They were not at all what Maggie had envisioned Madame Mennon was wearing casual country clothes, her silver hair dressed simply. Her blue eyes expressed the warmth of her outstretched hands as she welcomed Maggie. Except for the color of his eyes, Marcel's good looks were obviously inherited from both parents. His father was a ruggedly handsome man, taller than his son, and very thin, too thin for a man his size, Maggie thought. Streaks of white ran through his dark hair and his brown eyes also held a sincere welcome. Maggie's fears fell away as Madame Mennon kissed her on both cheeks and embraced her. M. Mennon, then took her hands and kissed her forehead.

"Come children, we'll be more comfortable inside," said Mme. Mennon, leading the way through the great double doors. Hand in hand, Maggie and Marcel followed as they entered the Great Hall. Once again Maggie gasped. "This is fairyland!" She had been in many beautiful homes but none as magnificent as this. The tremendous hall had a marble floor veined in black on top of which lay a pastel Aubusson rug. The vaulted ceiling, Marcel explained, was covered with gold leaf, not paint as Maggie had thought. It was so vast that ten chandeliers were needed to shed a proper light.

They went into the drawing room which, in a quieter way, was also breathtaking. The walls were covered in dark red brocade and the furniture was dark, velvet covered and very comfortable. Love seats faced each other in front of the large marble fireplace where they sat to drink Champagne and eat the little *biscottes* that were served by a uniformed butler and maid.

Madame's English was excellent, which made the situation easier as Maggie knew only a smattering of French.

"Marcel, you have chosen well," said M. Mennon in French which Marcel translated for Maggie. "I can see why you are so obsessed by this little beauty."

Marcel tenderly kissed Maggie's hand. "I knew you would love her as much as I do." His parents turned to her, a question in their eyes, and she hastened to reply, "I love your son very, very much! I shall always love him!"

They hugged her and kissed both Maggie and Marcel on both cheeks. Soon afterward, Maggie was shown to her room, and a maid was sent to unpack her belongings.

Maggie had been under a great deal of nervous tension and was emotionally exhausted. She took off her shoes, then said to the maid, "I'm going to lie down for a few minutes . . ." but she was asleep the minute her head touched the pillow. The maid, Felice, pulled a light cover over her, finished her work on tiptoe and didn't return to awaken her until it was time to dress for dinner.

The next two weeks were idyllic. The chateau had its own private park, tennis courts and stables. Maggie and Marcel spent their days enjoying one or the other of these outdoor sports. Sometimes they played croquet, at which Maggie excelled. At tennis, Marcel had the advantage of knowing the game well and having a stronger arm, which brought her down to laughing defeat each time they played. Maggie blossomed under Marcel's devotion and the tender care of his loving family, feeling more like the young girl she actually was than the successful business-woman she had become. Marcel's mother asked her, one day, if they had set a date for their marriage.

Maggie hesitated before replying. "You have accepted me so wholeheartedly without question, I wonder if Marcel has told you that I am one of the few women designers in the fashion business—perhaps the only one?" she said with pardonable pride.

Madame Mennon nodded. "He has told me

something of this. Will it present a problem?"

"I don't think so . . . It is one of the things Marcel and I have to discuss at greater length. He is a businessman and I trust he—and you and Monsieur Mennon, too—will understand that I cannot retire from my own business. It means so much to me and I would be unhappy without it."

"But surely after your marriage . . ." Madame began.

Maggie shook her head. "I would make arrangements so that I could spend most of my time with my husband when he was free, but I could not relinquish the career I have worked so hard to achieve. I am not yet ready to set a date for the wedding. Will you please try to understand?"

"It is most unusual for a wife to work, particularly in our social circle," said Mme. Mennon, "but," she shrugged, "Marcel has never done anything in the usual way. If he accepts it, I'm sure we can; at least I can, I'm not too sure about his father."

"Do you think I should speak to him?" Maggie asked.

Madame remained quiet for a moment, then slowly answered, "No, not yet. Although in his youth he was considered somewhat *avant garde*," Maggie nodded to show she understood the phrase, "he has become more conventional with advancing age."

"That doesn't surprise me," said Maggie. "And yet, I have felt a bond between us . . ."

"Do you know that my husband is an artist?" Madame asked with a hint of pride.

"He is? I guess that explains it! Do you think he would let me see his work?"

"He's very modest . . ." said Mme. Mennon hesitantly.

"I won't mention it unless you give your approval," Maggie assured her.

"You might bring the subject up, but gently. I would prefer that Marcel does not know this, but his father has a weak heart. As you can see, we live a very quiet life and nothing must disturb Etienne. If you meet any resistance, I want your promise that you will not insist."

Maggie rose and kissed her on the cheek. "You have my solemn promise. And I will not mention anything about my career unless he asks me."

"I doubt that he would do that. You see, as far as Etienne is concerned, women don't *have* careers and any talk of marriage is left to the women in the family." She laughed lightly as she remarked, "*bon chance*, Maggie."

"*Merci*," she answered self consciously. "That's about the only French I know! But I study the language. It would certainly lessen the barrier between Monsieur Mennon and me, although we manage fairly well. You and Marcel are very fluent in English."

"And Italian and German and a smattering of others," said Mme. Mennon. "I was raised in a very strict fashion and was tutored in languages and music and all the ladylike graces of my social world. Etienne, on the other hand, came from financially comfortable, landed people. He left the University to pursue his first love, painting. He was doing well when I met him. I was quite young and with a group of girls attended a chaperoned trip to Monmartre to study the art exhibits. It was quite daring; our parents

328

thought we were going to a museum." She smiled, remembering. "Attired in an artist's smock and beret, palette and brush in hand, Etienne made a handsome picture as he allowed himself to be surrounded by us. He asked to paint my portrait, and—well," she broke off bringing herself back to the present, "that's how we met. We fell in love almost at once. One day I'll tell you the rest of the story. We married against my family's wishes and it wasn't until Marcel was born that they became reconciled to Etienne." She put her hand on Maggie's arm. "I forgot to say, I have never regretted a moment of it. We have been very happy together and Marcel, our only child, is our greatest triumph. We love him very much."

Maggie smiled. "Thank you for telling me. I will be gentle with both your loves. Trust me!"

"I do, or I should not have told you the story very few people know."

"I'll let you know how your husband receives me," Maggie promised.

Immediately after she left Mme. Mennon, Maggie fetched her sketch pad and pencils and proceeded to the park where she had been told he would be taking his daily walk. She selected a bench with a view of the formal gardens and the statuary dotted on the lush green grass. Although she was waiting for him, she became so absorbed in what she was sketching, she jumped when he greeted her. "Maggie," he pointed to her and the pad. *"Artiste?"*

"Oui, Monsieur." She handed him the pad and he slowly leafed through it. To Maggie's great relief, at that moment, Madame came up the path. She was greeted with a rapid volley

of French as Etienne again went through the pages, showing her Maggie's sketches. She answered him in the same rapid speech then turned and translated what they had just said.

"I have explained to my husband that the fashion sketches are what you work at, and I have also told him you are a successful fashion designer. He wants to know if you work in Paris."

"No, America," said Maggie. He understood that. "I have a partner who executes my designs." Madame explained *that*.

"Please tell Monsieur Mennon that one day I hope to paint," she asked Madame.

When Mme. Mennon had translated, M. Mennon put his hands on Maggie's shoulders and kissed her on both cheeks. "Ah, that Marcel," he said in French to Madame, who translated for Maggie, "he is a most satisfactory son! Not only does he bring us a daughter to love, but a fellow artist for me."

"*Merci,*" Maggie said as she winked at Madame.

Through his wife, Etienne extended an invitation for Maggie to see some of his paintings. They spent the next hour looking at them. "Have you ever exhibited?" she asked, impressed by his talent and technique.

"*Oui.*" He looked to Madame to help him reply.

"Not lately," she said. "Now he paints only for the pleasure of it. He hopes that when you and Marcel are married, you will visit and you and he can paint together."

At Maggie's request Madame told him that until that time, she and Marcel would come on weekends while Maggie was in France. "But," Maggie said, "tell him he will have to teach me."

Madame translated his reply: "I have so much knowledge to impart and no one to give it to. Your drawing skills, so far as I have seen, are excellent. I can teach you to work with water colors, oils . . ." At this point he took Maggie's hands in his, and she didn't need an interpreter to tell her he was thrilled at her interest and wanted very much to teach her. He spoke again to his wife and she in turn asked Maggie, "What would you like to call us? 'Monsieur' and 'Madame' are far too formal."

"I have given that a lot of thought," said Maggie. "I call my own father Da—I am from Scotland, you know. But I have lived in America for some time now and they call their parents 'Mother' and 'Father,' but I think that's too cold. Would you mind if I call you Mama and Papa?" she finished shyly.

"*Bon, bon,*" he smiled after Madame had translated. "*C'est bon!* It . . . is . . . good," he said in English. They walked back to the house, Maggie setting the pace so he could walk slowly. "I promise to learn *francaise,*" she said to him. "so we can converse." He looked at Madame, thoroughly puzzled and Maggie tried again. "*Parle?*" He nodded. She gave up and asked Mama to finish the sentence, " . . . if you are going to teach me to paint."

Marcel had stayed in the background through most of the visit, although he and Maggie spent many hours together. He wanted

331

his parents and Maggie to get to know each other with none of them depending on him as the intermediary.

By the time Maggie and Marcel left for Paris, they were a loving family.

XXVI

PARIS

At the end of their first week in Paris, Marcel was beginning to be annoyed that Maggie was usually too busy to see him during the day. He said to her over dinner one night, "Maggie, it is time to tell me what you do all day. I never see you until the evening."

Maggie, who had been bursting with the project she'd kept secret for so long, said, "Yes, darling, it is time. I wanted to be sure before saying anything about my plans but now, I need your help."

"What is it, love? You must not keep secrets from the man you intend to marry," Marcel chided.

So Maggie told him of her plans to open her own salon in Paris. He was overjoyed since he had feared he would never be able to persuade her to give up her business in America and settle down in France with him. "You mean we can be married and you will live here with me?" he asked.

Maggie hesitated. "That's one of the things we must discuss. I cannot give up my American business, but I can put Lily in charge and visit there three or four times a year. Will you accept that?"

"That presents no difficulties. I visit America almost that often anyway," said Marcel cheerfully.

"But will it bother you to have a wife who works?" Maggie persisted. "I know it is unconventional, but I can't give it up." He hesitated briefly, frowning. "Would you like to think about it?" she asked.

But Marcel's frown had been replaced by a smile. "It is not necessary, *ma cherie*. While it is unusual for a wife, particularly the wife of a wealthy man, to run a business, I will be proud of your creativity." She leaped up and threw her arms around his neck.

"I love you, Marcel, so much!" she cried happily.

"And you know I love you and anything you want to make you happy, makes me happy." Marcel held her close. "You still haven't told me what has kept you so busy."

"Oh, well . . . I have been trying to find the right location to live and to show my designs," Maggie told him excitedly.

"Together in the same place?"

"Yes—that's how I work at home. I showed you my house, and Lily's."

"You are looking for a house?"

"No, no! After looking at the places of fashion on, among other places, Avenue Montaigne, I have decided I want something very different." His amused look said, "of course." "I will need you to bring the pressure of your prestige to bear on Monsieur Albert of the Grand Hotel."

The frown came back. "I am completely confused. Tell me again what it is you wish. Le Grand Hotel? I don't understand."

Maggie spun away from his embrace, too excited to stand still. "I have seen the top floor of the hotel and it is perfect for my needs! It is bright, with good light, and spacious. I could use half for living quarters and the other half for the salon."

"You, my dear one, are most innovative," said Marcel, concealing his dismay. Would she continue to live there after their marriage—insist on separate residences? *Mon dieu!*

"Thank you for not being shocked at my ideas. Monsieur Albert threw up his hands in horror when I expressed my desire to have that space," Maggie chirped.

"Would that not be prohibitive in cost?"

"That's what I would like you to find out for me. I don't understand the French monetary system and I'm at a complete loss there. Also, he is a little reluctant to have any kind of business in the hotel. But if you could assure him that only the very best people would be going in and out, I think he would permit it. I told him this, but all he did was shake his head —in spite of which, he made another appointment so that I could bring you to speak to him."

Marcel drew her back into his arms. "I have an idea our life will be a series of surprises and, my darling, I will be there for you whenever you need me. When do we see Monsieur Albert?"

And so the appointment was kept, the contract signed, and arrangements were made for Maggie to have the necessary renovations attended to by Marcel while she returned to America. In any other circumstance, she might have resented the carpenters and decorator and hotel staff taking their orders from someone other than herself, but in this case it was for the best as Marcel would be sure to see that her plans were carried out.

Maggie tucked a duplicate set of plans in the bottom of her carryall so she could study them on the long voyage home, and filled the last week of her stay in Paris with Marcel and gaiety and meeting his friends. There was a party every night—although Marcel said they were not parties but a way of life. The Left Bank was where they usually wound up and where Maggie met the most interesting people —poets, artists, writers, practitioners of all the arts she knew and some she had only heard about. Wherever they went, Marcel was greeted with open arms, particularly, she was quick to notice, by the ladies. They embraced him and kissed him and when he had freed himself from their embrace and introduced his fiancée, they would give her a cursory glance and a nod and continue their caresses until Marcel, laughing, uncoiled their arms. This happened time after time and after the third night, Maggie accepted it with an equanimity she had to pretend. However, by then she, too, was greeted with kisses by the men at the various soirees they attended. It seemed to be customary, even obligatory among Marcel's arty set. Marcel watched her closely to judge her reaction. These were his friends and she must learn to share them and be one of them. Maggie was not really comfortable with this free and easy way of life, drinking and dancing and loving, it seemed to her, with whoever happened to be near at the moment, but she was a better actress than he knew. As her sophistication grew, her revulsion was buried so deeply that sometimes she forgot it was there.

By the Friday before their last weekend together, Maggie was exhausted. They visited Marcel's parents at the chateau, and Maggie spent a delightful few hours with Papa Mennon. He sat her down beside him in the formal garden where he had set up his easel and explained what he was doing as he painted the scene before him. He showed her how to mix colors, a subject she was familiar with in water-colors though not in oils, and had her paint a crimson rose before she left. Maggie told him all about her chosen profession and that she intended to continue after marriage, this by courtesy of Mama, who had joined them. She smiled as she translated, "You have too much talent to bury it. Use it the best way you know how. We are all proud of you."

Marcel came along in time to witness the kisses and Mama's tears of happiness and relief. He kissed them both, then took Maggie in his arms. Mama and Papa Mennon beamed as they watched the love-birds. Suddenly self-conscious, Maggie gently pushed Marcel away.

"Now, children," Mama was still dewy-eyed, "have you set a date for the wedding?"

"Maggie?" Marcel said hopefully.

"We haven't talked about it, but I know when I would like it to be—if, sweetheart, it is agreeable to you," said Maggie with a shy smile.

"Any time, any time you say!"

"Let me explain. When I return to New York, Lily, my partner," she began, "and I will

337

have to go over schedules and make decisions that each of us will be handling separately in the future, she in America and me in Paris." She smiled. "It's ironic, you know—Lily is French and she should be taking care of the Paris branch."

"Oh no, *ma petite chou*, not with me!" Marcel laughed.

"Chou?" Maggie repeated, puzzled.

"Cabbage," he answered with a grin.

"You call me a *cabbage?*" Maggie cried. The Mennons laughed heartily at her consternation.

"It is a term of endearment, Maggie," Mama assured her.

Maggie gave a very Gallic shrug. "Then I guess I'll have to get used to that kind of endearment." She joined in the laughter. "But in Scotland, to call someone a vegetable wouldn't exactly be a compliment!"

"When, darling? When?" Marcel asked impatiently, reverting back to the original topic of the wedding date.

"How does the first of May suit you?" Maggie asked.

He frowned. "That's a long time away," he objected.

"I was about to tell you how I came to that. It will be the first week in November when I arrive in New York. I will have a million things to do, both personal and in my business. I want to be able to fully relax and enjoy you, my own, when I return. Besides, it will take at least that long for you to get the salon and our living quarters ready."

Marcel shook his head in reluctant agreement. "I guess that's so. All right—May first it is."

Papa had the best champagne brought out and in the formal garden, they toasted the wedding date and drank until they were all teary over M. and Mme. Mennon gaining a daughter and Maggie, the husband she adored.

The November wind off the river was brisk, and Ellen Colton shivered slightly as she waited for Maggie to disembark. At long last she spotted her, wrapped in a seal cape and wearing a smallish hat to match, coming down the gangplank. "Maggie, here!" Ellen cried, waving wildly. Maggie ran to the bottom and into her friend's arms. "Oh, my dear, you look *so* French," said Ellen, holding her at arm's length to admire her stylish garb.

"Merci, Madame Colton," Ellen was impressed by this brief burst of French and looked closely at Maggie, who was not able to contain her mirth. "Don't answer me in French —that's just about all I know—but next year this time, I will be able to converse with you in fluent French. After all, Ellen, when one's husband is French, one must learn the language!"

As soon as they were seated in Ellen's carriage, Ellen said excitedly, "You've set the date! At last! I want to hear all about your trip and Marcel and his parents and . . ."

"Wait," Maggie laughed. "I'll tell you at lunch." She looked out at the hustle and bustle of the city as they drove along. "I love Paris, but I'm afraid I'll miss the stimulation of New York," she sighed.

"You're going to *live* there?" Ellen was dismayed. "Oh, Maggie, what will I do without you?" She had been so entranced by Maggie's romance it hadn't occurred to her that of course she would live where her husband made his home.

After they reached the Coltons' house and had removed their outer garments, Maggie spent a half hour playing with Little John, who had grown tremendously, and then she and Ellen sat and talked about the forthcoming wedding. "We will be married at the chateau; you will love Marcel's parents, Ellen, they are so wonderful!" Maggie bubbled. On and on they went, going from one topic to another, barely tasting the lunch that was set before them. Finally Maggie said, "I must go home now. I have so much to do to get our business situation straightened out." She had told Ellen all about her new salon that was being designed and how competently Marcel was taking charge and how open-minded Madame and Monsieur Mennon had been about her career.

"But we haven't discussed what you'll wear to the wedding," said Ellen as Maggie put on her wraps.

"I have a few ideas, but that will have to wait. We have over three months to decide. My first project will be to spend time with Lily, get our books in order and make up announcements to send to our customers here, informing them about our Paris Salon. The more we can do in advance, the less we will have to worry about the correspondence that takes so long to cross the ocean."

Ellen hugged her. "I am so proud of you,

dear! You have managed the business so well and now, a happy marriage."

Maggie returned her hug. "All thanks to you. If you and John hadn't rescued me from the Horrible Hendersons, only God knows what would have happened to me! And," she added quickly, "if you hadn't pushed me into designing, I'd still be doing little sketches for my own amusement, and I'd probably be somebody's governess in a plain black frock!"

"And now, we'll have an ocean between us," Ellen sighed. "Methinks, my dear Maggie, I have created a monster!"

Maggie kissed her. "Not at all. I'll be here at least four times a year, and there's no reason why you can't visit me . . . *us.*" She grinned. "I must remember I will no longer be 'me' but 'us.'"

Lily was overjoyed at Maggie's description of their Paris salon and modestly accepted her fervent praise for being the inspiration for such a venture. Although she gave no indication of her disappointment, she had hoped to be the Director of the Paris branch. However, she was happy for Maggie's forthcoming marriage to a scion of the champagne industry, and naturally, whither Marcel went, there must Maggie go also. Every day of the ensuing months was filled with meetings with Lily and the accountant and finally, with an attorney to draw up the proper papers that would make Lily Landré a full partner in both establishments.

Ellen wrote to John to apprise him of Maggie's approaching marriage in France:

"Please get in touch with my father and ask him to arrange your schedule so that you can be present." Between John and Mr. Twombley they worked out a fine schedule. John would return to New York in April and Ellen would go back to France with him on his ship, where he would relinquish his command for a month. "It will give us time for the wedding and a second honeymoon," he wrote. Ellen was thrilled when she first read the letter but then doubts assailed her. She had never been away from Little John and while he had a perfect nanny, she would miss him terribly. It took a little while and a lot of talking to herself to adjust her thinking. John's profession took him away a good part of the time and he would occasionally want her to travel with him. This was the first time and therefore the most difficult. Eventually, she knew, as the boy grew older he would accompany them. And besides, she wouldn't miss Maggie's wedding for the world! Having come to this conclusion she put all doubts behind her as she prepared for the trip.

Ellen also sent out invitations for a party in Maggie's honor, both as a *bon voyage* and a celebration of the forthcoming marriage. Gifts tumbled in one after the other. Maggie displayed them in her home and gave a small reception so they could be viewed, after which she told Letty to make a list of names and addresses of the guests and note what each had given. "Have it ready before I leave and I will write my thank-you notes on the ship," she said. She also told Letty to take anything she would like to have, then distribute the rest around the house or pack them away for future use. The only gift she kept, oddly enough, came from Mortimer Sheldon; it was a clock of gold, with a singing bird which signalled the hour with the fluid notes of a lark. This she packed herself to take to France. Morty had enclosed a sad little note: "This little bird reminds me of you. I hope that when he sings, you will sometimes think of me." It wasn't the sentiment that impressed her but the exquisite workmanship that brought the little cloisonne bluebird, covered with real plumage, out of his gilded cage as his melodious notes floated into the air.

On the day of her departure, Maggie walked through the rooms of the home she had created with such care. She felt almost guilty at her sudden reluctance to leave it. Her housekeeper was sadly waiting for her at the door. "Take care of my lovely things, Letty," Maggie told her. "I have left money for you on the kitchen table, and Lily will give you a check every month. If you need anything, ask her." Letty broke down and started to cry. "Don't cry!" Maggie embraced her. "I will be back soon."

The coachman came at that moment. There was little baggage to be loaded, as the trunks containing Maggie's trousseau and wedding dress had been sent ahead to the ship. Letty dried her tears and stood in the doorway as the carriage moved off down the street, waving a sad farewell.

Marcel was waiting for her at Marseilles and bounded halfway up the gangplank to greet her with hugs and kisses. "Six months, *ma petite chou*—I thought it would never end!"

They embraced again and not until the passengers waiting in back of them to disembark made loud comments, did they realize they were holding up the line. Happily, Marcel put his arm around her waist and guided her down. "Let me look at you, my love! You are more beautiful than I remembered. You look like a saucy little girl in that French sailor's beret," he told her.

"Not quite, dear. Actually, it is a modified tam-o'-shanter, worn straight on my head like a French sailor's hat. I had it made to match this traveling suit." She didn't explain that she had adapted the Maccrae tartan in silk poplin. The dark background made it practical for taveling and the turquoise was flattering to her eyes. It was the only reminder of her heritage that she permitted herself.

"I never knew your eyes were so blue," he commented.

"Enough about me!" Glowing with love, her expression suddenly changed as she looked at him closely. "You look pale, dearest. Have you been ill?"

He laughed and shrugged off her concern. "No—there was a party given me last night— I think you would call it a 'bachelor party'."

She nodded. "Yes—it is a terrible tradition, but I guess it is celebrated the world over. If that's all it is, I won't worry." She put her arm through his. "Will we have time to stop at the hotel before we go to the chateau? I'm so anxious to see how everything turned out!"

"I hope you like it, Maggie. We worked very hard to make it exactly as you planned," he said enthusiastically.

They went to the salon first. When Maggie

saw what had been done, she was ecstatic. "You've done a beautiful job, darling!" she cried. "It's even more handsome than I anticipated."

"Where do you get your ideas? I have never seen a salon set up like this," said Marcel. "But I followed your instructions word for word."

"You mean the lowered platform that runs the length of the room, and the seats on either side of it?" He nodded. "I thought I had explained that. I will, of course, show my clothes on models, and it is difficult to see from seats that are lined up all across the room, particularly if all seats are on the same level. That's why I wanted the floor raked on either side. This way, the audience can get a full view of the garments as the models walk down the runway."

"It's a tremendous innovation," he said with a kiss.

"I hope it works," said Maggie, crossing her fingers.

"Oh, it will, Maggie," he assured her. "I can't wait for Charles to see it."

"Charles?"

"Charles Worth."

"The famous designer?" Maggie gasped.

"He's become a friend of mine. I met him recently and he made no effort to hide his amusement that an American, and a female to boot, would try to compete with him."

Maggie shook her head. "He was wrong, dear. I have no intention of competing with him. I am confident that I can build my own following." She walked around the large theatre-like room, gazing enraptured at the champagne silk walls and Empire furniture with coral brocade seat cushions. Instead of the currently popular heavy brocade drapes at the long floor-to-ceiling windows, Maggie had designed champagne-colored voile drapes with tiny coral "mermaids" woven into the design. She threw her arms around Marcel. "Thank you, dearest! It is absolutely *perfect*. If you didn't have your own business, we could work well as a team."

Marcel held her close. "My dear, sweet, Maggie. I wouldn't go through this again for all the money in the world—but I'm delighted that you approve. Come—you haven't seen our living quarters yet." He took her hand and they walked down the long corridor to the front of the building and the entrance to the apartment. Maggie stepped into the foyer and let out her breath slowly. "Beautiful," she murmured. The walls were ivory with a stripe of the same color in satin. A pink marble-top commode with a porcelain card tray on it and one small gilt chair were the only pieces of furniture, but set the pattern for the authentic Louis XIV furnishings throughout the other rooms. The bedroom made her blush; a sunburst of very pale pink satin served as a canopy over the ivory and gilt bedstead which was covered with lush lace and had a ruffled counterpane and heaps of lace and satin pillows.

Marcel waited for some comment and when none was forthcoming, asked, "How do you like our bridal bed?"

While the decorations of the flat were hers, the *boudoir* was his contribution. It took her a long moment to find the proper words. "It is extravagantly exquisite," she said at last.

He stood behind her, placing his hands on her breasts. She loved him so much, and his touch thrilled her, but it came as a shock that he was deliberately trying to arouse her. Still standing behind her, with his hands now in full possession of her breasts, he leaned his body against hers, gently propelling her toward the bed. Maggie felt her resistance ebbing; she was passionately excited but still had enough strength of will to be angry.

She whirled and pushed him away. "No, Marcel, *No*—not yet!" She put her hand to her head. "I am so confused . . ."

She didn't recognize that his grin was sardonic. "We've got to be married first, is that it?" She knew he was amused by her naivete. "Very well, my pet, I can wait."

He made her feel guilty for her reaction, and she attempted to explain why she felt as she did.

"Please remember, Marcel, that I have had a lot of male friends but never an—*intimate* one. I . . . I am not sure what is expected of me."

"You mean you and Ellen didn't discuss the duties of a married woman?" asked Marcel, astonished.

Maggie didn't much care for this conversation and she shook her head self-conscioiusly. She felt compelled to say something. "We had sort of planned to, but I was so busy, we just didn't have time."

Her innocence and youth never failed to delight him. "Don't worry. I shall teach you slowly and tenderly," he promised, kissing her chastely on the cheek and releasing her from his embrace. "For want of a more interesting activity, let's look at the rest of the rooms."

The kitchen was as she had planned it and the bath, again a sensuous touch by Marcel, was in pink marble. The parlor repeated the colors in the foyer and the long French doors which opened on a balcony were draped in the palest pink. On the floor was an exquisite Aubusson rug of cream, pink and blue. The Louis XIV furniture had been upholstered in the blue of the rug. Maggie, delighted, stood in the middle of the room. "It is lovely, dear! I love it."

"It is you, darling, just you."

"Mmm . . . that's the only thing I'm concerned about," Maggie admitted. "When you changed the bedroom accessories . . ." (she hated to bring up the subject of the bedroom) "well, I had planned to have a Dubonnet bedspread and drapes to provide a masculine touch so you would be comfortable. Will all those delicate frills bother you?"

Marcel smiled to himself. If she only knew! he was thinking. How many boudoirs have I been in that look exactly like this one? Aloud, he said, "Anything that will remind me of you, my sweet, is what I will be comfortable with." He had no intention of telling her that he would not be giving up his own bachelor flat, furnished as befitted his status and lifestyle. His rooms were on the Left Bank in a building he owned; the extra rooms were often used by any of his guests who were too inebriated to make it home after one of his famous parties.

Maggie didn't notice his silence. She was wandering through the flat again, looking in cupboards, checking the housekeeper's room off the kitchen with its own bath and finally, coming back to the bedroom to unpack. When she came to the gold clock, "Darling," she called, "come and see this beautiful gift!" Marcel admired it and carried it very carefully to the pink marble mantel over the fireplace in the bedroom.

They stood, their arms around each others' waists. Impulsively she turned and threw her arms around him. "Oh, Marcel, it is *perfect!* Everything is absolutely perfect. I love it, and I love you. Just think how lovely it will be to come here and relax after a hard day's work!"

Again Marcel didn't commit himself, knowing full well that he would spend many a night in his "bachelor" flat. He went into the kitchen where he had stored a few bottles of champagne and returned with a tray on which there was a crystal ice bucket in which a bottle of the wine was being chilled, and two fragile goblets, part of a set of Baccarat crystal given as a wedding present by his parents. They drank a toast to each other and Marcel filled their glasses a second time. After Maggie had drunk half of hers, she reminded him that they would have to leave immediately for the chateau or stay over until the next day.

"Would you rather stay here tonight?" Marcel asked.

"No, I'm eager to see your parents. I'm sure they're waiting for us. Is Papa feeling better? You told me in your letters he hadn't been well."

"No, I'm afraid he isn't improving. He never complains, but he doesn't have much strength."

"I am so sorry," Maggie sighed, putting down her glass. "Are you ready?" He nodded and quickly finished the champagne left in the bottle.

XXVII

THE WEDDING

The wedding was simple, with no attendants for either bride or groom. Maggie didn't have an heirloom dress, not even from Mama Mennon, who had eloped. So she had done research in libraries and museums and then went to work to design a wedding dress different from all others, one which she hoped would one day become an heirloom in her and Marcel's own family. Her basic inspiration was the dress of a famous ballerina, and when it had been completed, it was perfect for one as petite as Maggie. The bouffant skirt was made of layers of pointe d'esprit, with a U-neck edged with the tiniest moss roses, puffed sleeves tight at the wrists and each fastened with a rose. Her veil, of the same net, was shoulder length in front and longer in the back. She wore a wreath of roses and carried Mama Mennon's family bible with a cascade of ribbons and roses. Her tiny pink slippers were styled like a ballerina's. Papa made her promise to pose for him in her wedding dress when she and Marcel returned from their honeymoon.

Maggie's heart was in her eyes when Marcel lifted her veil and they sealed their troth with a long, loving kiss. "Now," she whispered, "I am truly yours, forever and ever."

"This is the most beautiful moment of my life, my very own Madame Mennon. Now I know why I remained a bachelor for so long," said Marcel, smiling.

Maggie had suggested the ceremony be held on the first terrace; it made it easier for Papa, now in a wheelchair, to attend. Maggie called him Marcel's "best man," which made him laugh. He didn't laugh very often these days since his health had begun to fail.

Only a few close friends had been invited, among them John and Ellen Colton, who were slightly in awe of their impressive surroundings. The second terrace had been lavishly decorated with fresh flowers. A sumptuous buffet was set up and the wedding cake wheeled in a little earlier than it might have been if Papa had been feeling better. It was obvious that his strength was waning and Maggie and Mama wanted him to enjoy as much of his only son's wedding day as possible.

After Maggie had changed into her traveling costume, the bride and groom left with a kiss and a hug for everyone and a special one from Mama and Papa. "We won't be gone long, Mama," Maggie whispered. "You need us with you." Marcel had offered to delay the honeymoon but Mme. Mennon had insisted that they leave. Maggie told Papa, "Rest until we come back. Remember, you have so much to teach me about painting that you'll need to save up all your strength!"

Papa Mennon feebly waved goodbye. He waited until they could no longer see him before he permitted tears to flow down his cheeks. His nurse wheeled him back to his room as Mama bade the guests farewell.

Because of Marcel's father's illness, the honeymoon plans had been changed. Their original intention had been to go to Rome, Venice and Florence and spend a month enjoying those places which Maggie had never been. Instead, Marcel agreed with Maggie that they should not stay away for more than ten days. "I'll show you a part of France that will surprise you," he suggested. "You've seen Paris and our Champagne country—now I'll show you Normandy."

The choice was inspired. Maggie's first sight of the great spired monastery of Mont St. Michel was awesome. Though Marcel was jealous of anything that distracted Maggie's attention from him for more than ten minutes at a time, he suggested she bring her sketch book along. Hand in hand they explored the fishing villages, the markets at Rouen, and the great cathedrals, and steeped themselves in the history of Normandy. While Maggie did not usually set up her easel with other artists, she did join them for a while to paint the picturesque fishermen and their little boats which were decorated with flowers on special occasions.

Marcel had kept his promise to initiate Maggie into the ritual of the marriage bed gently. Frightened by the unknown and anxious to please, she let him guide her, and discovered an ecstasy she had never dreamed existed, but his own desire was quenched somewhat while trying to elicit from her a

353

more passionate response. He knew this would happen eventually and suppressed his own impatience at her maidenly reserve. His reward at this early stage of their marriage was the new radiance that surrounded his young bride.

When they returned to Paris, they went straight to their elegant flat in the Grand Hotel. Marcel swept Maggie up in his arms and with much laughter, carried her over the threshold and straight into the bedroom where he placed her on the bed and threw himself on top of her. They were both fully clothed—in fact, Maggie still had her hat on. "No, no, Marcel," she cried, still laughing. "Not now, dear—not in broad daylight!"

"Oh, Maggie, how long will it take for you to reach for me at any time of the day or night? You still have so much to learn!" There was a little edge of anger to his voice as he petulantly strode out of the room and poured himself a tumbler of cognac.

Maggie followed and put her arms around him. "Please, dearest, you know I love you. It's just that I . . . well . . ." she didn't know quite how to explain, "I guess I feel that nighttime is the time for lovemaking."

Marcel laughed a mirthless laugh. "Where did you get that interesting piece of misinformation?"

She felt guilty as she faltered, "It—it's just the way I feel."

He shrugged. "All right, *ma cherie*, have it your way—until I teach you that you are wrong." He kissed the tip of her nose and handed her a snifter of cognac. She didn't want that, either, but thought it best not to say so. Instead, she offered a toast: "To our new home and happiness, now and forever!" He poured another drink for himself as he joined in the toast, and then another.

Maggie turned away to go into the bedroom. "I'm going to change into fresh clothes, dear. It's almost time to leave for the chateau." She said nothing about his drinking, but for some time now she had noticed he drank more than she considered necessary, and it disturbed her.

"We just got home. We can go tomorrow," said Marcel casually.

"But your parents are expecting us; it's early—we can be there in time for dinner. Aren't you a little anxious about your father?"

Marcel, irritated, took a swallow of cognac. "You know, we could go tomorrow and stay a few days," he suggested.

"You're forgetting, sweetheart, we only have tonight and tomorrow. We'll have to return on Sunday."

He raised his eyebrows. "Why?"

"You have to go back to work on Monday and I can't wait to get into my new studio!"

Marcel shrugged mentally. He began to doubt he would ever get used to a working wife, particularly one as dedicated to her career as Maggie. He took several drinks in quick succession while she was changing; then, holding her hand, he slept most of the way to the chateau.

It was a beautiful late spring day, the air sweet with the fragrance of budding trees and flowers. Papa had just been wheeled in from the terrace with Mama at his side when Maggie and Marcel arrived and their greeting was warm and emotional. Papa's nurse pointed out that it was time for him to go upstairs for a rest, but he insisted on hearing about their honeymoon in Normandy. Maggie had brought her sketches with her and she and Papa sat side by side as she showed them to him. He had been working hard for months at improving his command of English, so Mama no longer had to act as interpreter. Marcel, bored with rehashing their trip, excused himself to go, as he said, "to the vineyards."

"I am planning to base my new collection on the native styles," Maggie said. "Look at this!" She showed a drawing of a man wearing a puffed black cap and a bright blue smock with a red scarf knotted loosely around a short, pointed collar of white. "So picturesque," she said as Papa nodded his agreement. "We went, briefly, from Mont St. Michel into Brittany and there—look here." She pointed to a sketch of two women, both in black and wearing the traditional headdress, a tall, cylindrical starched lace hat, easily a foot tall, tied under the chin. "Of course," she said, "I will cut it down to a proper size and perhaps add a small brim."

Papa picked up her hand and kissed it. "You are a beautiful artist with great perception," he said gallantly. Blushing with pride, Maggie thanked him.

"*Merci*, Papa." She stroked his cheek and kissed the top of his head. His nurse, who had been standing by, insisted that it was time for him to rest, and Maggie and Mama accompanied his chair into the chateau.

Over the next six months, Maggie's sophistication in living and lovemaking increased, but she was never aggressive in either. Although she went along with Marcel's desire to be with his artistic friends every night and drank a little more champagne than she wanted, she did it only as her duty as a wife. She did not enjoy spending virtually every night in a cafe and she had decided that she did not particularly like his friends. She did enjoy going to bed with Marcel and making love, but by now he despaired of her ever participating in the wild, hurting passion he craved.

One Friday Marcel left his office in the middle of the day and went to Maggie's studio. She was working out a complicated design and didn't hear him come in. He tiptoed up behind her and put his hands over her eyes. "Guess who, *petite,*" he said, kissing her neck. He hoped for an ardent response to match his desire. She stopped drawing, the tip of the pencil in her mouth, looked up at him, smiled and patted his cheek, then returned to her sketch.

Marcel frowned, annoyed at her lack of response. "Maggie," he put his mouth close to her ear, "it's your husband, come to make love to you. Come inside, darling."

"Please, dear, you're in my light." She gave him a little push.

"Will you put that damned pencil down?" His voice rose.

Maggie frowned, did as he asked, and scolded, "I can't leave this now." She looked at her watch. "Why aren't you at your office?"

For answer, Marcel lifted her out of her chair and started to carry her out of the studio. Maggie, unamused, struggled and pushed at him. Marcel only held her more tightly. "What's wrong with you?" he grumbled. "I came to make love to you and you look at your watch! You do everything by the clock," he went on, "even make love! It's time you learned that your husband is a Frenchman. We make love when our passions are stirred."

By now Maggie was getting angry. "It seems to me your passions are stirred all the time! Let's not have a scene, Marcel. *Put me down.* I wanted to finish my work so we could go out and visit your parents." When at last he put her down, she marched over to the drawing board, stacked everything neatly and put her drawings to one side.

"I'm tired of this routine, Maggie!" Marcel shouted, equally angry. "If it's not your work that keeps you from me, it's my parents. I think you care more for my father than you do for me!"

Maggie sighed. "You sound like a jealous child. I can't get up from my desk and have someone take over for me, as you do. As for spending time with your father, you should be ashamed of yourself. You know he's very ill and the time we spend there helps both Mama and him. You're full of surprises, Marcel, and some of them I don't like very much."

"We haven't been married long enough for us to have arguments," said Marcel, beginning to calm down. "I just—well, I thought we'd be together more than we are. I didn't mean it about my father," he was remorseful. "I just wish we had more time to ourselves."

In the few months they had been married, Maggie had seen more and more a side of her husband she hadn't known; a spoiled child who had not fully grown up; a child whose every wish had to be instantly granted. But she loved him, and now she made a suggestion. "There's one way we can accomplish that, darling. If we stay home a few nights instead of partying all the time . . ."

"How many times must I tell you we do not 'party,' as you call it. We just join our friends. Do you want me to give them up?" he asked petulantly.

Maggie sighed. "It's time for lunch. I'll close up the studio. I promised your mother we would be out early today."

"Good. We can eat here and then . . ."

"No, not today. We'll eat downstairs in the dining room and leave from there." Marcel was sulking. Maggie knew she was being mean but he had to learn, she was determined, that she couldn't jump into bed with him whenever he wanted, which seemed to be all the time.

They didn't speak much on the way to the chateau. Maggie filled her eyes with the golden fields of mustard blossoms they passed and thought about the painting she was going to do at Papa's bedside. He was wheeled down to the terrace for an hour whenever she and Marcel visited, and with hand signals, more than with his weak voice, he would instruct her. She had learned much and he was pleased that she was becoming a fine artist. Marcel would chat with his mother for a while and then wander off, ostensibly to read a book or take a walk. He would reappear at dinner, not quite sober. After dinner, he continued to sip cognac and resisted all Maggie's efforts to get him to retire early. When he did stagger to their bedroom, he would make love to her in a brutal fashion that left her aching and unfulfilled. Often she thought he murmured someone else's name. Maggie was at a loss, not knowing how to handle him when he was this way. She couldn't talk to his mother about it, and knew no one else to confide in. Marcel was always contrite the next day. He excused his indulgence in drink by saying that a weekend at the chateau was boring with nothing for him to do. Marcel had never been a devoted son. Before his marriage to Maggie he had visited the chateau occasionally, when he had no important social engagement elsewhere.

"What would you be doing on a weekend if you weren't here, love?" Maggie asked once.

He answered irritably, "How can you ask such a stupid question? Do you realize how much fun we're missing? Weekends in Paris are fantastic!"

The retort that rose to her lips was an angry one, but rather than get into another one of the endless arguments that took place each week, she shrugged and walked away.

They had been married ten months when Marcel told her he had urgent business that would keep him from going to the chateau with her on Friday. "I'll try to join you on Saturday," he added. It was a difficult time for Maggie. The January collections were coming up and she had much to do, so much, in fact, that she had asked Lily to put Madeleine in charge of their New York operation and come to Paris to give her valued assistance. Lily had duly arrived and had been installed in a suite on the floor below.

Marcel did not come to the chateau on Saturday. On Sunday morning it was discovered that Etienne Mennon had gone to his eternal rest. Maggie found Mama sitting beside his bed holding his cold hand. There were no tears —she was in shock. Maggie too felt bereft but did her crying secretly. There were many details to be attended to and as she always had, Maggie rose to the occasion and did all the things that were necessary to ease Mama's burden.

Marcel arrived at two in the afternoon to fetch Maggie home. When he learned of his father's death, he immediately retired to his room, fortified with two bottles of brandy. The household had quieted. Maggie had put Mama to bed with a sedative to give her the rest she needed. When she searched for Marcel, he was nowhere to be found. Maggie walked into their room and found him sprawled in a chair. His eyes were closed, his mouth sagging open. "Marcel!" she said sharply; there was no response. She called his name again, louder, and shook him; she tentatively slapped his face, her anger mounting as she slapped him again and again, hard enough to leave the print of her hand. He stirred at last and she tried to pull him to his feet, but he shoved her away and sat down hard on the floor, pulling him with her. Angry tears were flowing as she picked herself up and looked down on him in despair. She grabbed him under the arms and literally dragged him to the *salle de bain* where she emptied a pitcher of cold water on him. He shook his head and opened his eyes. "What the hell . . . ?" he muttered.

Maggie didn't let him finish. "Get up, damn you, get on your feet!" she hissed.

He got to his knees and with a silly grin, pointed a wavering finger at her. "Oh, what you said!" he giggled. She took advantage of having his head at the right height and, praying that God would give her the self-control not to drown him, she grasped a fistful of hair and dunked his head up and down in the sink, occasionally bumping it against the edge. He spluttered and tried to strike out and finally cried, "Enough, enough!" Maggie then turned him over to his valet who had, at her request, prepared a cold bath. She closed all the doors to keep his shrieks from reverberating through the rest of the rooms.

An hour had passed before he joined her, pale and with dark shadows under his eyes. "I'm sorry, Maggie dear, truly sorry that I behaved in such a manner. It was such a shock to find Papa had . . ." he gulped, "died. I just couldn't stand it."

"Don't apologize to me," she said coldly. "Find your mother and see what you can do to ease her grief. I will join you later."

"I don't look very well," he said, looking at his image in the mirror.

"Under the circumstances—and I don't mean your drinking—you will be expected to look poorly," Maggie snapped. She couldn't resist adding, "If you don't change your dissolute way of life, what you see in the mirror will be only the beginning of your deterioration!"

"Maggie, don't be cruel," Marcel whined. "It was such a terrible shock—I didn't even have time to say goodbye." He stepped closer, encircling her waist with his arm. "Please, dear," he begged, "kiss me to show you forgive me."

She pushed him angrily away. "Don't play the little boy with me, Marcel! You escape into a bottle of brandy whenever there's a problem and sometimes even when there isn't. You have exhausted my patience. Now please go to your mother!"

He was a disconsolate figure as he walked away, head hanging in shame. When he realized Maggie had left and was no longer watching him, he shrugged, straightened up and went to his mother's room.

For Maggie, the loss of Etienne was one of the saddest events of her life; she had loved and respected him and vowed she would treasure his teachings always and try to go forward as he would have wanted her to. She was glad he had never seen Marcel in a drunken state. These were her thoughts as she bathed and changed into fresh clothing. She dismissed the maid so she could be alone for the first time since the discovery of Papa's death.

After she had mourned in private for a while, Maggie had a tray of light food prepared for Mama and took it up herself. When she entered the room, Marcel was sobbing on his mother's shoulder as she stroked his hair and soothed him.

Rather than being glad that Marcel's emotions had finally broken through his indifferent exterior, Maggie was disgusted at the sight of his alcohol-fostered tears. "Marcel," she said, hoping it sounded kindly, "I have brought something for Mama to eat. There's enough for you, too, if you would like to stay with her."

"I'm too upset, Maggie. I'm going for a walk. I'll see you later when you come downstairs," he murmured brokenly.   ·

She placed the tray on a table and walked to the door with him. "Don't you *dare* take anything to drink," she said quietly.

"Don't worry, I'll be all right." He walked quickly away to avoid further orders.

The funeral was simple but with more pomp than Etienne would have desired—or Mama, for that matter. However, Marcel felt that a splendid funeral procession was due his father's position . . . and his, as the only heir to the vast Mennon fortune.

XXVIII

MARCEL THE MAN

Maggie stayed with Mama for two days after the funeral. She was proud of the way Marcel had gotten hold of himself. After his brief breakdown the first time he saw his mother, he had taken charge of all the arrangements. He also made appointments for the following week with the manager of the vineyards and the winery and had ledgers brought to him at his mother's estate. The last appointment was to be with the attorney, M. Claude Galle, who handled the family affairs. Marcel told Maggie he could afford the time; therefore, he would stay with his mother as long as necessary. His tenderness toward his mother lessened her pain at the terrible loss; his presence gave her the strength to go on living without her beloved Etienne.

By the time Maggie returned from Paris for the weekend, Marcel had accomplished everything but the meeting with the attorney.

"I knew," she said lovingly, "that all you needed was the responsibility of taking care of someone. Perhaps, dear," she apologized, "I robbed you of that need by being so very independent."

Maggie was quite sincere. Living in Paris

without Marcel had given her time to think. Somewhere in their short marriage they had lost each other, or almost. She knew he loved her as she loved him, but something was missing. He complained often that her mind was always occupied with her work, which she had to admit was true. She disliked his friends and fast style of living but endured it without either joy or protest. By the time they were ready for bed, she was usually tired but willing to perform her wifely duties . . . her mind stopped in midstream and she realized what was wrong with their relationship. She said it aloud: "I perform my wifely *duties.*" Not once had she initiated their lovemaking. Telling her husband she loved him was not enough. She would have to endeavor to match his passionate nature, the only way he could measure love. She sighed deeply. "Thank God for these few days! If it is not too late, I'm sure I can heal the breach."

Now was the time to put her theory to the test. Mama was already asleep when Maggie arrived at the chateau. After a late dinner, she and Marcel walked a little in the garden. "I think these few days away from each other have done us both good. Marcel, dear, you look very well. I missed you," said Maggie softly. She put her arms around him, pressing ever so slightly against him as she kissed him, opening her mouth. He held her to him, then tilted her face and looked into her eyes.

"You *did* miss me! *Cherie, cherie,* I love you!"

Taking him by the hand, she led him back into the chateau and up the winding staircase to their room. She disrobed in her dressing room; he was waiting for her. She stood before him in a jade Chinese silk robe. Her every movement was sensuous as she opened the robe and slowly let it drop to her feet. It was the first time she had ever stood naked before anyone and also the first time she was not self-conscious with her husband.

Marcel was in a frenzy of desire. He picked her up in his arms and brought her to the bed. *"Ma petite poupee,"* he whispered as he caressed her bare breasts. "My little doll!" He kissed her from head to toe and back up again and finally knew she was ready to receive him as he desired. He nibbled and stroked and played with her, and when at last he entered her, Maggie was delirious with sensation and held on to him tightly until she was limp with exhaustion. Marcel stroked her face as he pushed her tumbled hair off her forehead, then gently covered her. "My sweet Maggie," he said softly, "now you know how a Frenchman makes love . . . You have made me very happy."

Smiling drowsily, Maggie snuggled next to him, and in moments, both were asleep.

They were in a mellow mood when they visited Mama the next day. "It is good to see you both looking so content," she said approvingly, and in answer to their question, said she would come down to dinner the following day. "Marcel has been so kind," she told Maggie softly. "He has helped me to become reconciled to my deep grief."

Later that day Maggie complimented Marcel again on his ability to take charge of the affairs of the household, and he replied solemnly, "I have recognized my responsibility, Maggie. I must oversee my mother's affairs, my wine business and the vineyards, the entire estate and all that it encompasses; as the only heir, it is incumbent upon me to take my place as head of the family. I'm afraid my father was too much the artist and too little the businessman to be as successful as he might have been.''

It hurt Maggie to hear him say this. She replied, ''The estate seems to have been managed very well, Marcel. If it wasn't your father, then who took care of everything?''

''The estate and the vineyards belonged to my mother. He married into great wealth and never really appreciated it. Mother had excellent supervisors and met with them once a month.''

''Your father didn't meet with them, too?''

''Yes,'' he said slowly, ''but I'm sure mother had the better head for business.''

Maggie was confused. ''If the estate was not your father's, how could he leave it to you?''

Marcel was fast losing patience with Maggie's endless questions. ''You know nothing of our French laws, my dear. When a woman marries, all her property becomes her husband's.'' He promptly turned his back and pretended to be absorbed in his ledgers to cover his annoyance.

Maggie said no more, but what Marcel had just told her was an unpleasant surprise. It was a very unfair rule and she wondered if that applied to her situation. It was something she would have to look into in the not too distant future.

Marcel stayed at the chateau another week

during which time he met with M. Galle, the attorney. He greeted him cordially and they went into the library together, where his mother was already seated. "It isn't necessary for you to be here, mother," said Marcel firmly. "I'm sure we can get everything settled."

"Excuse me, Marcel," M. Galle said. Although the attorney had known him from the time he was born, Marcel was annoyed at the use of his first name. "It is necessary for Madame Mennon to be here."

Marcel shrugged. "Very well. Suppose we get on with reading the will."

Mama looked at him somberly. "I thought you knew, son. There is no will. Your father had nothing to leave."

Marcel's voice had the edge of hysteria. "What do you mean? This estate, the vineyards, the company—" He glared at M. Galle. "What have you done with my inheritance!"

The attorney took a deep breath. "Sit down, Marcel. Your mother has asked me to let her explain."

He threw himself into a chair, then sat very straight as though ready to do battle. Turning to his mother, he said, "Your property became father's when you married."

But Mme. Mennon shook her head. "No, Marcel. Listen to me. You know something of how we met. Your father was an artist. He could have lived comfortably with his own family but chose to be part of the colony at Monmartre. We were very much in love, but he refused to marry me under the property laws of France since he felt it unfair to me. So," she said lamely, "we were united out of the

369

country. He renounced, in writing, all rights to my property." M. Galle shoved a paper across the desk. Marcel recognized his father's handwriting.

"You couldn't marry in any country, even with that paper. It's not a legal document," he said, after he had glanced at it.

Mama bit her lip. She had hoped she would not have to explain further, but now she knew she must go on. "That is true."

"What are you telling me?" Marcel's eyes were wide with horror.

"Dear Marcel—son—please understand . . . we were never married, at least not by clergy or magistrate. Our love was so . . ."

Marcel jumped up and towered over his mother, fists clenched. "You're telling me I'm a . . . *bastard?* You filthy . . ."

Claude Galle shoved him away from Mme. Mennon, who cowered in her chair, crying. Marcel ran out of the room in an hysterical rage, knocking a chair over, leaving doors open behind him as he left the chateau.

"I wanted him to understand how much his father and I loved each other," Mama sobbed. "He was a child of love. We couldn't have been more married. It lasted more than twenty-five years and we never fell out of love with each other!"

"I know, I know." M. Galle put his arm around her shoulders and murmured soothingly, "He'll get over it." He poured her a glass of brandy. "Drink this, Marianne." It was the first time in all the years they had known each other that he called her by her first name. "Let me send a message to your doctor to come and see you." But Mama negated the suggestion.

Calling on all her aristocratic background, she composed herself and bid M. Galle a dignified goodbye. She kept that pose until she reached her rooms, where she collapsed. Her maid put her to bed.

Maggie knew nothing of this until she returned on Friday. Marcel was not there to greet her. It was with great alarm that she learned about Mama's collapse. She went quickly to Mme. Mennon's room which she hadn't left since M. Galle's fateful visit. Papa's nurse was in attendance. "What is it? What is wrong?" Maggie asked the nurse frantically.

"Madame is depressed; she cries constantly," sighed the nurse, twisting her apron.

"Mama?" Maggie whispered, going over to the bed. She was shocked at the change in the older woman since she had seen her last.

Mama opened her eyes and sobbed, "Maggie, dear Maggie—I am so glad you are here!"

"Where's Marcel?" Maggie asked.

Mama cried harder. "I don't know. I haven't seen him since . . . since . . ." She couldn't continue.

"Don't cry, dear," Maggie begged. "I will find him. You look as if you haven't eaten in a week!" She scowled at the nurse.

"Madame is a very stubborn lady. She has not eaten," the nurse mumbled.

"Mama," Maggie scolded, "you cannot do this! I'll be back shortly and I will expect to see you freshly washed and in your best robe, sitting in that very comfortable chair by the fireplace!"

"I don't think I can . . ." Mama moaned. The

nurse was grateful to have someone in authority give her permission to do what was necessary for Mme. Mennon. She immediately fetched a basin of warm scented water and began to bath and change her patient. Over Mama's weak protests, the nurse helped her out of bed, and into the chair Maggie had indicated. A few minutes later, Maggie returned with a glass of milk with an egg and sherry whipped into it. Although Mama continued to protest, she drank it.

"Thank you, Maggie, that was very good," she admitted. She was silent for a moment then said, "Maggie, I must tell you . . . about Marcel. I should have told you before, but . . ." her voice trailed off feebly.

"Mama?" Maggie asked, gently. "What is it you want to tell me about Marcel?"

"It was all my fault. I tried to explain but I did it badly." Mama began to tremble. "And then Marcel went away."

Maggie held her hands to quiet them. "We won't talk about it now, dear. I'll find Marcel, don't worry. You must be strong. Whatever it is, we can take care of it together." She bent down to kiss her cheek and Mama put her hands on either side of Maggie's face.

"Please don't judge me too harshly," she whispered. "I only did what Etienne wanted because I loved him so much." She was getting agitated again.

Maggie, completely puzzled, said, "I want you to know this. I never knew my own mother. You are so dear to me, you could commit *murder* and I would be there to defend you! I love you and I thank you for the kind of love I never thought I would know."

372

Most of the tension seemed to have left Mama and she said quietly, "Tell me that after you have seen Marcel. You may change your mind."

The servants knew where Marcel was but they hadn't dared tell Madame. He was holed up in the drawing room with the doors closed and had threatened violence if anyone came near him. Maggie wasn't ready for the sight that met her eyes when she walked into the room. He was not dead drunk in a chair as she had expected, but face down on the floor, conscious but not coherent, an empty bottle clutched in his hand. She tried to pull him to his feet but he was too heavy. Maggie rang for his valet and told him, "Get someone to help you and take Monsieur Mennon upstairs. I can't imagine why you haven't done this before. Why did you wait?"

Jean, who had kept his head turned away until now, faced her. He was sporting a black eye. "I tried, Madame."

"Oh, my God!" Maggie gasped.

He nodded. "Monsieur Mennon was—difficult."

"You had better get two men to help you," Maggie said. Jean understood—Marcel was beyond putting up a fight but he was dead weight.

The doctor was summoned and came once again to the Chateau Mennon. After examining Marcel, he explained the course of medication to Jean. A burly male nurse arrived and stayed with Marcel in a wing of the house where his drunken ravings could not be heard.

Maggie was at her wits' end. She had to go

back to Paris but she couldn't leave Mama. In a flash of inspiration, she persuaded Mama that she was well enough to accompany her to Paris. Maggie explained that Marcel was somewhat unwell and would join them later. She still didn't know what the problem was, although she guessed it had something to do with his inheritance. In order to put Mama's mind at ease, Maggie told Mama she had talked with Marcel. Assuming that Maggie knew the facts, Mama was grateful that her attitude had not changed.

Mme. Mennon still wasn't well enough to be left alone, so she was installed in Maggie's Paris apartment with her maid. There was more than enough room for all of them, including Marcel when he returned. After four weeks in which Maggie had received no word from her husband, Jean sent a message that M. Mennon was returning to Paris and was in good health. Maggie waited day after day, but heard nothing from him. Meanwhile, the new MerMaid collections were only a few weeks away and the pace in the studio was frantic.

Mama's health had been restored, but she spent most of her time sadly gazing into space. After much thought, Maggie came up with a remedy. "Mama, we desperately need another pair of hands. Do you think you could help us?" she asked.

Mama laughed. "Me? My dear child, you know I would do anything to help you, but what can I do? I can't sew, or cut, or pin, or do anything that would be helpful."

"I can't either," Maggie answered cheerfully.

"Ah, but you are the artist behind your

374

successful establishment and you can draw."

"And you can write. I've seen some of your letters—you write a fine hand."

Mama nodded in agreement. "Yes, I suppose it sounds immodest to say so, but that is true."

"That is exactly what we need!" Maggie continued. "We have over a hundred invitations to send out and no one to address the envelopes. If you don't think it would be too tedious or tiring, I thought you might do that. Would you like to try?"

Mama was enthusiastic and immediately a desk was set up in Maggie's private office, complete with the proper writing instruments, a long list of names and addresses, and a large box of envelopes for the invitations, which Mama would insert as she addressed them. Her assignment, as she proudly referred to it, kept her busy and succeeded somewhat in keeping her mind off her loss . . . or rather, losses, for she realized she had lost not only her husband but her son as well.

The day before Christmas was very quiet. Maggie's employees had been given two days' holiday and the usual busy hum of the workshop was silent. Lily had gone off to visit her family, which left the entire floor empty with the exception of the two Mennon ladies. All day Mama had sat silent, her eyes constantly straying to the door, waiting, hoping Marcel would come in. Maggie hoped so, too. As the day wore on, she could see disappointment set in, and as it did, Maggie's long-suppressed anger mounted. "Mama," she said suddenly, "I have some errands to do. I hate to leave you alone, but I should be back quite soon. Will you be all right?"

"Of course." Mme. Mennon roused herself to sound convincing. "I didn't sleep to well last night and I am rather tired. Perhaps I'll take a nap while you're gone."

"Good! I'll be back in time for dinner."

Some time ago, Maggie had learned from one of Marcel's friends that he still maintained his bachelor apartment. She had never told him that she knew and he had never mentioned it. Now, with fire in her eye she was determined to find him and see to it that, whatever was the matter between himself and Mama, Christmas would not pass without a visit to his mother.

It was a twenty minute carriage ride to the Left Bank where Marcel's house was located. Maggie had the driver wait for her. As she neared the door of his flat, the noise gave evidence of a party inside. She knocked long and loud and finally the door was opened by Armand, Marcel's best friend. She couldn't see beyond him because of the dim light suffused by the red globes on the fixtures and the haze of smoke which had a sweet, acrid odor. As her eyes adjusted, she could see Armand had his arm around a statuesque brunette—not Flame, his exquisitely beautiful Eurasian mistress. One of the long-running arguments between Maggie and Marcel had been over the fact that he would go nowhere unless Armand and Flame were with them.

"Maggie!" Armand made an elaborate bow and almost fell over. "My dear Maggie . . ." He didn't move from the doorway and, turning, he called out to the shadowy people in the room, "Everybody, ladies and gentlemen, our very own Miss MerMaid." No one paid any attention.

"Madame Mennon," Maggie snapped. "Where is my husband?"

Armand stepped away from the door and cleared a path for her through the crowd. No one noticed her expression of utter disgust as she threaded her way over and around countless bodies. She turned and asked again, "Where is my husband?" Armand jerked his thumb toward the bedroom. Past experience told her Marcel was probably drunk; she wondered if she could expect any help from the weird assortment of guests in getting him out of there. She did not see the wicked grin on Armand's wide, lascivious mouth as she opened the bedroom door and stood, frozen to the spot. Marcel was drunk . . . and naked . . . and in bed with Flame. Their arms and legs were entwined and they seemed to be trying to consume each other.

"*Marcel!*" she shrieked.

He pushed Flame away so he could sit up. "What are you doing here?" he gasped. He threw a bedcover to Flame who was lying back, hands clasped behind her head, her breasts exposed. "Get out of here, Flame!" She got out of bed, but did not use the cover to hide her nudity. Instead she draped it over her shoulder, letting it drag behind her. She said nothing but smiled contemptuously at Maggie and slowly walked into the bathroom. Marcel turned back to Maggie. "Don't look so shocked, dear wife," he sneered.

"I am shocked but more than that, I am bewildered. Why have you degraded yourself like this . . . and with your best friend's mistress? I don't understand any part of it!" cried Maggie.

Marcel had by now wrapped a sheet around himself. "You are so naive, it is painful," he sighed. "Flame is and always has been *my* mistress. We always brought Armand along with us so you wouldn't suspect. A Frenchwoman would have guessed immediately." Maggie's eyes were wide and her face pale as he thrust the truth at her. "Did you really think your pallid lovemaking could satisfy a man like me?" he asked insolently.

Maggie finally found her voice. "I thought our love was strong and beautiful. What happened to all the romance you courted me with? What happened to all the honesty and sweetness we had between us? What has come over you? Is this shameful behaviour intended as revenge on me? I loved you, Marcel, and I thought you loved me," she said miserably.

He covered his guilt with defiance. "I did love you and if you had paid more attention to me than you did to your studio, I wouldn't have resumed my former way of life." He seemed sober now, and as Flame came back into the room, he directed her to get everybody out of the flat. "I'll see you later," he told her. She left with a toss of her head, showing her anger. "If you had half her fire," he said to Maggie as he watched her go, "this might not have happened."

Maggie's shock had now turned to boiling rage. "If I had half her fire, I'd be a prostitute, walking the streets!" she snapped.

Marcel made no response, only excused himself and asked her to wait. When he returned, fully dressed and presenting a some-what better appearance, Maggie noticed that his good looks were deteriorating.

"It's time we talked, Maggie," he said, offering her a seat.

"Before you start, Marcel, I am not here for myself," said Maggie. "I find it hard to believe that your father's death grieved you so much that you were forced to find relief in debauchery."

"You are right, it did not."

"Then what is it? Your mother needs you. Why have you turned your back on her?"

"You mean she hasn't told you?" he said, astonished.

"Your mother has been incapable of saying anything about you whatsoever. She has been very ill. I try to keep her busy, but most of the time she sits while the tears roll down her face. Why have you done this to her?" cried Maggie.

Marcel's expression hardened. "I don't wonder she hasn't told you. She is no better than a whore. Not as good, in fact, because she covered her sins with a false facade." Maggie put her hands up as though to fend off his terrible words. "Let me finish! She *said* Etienne is my father, though I even have doubts about that. They were . . . *never* . . . married! They produced a *bastard! Me!*" he shouted.

"Who told you these lies?" gasped Maggie.

"They are not lies. And it was my sainted mother herself who told me. It is a wonderful story of selflessness—because my mother's property would have gone to Etienne when they married, he refused to marry her so it would remain in her name. If you don't believe me, ask Galle, who came to the chateau to inform me I had no inheritance. The property which should have passed to me remains my mother's. This is the story *my mother* told me."

Maggie remembered Mama's plea not to judge her too harshly. When she had recovered sufficiently to speak, she said, "It was a terrible thing for you to have to learn, Marcel, but I wish you had your father's pride. That's all it was, you know—you were the issue of a great love. There was no intent to cheat you out of anything. Whatever your mother has will be yours one day." She got up to leave.

"Maggie," Marcel said hesitantly, "I do love you. It's just that I need more than you give me. If . . ." she could see the effort he was making to continue, "if I change my ways, will you take me back?"

She made a gesture of revulsion. "I don't think so, not after tonight. I find you and your ways disgusting!"

"Wait, Maggie. I'll make a bargain with you. I'll ask my mother's forgiveness and be a dutiful son if you take me back."

Marcel had put the responsibility for his mother's peace of mind squarely on Maggie's shoulders. She thought about the proposition so long that he finally said, "Maggie?"

"It is not a decision I can make quickly," she said at last. "You are taking unfair advantage. You know I love your mother and will do anything to make her happy. I'll have to think this through in depth. Meanwhile, I will meet you this far: visit your mother tomorrow. Tell her you became ill—that will account for your condition. Bring her a token remembrance for

Christmas. No recriminations—be kind and gentle with her. Then spend New Year's Eve and New Year's Day with us."

A smile glimmered at the corner of Marcel's mouth. "At our apartment?"

"This is a probation period, Marcel. You will stay here, in your own flat, *alone*, until such time as I can bring myself to forgive you and erase the horror of what I saw tonight. Then, and only then, will we talk about your moving back." She paused. "Do you accept my terms?"

Marcel shrugged. "I have no choice. I wish you loved me as much as you do her," he added wistfully.

"I wish you deserved it as much," she retorted and walked quickly out of the flat.

XXIX

NEW YORK

As agreed, Marcel visited his mother the next day. He came bearing flowers and candy —her favorites, chocolate covered cherries in cordial and cream. Maggie greeted him coolly, then returned to her workroom. As she left she could hear his tearful, "Oh, Mama, I am so sorry I was bad. Please forgive me. I love you." Without looking back, she could hear Mama's rejoinder, also tearful.

"My son, my son, it was my fault! I should have told you sooner and explained better than I did." Maggie glanced over her shoulder and saw Marcel put his hand gently over his mother's mouth.

"I understand everything. Believe me, I do. We will talk no more about it." He sounded sincere and was, again, his mother's darling naughty boy. If it hadn't been for the revolting scene she had witnessed with Flame, and if he hadn't confessed that she was his mistress, Maggie might have been fooled into belief in his total innocence of any wrongdoing. Mama's health had been restored and now that Marcel had returned, her spirit revived as well. Marcel put in a full day at his office, then ate dinner every evening with Maggie and

383

his mother. Because she retired early, Mama did not know that he was not living there as well. Maggie played her part well and Mama never knew the true state of affairs between them.

The big day of Maggie's January collection was at hand and all was in readiness. As she told Mama later, "I couldn't have done it without you." Mme. Mennon had added to Maggie's invitation list by sending notes to her many friends. They all came and bought, ensuring that the Paris House of MerMaid was well and securely launched. The unusual runway Maggie had installed brought applause; the models she had hired were girls who had not been seen before. They were fresh and wholesome, unlike the more sophisticated ones who modeled for the other fashion houses which were beginning to spring up. M. Worth's specialty was elaborate ballgowns—Maggie showed only a few and none with bustles, hoops or cages to support yards and yards of draped satin. She employed the same simple Grecian lines she had used in America. They were received enthusiastically and all the customers who had to be first with a new fashion snatched them up quickly. The *piece de resistance* was the segment devoted to sports clothes. No designer had previously bothered much about them, but Maggie did. There were split skirts for riding, tennis dresses three inches shorter than convention decreed—for comfort, she explained—and the sleeves were short and full to allow for easier movement. Everything had either a satin label with an embroidered MerMaid emblem on it, or the design was incorporated into the pattern of the trim or even the fabric itself. She showed bathing dresses, again shorter than the current length, with striped or polka-dot bloomers and caps to match.

The final applause was spontaneous and enthusiastic. By the time the last customer had left, the last order taken, the last crumb of the buffet eaten and the debris cleared away, the ladies of the House of MerMaid were in a state of near-collapse. Marcel had been present during the showing. He kissed Mama and Lily and said to Maggie, "You were splendid!" as he came to embrace and kiss her. Unnoticed by the others, she suffered his embrace but turned her face to receive his kiss on her cheek. He said softly, "Not yet?" She didn't answer. Tentatively he suggested to all three women, "Shouldn't we celebrate, get away from the salon and see some nightlife?" Again he got no answer from Maggie and the others said it was impossible—all they wanted was a good night's sleep. He sighed heavily as he said, "In that case, I shall leave you ladies to your rest." He kissed Mama goodnight and blew kisses to the others as he left. Maggie was certain he would do enough celebrating for all of them.

Life slowed to a more normal pace the following week. Lily was busy seeing to the making up of the clothes that had been ordered, and the bookkeeper took care of the billing. Toward the end of the week at dinner, Mama, now rested and adjusted as much as she would ever be to her husband's death, said, "Children, it is time for me to go home." Maggie started to protest, but she continued,

385

"No, dear, I am in good spirits and I miss my home. You saved my sanity, dear daughter, and I shall be ever grateful but now I am ready to return to my own quiet life. You will visit me?" she asked Maggie and Marcel.

"Of course we will," Maggie promised, "but for the next few weeks, Marcel will be visiting you alone." She looked in his direction with a warning in her eyes. "As you know, having been absent so long, he has much to catch up with at his office, so we have decided I will take a short trip to New York to check on my business there."

"Marcel dear, that doesn't seem fair to either of you. Is there no way you can arrange to have someone do your work for you?" Mama asked.

Marcel had understood Maggie's intent and although it rankled, he agreed that he could not be spared for a holiday just then. But he added, "She won't be gone long—will you, *dear?*" Maggie glanced at Mama to see if she had caught the sarcasm in his voice, but saw no reaction. She shook her head, then changed the subject. "When would you like to leave, Mama?"

A little shamefaced, the older woman answered, "I knew yesterday I was ready to go home and," she blushed, "please don't think I'm ungrateful, but I started packing then."

Marcel rose to the occasion. "Of course we understand, Mama. We all like our *own* homes." Maggie ignored the remark.

Mama's return to Chateau Mennon was pleasant. She was greeted enthusiastically by all the staff, then went upstairs to freshen up. A little later Maggie walked into the drawing room and found Mama standing in front of a portrait Etienne had painted a long time ago of the two of them standing together, holding hands. Maggie excused herself for intruding, but Mama said, "Don't go, dear. Etienne loved you, too. It makes me feel good to remember how happy we were. The next time you visit we must go through his paintings. He wanted you to have as many as you like."

"I couldn't take them from you," Maggie protested.

"It was one of his last wishes. He said, 'See that the little one takes some of my paintings.' "

Maggie's eyes glistened with sudden tears. "I wish I could have thanked him," she said softly.

"He knew you loved him—that was enough." Mama was smiling when she turned away from the double portrait. "It's almost time for dinner, dear. I'm not going to dress tonight."

"I'm glad. I'm still very tired," Maggie admitted. "I think after dinner I'll get a book from the library and read in bed." It had been privately agreed that she and Marcel would have separate rooms, not uncommon practice among even the most devoted married couples.

Marcel joined them at dinner and although wine was served, he did not touch it. He continued to be solicitous of his mother and his self-satisfaction was easy to see. Though he waited for some private word of praise from Maggie, none was forthcoming.

Maggie left for America on the first of February. After spending a few days with

Mama, she had returned to Paris. Marcel arrived at the apartment the day before she embarked, to take her to the ship. "For your information, Lily will be staying here while I'm gone," Maggie told him coolly.

"Oh," he said, taken aback. He had intended to move in as soon as she left, but he quickly regained his composure. "Of course, I had no intention of staying here. I can wait until you return."

"About your mother . . ."

He cut her off. "Don't worry about my mother. I shall take very good care of her. I will see her every weekend."

"Good!" There was no other, more tender farewell.

The voyage to America was reminiscent of Maggie's first one. The seas were rough and it was cold. Maggie slept most of the way, but she was still a good sailor, and was one of the few passengers who didn't miss a meal.

When she entered her house, Letty was overjoyed to see her. "We missed you, Miss—I mean *Mrs.* Mennon!"

Maggie hugged her. "I'm so tired of formality! You will have to start calling me Maggie." Letty giggled and brought her a cup of strong coffee, saying, "I have several messages for you, Mrs.—uh—Maggie. I think you'll want this one first." She handed her a small envelope; the engraved announcement inside was edged in pink. "Captain and Mrs. John Colton are proud to announce the birth of a daughter Maggie Ellen, born January 25, 1885."

Maggie was delighted. "I didn't even know

Ellen was expecting! A little girl—and named Maggie! Oh, I must go there!"

"Well, Mrs. . . . . Maggie, here's another note that came this morning."

Maggie read through tear-dimmed eyes, "Dearest Maggie, If you are not completely exhausted when you arrive, please have dinner with us tonight and see your—would you accept?—Godchild. All our love . . ." "Do you think it's too late to go?" She didn't wait for an answer. "Help me change, quick, Letty!"

"I took the liberty of sending a note saying you would be there. I was certain you would," Letty told her.

"I love you, Letty!" Maggie cried.

When she entered her room she saw that her housekeeper had laid out a dinner gown with the proper accessories. She had thought of everything. Maggie's carriage was waiting at the door when she descended from her rooms. The coachman greeted her with a big smile and a "Welcome back, Ma'am!" She sank back against the velvet cushions and thanked God for letting her rediscover how precious her own home and country were. She hadn't been so happy in almost a year.

Maggie's reunion with Ellen was a joyous one. They tiptoed into the nursery and looked at the sleeping infant in her cradle. "I think she's going to have red hair," Ellen whispered.

"She *is* beautiful, Ellen," Maggie whispered back. "And how is my handsome boy?"

"Probably still fighting sleep," Ellen laughed. With his nursemaid's permission they went in to see young John, who contrary to his mother's prediction was sound asleep.

Maggie would have liked to pick him up and hug him, but that would have to wait for another day.

"Oh, Ellen," Maggie sighed, "how *intelligent* of you and John to have two such beautiful children!" It wasn't until they went to dinner that she asked, "Was little Maggie's birth easier than John's?"

Ellen snapped her fingers. "Like that! Apparently all I needed was dry land! I'll never stop being thankful that you were with me when Little John was born."

They spent the rest of the evening talking as only very dear friends do, catching up on everything that had happened since they had last seen each other at Maggie's wedding.

Maggie spoke of her close relationship with Mama and Papa Mennon and how much she missed him; of their shared interest in art and his patient instruction. She spoke of her satisfaction with her new salon and the success of her first collection and the ensuing avalanche of orders. She praised Lily and once again thanked Ellen fervently for starting her off on such a lucrative and rewarding career.

Ellen listetned without comment. When Maggie had finished the recital of all the stupendous happenings which had come about, Ellen remained quiet for a moment. There was speculation in her eyes as she finally said, "You have told me about all the good things in your new life, but not a word about Marcel or your marriage."

Maggie fluttered her hand up in a very French gesture that brushed aside the subject. "Ellen, I really don't want to talk about that; in fact, I can't put my feelings into words. Suffice

390

it to say that in spite of all the good things that have come about because of it, I made a terrible mistake. Marcel is not the man I thought he was," she admitted.

Ellen murmured, "I'm so sorry," and asked no more.

XXX

REUNION

Two months passed for Maggie, the best two months of the past year. She tried to put off the thought of returning to Paris, but the time to show her new collection was nearing and she had to prepare for them. Lily wrote regularly, and in her last letter asked if Maggie had set the date of her return. In the most recent of many letters from Marcel, he also importuned her to return, reminding her that their first anniversary was only a few weeks away. He assured her he visited Mama every weekend, that she was well and missed her daughter-in-law. He finished by writing, "I have been a model husband and son, concentrating on business and waiting impatiently for your return." The letter troubled Maggie deeply. She had lost every vestige of love for Marcel and knew she could never resume their marriage, as such; it would have to be a marriage in name only, a dreary outlook for both.

Maggie buried herself in work, sketching for the July collection. Madeleine had been trained well and never interrupted her, until one day at the end of March she came flying into the studio without knocking. She came in with such speed that Maggie jumped and spoiled the sketch she had been completing. Annoyed, she was about to chastise her when she noticed her agitation. "What is it, Madeleine?" she asked with some irritation.

"Forgive me, Madame, I'm sorry to bother you but you must see this!" She thrust a swatch of silk on the drawing board. Still annoyed, Maggie picked it up. "Madeleine, you now you must place nothing on my sketches." She really looked at the small square of silk for the first time. "Oh, my goodness!" It was a lovely paisley design.

"See? It is *your* design. Someone has stolen it!" Madeleine cried melodramatically.

"Where did you get this?" Maggie asked.

"A man—here's his card." Maggie grabbed at the card and whispered, "Oh, my God . . . *MacConnack!* No wonder I never found them!" She felt like a balloon slowly collapsing. Her mind flashed back briefly to the visit to Paisley of the silk mill owner and his sister. She had felt so neglected at the time, so angry at not being allowed to come to America, that she hadn't really listened to the name. In her sporadic search over the years, she had been looking for a MacCormack. "Is he still here?" she asked, rousing herself and still looking at the paisley in her hand.

"I asked him to wait."

When Maggie worked, she always rumpled her hair by distractedly running her fingers through it. Consequently, she had had it cut shoulder-length, long enough to put up sedately when circumstances demanded. Now, she didn't take time to arrange it, but dashed out of her studio, still in her smock.

Donald MacConnack was congratulating himself on his good fortune that he was about to see, in person, the famous designer of MerMaid, who had a reputation for never leaving her drawing board to see anyone. How lucky, he thought, that I could catch her while she is in America! He was astonished when a pretty little slip of a girl came running, hands outstretched, to greet him. "Donald MacConnack, I am so happy you are here!" she cried and kissed him, French fashion, on both cheeks.

"Well," he said to cover his confusion, "I thank you for the warm welcome."

"You don't recognize me?" Maggie still held his hands and at arms' length, he scrutinized her closely. He had had little to do with Maggie during that first visit to Scotland and had paid her scant attention.

Maggie was all but jumping up and down with excitement. "I am *Maggie*—Maggie Maccrae!"

Donald's response was the same as hers had been initially. "Oh, my God!" he gasped. "Maggie! Our long-lost Maggie! I should have known—the little MerMaid and the capital M's, your initials. Wait until Annie sees you! Please God she will regain some of her strength."

"Annie is here? In America?"

"She is my wife, Maggie. We have a little boy almost four years old. I can't tell you what finding you will mean to her. She has never stopped wondering what had become of you."

As soon as Maggie had fixed her hair and changed her clothes, they were in his carriage on the way to Tarrytown, and Donald had brought her up to date on the doings of the Maccrae clan.

"I have been . . ." she thought for a moment seeking the right words, "not *thoughtless*, because I thought of disclosing my whereabouts many times, but selfish. At first I wanted to prove I could succeed on my own and then so much time elapsed that I felt the family had probably forgotten all about me. I knew about the girls getting married—I read about it in the Glasgow paper—but I *didn't* know about you and Annie, and Da. I do hope he is happy!" The rest of the trip was spent hearing about each member of the family. Each girl had children. "I am an aunt many times over," Maggie said, bemused. "Imagine that! Now I am anxious to see them all!"

"We are here," Donald said at last, as they turned into the long drive to the MacConnack mansion.

"Ah, how beautiful!" Maggie sighed. "Your flowers are beginning to bloom."

"An early spring. Next month the azaleas will be in flower. Maggie dear, I hope you'll be here to see them."

They alighted from the carriage, having agreed, considering of Annie's delicate health, that Donald would prepare her for Maggie's appearance. Maggie waited in the drawing room, pacing back and forth in an agony of anticipation.

Annie burst into the room, as close to running as her strength would permit as Maggie ran to meet her. "Maggie, my darling little one! My Maggie, we've missed you so much!" She was hysterical, laughing and crying and hugging and kissing her "little one" until she was weak with emotion.

"Hush, Annie, hush," Maggie soothed as she tried to control her own tears. But it was impossible, and they mingled with Annie's. She was crying for so many reasons—joy at seeing Annie after five long years, and sorrow, remembering her as she was, the stalwart of the family, scolding and vibrant with health. Now she was a wraith, thin and drawn, with the lustre gone from her eyes and the color from her face.

Donald ran to them as Annie's knees buckled. He picked her up in his arms as one would a child. Her happy sobbing ceased. "I am all right, Donald," she said as her personal nurse hurried forward with lavender salts and waved it back and forth under her nose. "Maggie dear, don't be alarmed. I'm really perfectly fine! Come, we have much to talk about."

Over her head Donald shook his head and mouthed, "Later," to Maggie, who said, "This has been a shock to you, dear. Get some rest now. Donald has invited me to stay overnight. We can talk later, or all day tomorrow, when you are not so over-excited."

"You *must* stay with us. I don't want you to disappear again!" Annie cried.

Maggie kissed her. "I promise, I won't. I am just as happy to find you as you are to find me!" Annie's nurse gave her a potion which Donald said would quiet her, and after he had helped her upstairs, he returned, to ask Maggie, "Would you like to see our son?"

"Indeed I would! May I see him now?"

Donald led the way up the staircase and into the nursery. The child had just been bathed and his nursemaid was rubbing him dry with a large, soft towel. He was the most beautiful little boy Maggie had ever seen—even, she thought guiltily, more so than Ellen's children. He had the dark, curly hair and almost black eyes of his father set in the fair complexion of his mother. His firm little body was rosy from his bath and the friction of the towel. Wriggling out of the nursemaid's grasp, he ran to his father's arms, naked and exquisite. They exchanged hugs and the little fellow kissed him several times.

"Young man, here is a lady come to see you. She is your Aunt Maggie. Say hello," Donald prompted.

In all his nakedness, he made a formal bow. "How do you do, Aunt Maggie." She put her hand to her mouth to hide her laughter as Nursie caught up with him and hastily covered him with a robe. "Papa, I have an Aunt Amy and an Aunt Kate, and now I have an Aunt Maggie?" the child asked his father.

"Indeed you do, not to mention an Aunt Robyn, Aunt Laurie, Aunt Frances . . ."

"That's too many aunts," said young Donald firmly, and Maggie and Donald burst into laughter. "You're probably right, and I apologize," said Maggie, grinning. "But I am happy to meet you, Donald Ian MacConnack." He giggled at the use of his full name. "I would like to kiss you. May I?"

He ran to her immediately, snuggling in her arms. "You smell different than mama, but pretty, too," he said as he sniffed at her neck.

"Well, Donald," Maggie said, "you are going

to have to watch this young man—he's obviously going to be a lady-killer!" She kissed him again and got a bear hug in return.

He then kissed Donald. "Will you read me a story, papa?"

"Not tonight, son, we have company . . ." Donald began, but Maggie immediately interrupted. "Don't be silly, Donald. I haven't had a chance to freshen up yet. Perhaps I could go to my room while you're reading to him."

He smiled gratefully. "Of course. Show Aunt Maggie how a gentleman says goodnight," he urged the little boy.

Young Donald trotted over to Maggie, reached for her hand, and bowed as he kissed it. "I am very flattered, sir," she said to the child. "I may never wash my hand again so I can keep that kiss!" The child went off into peals of laughter.

After a solemn promise to return for story time, Donald showed Maggie to her room and when they reached it, he put his hands on her shoulders and lightly kissed her cheek. "I have never heard my son laugh like that," he said huskily. "I think God must have sent you. Ian needs a little heart near him—by the way, we call him Ian to avoid confusion."

After Maggie had dressed for dinner, she sat with Annie and coaxed her to eat. In an effort to please her little sister, Annie did a better job on her cup of broth and small piece of chicken than she usually did. When she had eaten all she could, Maggie kissed her goodnight and left the room with a heavy heart.

At dinner that night, Maggie suggested to Donald that barley and lambbroth should be prepared for Annie. "She used to cook it for us. I hated it, but she always said I had to eat it to make me strong."

"I shall certainly try it," said Donald. "Come with me later and you can instruct the cook. Everyone here tries to make life easier for Annie . . ."

"It's not easy for you either, is it?" said Maggie shrewdly.

"No, I'm heartsick over her prolonged illness."

"What exactly is wrong with her? How long has she been ill?"

Donald sighed. "You won't believe this, Maggie. After we were married, we left immediately for America on our honeymoon. We had a wonderful wedding night. She became seasick the next day and was ill for the next two months, when we discovered our one night of love had resulted in the conception of a child."

"You mean . . . ?" Maggie faltered.

"That's right. We have never been together as man and wife since. She was a wonderful lover that first night," he seemed to be thinking out loud. "I sometimes think she had saved all her passion for her wedding night. She—never wanted me again." Maggie felt his anguish, and suffered for him. "Annie loves me and I love her, but sometimes desire rages in me. If I were a different man, I could relieve myself elsewhere—but I can't do that."

Maggie looked at him compassionately. If only, she was thinking, Marcel had even a small part of that fidelity! "Her doctor?" she said at last.

"I have had every specialist I could find

examine her. They all say that physically they can find nothing wrong."

"Do they imply it is mental?" Maggie asked in alarm.

"No one has said that in so many words . . . melancholia, they call it."

"I wish . . ." she broke off, then said, " If only I had known sooner! I have so little time to see if I could help. I have to leave for Paris next week to prepare for the spring collections."

"I keep forgetting you are the great Mademoiselle MerMaid," said Donald, forcing a smile.

"Actually, Madame Mennon," Maggie corrected, wondering if there had been a trace of sarcasm in his voice.

"That didn't come out the way I meant it, Maggie. I think it is amazing how much you have accomplished all on your own. You are to be congratulated." She acknowledged her acceptance of his explanation with a smile. "Did you say *Madame* Mennon?" Donald added.

"Yes. My husband is director of the Mennon Champagne and Wine Company. His headquarters are in Paris where I . . . *we* live."

He noticed her slip but let it go. "How long have you been married?"

"It will be a year on the first of May— another reason I suppose, I should return to Paris."

"You are not happily married?" Donald asked bluntly.

Maggie took her underlip between her teeth and hesitated before answering truthfully, "I suppose part of my empathy for you stems from the fact that I, too, have a husband who is sick—has an illness, different, but . . ." she shrugged and did not finish.

Donald did not question her further, but reached across the table and took her hand. "It shouldn't happen to anyone; perhaps we can support each other," he suggested.

"I have told no one else, Donald, not even my best friend," Maggie whispered.

"I shall respect your confidence, Maggie."

Both were equally grateful for the bond of understanding that had been forged between them.

At eight the next morning Annie's nurse, Emma, came in with her breakfast tray. Annie was stirring; Emma waited for her to open her eyes. Her gaze finally focused on the nurse and the dawn of remembrance brightened her face. "Did I dream it, Emma?" she said fearfully. "Did Maggie really come?"

Emma answered, "Yes, Miss Annie, she is here and dressing for breakfast. Shall I ask her to come in and join you?"

"No, no!" Annie's excitement rose. "No—help me dress. I feel very strong this morning. I shall go downstairs and have breakfast with her and Donald."

Donald was finishing his morning coffee and Maggie had just joined him when Annie came into the breakfast room. "Darling!" He sprang up. "How wonderful to see you here. You must be feeling much better!"

"I haven't felt this strong in months. See, Maggie, what you have done for me? I am so happy that you are here!"

Without any assistance, Annie went to the sideboard and helped herself to eggs and sausage and hot muffins on which she put slabs of butter. "I'm hungry," she said, apologizing for her laden plate.

"That's the best news I've heard in ages, darling!" said Donald, beaming. "Enjoy your breakfast." He squeezed Maggie's shoulder in an unspoken thank-you. "I know you two have a lot to talk about so I'll leave you, but I'll try to be home early."

After he had left the room, Annie said, "It's good to see him smile. I've laid a heavy burden on him," she added regretfully.

"He loves you very much, Annie. I'm dying to know how you and he came together. I didn't know there was a romance there," said Maggie.

And so they talked. After Annie had told the story of her courtship, she insisted that Maggie tell her everything that happened from the day she stowed away on the *Red Rose*. When Maggie had finished, Annie said, "So you are Mademoiselle MerMaid! Do you know I have a gown that Donald brought to me from Paris with your label on it? Strange, I never connected the mermaid with the paisley design. I am very impressed, dear, and so proud of you. And you are married, little Maggie . . . what is it?"

"Mennon—Madame or Mrs. Mennon."

"The Champagne people! You're done very well for yourself," said Annie admiringly.

Maggie smiled. "So have you. Who would ever have thought you'd be Mrs. Silk Mill?"

Annie laughed out loud. "Mrs. Silk Mill—

how funny! I must tell Donald." They were interrupted by Ian on his way to play in the park with nursie.

"Mama! Mama!" he cried, so glad to see her that he ran to her and flung his arms around her.

Annie flinched slightly and bent her head so he could kiss her cheek. "Don't shriek so, Ian. Say hello to Aunt Maggie." There was no warmth in her voice, Maggie noticed.

Ian's enthusiasm had dissipated. "Would you like to play with me?" he asked Maggie wistfully. "I have a ball."

"I'll come out," Maggie promised, "in a few minutes and we'll have a game of catch." He skipped out of the room, high spirits restored.

Annie sighed and shook her head. "I keep wondering how I ever had the patience to bring up six girls. Children are very noisy—especially Ian, always pestering to be picked up or kissed."

"You forget how noisy we were," said Maggie.

"No," Annie shook her head. "Boys are different. He's really too much for me."

Maggie changed the subject. "Shall we take a walk?" she suggested. "It's a beautiful day."

"No—here's Emma." The nurse came into the room. "It's time for me to rest. We'll talk more later," Annie told her.

Maggie waited until they had gone upstairs, then went in search of Ian. He spotted her coming toward him and called out, "Aunt Maggie, here—catch!" He threw the ball quite well for such a little tot. Maggie caught it and bobbled it and bent into funny postures trying to hold onto it. Ian was laughing so hard he rolled on the grass. They played for quite a while. When at last they walked back to the house, Ian took her hand. Before he left her, he said gravely, "I love you, Aunt Maggie. I hope you will be here always!"

Impulsively, Maggie said to the nurse, "Let me take him upstairs." The nurse agreed, following softly behind. "I'll tell you a secret, Ian," said Maggie. "I don't know any place I'd rather be than right here with you. But I have to go home soon." A fierce frown made his eyes squint. "I live way across the ocean. Do you know what the ocean is?" He shook his head. "It's a great big space filled with water."

"Like our pond?"

"A hundred times bigger."

"A *hundred* times?" That must be very big, he thought. She nodded, and handed him over to his nurse.

"Take your nap now, darling. I'll see you when you wake up." The conversation about the water had been an inspiration. She would ask Donald to bring Ian to the ship to see her off. She knew Annie would have no objection.

That night Annie came downstairs again, dressed for dinner. Donald was overjoyed. It was the first time since Ian's birth that she had attempted it. Her conversation was light and she still had a great curiosity about Maggie's life during their long separation; she would not, however, be drawn into any discussion of her own. "How long can you stay with us, Maggie?" she asked.

Maggie had already told her but Annie had closed her mind to the answer.

"I'm sorry, dear, that this reunion has to be so short. I am going back to the city on

Wednesday and sail for France on Saturday."

Panic flared in Annie's eyes. "You can't do that, you have just come!" Her voice bordered on hysteria.

Maggie explained patiently about the showing that she had to prepare. "I want you to get strong, Annie dear. I promise I will return as soon a the collection is shown."

"When will that be?"

Concerned with her possible reaction, Maggie avoided a direct answer with a careless, "Some time this summer."

Donald looked anxiously at his wife and was relieved that her hysteria seemed to have lessened. But her face took on a pinched look; her eyes seemed smaller and clouded. "Donald, will you call Emma? I'm tired and must rest," Annie said in a small, weak voice.

Like a thunderbolt, the realization struck Maggie that this was Annie's escape from reality. "Don't go yet—you haven't said a word about Kate. I would like to have seen her," Maggie said urgently.

"Perhaps if you ever find your way here again, you shall," Annie replied. Her mind seemed clear as she continued coldly, "Have a good voyage."

"I won't be leaving until Wednesday. We can talk more when you're rested," Maggie told her, but Annie shook her head.

"No, this is goodbye." Emma came in then and Annie leaned heavily on her as they left the dining room.

Maggie was upset. "What have I done, Donald?"

"Nothing," he sighed.

"Clearly she is punishing me," Maggie said sadly.

"I'm sorry you had to recognize that. Yes, that is her way—and yet, since your arrival, she has been in so much better spirits."

They went into the drawing room for coffee and brandy, but both were depressed, and conversation lagged. Emotionally and physically exhausted, Maggie went to bed early.

The next morning, Maggie stopped at her sister's room.

She asked Emma, "Is Mrs. MacConnack coming downstairs for breakfast this morning?"

Emma shook her head and whispered, "She won't even eat the nice breakfast I brought her!"

"I'll sit with her—maybe I can get her to take something," said Maggie, but Emma shook her head again.

"She doesn't want to see you, Mrs. Mennon. She wouldn't even say good morning to Mr. MacConnack."

Rebuffed, Maggie joined Donald in the breakfast room. "What do I do now?" she asked wearily. "Should I insist that she see me?"

"No, let her alone today. She's moody. She'll rest in bed and by tomorrow, in all probability, she will have forgotten anything was ever wrong," Donald told her.

"I'm sorry I upset her. I'm truly puzzled; she acts like a spoiled child . . ." Maggie became silent and thoughtful for a moment as she heard her own words. "You know, Donald,

Annie never really had a childhood. It seems to me she is acting out the role of the child she never was."

Donald made no comment, so Maggie changed the subject. "I would like to see Katherine. Perhaps today would be a good time to go," in spite of herself she grinned, "to Sullivan's Saloon."

Donald returned her grin. "If you would like, I'll take you there tonight," he offered.

But Maggie refused, saying, "I think it would be best if I see her alone. How do I get there?"

She walked to the door with him and he pointed out the path to town and told her it would take her right to Kate's door.

"So close? Do you see her often then?" Maggie wanted to know.

Donald shook his head and told her something of the delicate situation that existed. "She upsets Annie." No further explanation was necessary.

The walk to town was a pretty one. Maggie had not had time to explore the grounds surrounding the mansion. Now she could see, off to the right as she walked, a beautiful pond. That must be Ian's pond, she thought. We'll have to go down there and skip stones one day. Beyond the gates of the estate, the path wound round and as Donald had said, eventually led right past the door of Sullivan's Saloon; the name was announced in big gold letters over the entrance. She didn't see the arrow that pointed to another door labeled "Family Entrance." Maggie turned the knob but it resisted her efforts. Finally she knocked, timidly at first, then louder. She could hear children, several children, and had to knock even louder to be heard over the noise they were making.

A male voice called out, "We're not open yet, not until noon." Maggie knocked harder. She could see the curtain on the glass door pulled to one side and eyes on her. She didn't hear Rory say over his shoulder to Kate, "Here's one of your society friends, slumming."

"Open the door, Rory," Kate laughed. "If it's one of my 'society friends,' she won't stay long."

Maggie didn't realize how much her Parisian style and sophistication made her stand out in these surroundings. When the door finally opened, it took a moment for her eyes to adjust to the dim interior. Though Donald had prepared her, she couldn't believe at first that it was her dashing sister behind the bar, washing glasses. Kate had on one of Rory's shirts, sleeves rolled over her elbows, and a long, pink coverall apron. Her hair was pulled up on top of her head in an untidy bun. Her eyes were bright as she offered a smile of greeting. "Good morning, what can I do for you? As my husband said, we don't open until noon." Like three little kittens, the children romping around the saloon had quieted and followed Maggie with their large, very blue eyes as she walked over to the bar and stood directly in front of her sister. "Kate?"

Kate wiped her hands on her apron, pushed back the tendrils of hair which had escaped from her topknot, leaned on the bar and peered into Maggie's face. "Oh, my Gahd . . ." she drew it out, "Rory, come here! It's Maggie

—Maggie, my naughty, runaway sister!" Her excited shrill voice caused the children to start crying again. She dashed out from behind the bar and gave Maggie a hug that all but squeezed the breath out of her.

Rory came quickly, hand outstretched. On the way, he ruffled the hair of one of the children, saying affectionately, "Shut up, ye little brat!"

Maggie refused the beer and pretzels they eagerly pressed on her. "Too early" she said, and they agreed, so Rory disappeared and came back with soda bread and tea. Kate winked as she said, "You can see we're a typically Irish family." The children were each given a drop of tea with a lot of milk in it and a huge slab of bread thickly spread with butter. The twin boys were named Rory and Robert, "for Robbie," Kate explained, and the two year old girl, Macushla. They were extremely active, their bright red hair peeking suddenly from under the table or around the back of a chair. Ever so often Rory would call out, "Will ye shut up?" The words were crude but never angry, rather like a rough caress.

"It's time for their naps, darlin'—I'll take them upstairs," Rory said at last. He lined the children up and they marched after him; bringing up the rear was a big, black cat with a white blaze, white socks and a tail that stood straight up in the air.

The girls exchanged amused glances. "That's my family," Kate said with pride.

"They're wonderful, Kate! You have done well," said Maggie sincerely. It was evident that her sister was a perfectly happy woman, and Maggie couldn't help feeling a little pang of envy.

"I thank God—and Annie—that for once in my life I did the right thing; I am happier than I deserve to be," Kate confessed. They then talked about Annie. Both felt some of the blame for her condition was theirs. Kate summed it up rather sadly: "Annie was all worn out even before she came to America, from taking care of Da and all of us. It would have been better if she had stayed at home, never married and lived her life through her nieces and nephews. The wealth, grandeur and elegance of living on the MacConnack estate almost did me in, but thank God, as I said before, for Rory!" She hesitated for a moment. "I guess we don't look like much to you, Maggie, but we are a very happy family and I truly love my life."

"That's easy to see, Kate. Neither Annie nor I came out as well," said Maggie with a wry smile. She rose to leave. "I have to go back to Paris this week—I return to New York tomorrow."

Kate threw her arms around her. "Little sister, please let me know when you return! I don't want to lose you again." Rory, who had just come down, repeated Kate's invitation. Maggie refused his offer to call a cab, preferring intead to walk, as she had come. Her heart was lighter on her way back to Annie's; she looked forward to being friends with Kate and her family when she returned from France . . .

Ian MacConnack was an excited and happy

little boy as Captain Colton showed him around his ship on which Maggie would be making the crossing. "Ian," John said, "when you go ashore your papa said he would wait until I send a message just for you. When you hear two toots, you will know Aunt Maggie and I are saying we will see you soon."

Before he left the ship, Ian asked Maggie, "Do you *have* to go?"

"I do, sweetheart, but when I come back I will stay a long time," she promised.

Donald took her hand. "I hope you mean that, Maggie. You have brought life to our home; Ian laughed and had someone to play with and I . . . well, I can't tell you how much I enjoyed your visit. Even Annie . . ."

Maggie cut him off. "I think you had better stop there. I didn't help Annie one little bit; all I did was confuse her and make her angry," she said sadly.

"Oh, no, Maggie. She made an effort to come to breakfast and dinner, something she hasn't done since . . ." he nodded in Ian's direction. She understood what he meant.

"But at the end, Donald, she was so angry she wouldn't see me."

"When you return, you will see she will act differently. She thought you had come to stay; Annie forgets things so easily."

It was time for the visitors to leave. Ian and Maggie exchanged bear hugs, John Colton saluted Ian, who proudly returned the salute, and they all exchanged warm handclasps. Ian parroted his father's, "Come back soon, Maggie," and Maggie watched as they went down the gangplank to make sure she could see them on the pier. Ian was perched on his father's shoulders, and when he heard the two toots which John had promised, he became so excited he almost fell off. Maggie stood at the rail, waving until they were out of sight.

XXXI

PARIS

Maggie could hear a subdued hum of activity as she entered her room in the Grand Hotel. Her salon was, indeed, a place of beauty, but she had no feeling of coming home. She had not notified anyone of her time of arrival and therefore made the initial readjustment alone, which had been her intention. She went into her living quarters, bathed and changed before going to the studio to look in on Lily. She was greeted with hugs and kisses and "You look wonderful! Why didn't you tell us you were coming? We could have met you!" and finally, "Is Marcel with you?"

"I didn't tell anyone when we would dock, Lily." She quickly changed the subject. "Everybody busy?"

"We've been working on the designs you sent. They're truly beautiful, Maggie! The show should cause a sensation. Do you want to see what we're doing?" said Lily, obviously eager to show Maggie how well she had managed on her own.

"Glad you like them. Yes, I do," Maggie answered as they walked toward the workroom where the seamstresses were cutting, pinning and sewing industriously.

"I've managed a few more sketches on the voyage," Maggie told Lily. "Do you think you'll need them?"

"If you want to discard some of the first ones, we still can," said Lily. "Otherwise, I think we have more than enough." This was Lily's end of the business and Maggie was more than glad to leave the decision to her.

Lily asked tentatively, "Does Marcel know you're here?" Maggie shook her head. "He's been haunting me to find out when you would return," Lily continued.

"I'll get in touch with him. Has he said anything about his mother?"

"No, but he has seen her." (Lily didn't know how seldom.)

Maggie turned her attention back to her studio, greeted each of the women working on her designs, examined some of the almost finished pieces and was satisfied that they were, as she had hoped, unusual and attractive. "Lily, you're doing an excellent job. I can see that my part is finished, or almost, and I'm not needed now."

Taking advantage of their close and long friendship Lily ventured, "Maggie, you *look* well, but you don't sound it. Is anything wrong?"

Maggie sighed. "I've got a lot on my mind. I finally located my sisters, Annie and Kate. It was hard to leave Annie—she's not well."

Lily murmured her sympathy. She was dying to hear how Maggie had found her two sisters, but it was obvious that Maggie didn't want to discuss it just then.

Maggie left the workrooms, realizing that she must inform Marcel of her arrival. Since it

416

was still early, she decided to walk to Marcel's office instead of sending a messenger or hiring a cab. The trees had started to bud. The wide boulevards were uncrowded and although Maggie still did not feel quite at home, she knew she would always have a love affair with Paris. She was thinking thus as she reached the headquarters of the Compagnie Mennon. It was a handsome building and, like the more modern ones, equipped with an elevator. The executive suite was on the fourth floor. A pert little secretary, black spitcurls framing a heart-shaped face, greeted Maggie politely as she entered. The girl was new and did not recognize Mme. Mennon. "Monsieur Mennon is not in. Would you like to leave your name?" she asked.

"I will leave a note for him. May I have that?" Maggie pointed to a pad. The secretary raised her eyebrows at the request but handed her the pad and a pencil. Maggie wrote a quick note, saying she had returned and would have dinner in the hotel dining room at eight, if he would like to join her. The girl, Janine, waited until Maggie left before reading it with some amusement. She would give it to him but it would do no good—she herself was having dinner with Marcel at his apartment.

Marcel didn't reach his office until four o'clock that afternoon. With a wink, Janine handed him the note. She didn't expect the excitement it engendered.

"She was here?" Marcel slapped his forehead with the palm of his hand. "I should have been here when she came!"

Janine said archly, "She must be someone very special."

Marcel stared at her. "You don't know? She is my wife—I've been waiting months for her to come home. Of course she's special!"

The signature had been just "M." It hadn't signified anything to Janine. "Does that mean we won't be having dinner tonight?" she pouted, her disappointment showing. "There's lots of time—we could at least spend some of it together, have a drink or . . ." she said provocatively, "something."

"You're talking nonsense, Janine," Marcel snapped. "I must go home and change into appropriate clothing for dinner."

Janine was aghast. "For your *wife?*"

He didn't answer but dashed out of the office. He needed a massage and a facial massage as well—Jean would erase most signs of his recent dissipation. Marcel was nervous and excited; Jean's work was cut out for him. By seven o'clock, Marcel had slept and bathed and dressed. Checking his appearance anxiously in the mirror, he was satisfied that Jean's ministrations had been fairly successful. To steady his nerves, Marcel rapidly drank several ounces of cognac.

He stopped at the florist and had two dozen roses sent to Maggie's flat, keeping one to give her when they met.

Marcel's plan to embrace Maggie and smother her with kisses was thwarted when he discovered she was already at her table in the hotel dining room, fragile and lovely in sea-green moire. He hurried in and welcomed her with a kiss on the hand she extended. "Maggie, my darling wife! I am so happy to have you back," he said warmly. He extended the rose, which she accepted.

"Thank you, Marcel. How have you been?" It wasn't exactly the passionate exchange he had hoped for.

"Very well, thank you," he said, seating himself. "And you?"

"I am well. How is Mama?"

"She is in good health and, I think, finally has accepted the fact of my father's . . . of Etienne's death," he told her.

"I plan to see her this weekend," Maggie said.

"We will both go. Mama will be so happy to see you."

Maggie noticed that the flush on Marcel's face was a little too high, his eye too bright. It wasn't difficult to see he had reverted to his former style of life.

"As you wish," she agreed. The rest of their tepid conversation during dinner brought Marcel no closer to the intimacy he looked for. When they finished, they walked to her private elevator. "Goodnight, Marcel," she said, once again extending her hand.

"*Goodnight?* I'm not coming up with you? Is this what I've waited for? After all this time when I have lived as a monk . . ." Her look of doubt made him angrier. "I *have,* despite what you think—and now you say goodnight, just like that? You haven't forgiven me?"

Maggie's expression was stony. "There is nothing to forgive. The fault was mine. I should have known you better before we married. As you said once, I was naive." The elevator car arrived and she stepped in. Marcel fumed as the elaborate grillwork closed behind her. Furious, he returned to his own flat where Janine was waiting for him.

She enjoyed the brutal lovemaking Maggie could never understand.

Maggie kept herself busy and did not see Marcel again until Friday. She had sent a note to his office to inform him she would be leaving for the chateau at two in the afternoon. He accompanied her. Their stilted conversation was of Maggie's trip to America and the mixed joy of finding her sisters. Marcel made several efforts to steer the conversation to more personal topics, Maggie adroitly evaded the issue.

Mama greeted them with tears. "I am so glad to see my dear children!" she sobbed.

Maggie embraced her lovingly. "And we are happy to see you. Don't cry, dear."

"You cry too much, Mama," Marcel said as he kissed her cheek.

"They are tears of happiness—it is so long since you have both been here! You don't look well, Marcel. Have you been ill?" she asked, peering into his face.

Marcel turned away. "Not really. I missed my wife and spent my time pining for her. I thought she'd never return," he told her. Mama fortunately missed the skeptical look Maggie shot at him.

It was a lovely weekend for Mama and Maggie. They had much to talk about. Mama invited them both to look over M. Mennon's paintings, an offer which Marcel declined. Maggie selected several saying, "I will cherish them and one day, because of his teaching, I may show you a few of my own." As always, Marcel was bored but he kept his drinking to a minimum during the day. Each night, however, angry and frustrated by Maggie's insistence on separate rooms, he retired early and drank himself unconscious.

Mama did not know of their sleeping arrangement. On the way back to Paris, Marcel threatened to tell her the next time they visited the chateau. "You are not keeping your word," he accused. "You said if I became a dutiful son you would take me back."

Maggie was unmoved. "That was only part of the problem. I also said I would have to see if I could forget the scene I walked in on that dreadful night. As for being a dutiful son, I have learned that you saw your mother exactly *three times* while I was away. I don't consider that you did much to comfort her during her period of mourning."

Marcel sighed. "You know how boring I find a visit to the chateau, Maggie. Why do you nag me?" he asked petulantly.

"When you can forget yourself and give love to those who love you, you will be a better man," Maggie shot back.

"I do love you, yet you continue to reject me," he whined. "I know you are still angry about Flame, and," he lied, "I haven't seen her since—at least, not like that."

"You are mistaken," said Maggie quietly. "I am not angry. I feel sorry for you. You don't know what it means to love someone. I hope one day you will discover that it doesn't mean just going to bed." Seeing his bewilderment at her statement, she knew he never would.

"Does that mean we will not resume our marriage?"

"It is finished. We will go our separate ways," she replied.

"Then I won't go see Mama anymore!" threatened Marcel, knowing Maggie's weakness.

Maggie was angry. "Don't try to blackmail me! I hope for your sake you *will* visit her. However, I will leave that to your conscience." They had used her carriage for the journey and she dropped him off at his flat. He slammed out of it, flinging the door open and leaving it that way. The disapproving coachman had to come down to close it.

Mama came to stay with Maggie a month before her new collection was to be shown. "You were such a help to me last time," Maggie told her, "I would like you to do the invitations again; and this time, I would appreciate it if you would act as hostess to the friends you invite."

Mama hesitated. "I'd love to do it, dear, but I don't want to detract from the professionalism of your presenation." But it took very little persuasion from Maggie to convince her.

The summer MerMaid collection was the sensation Lily had predicted. Applause met every piece that was shown. Her bathing dresses, even more daring than the year before, acted as the bellwether, appropriately enough, for the direction in which the House of MerMaid would go forward. The greatest compliment Maggie received was on House of Worth stationery: "My initial amusement has been transformed into the highest admiration. (signed) Charles." The note was tucked into a basket of *muguet du bois*, the fragrant lily-of-the-valley, so prevalent at that time of the year that all Paris seemed scented with it.

Maggie spend the next week taking care of business with Lily. She then joined Mama at the chateau, were she spent the next month. Marcel was not in evidence the whole time she was there, and his mother, sensing unspoken tension, never questioned his absence. Maggie told her the story of her first voyage to America; and of her search for her sisters. She had already mentioned on her last visit to America; and of her search for her sisters. She had already mentioned her last visit to Mama, and I have had to come to a decision about going back to America to live." Mama listened with her eyes closed so as not to reveal the pain she felt at the prospect of losing her beloved daughter. "And now, although I don't want to burden you further, we must speak of Marcel and our marriage," said Maggie at last.

"I know something is wrong, dear, and I can almost guess what it is," Mama sighed, then motioned Maggie to continue.

"I have not been the right mate for your son," she confessed. "He needs a playmate, not a wife. I am consumed with my career. I do not enjoy his companions or their nightly debauchery. I guess I'm not sophisticated enough to participate in their 'fun,' as they call it. We are wrong for each other and neither of us can or wants to change." She paused, not wanting to go into deep or specific accusations.

Before she went on, Mama spoke. She reached over and took Maggie's hand. "I hope you will forgive Etienne and me. We knew about Marcel's escapades, and we looked the other way because we loved him so. We were

423

so happy when he met and married you! We thought you would supply the balance he needed. His father and I often spoke of the unfair burden we had placed on your shoulders." She sighed. "I could see things were not going well. I know the signs of dissipation in my son; I could see his good looks and healthy body deteriorating more each time he visited."

". . . which wasn't often," Maggie interjected.

"True. Perhaps Etienne and I kept too many secrets from you. I'm sure you don't know that Jean is more nurse than valet. We pay . . ." she corrected herself, "I pay him handsomely to look after Marcel's well-being. Jean does the best he can."

Maggie sighed. "I am relieved that I have not shocked you by my recital. I am so sorry, Mama—I really wanted our marriage to work."

"Will you divorce him?" Mama asked, almost in a whisper.

Maggie wrung her hands in agitation. "I don't know what to do. We should no longer be tied together and yet, a divorce is scandalous."

Surprisingly, Mama said, "I will help you, dear. Etienne and I had such a loving life that I can't bear to see you in an unhappy situation. How much longer do you plan to stay with me?"

"I have made reservations to go back to Paris on the fifteenth of September—another two weeks," Maggie told her. "And then I must return to America."

"I will send word to Claude Galle to come for dinner on Friday," said Mama. "He will

424

know what to do. Oh, my dear, I wish you were not leaving France!"

They rose and came together in a warm embrace. "I love you, Mama and I shall miss you. But I will be here twice a year for the collections and we will spend lots of time together then."

"You will keep your Paris branch?" Mama asked, drying her eyes on a lacy handkerchief.

"Yes—it will work out very well. It doesn't matter where I am—all I need is my sketch pad and drawing pencils. I shall continue to send sketches to Lily, who will be in complete charge."

"How does Lily feel about settling here permanently?"

"Delighted! You know, of course, she was born in Paris. Her family is here and, with the new arrangement, she told me she will marry a gentleman who has been paying her court."

Mama's tears began again. "I am so sorry, Maggie, that Marcel was not a better husband," she said.

Maggie hugged her briefly. "I'm over my disillusionment and besides, I feel I got more out of the marriage by finding you and Papa than I will suffer by losing a mate."

"It has been a blessing for both of us," Mama sobbed. "I couldn't love you more if you were my own daughter, dear."

When M. Galle arrived, he said a divorce wouldn't be necessary. He would start annulment proceedings, based on the evidence of Marcel's decadence. He didn't think Maggie's presence would be necessary and would contact her immediately if she had to be present for some reason. Through Maggie's tears as she left the chateau, she was somewhat comforted by the sight of Claude Galle holding Mama's hand. Mama would not be alone.

XXXII

CONFESSION

Donald met Maggie when her ship docked in New York. Although she had written to say when she would arrive, she was surprised to see him. Her first reaction was alarm. "Is it Annie?" she asked, clutching his arm.

Donald didn't answer, but said, "I need to talk to you, if you have time."

"My carriage is waiting," said Maggie. "Please join me—we can drive to my home and talk when we get there."

Letty greeted Maggie with a hug, then stepped back when she saw she had a man with her. "Letty, this is Mr. MacConnack," Maggie said, "my brother-in-law. Will you bring us some sherry and those little French biscuits? We'll be in the parlor." Donald waited while Maggie changed out of her traveling costume into a more comfortable dress.

When she returned, he said, "You must be a good traveller. You look splendid."

"I have much to tell you—but I want to hear about Annie first."

Donald's news was not good. Annie hadn't come downstairs since Maggie had left. The only reason she would give was that Maggie

427

had disappeared. She seemed to have retired into the past, and Donald feared for her mind. "Maggie, I know you're tired and probably have many things to do and possibly personal problems to solve as well, but if you can spare the time to come home with me . . ." there was an urgency in his voice. "I know I'm being selfish—I haven't even asked how things went with you and . . . ?"

She supplied the name. "Marcel." He nodded. "I'm happy to tell you that it is coming to a satisfactory conclusion." She told him about the imminent annulment. "I have no regrets. I feel as if a tremendous burden has been lifted from my shoulders. And I will come with you, Donald, but not tonight. I intend to settle here permanently and must get this house in order. Don't tell Annie that I have arrived. This is Wednesday—I can leave here at . . . let us say, ten o'clock Sunday morning." He looked troubled at the delay, but brightened when she added, "I will have everything in readiness here so that I can stay with you for at least a month."

"Oh, Maggie, if you can spare that much time . . ." he didn't have to finish the sentence. He held her hand tight in his. "I would be ever so grateful. I'm sure Annie's health would improve. As for little Ian, he still asks about you and . . . " he broke off, embarrassed by the tears he could feel stinging his eyes.

Maggie reached up to put her hands on either side of his face, pulled him to her and kissed him lightly. "I love you, Donald MacConnack, for caring so much!"

The emotion-filled moment passed. "I will

come and pick you up on Sunday," Donald announced.

"No, I'd rather use my own carriage. Then, if for any reason there is an emergency here, I can come back without disturbing you. I don't anticipate any such, but just in case . . ."

"Any way you want it, Maggie, as long as you come," he said gratefully.

"Not to worry, my dear. I will be there."

Donald left then, declining her invitation to dinner. "I don't like to be too far away for too long," he explained.

"I understand."

"We'll see you Sunday then, for lunch."

After he had gone, Maggie walked around her flat, mentally renovating and making decisions about changes. She would convert Lily's house so the entire workspace would be occupied by the cutters and sewers and she would install dressing rooms for the models. Her house would become only where she lived, not where she also worked.

Maggie retired early and spent the rest of the week contacting carpenters and other workmen. All she wanted to do at this time was begin the renovations to Lily's place; hers could wait until she returned from Tarrytown.

On Sunday promptly at ten, Maggie was on her way. She had managed a brief luncheon the day before with Ellen, long enough to fill her in on the sad details of her almost defunct marriage and the happy news about her discovery of Annie and Kate, and to give her and the children the specially designed clothes she had brought back with her from Paris. Maggie enjoyed the drive—it was a beautiful autumn day, warm enough to be comfortable in a light shawl. Still, the air was fresh and invigorating.

When Maggie arrived at the MacConnack mansion, she found Annie seated on the veranda with a light blanket tucked around her, waiting. She greeted her sister with weak tears, sobbing, "You came back, little one! I didn't think you would."

Maggie kissed her and assured her she would never "disappear" again. Annie believed her when she saw the quantity of luggage Maggie had brought. "What is that?" she asked as a large square case was brought into the house.

"That's my drawing board. If I'm going to stay here, I must work," Maggie told her.

Donald had directed the servants to bring all Maggie's luggage to the wing that had once been occupied by Robbie and Kate. It was perfect—the long windows gave Maggie the light she needed. One room had been set up as a studio for her, an example of Donald's thoughtfulness.

At noon, Annie, supported on either side by Maggie and Donald, walked into the dining room. Amy and Gunther Crismann had been invited to meet the long-lost sister. As Maggie remembered, she and Amy were almost the same age. "I am happy to meet you again," Amy said. "You ran away and hid when we came to visit that first time!"

Maggie blushed. "I apologize to both you and Donald for my anti-social behaviour then. I felt terribly neglected—I wanted to go to America more than any other member of the family and no one paid any attention to me. I was spoiled, you know, and determined to have my own way, so I stowed away on the ship I thought you and my sisters were on. As Donald has no doubt told you, it turned out to be a different ship, but I got here all the same."

Donald added, "It worked out well." He went on to explain her success as a *couturiere*. Amy was very impressed—she was very fashion-conscious and was familiar with the MerMaid label.

After the first few bites of food, Maggie noticed Annie was barely nibbling; her hand shook as she attempted to lift her fork. Emma as usual was standing by. Annie nodded to her and as her nurse approached she said in a small voice, "If you will excuse me, I would like to rest. The excitement has tired me." Donald helped Emma take her to her room.

They were all concerned and Maggie's heart sank as her eyes followed her eldest sister. "I hate to see Annie this way," she sighed. She turned to Amy. "You remember how strong and healthy she was when you and Donald came to Scotland. Now she's like a different person."

"She's brighter than usual," Amy consoled. "Perhaps when she has you with her for awhile, she'll pick up her strength again."

"That's why I'm here," said Maggie. "She was always so vibrant and in charge of everyone back home. Her authority was almost as strong as my father's. She brought us up, you know, even though she was only a child when Mother died. We each had our chores to do—although I always got the easy tasks. She cooked for us and ran the household as our mother would have done. And now, with this beautiful home and family, with servants to do all the work, she seems to have lost interest in living. Ian is a beautiful child, bright and loving and yet he seems to irritate her."

Amy, in an effort to lift the sadness that had descended on them, said, "Ian speaks of you constantly, Maggie. He told us of his Aunt Maggie who was on a ship going across the ocean, and that the ocean was much bigger than our pond."

Her effort worked. Maggie smiled as she said enthusiastically, "Isn't he a darling?"

When Donald returned to the table, he was delighted to find everyone talking about his son. "Ian says you promised to play ball with him again," he said to Maggie.

"Indeed I did! After I settled in, I stopped by the nursery to see him. I was so pleased that he remembered me. We exchanged bear hugs and promised to play ball. Will he be coming down soon?"

"In about half an hour," said Donald.

"Won't you join Ian and me?" Maggie suggested. "A game of catch might be fun for all of us."

And so it was. Maggie and Donald took turns tossing the ball to Ian, who was becoming very adept at catching and returning it, and Amy and Gunther cheered them on.

Each morning Maggie would have breakfast with Annie in her room. When Annie expressed interest in Maggie's work, she was brought into the studio to watch her sketch, but Annie's interest waned after the first few days and thereafter the sisters parted after break-

432

fast and didn't meet again until the afternoon.

One day, toward the end of the first week, Maggie asked Annie to join her and Ian as they romped outside. "Watch us play and see how much fun it is to run around," Maggie urged. Annie permitted herself to be brought to a chair on the lawn, bundled in shawls and scarves, as the air had turned nippy, the ever-present Emma in attendance. Maggie tried to watch her sister, hoping for some response to the boisterous activity of a game of catch. But when she saw Annie put her hands over her ears to shut out the sound of Ian's high, childish laughter, she was ready to admit defeat. Ian was in high spirits, rosy-cheeked and adorable in the bright blue knitted cap and sweater Maggie had brought for him. He ran over to Annie and stood a few feet away, calling, "Catch, Mama!"

"No, no, no!" Annie cried, but it was too late. The ball, not too well aimed, hit her arm, then landed in her lap. With a look of revulsion she swept it away with one hand and beckoned to Emma with the other. "Take me upstairs, Emma," she ordered, effectively ending the game since Emma would need Maggie's help in taking her to her room.

Ian stood in front of her, frozen with misery at what he had done. "Mama, I didn't mean to hurt you! Mama, please, I didn't mean it!" he wailed.

Maggie was angry; sick or not, Annie could have controlled her reaction. She hugged the little boy, and said, "There, there, love, it's all right. You didn't hurt your mama, did he Annie?" But Annie didn't answer. As Emma helped her to her feet, Maggie called to one of the gardeners, "Help Emma take Mrs. MacConnack back to the house. I don't want to leave Master Ian alone." The gardener tipped his hat and dutifully took Annie's other arm.

When they were on their way, Maggie knelt down and swept the sobbing child into her arms. "Don't cry, darling. You didn't hurt Mama. She has forgotten how to play. She was surprised, that's all." His sobbing finally subsided and Maggie took him upstairs for his nap. She stayed with him until he slept.

From that time forward, Annie kept to her room and Maggie lunched with her there occasionally. She cut her working time short one day and decided to visit her sister earlier than usual. She found Annie was lying prostrate on the bed, and as she turned her face to Maggie it was evident she had been crying.

"What is it, dear, what troubles you so? Tell me what it is, perhaps I can help," Maggie soothed. She stroked Annie's tangled hair away from her face, then put a drop of witch hazel into the basin and gently bathed her face with a damp cloth, but the tears didn't stop.

Annie grabbed her hand and clung to it. "I am so glad you are here, but it isn't enough. Oh, Maggie," she burst out, "I am dying and I want to go home to die!"

Maggie suppressed her own anguish, saying tartly, "If you will it so, you *will* die! You can be just as determined to live and get well."

"No, I will not be here much longer. Please, Maggie," she begged pitifully, "take me home!" The dam had broken and a river of sorrows released as Annie at last bared the secret places of her heart. "I hate America and the casual ways of Americans; I hate this big house and all the servants. I have had six children and I loved them all and took care of them. I have another now, and I have done my duty to my husband by giving him a son. I love Donald, but it doesn't make up for my loneliness."

"He's a good husband, Annie. He spends all the time he can spare from the mill with you," Maggie reminded her.

"I am lonely even when he is here! I want to go back to my own country, to Scotland. It is all I desire. I'm afraid I'll never see our sisters or Da again. That is the grief I have carried for five years. Love isn't enough." She wailed, "I want to go home!"

Emma, as always, had been near and now bustled over with medication, which she administered. Shortly thereafter, Annie was asleep. "Did you know this, Emma?" Maggie asked.

"No, Miss Maggie, as far as I know she has never told anyone how homesick she was," said Emma sadly.

Maggie spent the afternoon in deep thought. Sheets of cold rain had been drumming against the windows all day, which added to her gloom. Instead of their usual playtime outdoors, she had brought Ian into her studio where she set up a small makeshift easel. She gave him crayons and drawing paper and the sight of him in deep concentration gave her the only pleasure she experienced all day.

When Donald came to read to Ian that night, he was presented with several oddly colored landscapes, each one having in common a brilliant, yellow sun with a smiling face.

435

"These are for you, Papa," the child said eagerly. "Aunt Maggie and I drew today because it was raining outside."

Donald held one drawing at arms' length, exclaiming, "This is the most . . . *unusual* picture of trees I have ever seen. They are *so blue.* Thank you, son. I shall have it framed and hang it in my office."

"Aunt Maggie said I am crative," Ian said with pride.

"Crative?" Donald repeated. Then light dawned. "Oh, creative . . . cre . . . a . . . tive," he pronounced carefully, expecting Ian to repeat it correctly.

Ian shook his head vigorously up and down. "Yes."

His father laughed out loud and picked him up, holding him high in the air. "You are a wonderful boy . . . very, very wonderful!"

"You are, too, Papa, and so is Aunt Maggie."

That sent both Donald and Maggie into gales of laughter, which Ian didn't understand but joined in anyway.

In the early evening, Donald stopped by to see Annie. Emma, meeting him at the door, told him she was sleeping. It was not unusual for her to sleep through the dinner hour, and his mood was light as he joined Maggie for dinner. "It seems I'm always saying thank you for all the time you spend with Ian," he told her. "He is a different child since your arrival. Right now, he considers himself an artist. In fact, I fully intend to have that painting framed as I told him."

"Oh, yes, the one with the blue trees was his very best," Maggie agreed. With an effort she tried to match Donald's mood; she had much to say but would wait until after dinner. When the dessert was served she waved hers away.

"I'll wait, too," he said. "We can have it later. Shall we have coffee in the library?"

Maggie walked rapidly ahead of him. When the coffee service was brought in, she poured, gave a cup to him and accepted the brandy he offered, then walked restlessly across the room to the long windows and back.

"You seem nervous, Maggie. Is something wrong?" Donald asked.

"Not exactly, but . . ." she picked up the snifter of brandy and drank it down in one gulp. "I have something I must discuss with you."

"About Annie?"

Her "yes" came out as a sigh. "This is very difficult for me, Donald. The last thing I want to do is cause you more distress," she began. Although she was apprehensive, he motioned her to go on. "I visited Annie earlier than usual this morning. I thought at first she was sleeping; then I noticed she was crying uncontrollably, with her face buried in the pillow so no one would hear." Donald frowned. She continued quickly, "I called her name and she turned to me, grabbed my hand fiercely and sobbed and clung to me. I tried to soothe her and asked her to tell me what troubled her . . ." She paused.

"And?" Donald prodded.

"How can I tell you this easily?" she murmured, almost to herself, then plunged into the heart of the matter. "Annie wants to go home."

He raised his eyebrows in question. "Doesn't she know where she is? That she is home?"

Maggie shook her head. "She meant home in Scotland . . . in Paisley."

"If she had told me she was homesick . . ." Donald began.

"No, Donald, it is not simply homesick. It is an obsession with her. From what she told me, she has never been," she searched for the word, "*comfortable* here. She misses the family, and says she will never get used to America and the casual American customs; she says she has given you a son and now she wants to go home; I wish I could spare you the rest of it, Donald, but . . ." Maggie swallowed hard, "she said she is dying and wants to go home to die."

Hand covering his eyes, Donald paced the length of the room as she finished her recital. He could not conceal his tears. He cried out from the depths of his being. "Jesus Christ!" Maggie didn't know whether it was a prayer or an epithet. "I am a blundering idiot! I should have known." His voice lowered until it was almost a whisper. "Perhaps, way down deep I suspected, but I refused to let the thought come to the surface. I have been abysmally selfish and have given Annie nothing but the wish to die." He had opened the French windows and stood there now with the rain beating in on him as he clenched his fists in self-anger. "Why didn't I know? Why didn't I see?"

Maggie gently put her arm around him and led him out of the rain, back into the room. He slumped into a chair and she sat at his feet.

"Know this," she said as she took his hand. "Annie never would have admitted it to you, or me, if I hadn't caught her at her weakest moment. My sisters and Da were her life; I didn't help matters by running away from home, nor did Kate's behaviour. More, the fact that Da wanted to marry again probably shocked her. As much as she loves you, Donald, she would have been content to stay with him."

Donald shook his head and said wearily, "Not enough. She doesn't love me enough . . ."

"Not enough to overcome her longing for our homeland. She told me once that when you consummated your love on your wedding night, it was the culmination of a life that seemed much longer than her actual years, and she was ready then for it to be finished. It is more terrible for you than for her—it was the beginning for you; for Annie, it was the end."

Donald buried his head in his hands. "I should have been more sensitive to her needs. You know, she had refused my proposal many times because she didn't want to leave your father alone. When I learned he wanted to remarry, he and I put great pressure on her. I knew she loved me and I gave her no choice but to come with me to America. But the truth is, she used your father as an excuse; she was content with her life as it was." Maggie didn't interrupt him; it was good for him to talk. "I would have taken her back any time, but she had such a fear of crossing the ocean, I didn't suggest it."

He was silent for a moment. There was pain and confusion in his eyes as he turned to

Maggie and asked, "What can we do?"

Maggie said promptly, "I think we should have a talk with her doctor."

The doctor, armed with the information Maggie had given him, used it to advantage the next time he visited Annie and managed at first to avert hysteria which had accompanied her plea to Maggie to take her home. "I understand, Mrs. MacConnack, you want to visit your family in Scotland," he said cheerfully. "And I see no reason why you should not do so. But you must work a little harder at getting your strength back. You must get out of bed and walk a little every day, and . . ."

Annie started to scream, "No, no, no! I don't want to *visit*. I want to go *home* to Da and the girls. I am dying and I don't want to die in a foreign land!" She started to feebly beat at the doctor with her fists. "Why don't you understand? Why doesn't *anybody* understand? Da would know . . ." Dr. Wilson did his best to calm her as Emma came running with a sedative. He waited until the sedative took effect, then went down to speak with Donald and Maggie, his expression grave. "Mrs. MacConnack is very upset and insists she wants to go home to Da—her father I assume—" they both nodded, "and the girls. Do you know what girls she is referring to?"

Maggie explained the situation, finishing by saying, "The girls are all married now—one of our sisters lives nearby, in fact—father no longer lives in the house where we were raised. If it were up to me, I would take her home."

"And you, Mr. MacConnack?" Dr. Wilson asked.

"If that's the only thing that will make her happy, yes."

"When would you do this?"

Maggie and Donald looked at each other and Donald answered, "We would have to wait for better weather . . . perhaps in the early spring."

"Yes. The water is much too rough at this time of the year for a woman in Mrs. MacConnack's delicate state of health," the doctor agreed.

"I am leaving next week as I have to be in Paris on business," Maggie put in. "But I will return as soon as possible and stay until May, when I have to go back."

The doctor was impressed. "You travel a lot, Mrs. Mennon."

"Yes, I have business in France and in New York as well." Maggie closed her eyes, trying to work out a schedule. "If we leave the beginning of April, we could bring Annie home before I go to Paris," she suggested.

Donald, grim-faced, asked, "Can we wait that long, Dr. Wilson?"

"I think so," he said, concealing his reservations. "Tell her your plans. The prospect will no doubt give her hope and the will to live."

The following morning, Donald sat on Annie's bed waiting for her to show some sign of recognition. "Darling," he finally said softly, "are you awake? I have some very good news to tell you."

Annie opened her eyes. It was obvious that she had not been sleeping. She didn't speak, neither did she close her eyes again. He took her hand; it lay limp in his. "Maggie and I are going to take you home to be with Da and the girls." Annie still didn't speak, but tears began to roll down her cheeks and Donald kissed them away. "It is winter now and the seas are rough. Dr. Wilson says you must gain some strength before you make the voyage, and that will be just right, because as soon as it is spring we shall leave for Scotland; by then you will be strong enough. Ah, my love, you are smiling!"

"Thank you," Annie whispered.

When Maggie sailed for France, there were still many questions to be resolved, Would Annie be willing to come back to America when her health was restored? Would she keep Ian with her if she did not? If she decided to remain in Scotland, what would Donald do about the silk mill? These questions plagued her all the way to Europe.

The same questions obsessed Donald, but he could think no further than getting Annie better. He couldn't tell if she had improved, except that she had not forgotten his promise. Every morning she would ask, "Is is spring yet?"

Once again the House of MerMaid had a triumphant showing. The high standards she and Lily had set, Maggie vowed, would have to be maintained and to that end the week following the showing, they met together constantly, making momentous decisions. They agreed they would expand their Paris workrooms to accommodate more employees, perhaps even look for a new location. Perhaps, Lily suggested, she would have to send the overflow of customers to New York. It was amusing to think that perhaps the Parisians would start the semi-annual fashion pilgramage in reverse.

Maggie stayed another week to attend Lily's wedding to her doctor. She had met him when he was called in to attend to one of the girls who had cut her finger instead of the fabric she was working on.

"I never expected I would marry again, Maggie," she confessed, blushing girlishly.

"Be happy," Maggie told her. "Above all else, love him and be happy!"

Mme. Mennon had come to Paris for the ceremony and after the wedding she and Maggie went to the chateau. During Maggie's visit, Claude Galle came often.

"The annulment has not yet been finalized, but I have been assured it will," he told her. "I have tried to speak to Marcel but he becomes violent whenever he sees me."

"Unfortunately, that is true," Mama sighed. "He has been here only once since you last left. When he arrived, Claude and I were having dinner. The moment he saw us, he shook his fist at Claude and would have attacked him if not for Jean. He had tried to prevent Marcel from coming here, but Marcel got away. Jean followed him to the chateau and managed to subdue him before any harm was done. They returned to Paris that same night." She shook her head sadly. "Marcel was very drunk!"

"It is a terrible situation and it grieves Marianne," Claude said with concern.

"No, Claude, not any more. It is his wild life

and his drinking, and God knows what else he does that has made him this way. I no longer have a son. This man is a stranger." Mama spoke with sorrowful conviction.

On the twentieth of January, Maggie sailed away, glad to be going to her home in America and anxious to see Annie, Ian, and Donald.

Again Donald met her at the dock and this time accepted her invitation to dinner. "Annie won't miss me," he said sadly. "She asks for you constantly and always with the question, 'Is it spring yet?' "

"Is she stronger?" Maggie asked.

Donald shook his head. "No, on the contrary. She seems to be fading away. Emma almost has to force-feed her, she'll take only liquids. Perhaps when she sees you . . ." his voice was hopeless as it trailed into silence.

"Don't fret," Maggie urged. "We both know I can't promise anything, but I'll do everything I can to help her. Has Kate been to see her?"

"She came once, but Annie refused to see her," Donald sighed.

They talked for a while longer. "My partner and I have made some changes which I will have to explain to my assistant here," Maggie finally said as Donald was about to leave. "Give me a few days. I will join you as soon as I can, I promise. If there is an emergency—and I pray there will not be—send for me immediately and I'll leave whatever I am doing."

He kissed her forehead. "Don't be too long, Maggie," he begged.

Instead of waiting until morning to talk to Madeleine, Maggie sat up most of the night writing out the changes that would be taking place. When Madeleine arrived, she had her read it. "I will wait and answer any questions you may have—I wrote it when I was very tired. Some of it may need clarification."

Madeleine had very few questions, saying after she'd gone over the material, "I understand. I guess I'll have to brush up on my French if we're going to have a Paris clientele coming to our door!"

"That's far in the future, Madeleine, and I know you don't have to brush up on your French—I have heard you and Lily chatter away like two French magpies."

Madeleine laughed in agreement. "That's so. But without Lily to talk to, I'm afraid I've become very rusty."

Maggie's luggage had arrived shortly before she had herself. She did not bother to unpack. The following day, she had her bags loaded into the carriage. As the coachman carried out the last valise, Maggie said to Madeleine, "I may send for my trunk. Letty will know what to pack. I'm leaving immediately for my sister's home—she has been ill, as you know. If you need me, you can always send a wire."

She herself had wired ahead, letting Donald know she would be arriving several days before he expected her. He was overjoyed to find her sitting in Annie's room when he came home from the mill that evening.

"My dear Maggie, how good to see you here!" he whispered. "Does Annie know?"

"She opened her eyes just once and asked me if it was spring. But I'm not sure she knows who I am." Maggie's face was tearstained. Donald took her gently by the hand and led her downstairs to the drawing room where he poured two glasses of brandy.

"I'm not sure I should, Donald," she said. "I haven't had anything to eat since morning."

"No food was brought to you?" He was instantly angry.

"It was offered. I didn't want it."

"We'll take care of that right away." He pulled the bellcord and when a manservant came in, asked how soon dinner could be served.

"We can serve whenever you wish, sir," he was told. A few minutes later dinner was announced by Jeffrey. Donald escorted Maggie to the table where they continued to talk as they ate, not realizing they spoke in hushed tones as though they were dining in a crypt. Donald was the first to notice and resumed his normal voice. "Have you seen Ian?" he asked.

"Oh, yes!" Maggie's voice immediately rose to meet the level of his. "He was so glad to see me. He is such a warm, loving child, Donald. You have done a very good job raising him."

"Me?"

"Certainly not Annie," said Maggie, her tone regretful.

"No, I'm afraid not," Donald admitted. "Wanda—Nursie—has done most of the bringing up."

"Not without your good influence. He adores you."

Suddenly Maggie glanced at the little gold watch pinned to her dress and Donald pulled out his pocket watch at the same time.

They spoke at the same time. "Time to read a story to Ian." Laughing, they went upstairs together, lowering their voices as they neared the top of the staircase and tiptoed past Annie's room.

Maggie got a goodnight kiss and the obligatory bear hug from Ian and promised to play with him the next day. "We'll play in the snow if we can and if not, you can come in and draw with me," she promised. Either one suited him just fine. When Maggie left them, Ian was settled down in his bed and Donald was opening his son's favorite animal storybook. . . .

PART FIVE

XXXIII

ANNIE GOES HOME

The last time Kate Maccrae Sullivan had set foot in the MacConnack home had been on the day when she had attempted to see Annie and been rejected. Now she stood in the great hall, waiting for Maggie. She was nervous and plucked at the tiny buttons on her form-fitting jacket. This day her dress was properly somber; still, the olive green ensemble and small bonnet perched atop her titian hair enhanced, rather than detracted from her milk-white complexion. The corset and many layers of undergarments made her uncomfortable and she longed for the freedom of her usual wide skirt and soft blouse with as few undergarments as Rory would allow. She clasped her prayer book and rosary beads, and murmured a brief prayer.

Maggie greeted her with a kiss, her eyes faintly red-rimmed. "Kate, I'm so glad you have come!"

Kate embraced her. "Does Donald know . . . has he given his permission for me to see Annie? She wouldn't see me before—I'm afraid she became very upset."

Maggie nodded. "Come. She may not know you or seem to be aware of your presence, but speak to her softly; she will hear you . . . I think. It's difficult to tell sometimes."

The shades were drawn and the light was dim as Kate followed Maggie into Annie's room. It took a few moments for her eyes to focus. As she made out the skeletal figure on the bed, her hand flew to her mouth and she turned and ran out into the corridor. Maggie followed and put her arm around the trembling figure. "That's not Annie, it can't be, Maggie!" Katherine sobbed.

"I thought you knew how ill she has been," said Maggie gently.

"I knew she was sick but I didn't know . . ." Kate couldn't continue as she made an effort to reconcile the emaciated creature she had just seen with Annie as she had last appeared at Amy and Gunther's wedding. "Just let me sit here for a moment to compose myself," she begged. Emma had witnessed the scene and told Maggie she would stay with Kate. She brought a glass of brandy and remained with Kate until her trembling had ceased. Then, steeling herself, Kate returned to the bedroom.

Donald relinquished his place at Annie's beside to her. "Only a moment, Kate," he whispered. He and Maggie moved away to give her the privacy she obviously needed. Kate took Annie's thin hand. "My darling sister, I am so very sorry I was so wicked and caused you so much pain. I do love you. Can you forgive me?" she pleaded. Annie's eyes remained closed but her claw-like fingers clutched Kate's wrist spasmodically. Kate bent down and kissed her forehead then, gently disengaging her wrist, moved away.

Donald and Maggie came back to the bedside. Donald took Annie's hand and knelt beside her. Suddenly she started to speak. Her voice was so low he could hardly hear. "Da—dear, dear Da—I'm so glad the spring has come. . ." Donald beckoned Annie to come closer.

Maggie said, "Annie, dear, it . . ."

For a moment Annie's eyes opened and seemed to hold a flicker of joyous recognition. "Mama? I have missed you so . . . Now I am coming to be with you always . . ." She reached out her arms in a feeble gesture.

Donald nodded to Maggie and she understood, embracing Annie. "Hush, darling, Mama is here. I will hold you close to me for all eternity. I love you, Annie. We will always love each other," she whispered brokenly.

Kate was sobbing as she stood near the windows with bowed head fingering her rosary, praying for Annie's soul.

Donald sat on the bed, raised Annie up and held her close. Her voice was a little stronger, her smile beatific. "Mama and Da and Annie—no one else. I am so happy . . ." She went limp in Donald's arms and he laid her gently back against the pillows. Maggie looked at him in alarm.

He sighed deeply. "Yes," he said softly. "She's gone." He tenderly kissed Annie's mouth, then gently closed her eyes.

Maggie, dazed by the finality of these last moments, could not cry.

Tears streaming down her face, Kate offered Donald her rosary. "I know it's not your religion, Donald," she choked, "but perhaps it will help Annie to forgive me when she gets to

453

heaven. May I leave them for her?"

Weeping silently, Donald took the beads and draped them through Annie's still-warm fingers. Kate kissed Maggie then left quickly, trying to stifle her sobs.

Annie returned to Paisley in the spring, but not as had been planned; for her it was a fearless journey. Maggie had collapsed just as they boarded the ship and Donald put aside his own grief for a little while to comfort her. "Cry, little Maggie—you've been strong long enough. It's time for you to cry," he whispered. They mingled their tears, two heartbroken people who had tried to fend off the inevitable.

For the Maccrae clan, the sadness of Annie's homecoming was mixed with the joy of having Maggie back. All the girls, their husbands and children, and Robbie on her own, had gathered at the home of Ian and Mina Maccrae to mourn Annie's death and to rejoice at Maggie's return. It was a few months short of six years since Annie had left Paisley as a bride. During that time, she had always been remembered and loved as an image in the hearts of her family, but her long absence made their loss somewhat easier to bear. As for Donald, his love for Annie had become that of a parent for a sick child who accepted his tender care. He grieved for her loneliness and the deep, hidden sorrow that had eaten at her heart, but could not in truth mourn her death.

Maggie nurtured in her heart the image of Annie as she had once been, stalwart and strong, and was eventually able to erase from her mind the frail, hollow-eyed creature with whom she had been briefly reunited.

Annie would always be cherished and loved—it was almost as if she had not died. She had indeed come home at last.

XXIV

UNITED IN SORROW

Donald stayed in Scotland for three days after Annie's funeral, spending most of the time with Ian Maccrae. They spoke of many things—of Annie and their deep sorrow of Maggie and Ian's joy at being reunited with his youngest child, of his pride in all his daughters and their accomplishments, and the happy marriage he and Mina enjoyed.

"I must go back to America immediately, Ian," Donald told him. "I have left your namesake at home. He hasn't been told much—he's too young to understand. You know, Annie spent very little time with him and when Maggie and I told him she had 'gone away,' he accepted it without question. In the brief time Maggie stayed with us, she was more of a mother to him than Annie's poor health permitted her to be," he admitted.

Remembering how well she had mothered her sisters, this was difficult for Ian to understand, but at last he said, "Perhaps she had nothing left for her own child." He shook his head sadly. "I have a heavy burden of guilt to bear."

"Don't blame yourself, Ian," Donald urged. "If anyone must bear that burden, it's I. I should have known, even without her telling me, how homesick she was."

The two men sat in brooding silence for a few moments. Then with great effort, Donald changed the subject, and they continued their conversation.

Maggie also spent a great deal of time with her father, telling him about her adventures, and though he scolded her for running away, he also grudgingly praised her success. She visited her three sisters and their families, then accompanied Robbie back to Edinburgh where she stayed overnight. They compared notes on the unforseen results of their various sojourns in America. The conversation finally came around to Kate. "I suppose she cried crocodile tears about Annie," said Robbie, whose opinion of Kate had never been very high.

"No, Robbie, she cried real tears and was truly grief-stricken," Maggie told her.

"That surprises me. How is she getting along?"

Maggie paused, then said thoughtfully, "I would say that Kate is the happiest, best adjusted member of our family—with the notable exception of you," she said quickly as Robbie was about to protest. "And I don't really know much about Mary, Frances and Laurie. They seem happy enough, but Kate *glows*. Have I told you that she and her husband own a saloon?" Robbie let out a whoop of laughter. "Don't laugh—she works behind the bar, waits on tables, and her husband adores her. She has three very lively children—twin boys who look like pictures I've seen of Da when he was little, and a darling little girl named, sentimentally, Macushla. She has converted to Catholicism and is very devout." Robbie let out a little squawk. "She thanks God—and Annie—for sending her Rory Sullivan," Maggie added. "I can only hope that one day you and I will be as loving and as loved."

"I'm amazed and I'm also glad. I never thought Kate would be content in any situation that didn't involve lots of money and fine clothes," Robbie admitted.

Maggie then told Robbie that she was waiting for an annulment from her marriage to Marcel. "I hope to receive the final papers when I return to France—I must be in Paris for our July collection and then I'll spend a few weeks with my mother-in-law, a dear lady whom I love."

"Will you see your husband?" Robbie asked.

"I hope not," said Maggie. "But I will see my lawyer to find out why the annulment hasn't come through as yet. It is taking far too much time."

Before Maggie left, she promised one and all that she would return in November and possibly spend the Christmas holiday with them. Not wanting to make any promises she might not be able to keep, she didn't say she would try to bring young Ian and Donald, if he would come.

The House of MerMaid had another successful showing. Maggie's new designs were exciting, the congratulations effusive and the applause loud and long. Afterward, she and Mama, who had again given her invaluable assistance, left Paris and drove to the chateau.

"I'm so tired, Mama, I just want to sit in your beautiful gardens and relax," sighed Maggie.

"Then that's precisely what you shall do," said Mama. "The strain of your sister's illness and death, and the work you have put in on the show has been more than anyone should have to bear. When you have rested, we can talk."

After only a few days in the picturesque surroundings, Maggie's peace of mind and vitality of body began to return.

Claude Galle came for dinner on the third night of her visit and he was most apologetic. "The annulment is being blocked," he said bluntly in answer to Maggie's questions. "I don't know what Marcel has in mind because when I approached him initially, he was most agreeable about dissolving the marriage. Now he has instructed his attorney not to go further with it and . . ." he sat back, his face reflecting his chagrin, "he seems to have disappeared."

"Why would he do that?" asked Mama, obviously puzzled and perturbed.

Claude shrugged. "With all due respect to you, Marianne, it is impossible to follow the thinking of a man like Marcel." She nodded in sad agreement.

"Do we have to wait until he turns up?" Maggie asked anxiously.

"If you still want an annulment, yes. This has to be done by the Church. But if you want to institute divorce proceedings, I can do that immediately."

Maggie hesitated and turned to Mme. Mennon. "Mama, would that bother you?"

Mama shook her head. "No, dear. I think you should get out of the marriage whatever way you can."

The next morning Maggie said a fond farewell to Mama, who promised to meet her in Paris for the next collection in January. On her way back to the city, Maggie stopped by Claude's office where she filled out numerous forms relating to the divorce proceedings. She spent her last day in Paris with Lily Landre Juneau, then set sail once again for New York.

Maggie's mind was still in turmoil. Annie's death, her reunion with her family, and the news of the stalled annulment gave her much to digest. Not finding any answers to the most recent problem with Marcel, she decided that a visit to Donald and little Ian was just what she needed to take her mind off herself, and two weeks after her return, she set off for Tarrytown. Because she knew it was about time for Ian's nap when she arrived, Maggie told her coachman, on an impulse, to drive to the silk mill instead of to the MacConnack's mansion.

Donald was so surprised and pleased to see her walk into his office that he jumped up from behind his desk, sending his chair rolling. "Maggie, it is so good to see you!" he cried. "I was beginning to think you had disappeared again." He put his arms around her and they kissed. The warmth of that kiss startled them both. Almost guiltily they sprang apart. Trying to cover the confusion of the moment, Maggie walked around the spacious office, examining the paintings on the walls, and exclaiming with pleasure when she saw Ian's painting of the blue trees. Donald took control of the awkward situation. "You've never been here before, have you, Maggie?"

"No, but I decided to take advantage of the many invitations you have extended," she replied, smiling.

"I'll order lunch and while it is being prepared, I will give you the grand tour," he suggested.

At Donald's request, Gunther joined them and showed Maggie the new machinery they were using, adaptations of the looms her father had designed. He pointed with pride to the improvements Robbie had made. "She's a genius," he said.

"Every family should have one," Maggie replied, laughing.

"It seems your family has a surplus," Donald remarked.

They continued their tour through the factory, and when Maggie saw the fabric that was being woven on one of the mechanical looms, she exploded. "Donald, how *dare* you not bring this to my attention?" she cried. It was an adaptation of the paisley pattern in vibrantly colored silk.

"If you remember, I did submit a sample," Donald reminded her. "That is how we found each other."

Maggie thought for a moment. "That's right! I was so excited I put it down and forgot all about it. My apology, sir. Now let's get down to business. Before I go home, I'd like to come here again and give you an order. It was my father's intention, as I recall, that the paisley design be known worldwide. In fact, it was one of the reasons he permitted Kate and Robbie to come to America in the first place."

"Well, Maggie, your little MerMaid symbol does that!" said Donald.

"In a very small way. It is only part of the overall paisley design." She held the silk fabric in her hands, admiring it. "I shall design an entire wardrobe in paisley, from ballgowns to bathing dresses!"

Her enthusiasm was contagious and as they all went back to Donald's office for lunch, he and Gunther caught her excitement. They discussed silk paisley, wool paisley and even the possibility of velvet paisley. Finally Gunther pulled out his pocket watch and said regretfully, "I've got to get back to work. Maggie, please keep an evening open." He turned to Donald, "Amy will be desolate if you don't bring Maggie to dinner before she returns to the city."

"It's a promise," said Donald.

After he had signed a few letters, Donald left the mill with Maggie. He wanted, he said, to see Ian's face when she arrived. He wasn't disappointed. Ian flew into Maggie's arms, shouting, "Aunt Maggie, Aunt Maggie!" She picked him up and twirled around with him. He threw his head back and laughed and when she put him down, he ran around the room like an excited puppy. "Papa, Aunt Maggie came to see me!"

"Imagine that!" he said as he picked his son up and hugged him.

"Can we play now?" Ian asked eagerly.

"It's too late for that now, I'm afraid, but we'll play all day tomorrow," Maggie promised. The child's face fell with disappointment. On impulse, Maggie said, "Donald, this is a very special day. Do you think Ian could have dinner with us instead of upstairs in the nursery?"

Ian jumped up and down. "At the big table?" She nodded. "Please, Papa?" he begged.

Donald answered, "I think that is a splendid idea." Nursie had just entered to retrieve her charge, and he said, "Wanda, see that this young man is properly attired—with *clean hands*—" he looked meaningfully at Ian, who put his hands behind his back, "to have dinner in the dining room with Madame Mennon and me."

Delighted, Ian raced up the stairs and had already started to take off his clothes by the time she reached the nursery.

Maggie turned to Donald, embarrassed at her temerity. "Before you say anything, please forgive me for making the suggestion without consulting you first. I promise never to do it again."

Donald smiled. "It was an excellent idea. He's a happy child today, happier than he's been in a very long time."

The dinner hour was pushed up to six o'clock, which put the kitchen staff in a swivet. Promptly at six, Ian presented himself in the drawing room dressed in a navy blue jacket, knee pants and a blouse with a starched white collar. His face was shining. Nursie had tried to slick his hair back, but the stubborn curls refused to cooperate. He was growing up, Maggie knew, but he still looked like a cherub in her eyes. When dinner was announced, Ian offered his arm to Maggie, which she accepted solemnly. Fortunately for Ian's dignity, Maggie's small stature made it possible for him to reach her arm without straining too much. She didn't dare look at Donald; she couldn't spoil this moment by laughing.

During the meal, Ian watched his table manners and tried not to chatter too much, though he had much to tell his Aunt Maggie of his activities during her absence. Dessert was a concoction such as had never come out of their kitchen before—chocolate pudding, piled high with whipped cream and a bright red cherry on top. The youngster relished every bite and would have licked the plate, but he knew that was forbidden.

When the gala meal was over, Ian went to his father and said very formally, "Thank you for inviting me to dinner." Donald hid a smile. Ian then walked to Maggie, bowed and kissed her extended hand, after which he said goodnight. He was at the foot of the stairs when suddenly ran back, threw his arms around Maggie's waist and said, "I love you, Aunt Maggie!" She smiled at Donald through her tears as the child ran up the stairs without a backward glance.

A pattern had been set—every Thursday, Maggie would meet Donald at his office where they would discuss business, then leave early in order to play with Ian. Every Friday Ian joined them for dinner in the dining room. On Saturday, depending on the weather, they would picnic in the park or if it were inclement, Maggie and Ian would play checkers in the library—Donald played the winner. A warm sense of family enveloped them and Ian blossomed before their loving eyes.

XXXV

THE WIDOW

On the fifteenth of October, Maggie received a long letter from Claude Galle: "Dear Maggie, As you know, I cancelled the annulment proceedings when I filed divorce papers for you. I found it necessary to employ an investigative service to try to locate Marcel . . ." He went on to describe the service and the difficulty they had had tracking Marcel down. "He was finally traced to Switzerland, where he had rented a chalet in the Alps. There is no way to break this to you gently. Marcel and two other people (I only have first names), Janine and Armand, were found in the chalet with him. All three were dead. From what the authorities could discover, a blocked flue in the fireplace caused their death by smoke inhalation. I don't think, Maggie, they knew what had befallen them. There were many bottles in the room, all empty. The consensus is that they were all in a stupor from drink. There was no sign of an attempt to get outside. Marcel had rented the chalet under another name, but has been positively identified by me. Marianne knows this. She is not surprised that Marcel has come to a tragic end, but is desolate that it should have happened in such a manner. I have of course cancelled the divorce proceedings. I will await word from you before setting a date to read the will, though Marcel's estate is, as you are aware, negligible, since the Compagnie Mennon as well as all the family lands are in Marianne's name. May I hear from you soon?''

Maggie was stunned. For long moments she sat as if turned to stone; then, taking several deep breaths, she reread the letter, this time more carefully. She would have to go to France—no, she wasn't prepared to leave just yet. . . Her mind was darting about like a flea on a cat. Poor Mama! She needed Maggie at her side . . . Wringing her hands, Maggie knew she had to speak to someone and sent an urgent note to Ellen: ''If you can get away, will you come to lunch with me today? I need to talk to you. I have had shocking news.''

Instead of answering the note, Ellen arrived in person on Maggie's doorstep half an hour later. She was more alarmed than Maggie appeared to be, but Ellen knew her friend so well that she was not fooled by the calm exterior Maggie tried to present; her eyes betrayed her. ''What is it, Maggie? What is wrong?'' Ellen asked.

For answer, Maggie handed her the letter. She read it quickly. ''Oh, my God, how could he . . . so sordid, to you . . . to his mother . . .'' She couldn't finish a single sentence.

''Ellen, I'm sure he didn't *plan* to die,'' said Maggie dryly.

''How can you say that? He had been working toward that end ever since you married him, and from what you've told me, long before that.''

Maggie sighed. "You're right; he was self-destructive. I'm glad for Mama's sake this didn't happen right after she told him he wasn't . . ." she stumbled, then "his father's heir," she finished lamely.

Ellen leaned forward, putting her hand on Maggie's. "I can tell that guilt is beginning to form. Don't let it! You are in *no way*" she emphasized, "to blame for any of this."

"I didn't help him very much," said Maggie wearily. "I was not a good wife to him . . ."

"Stop it! You were lied to! He misrepresented himself. He was a dissolute wastrel and pretended otherwise." She paused. "I hope you'll forgive me for saying this, but at least you won't have to go through a scandalous divorce now."

"That's true. But it's still a tragedy. Poor Mama! I hope she's all right . . ."

It wasn't until Ellen had left that Maggie had the strength to go through the rest of her mail, where she found a brief note from Mama. She had only comforting words for Maggie: "Feel relief, my dear, that your ties to him are severed. We can hope that he has found peace. If there is fault to be found, it lies with his father and me. We thought of Marcel as a pledge of our love and we indulged him in every respect. The only good thing he ever did in return was to bring you to us. Try to forget the bad things and remember, my daughter, I love you very much. Do come soon."

In answering M. Galle's letter, Maggie informed him that she would arrive in Paris sometime in December and would contact him shortly to let him know the exact date.

The letter to Mama was not easy: "I am

distressed about Marcel's tragic death, and very concerned about your welfare at this moment. I am sorry I can not be with you, but will come as soon as possible, which unfortunately will not be until December. Keep up your strength and remember I love you, too."

Maggie sat at her escritoire, pen in hand, suddenly engulfed in sorrow; the pent-up tears finally flowed. In spite of her alienation from Marcel, she felt a tremendous grief for a marriage that had failed; for a man who had so much and such potential; but mostly for Marianne Mennon whose devotion to her only son had resulted in nothing but rejection and heartbreak.

Maggie had stifled an almost overwhelming impulse to run to Donald when she had first heard the news of Marcel's death. She made her regular visit to Tarrytown the following Thursday, but did not stop at the mill. When Donald arrived at the house, he found her playing outdoors with Ian, shuffling through the leaves that had been raked into neat piles which the youngster was mischievously kicking apart. They each had a small collection of special leaves, gold and deep red and yellow, tinged with red. Donald joined them, and they sat on the autumn-brown grass, discussing the colors. Maggie promised Ian they would paint pictures of their few perfect specimens, much to Ian's delight.

Maggie didn't broach the subject of Marcel's demise until she and Donald were settled in the drawing room after dinner that evening. She requested brandy with her coffee and suggested he have it, too. He listened quietly as she told him what had happened, then moved close and put his arms around her. "Are you all right, dear?" he asked.

She nodded, sighed and put her head on his shoulder. It seemed the most natural position in the world. "I am now," she murmured.

"It's too soon for us to talk seriously, Maggie, but you must know that Ian and I love you very much. But one day, when the time is right, we *will* talk," he promised, looking deeply into her eyes. They kissed, and this time neither felt embarrassed or drew away.

As Maggie had promised, she returned to Scotland in November for a brief visit with her family, then left immediately for Paris. It was a whirlwind visit, first to see that the preparations for the January collection were proceeding well and to leave a bundle of new sketches, and second, to see Claude Galle. She went with him to the chateau, where Mama was anxiously waiting. They embraced warmly and Maggie, looking at her closely, saw that Mama was thinner, and looked a little older. Her eyes were not quite as bright until she turned them on Claude. Maggie experienced a surge of relief as she realized Mama had found a loving companion for her declining years.

Maggie had decided to spend Christmas with Mama, and so was unable to return to Scotland for the holiday, but Donald brought Ian to meet his grandfather, his aunts and numerous cousins in Paisley, Glasgow and Edinburgh. The two Ians loved each other at once. The aunts marveled at his beauty and the children vied for the attention of their

American cousin. Ian had never known there were so many children in the world.

Donald and young Ian spent the last few days of December in Paris with Maggie, then sailed for America on the second of January. Maggie herself left immediately after the showing was over.

XXVI

HAPPILY EVER AFTER

Several months later, on a beautiful summer day, Maggie, Donald and Ian were enjoying a picnic lunch on the green velvet lawn of the MacConnack estate. When the last of the cold fried chicken had been consumed and the last of the iced lemonade had been drunk, Donald caught Maggie's eye and, at her barely perceptible nod said to Ian, "Aunt Maggie and I have some news for you, son."

"What, Papa? Tell me!" cried Ian.

"We are going to be married. Do you know what that means?"

"Married?" A small frown creased his forehead as he considered the word. With very few playmates, Ian knew little about the world outside his estate. At last he turned to Maggie.

"Does that mean you will live here?" he asked eagerly.

Maggie took his hand. "Yes, dear—forever."

Tears of joy welled in the little boy's eyes. "I would be so glad, Aunt Maggie! Will you be my mama then?" There was sudden alarm in his voice as he turned to Donald and said, "And will you still be my Papa?"

"Come over here, son. I will *always,*" he said

as he put his arm around Ian, "be your papa and I shall always love you just as I do now."

"And so will I," put in Maggie. "You know, Ian, I will not be your real mama because you were not born to me. Do you remember your mama?"

"A little—I didn't see her very much. She was sick an awful lot."

Maggie didn't go into any details about her relationship to Annie, but told him, "In my heart you are my little boy."

He gave her one of his famous bear hugs, then asked, "Will I still call you Aunt Maggie?"

Donald shook his head. "After we are married, you could call her Mrs. MacConnack . . ." Ian went into peals of laughter at the thought, " . . . or Mama Maggie . . ." which made him laugh even harder.

The child was thoughtful for a moment, then very seriously he looked up at Maggie and asked, "Could I call you just plain Mama?"

Maggie threw her arms around him and kissed him. "I would be so *proud* for you to call me Mama!"

"When?" Ian wanted to know.

They explained about the wedding which would take place that autumn in Grandfather's home in Scotland. That night, an excited little boy took a long time to fall asleep.

A year to the day that Maggie had been notified of her widowhood, she and Donald were married. Amy and Gunther had planned their travels so they could attend, as had Ellen and John Colton, Mme. Mennon and Claude

Galle. Kate, however, was pregnant again and unable to make the crossing.

Maggie had little problem deciding on her wedding dress. Since it was her second marriage and she and Donald were widow and widower, she felt it unsuitable to wear white. Instead, she wore a very pale blue dress with the Maccrae tartan draped over her left shoulder, across her chest and pinned at the right hip with a turquoise and pearl pin. A wreath of heather crowned her head and she carried the Bible Mama Mennon had given her. Robbie, maid of honor, wore yellow and carried a bouquet of heather. (Frances had to be excused from the bridal party as she was big with her fifth child.) Da in his dress kilt and Mina draped in the Maccrae tartan looked every inch the proud father and stepmother of the bride.

The only problem was Donald's clothes. The family expected him to wear kilts, too, but he appealed to Maggie, saying, "I'll be very uncomfortable with my knobby knees showing."

Maggie giggled. "I'm sure your knees are beautiful, darling, but no one wants you to be uncomfortable at your own wedding." A satisfactory compromise was made; Donald and Gunther wore black trousers and formal Scottish black velvet jackets with silver buttons, but Ian was proud as punch in his very first kilt.

It was a lovely wedding; counting the friends and relatives, there were about thirty in all. Gunther was Donald's witness and Da gave the bride away. Ian was the ring-bearer which gave him a great sense of importance. After the ceremony he stood on the periphery of those who had gathered to give their good wishes, but finally made his way to his father's side. He kissed him, then put his arms around Maggie. "May I call you Mama now?" he asked.

"Yes, my little love—now and for all time!"

He whispered, "Mama, I am so glad you married us!"

The seventh sister had at last discovered the wonder of loving and being loved.

TOMORROW AND FOREVER

Francesca Macklem

ONE MAN'S LOVE
WAS
HER DESTINY

The shadowy rooms of the old family mansion seemed to echo with the loves and hatreds of generations past, or so it appeared to Donna when she was called to her dying father's bedside. There she encountered the enigmatic and dangerously attractive Dr. Paul Arnett, who aroused conflicting emotions in her heart, and eventually swept her away with a love she dared not deny...

0-8439-2155-2   Price: $2.75

UNDER CRIMSON SAILS

Lynna Lawton

Beautiful, spirited Janielle Patterson had heard of the reckless way pirate Ryan Deverel treated his women. He seduced them with the same abandon with which he plundered ships. To the handsome pirate, women were prizes to be won, used, and tossed away.

Ryan intrigued and repelled Janielle—and when they finally met, she was shocked to discover that her own nature was as passionate as the pirate's!

But while he was driven by desire, she was driven by a fierce hatred. Yet she knew neither of them would rest until she had surrendered to him fully.

LEISURE BOOKS   2002-5/$3.50

Make the Most of Your
Leisure Time
with
LEISURE BOOKS

Please send me the following titles:

Quantity	Book Number	Price
_____	_____	_____
_____	_____	_____
_____	_____	_____
_____	_____	_____
_____	_____	_____

If out of stock on any of the above titles, please send me the alternate title(s) listed below:

_____	_____	_____
_____	_____	_____
_____	_____	_____
_____	_____	_____

Postage & Handling _____

Total Enclosed $_____

☐ Please send me a free catalog.

NAME _____
(please print)

ADDRESS _____

CITY _____ STATE _____ ZIP _____

Please include $1.00 shipping and handling for the first book ordered and 25¢ for each book thereafter in the same order. All orders are shipped within approximately 4 weeks via postal service book rate. PAYMENT MUST ACCOMPANY ALL ORDERS.*

*Canadian orders must be paid in US dollars payable through a New York banking facility.

Mail coupon to: **Dorchester Publishing Co., Inc.
6 East 39 Street, Suite 900
New York, NY 10016
Att: ORDER DEPT.**